PENGUIN CLASSICS

THE NARRATIVE OF
ARTHUR GORDON PYM OF NANTUCKET

Edgar Poe was born on January 19, 1809, in Boston, the son of impoverished actors. Orphaned when he was not yet three, Poe was
taken in by John and Frances Allan of Richmond, Virginia. After a
major falling-out with his foster father in 1827, Poe left Richmond
for Boston, where he arranged for the publication of his first book of
poetry, *Tamerlane and Other Poems*. He published two additional
books of poetry—*Al Aaraaf, Tamerlane, and Minor Poems* (1829)
and *Poems* (1831)—and began to publish short stories and book reviews, gaining an editorial position at the *Southern Literary Messenger* in Richmond in 1835. Perhaps already privately married to his
thirteen-year-old cousin Virginia Clemm, he married her publicly in
May 1836. By this time, he had begun work on his novel, *The Narrative of Arthur Gordon Pym*, early chapters of which were published
in the *Messenger* of January and February 1837. But on January 3,
1837, Poe lost his job (very likely owing to his drinking), and he
moved to New York City, where he completed the book. *Pym* was
published by Harper & Brothers on July 30, 1838. Poe had by then
moved to Philadelphia, where he came to serve as an editor for two
periodicals—*Burton's Gentleman's Magazine* and, later, *Graham's
Magazine*—and where he published a collection of short stories,
Tales of The Grotesque and Arabesque (1840), as well as many additional short stories, including the prize-winning "The Gold Bug"
and the first modern detective story, "The Murders in the Rue
Morgue." However, his wife, Virginia, developed tuberculosis. Returning to New York City in 1844, Poe soon reached the peak of
his fame with the publication of "The Raven" in 1845. That year
also saw the publication of both *Tales* and *The Raven and Other
Poems*—but Poe's drinking led to the failure of his weekly, the
Broadway Journal. Settling in Fordham, Poe continued to write
and to care for Virginia; she died in January 1847. In his final
years, Poe wrote some of his most celebrated poetry—"The Bells,"
"Eldorado," and "Annabel Lee"—and his cosmological prose
poem, *Eureka* (1848). On October 7, 1849, Edgar Allan Poe died in
Baltimore.

Richard Kopley, associate professor of English at Penn State DuBois, is the author of numerous studies of Poe, Hawthorne, and Melville; editor of *Poe's Pym: Critical Explorations* and *Prospects for the Study of American Literature: A Guide for Students and Scholars*; and coeditor of the journal *Resources for American Literary Study*. He is also vice-president of the Poe Studies Association.

THE NARRATIVE OF ARTHUR GORDON PYM OF NANTUCKET

Edgar Allan Poe

EDITED WITH AN INTRODUCTION
AND NOTES BY
RICHARD KOPLEY

PENGUIN BOOKS

PENGUIN BOOKS

Published by the Penguin Group

Penguin Group (USA) Inc., 375 Hudson Street, New York, New York 10014, U.S.A.
Penguin Group (Canada), 90 Eglinton Avenue East, Suite 700, Toronto,
Ontario, Canada M4P 2Y3 (a division of Pearson Penguin Canada Inc.)
Penguin Books Ltd, 80 Strand, London WC2R 0RL, England
Penguin Ireland, 25 St Stephen's Green, Dublin 2, Ireland (a division of Penguin Books Ltd)
Penguin Group (Australia), 250 Camberwell Road, Camberwell,
Victoria 3124, Australia (a division of Pearson Australia Group Pty Ltd)
Penguin Books India Pvt Ltd, 11 Community Centre, Panchsheel Park, New Delhi – 110 017, India
Penguin Group (NZ), cnr Airborne and Rosedale Roads,
Albany, Auckland 1310, New Zealand (a division of Pearson New Zealand Ltd)
Penguin Books (South Africa) (Pty) Ltd, 24 Sturdee Avenue,
Rosebank, Johannesburg 2196, South Africa

Penguin Books Ltd, Registered Offices: 80 Strand, London WC2R 0RL, England

First published in the United States of America 1838
This edition with an introduction and notes by Richard Kopley
published in Penguin Books 1999

20 19 18 17 16 15 14 13

Introduction and notes copyright © Richard Kopley, 1999
All rights reserved

LIBRARY OF CONGRESS CATALOGING IN PUBLICATION DATA
Poe, Edgar Allan, 1809–1849.
[Narrative of Arthur Gordon Pym]
The narrative of Arthur Gordon Pym of Nantucket / Edgar Allan
Poe ; edited with an introduction and notes by Richard Kopley.
p.   cm.—(Penguin classics)
Includes bibliographical references.
ISBN 0 14 04.3748 7
1. Whaling ships—Fiction.   2. Stowaways—Fiction.
I. Kopley, Richard.   II. Title.   III. Series.
PS2618.N3   1999   98–50102
813'.3—dc21

Printed in the United States of America
Set in Stempel Garamond

For Leslie Fiedler,
who got me started

—R.K.

CONTENTS

INTRODUCTION

It could well be argued that the idea for the first episode in Edgar Allan Poe's great novel of adventure, *The Narrative of Arthur Gordon Pym*, came from a newspaper.

Poe was a devoted reader of reviews of his work. And as the editor of Richmond's monthly *Southern Literary Messenger*, he included reviews and extracts of reviews of the *Messenger* in a supplement in the January, April, and July issues of 1836. Notably, he regularly featured in the supplements reviews from the Norfolk *Beacon* and the Norfolk *Herald*. As a professional journalist, he could not well have missed these newspapers of a neighboring city. Our recognizing Poe's reading in the *Beacon* and the *Herald* in 1836 is important, for we can see in that reading the beginnings of *Pym*. Poe would have encountered in the *Beacon*, on February 18, 1836—one day after a very positive review of the February issue of the *Messenger*—and in the *Herald*, on February 19, 1836—adjacent to a highly favorable review of that same issue—a first-hand account of the destruction in a storm at sea of a Norfolk vessel named the *Ariel*, and of the escape and rescue of two men who had been on board. In all likelihood, Poe would have been reminded of James Fenimore Cooper's *Ariel* in *The Pilot*, Percy Bysshe Shelley's boat *Ariel*, John Milton's Ariel in *Paradise Lost*, and William Shakespeare's fairy Ariel in *The Tempest* (a part once played by Poe's mother, Eliza). But it was the Norfolk newspaper account that appears to have been the immediate prompt, and it was that account that most closely anticipates the events of chapter 1 of Poe's novel: the destruction of the *Ariel* and the rescue of two males who had been on board. The story had great possibilities for a general

audience: as a work in the public mind, it could perhaps intro-
duce a popular sea narrative, one characterized by what Poe
termed "the potent magic of verisimilitude" (the use of specific detail to promote belief and heighten effect). It could lead
to a work comparable to Daniel Defoe's *Robinson Crusoe*,
which Poe had so highly praised in the January 1836 issue of
the *Messenger*. Furthermore, the newspaper account of the
destruction of the *Ariel* had great possibilities for a literary
audience: it could conceivably suggest another story altogether. Addressing both the general audience and the literary
audience in *Pym*, Poe sought the resounding success that had
so far eluded him.

Edgar Poe was born in Boston on January 19, 1809, to Eliza
Arnold Poe and David Poe Jr., both actors. Edgar had an
older brother, Henry, and, soon, a younger sister, Rosalie.
David Poe Jr., a performer of limited talent, and given to
drink, abandoned his family in New York City in the spring
or summer of 1811. The children's beloved mother, Eliza, a
much celebrated ingenue, became sick in Richmond and died
on December 8, 1811. Henry went to live with his grandpar-
ents in Baltimore and Rosalie with the Mackenzies of Richmond; Edgar was taken in—but never adopted—by John and
Frances Allan, also of Richmond.

Obvious difficulties did not develop for a while. Several
people who had known Edgar when he was a young boy remember him to have been "a lovely little fellow . . . charming
every one by his childish grace, vivacity, and cleverness." In
London, where John Allan had taken his family so that he
could expand his import/export business, the attentive foster
father wrote in 1818, "Edgar is a fine Boy and reads Latin
sharply." While his schoolmaster considered him spoiled and
mischievous, Allan continued to state that "Edgar is a very
fine Boy & a good Scholar." And when John Allan returned
to Richmond in 1820, having suffered business reverses, he in-

quired of Edgar's new teacher Joseph H. Clarke whether a book of his foster son's poems (written to various girls in the city) should be published. (Impressed with the boy's imagination, Clarke nonetheless recommended that, to avoid inflating Edgar's already high opinion of himself, Allan should not have the book published. The poems have since been lost.)

Edgar continued to distinguish himself as a student, and showed skills as an athlete, as well—as a runner, leaper, boxer, and swimmer. But he was, in all likelihood, becoming aware that his status among his peers was uncertain, since he was the son of actors and dependent on the goodwill of the Allans. Also, he longed for the mother he had lost, and he sought maternal sympathy in his foster mother, Frances Allan, and his friend Rob Stanard's mother, Jane Stanard. Mrs. Allan was frequently ill, however, and Mrs. Stanard, though very responsive to the boy, soon died. Edgar was distraught and apparently moody at home—"miserable sulky & ill-tempered," John Allan wrote. Edgar's relationship with his foster father worsened—especially when this son of actors defied John Allan by joining the Thespian Society.

In the summer of 1825, Edgar had the second of two visits from his brother, Henry—a welcome interlude, surely. Also, Edgar became involved in a romance with Elmira Royster, but after he went to the University of Virginia in February 1826, her father intercepted his letters, and she eventually married someone else. Poe fared well academically at the university, excelling in languages, and he continued to write and revealed a talent for drawing. But he considered himself hampered by John Allan's inadequate financial support. He gambled at cards and lost, incurring great debts. And he began to drink, as well. In December 1826, John Allan removed Edgar from the university, refusing to pay some of his debts. In March 1827, after living with the Allans in Richmond and working in his foster father's business, Edgar had a final argument with John Allan and left the house for good. The impoverished young man voyaged north along the coast to Boston to try to begin his literary career.

Young Poe struggled in poverty, working as a low-level clerk and then a reporter, and eventually joining the army. But before his battery traveled south to Charleston, South Carolina, he arranged for the publication of his first book, *Tamerlane and Other Poems*, at his own expense. This volume of Byronic longing and conflict—now one of the most highly valued rarities in American book collecting—was printed by Calvin F. S. Thomas in June or July 1827 and met with little response.

Poe's two-year career in the army was reasonably successful but evidently unsatisfying. In 1829 he left to live with his aunt Maria Clemm (his father's sister), his brother, Henry, and his cousin Virginia, in Baltimore. His foster mother, Frances Allan, soon died, and Henry, a minor writer, was "given up to drink." Poe asserted in a letter to novelist John Neal, who had praised his poem "Heaven" (later "Fairyland") in *The Yankee*, "I am young—not yet twenty—*am* a poet—if deep worship of all beauty can make me one. . . ." He then went on to intimate his devotion to Henry and its cause: ". . . there can be no tie more strong than that of brother for brother—it is not so much that they love one another as that they both love the same parent. . . ." Here we have a critical insight into Poe's family life, one that may help to illuminate some of the less immediately accessible elements of *Pym*.

In December 1829, *Al Aaraaf, Tamerlane, and Minor Poems* was published by Hatch & Dunning; it elicited a small but appreciative critical response. Among the remarkable poems in this collection was the elegant "Sonnet—To Science," Poe's early critique of science as an enemy of the imagination. Then, in 1830, with support from his foster father and others, Poe won an appointment to West Point. But while he did well in his classes in languages and mathematics, he came to dislike the military regimen. And his relationship with the newly remarried John Allan was growing more problematic—very likely, in part, because of a letter that Poe had written offering criticisms of his foster father, including an indiscreet allegation about Allan's drinking. Responding to a rejecting John Allan in January 1831, Poe wrote an angry and defensive letter, which closed with a resolve to abandon his work at West Point. He followed through on this resolve, deliberately provoking a court-martial.

Returning to Baltimore in 1831, Poe published *Poems* with Elam Bliss, winning only a few notices and great resentment from the cadets who had subscribed to the book with the expectation that it would offer Poe's familiar clever satire. Still, this book, like all of Poe's works, offered compelling writing—it featured, among other poems, such now recognized classics as "Israfel," "The City in the Sea," and "To Helen" (his tribute to Mrs. Stanard).

Poe decided, though, to shift his efforts to fiction, hoping for the success that he had not yet won with his poetry. He entered the Philadelphia *Saturday Courier*'s short story contest, but he lost. Meanwhile, Henry had become sick, probably owing to excessive drinking. In light of the poverty of Maria Clemm's household, the two brothers probably shared a room—perhaps, given the custom of the day, even a bed. On August 1, 1831, Henry died. Edgar may well have witnessed his brother's death.

The earliest published short story attributed to Poe, a tale of the crucifixion of Jesus, titled "A Dream," appeared in the *Saturday Evening Post* on August 13. Then, in early 1832, the *Saturday Courier* published five of Poe's tales, including the supposedly comic work about the Romans' mockery of the besieged Israelites, "A Tale of Jerusalem." And Poe continued to write short stories, gathering them in "Tales of the Folio Club"—but the collection was never published.

Still, Poe won local attention when he submitted "Tales of the Folio Club" to the Baltimore *Saturday Visiter* competition in 1833. His tale of the Flying Dutchman, "MS. Found in a Bottle," was selected as the prize-winning story—it was published on October 19, 1833, and Poe was awarded fifty dollars. But personal problems continued. In February 1834, Poe visited his dying foster father, but Allan, uninterested in reconciliation, raised his cane to Poe and ordered him out of the room. In March 1834, John Allan died. And Poe was not mentioned in his will. However, one of the judges in the *Saturday Visiter* contest, John Pendleton Kennedy, took an interest in Poe, providing him with clothing and writing in his behalf to publisher Thomas W. White of Richmond, who had recently begun a monthly magazine, the *Southern Literary Messenger*.

Poe began to publish stories and poems and reviews in the *Messenger*. In August 1835, he moved to Richmond, perhaps to pursue a teaching position (which he did not get)—and he shortly begin to assist White editorially. Poe's drinking—probably aggravated by his anxiety about possibly losing Virginia to the guardianship of his second cousin Neilson Poe—led to his dismissal. Offered a warning by White ("No man is safe who drinks before breakfast!"), Poe was allowed to return. In October 1835, he moved back to Richmond from Baltimore, this time with Virginia (whom he may already have married secretly and whom he would soon marry publicly) and her mother, Maria Clemm. After many years of struggle, Poe had secured an important position and his own family—but not yet the popular and critical success that he desired.

On March 3, 1836, the intermediary for the Harper & Brothers publishing house, James Kirke Paulding, wrote to Poe's employer, *Messenger* publisher White, that the Harpers had declined "Tales of the Folio Club" because some of the tales had already been published and some were too obscure. He advised that Poe "lower himself a little to the ordinary comprehension of the generality of readers, and prepare a series of original Tales, or a single work." He soon thereafter wrote to

Poe, "I think it would be worth your while . . . to undertake a Tale in a couple of Volumes. . . ." On June 19, Wesley Harper himself wrote to Poe, clarifying the publisher's view: the book had been declined because many of its stories had been published, because "detached tales and pieces" were not usually successful, and because the works themselves were "too learned and mystical." "They would be understood and relished only by a very few," he added, "not by the multitude." Harper offered his considered opinion about the American readership: "Readers in this country have a decided and strong preference for works (especially fiction) in which a single and connected story occupies the whole volume, or number of volumes, as the case may be. . . ." While Poe tried once more to publish "Tales of the Folio Club," he also took seriously the advice he had received; his writing *Pym*, his only novel, was his response to that advice.

Seeking "the multitude," Poe borrowed the story of the wreck of the *Ariel* from the popular press in 1836 and began to elaborate a nautical narrative, probably in hopes of attaining the popular success of Defoe or Cooper or Michael C. Scott with *Tom Cringle's Log* (1833) or Joseph C. Hart with *Miriam Coffin, or The Whale-Fisherman* (1834). He would surely have been encouraged by his own earlier success with a sea tale, "MS. Found in a Bottle." (Notably, chapter 10 of *Pym*, the death ship chapter, relies on the "Flying Dutchman" motif of "MS.") Working in the genre of the sea novel, Poe clearly emphasized its sensational elements. He understood that the expectations of his potential readership had been shaped by tales of the extraordinary that appeared in monthly magazines and accounts of the extraordinary that were regularly published in the penny press. Defending his tale "Berenice" to publisher White in April 1835, Poe defended the sensational in literature, stating that literary success in the magazines was owing to "the ludicrous heightened into the grotesque: the fearful coloured into the horrible: the witty exaggerated into the burlesque: the singular wrought out into the strange and mystical." (He disagreed with Harper on the "mystical.") Poe summed up his position by explaining to White, "To be appreciated you must be *read*, and these things [stories with sensational elements] are invariably sought after with avidity." From popular gothic tales, Poe extrapolated a gothic sea novel—a series of tales, involving a character repeatedly on the brink of either death or discovery.

The language of *Pym*'s subtitle cries out the sensations of the book: "MUTINY," "BUTCHERY," "SHIPWRECK," "SUFFERINGS," "CAPTURE," "MASSACRE." Over and over, Pym is about to die; indeed, in one episode he appears as a dead man. Poe was drawing on the same fascination with death that he drew on in so many other works, including "The Fall of the House of Usher" (1839), "The Premature Burial" (1844), and "The Facts in the Case of M. Valdemar" (1845). He was appealing to readers' desire for pleasurable fear, and perhaps, too, to their longing for annihilation—at least vicarious annihilation—to what he later termed "the Imp of the Perverse." Furthermore, the "CAPTURE" and "MASSACRE" of Pym's shipmates would probably have had a particular interest for a large audience—the devious, deadly natives would have suggested to readers not only the fierce natives in other sea narratives but also, very likely, fearsome renderings of southern slaves. Poe invited an association such as this in Pym's voyage south by stating that "a singular ledge of rock" in a South Sea island looked like "corded bales of cotton" (chapter 17). Poe's characterization of the Tsalalian natives as a primitive people of great deceit and murderousness would probably have resonated with southern fears of slave insurrection—and perhaps with similar northern fears, as well. (Harry Levin, Leslie Fiedler, Sidney Kaplan, and numerous subsequent scholars have discussed the importance of race in *Pym*; J. Gerald Kennedy has recently posited that the rescuing "half-breed,"

Dirk Peters, may suggest an ameliorative view.) Finally, Poe's reference in his subtitle to "ADVENTURES AND DISCOVERIES STILL FARTHER SOUTH" would have engaged a public intrigued by nautical exploration. The belief that there were holes at the poles—with water rushing north to south according to Captain John Cleves Symmes Jr., and south to north according to his disciple Jeremiah N. Reynolds—and the effort of Reynolds to secure an exploring expedition to advance human knowledge of the southern waters—were very much in the news. The mystery of the southern regions was a great one in Poe's day, and could be taken as an emblem of all mysteries that perplexed and challenged.

Poe intensified the sensations of *Pym* by rendering them with what he termed in his September 1836 review of Robert Montgomery Bird's novel *Sheppard Lee* "the infinity of arts which give verisimilitude to a narration." Poe relied upon a variety of sea documents—not only works of fiction, but also mariners' chronicles, the writings of Jeremiah N. Reynolds, and, in particular, *A Narrative of Four Voyages* (1832), supposedly written by Benjamin Morrell but actually ghostwritten by Samuel Woodworth. The specific details that Poe provided may have occasionally slowed readers, but they also probably yielded a sharper contrast for the sensations of the novel. Clearly, the believability of the work—or the seeming good-faith effort to make the work minimally believable—could increase its readership. Strengthening the verisimilitude of the novel was Pym's earnest appeal to "progressing science." Although Poe had critiqued science as an enemy of the imagination in "Sonnet—To Science," he came to hold a more positive view in subsequent years, seeing science as an effort that could satisfy the imagination; his ultimate meditation on that subject was his prose poem on the nature of the universe, *Eureka* (1848). Pym's trust in science and the findings of the Exploring Expedition (1838–1842) might have held out to readers the possibility—perhaps only the apparent possibility—of empirical bases for Poe's improbabilities and impossibilities.

However, whereas Pym claims in the preface to the novel that the public recognized as factual the seemingly fictional narrative in the *Messenger* (roughly, the first three and a half chapters of the book), readers were not typically so credulous. It is true that in reading *Pym* Oliver Wendell Holmes's brother John was "completely deceived by the minute accuracy of some of the details." And, as Joan Tyler Mead has shown (in Kopley, *Poe's Pym*), John Murphy did include portions of *Pym*'s "stowage" section in a guidebook, *Nautical Routine and Stowage* (1849), identifying his source only as "Am. Pub." (If he recognized *Pym* as fiction, he still had sufficient regard for one of its digressions to include it in his work of nonfiction.) Yet an angry William Burton (editor of *Burton's Gentleman's Magazine*) called the novel "an impudent attempt at humbugging the public," and a British critic concurred, terming it "an impudent attempt at imposing on the credulity of the ignorant." An 1850 reader wrote in his copy of *Pym*, addressing any future reader, "I Don't believe A damned word of this yarn do you Sir" (University of Texas, Austin, copy). And while this reader must have believed in Pym, for he wrote beneath Pym's name in the title, "you are a Liar," another contemporary reader disbelieved in Pym, declaring at the novel's close, "It is my firm opinion that the whole of the preceding narrative is a base fabrication, & that such a man as Pym never existed[;] if any one should read this book[,] I think them void of common sense if they believe it" (UCLA copy).

Yet some could willingly disbelieve and still enjoy the story. An American critic asserted, ". . . this is a very clever extravaganza . . ."; a British critic exclaimed with amusement, "Arthur Pym is the American Robinson Crusoe, a man all over wonders, who sees nothing but wonders, vanquishes nothing but wonders, would, indeed, evidently, scorn to have anything to do but with wonders. . . ." And an 1852 reader, a nineteen-year-old bookstore clerk in Lancaster, Pennsylvania, Frank R. Diffenderfer, wrote:

> This is without a doubt one of the most remarkable books I ever read. I really do not know which to admire most[,] the story or its author. . . . Unfortunately for the truth of the story[,] a few years later the United States Exploring Expedition discovered a continent stretching 1500 miles in length from east to west being all the portion which Mr. Pym pretends he sailed over. This is of little account however. Centuries may elapse ere another such story is written. Future generations will appreciate the genius of its gifted but erratic author. (Franklin & Marshall copy)

The clerk (later a distinguished historian) overstated the problem, but he was correct in that there is a geographical difficulty in the final portion of *Pym*: the "Antarctic Ocean" that Pym sails over in this portion—from 84° S, 43° W, over a "vast distance to the southward"—is Antarctica itself. But this inconsistency was evidently not troubling to young Diffenderfer. Poe's occasionally unbelievable verisimilitude was apparently considered acceptable, and his many sensations considered sensational. It is relevant to note what Poe wrote in this regard in his *Sheppard Lee* review:

> The attention of the author, who does not depend upon explaining away his incredibilities, is directed to giving them the character and luminousness of truth, and thus are brought about, unwittingly, some of the most vivid creations of human intellect. The reader, too, readily perceives and falls in with the writer's humor, and suffers himself to be borne on thereby.

Appealing to the popular imagination with sensation and purportedly verisimilar detail, Poe did successfully reach some contemporary readers.

———

But Poe also still sought the "very few," members of the small, highly literary audience. Very probably, he sought readers interested in the solving of codes—another kind of adventure. Jean-François Champollion's solving the mystery of the Egyptian hieroglyphs with his analysis of the Rosetta stone in 1822 had made the issue of decoding a familiar and exciting one to a number of readers of Poe's time. Poe would later enjoy some success with his code-breaking articles in *Alexander's Weekly Messenger* in 1839 and 1840 and would publish "A Few Words on Secret Writing" in *Graham's Magazine* in 1841. And he acknowledged in his "Exordium" in 1842 that "The analysis of a book is a matter of time and of mental exertion. For many classes of composition there is required a deliberate perusal, with notes, and subsequent generalization."

Deliberate perusal reveals a subtext in *Pym* concerning Poe's family. We may trace it briefly here. Even as Arthur Gordon Pym suggests Edgar Allan Poe, Pym's friend Augustus suggests Poe's brother, Henry. Even as Augustus was two years older than Pym, taller, more widely traveled, and inclined to tell stories and to drink, so, too, was Henry two years older than Poe, taller, more widely traveled, and inclined to tell stories and drink. The early episode in which Augustus was rescued from the ocean and the later one in which Pym was rescued from the hold of a ship may suggest their births. And certainly Augustus's death on August 1 suggests Henry's death on August 1, 1831. Critically, attention to the mysterious close of *Pym* reveals more about Poe and his family.

A language correspondence can clarify the subtext. By virtue of the identical phrase "human figure," the "shrouded human figure" at novel's end (chapter 24) may be linked with the "human figure" in the chasms (chapter 23) and, more importantly, with the "human figure" to which Poe's Pym compares a penguin: ". . . the resemblance [of the penguin] to a human figure is very striking . . ." (chapter 14). This penguin connection for the phrase "human figure" is revealing. If we recall that at the novel's beginning the boat *Ariel* collided with the ship *Penguin*, then we may infer that at the novel's close Pym's canoe, approaching the "human figure" that is "very far larger . . . than any dweller among men," will also collide with the ship *Penguin*. The final chapter covertly reflects the first chapter: in both chapters, a small vessel is destroyed by the *Penguin* and those on the small vessel are rescued by those on the *Penguin*. Accordingly, we may understand how Pym returned from his Antarctic adventure.

If we move a step further and note the most "astonishing" characteristic of the penguin and its neighbor the albatross, as stated in chapter 14—their "spirit of reflection" (a phrase not in the Morrell/Woodworth source passages)—then we may conclude that the penguin and the albatross suggest a mirror. According to this reasoning, the ship *Penguin* that appears at the book's beginning, accompanied by the scream of what seem to be "a thousand demons," and the ship *Penguin* that appears at the book's end, accompanied by the screaming "gigantic and pallidly white birds," stand for mirrors, and the double appearance suggests two mirrors—facing mirrors, as in the cabin of the *Jane Guy* in chapter 18. (There is, interestingly, only one mirror in the source passage from Morrell/Woodworth.) Infinitely reflected between these facing mirrors in *Pym* is "Too-wit," the native chief, who was said to be "in the middle of the cabin." Correspondingly, in the middle of *Pym*—midway between the facing mirrors, in the eleventh of twenty-two paragraphs in chapter 13, the central chapter of twenty-five chapters—is the infinitely reflected death of Augustus/Henry on August 1. Arguably, Poe is providing for his literary audience a coded infinite reflection suggesting memory—what he termed in "The Philosophy of Composition" (his 1846 essay on the writing of "The Raven") "Mournful and Never-ending Remembrance."

The remaining portion of the novel's subtext involving Poe's family is implied by his aforementioned comment that "... there can be no tie more strong than that of brother for brother—it is not so much that they love one another as that they both love the same parent...." Richard Wilbur has noted that the name "E. Ronald" in the first chapter is an anagram for the maiden name of Poe's mother, "E. Arnold." Furthermore, the white "shrouded human figure" not only reflects Poe's brother but also itself signifies Poe's mother. This is hinted by the fact that the figure appears on March 22 surrounded by birds crying, "Tekeli-li!" In the Charleston *Courier*—a newspaper from which Poe would later borrow for the poem "Annabel Lee"—Poe's mother Eliza Poe was listed as appearing in a play titled *Tekeli*. The play, performed on March 23, 1811, had first been scheduled for March 22. Eliza's role in *Tekeli* was that of a bride—she probably would have been dressed in white.

Writing in the January 1836 issue of the *Messenger*, Poe praised an essay by Barthold Niebuhr, a piece asserting that in Dante's *Inferno* the allegory—the story beneath the story—is a personal one. It certainly seems as if the allegory here described, in *Pym*, is a personal one. The private nature of the novel may have been implied by the Tsalalian natives' cries of "Anamoo-moo!": in Poe's Morrell/Woodworth source for portions of the later chapters of *Pym*, reference is made to the native name for the southern of New Zealand's two islands—"*Tavi Poënammoo*" (365). While Poe did object to allegory if it was obtrusive, he accepted allegory if it was "judiciously subdued"—and Poe's familial allegory in *Pym* certainly is so subdued.

Pym is, then, a memorial volume, a book that honors Poe's dead mother and brother. Pertinently, Poe wrote of his mother in December 1835, shortly before he began *Pym*, that she was "a string to which my heart fully responds." And ten years later, he added: "The writer of this article is himself the

son of an actress—has invariably made it his boast—and no
earl was ever prouder of his earldom than he of the descent
from a woman who, although well-born, hesitated not to con-
secrate to the drama her brief career of genius and of beauty."
He apparently confided to a friend that from his mother he
had received "every good gift of his intellect, & his heart." If
we recall that Henry twice visited Edgar in Richmond, we
may readily imagine that the two brothers had many conversations about the mother they both cherished; the older
Henry would naturally have shared his more plentiful memo-
ries of her with his younger brother. Perhaps, like Pym and
Augustus, Edgar and Henry enjoyed an "intimate communion."

Poe's allegories of Henry's death and Eliza's performance
in *Pym* would have been difficult for the reader of Poe's time
to ascertain, since these allegories were dependent on knowledge of such personal matters. Probably only those people
who were close to the author fully fathomed the private con-
cerns of the novel. Yet perhaps more readers would have
found *Pym*'s other allegories accessible, since these were
based on a shared text, the Bible.

We must here return to the Norfolk newspapers' February
1836 account of the destruction of the *Ariel*. To understand
more of Poe's thinking as he read that account, we should
consult further his critical writing at the time. The February
1836 issue of the *Messenger* featured Poe's piece on "Palæstine," which closes with mention of the destruction of
Jerusalem. As a reader of the Bible, Poe would have known
that Jerusalem is there referred to as Ariel: "Woe to Ariel, to
Ariel, the city where David dwelt!" (Isaiah 29:1). Accordingly, when he came upon the news story about the destruction of the vessel *Ariel*, he would have realized the story's
potential for suggesting another level of meaning—the destruction of Jerusalem. Thus he would have seen an opportunity to solve a problem that the poet Samuel Taylor Coleridge

had declared insurmountable. In *Specimens of the Table Talk of the Late Samuel Taylor Coleridge*, which Poe read, and which he commented on in the April 1835 *Messenger*, Coleridge contended:

> . . . the destruction of Jerusalem is the only subject now left for an epic poem of the highest kind. Yet, with all its great capabilities, it has this one grand defect—that, whereas a poem, to be epic, must have a personal interest,—in the destruction of Jerusalem no genius or skill could possibly preserve the interest for the hero from being merged in the interest for the event. The fact is, the event itself is too sublime and overwhelming.

Coleridge was, as acknowledged by early Poe biographer George Woodberry, "the guiding genius of Poe's early intellectual life"; in fact, he was the author of poems that Poe would draw on for *Pym*—"The Wanderings of Cain," "Christabel," and, most important, "The Rime of the Ancient Mariner." Coleridge's assertion of a literary problem—and of his own failure to solve it—would have intrigued Poe. We can reasonably infer that Poe would have thought about Coleridge's challenging comment regarding "the only subject now left for an epic poem of the highest kind" and worked up the novel *Pym* in part to accomplish what his hero Coleridge could not—to offer the "genius or skill" to "preserve the interest for the hero" by allegorizing the destruction of Jerusalem.

We can see that Poe anticipated the destruction of Jerusalem in *Pym* in chapter 19 with an allegory of the siege of Jerusalem: Pym and eleven shipmates (the twelve tribes of Israel) sit in the native chief's tent (a word associated etymologically with "tabernacle") while the Tsalal natives surround the tent (the Romans surround Jerusalem) and the "palpitating entrails" of a slim-legged hog are passed to Pym and his friends for dinner (a hog is passed by the Romans to the Israelites as a supposed joke). (This was the same story that Poe had written less cryptically in "A Tale of Jerusalem.") And Poe rendered the destruction of Jerusalem in the story of the wreck of the *Ariel* in chapter 1 (and in its retelling in chapter 24) and in the inversion of the prophecy in Isaiah 33:20 regarding "Jerusalem a quiet habitation, a tabernacle that shall not be taken down; not one of the stakes thereof shall ever be removed, neither shall any of the cords thereof be broken": at the end of chapter 21, the natives of Tsalal pull on "cords" (mentioned four times) that are attached to "stakes" embedded in the earth (mentioned six times), thereby causing a landslide that kills most of the men from the *Jane Guy*.

Poe's use of the ship *Penguin* to rescue Pym and his allusion to the play *Tekeli* are clarified by the final allegory of the novel. Even as Jerusalem is destroyed, the New Jerusalem is prophesied. Notably, there are many suggestions of Jesus in the novel—for example, "the light of the blessed sun" (chapter 9), the "heavy cross sea" (chapter 14), "a series of cross questioning" (chapter 19), and the cry of the natives, "Lama-Lama!" (chapters 18 and 19), recalling one of the last words of Jesus: "Eli, Eli, lama sabachthani?" (Matthew 27:46; Mark 15:34): "My God, my God, why hast thou forsaken me?" The landslide itself (chapters 20 and 21) is described with language echoing that of the 1831 tale attributed to Poe, "A Dream," concerning the crucifixion of Jesus. (The fall of Jerusalem was often considered resonant with the crucifixion.) Critically, *Pym*'s white "shrouded human figure" has been seen as Jesus in the Vision of the Seven Candlesticks (Kaplan, Wilbur)— "one like unto the Son of man" whose "head and his hairs were white like wool, as white as snow" (Revelation 1:13–14). Observing Poe's association of the *Penguin* with Wales (chapter 1) and Poe's affection for the etymologies in dictionaries, we may note that in the Johnson and Webster dictionaries (with which Poe was familiar), the word "penguin" is derived from the Welsh for "white head" ("guin" is white, as in Guinevere, and "pen" is head). Accordingly, we may infer that the ship *Penguin* suggests the white head of Jesus, who has come to prophesy the New Jerusalem. The use of the term "Tekeli" is highly important, since Poe's mother appeared in the play *Tekeli* in the part of a young bride named Christine—that is, she represents, for Poe's purposes, a triumphant image in Christian eschatology: the union of bride and bridegroom— the Church and Christ—at the end of time.

If we wish to pursue the connection between the biblical allegories and the aforementioned issue of race in *Pym*—a book of black and white opposition—we might consider the special significance of Jerusalem in the American South in the 1830s. After all, Poe, living in Baltimore in August 1831, would surely have known of the widely reported rebellion of the slave Nat Turner and his supporters as they advanced on Jerusalem, Virginia. It is interesting to conjecture whether a secondary implication of Poe's biblical allegory of the destruction and recovery of Jerusalem may be the Turner insurrection and its eventual defeat.

If we wish to assess the connection between the biblical allegories and the literal and biographical levels of the novel, we may readily realize that the complex work has a thematic unity—all three levels concern loss and recovery. Even as the *Ariel* is lost, the *Penguin* recovers the survivors; even as Jerusalem is destroyed, the New Jerusalem is prophesied; even as Henry and Eliza Poe die, they are implicitly to be reunited with Edgar in the hereafter. *Pym* is a work of sorrowful memory and hopeful anticipation. And its dynamics are evident, in varied forms, throughout Poe's oeuvre, and nowhere more clearly than in his cosmological disquisition, *Eureka*. Here Poe discusses the expansion and contraction of the universe. He maintains that "A diffusion from Unity . . . involves a tendency to return into Unity—a tendency ineradicable until satisfied." And he later elaborates, "[The atoms'] source lies in the principle, *Unity. This* is their lost parent. *This* they seek always—immediately—in all directions—wherever it is even partially to be found; thus appeasing, in some measure, the ineradicable tendency, while on the way to its absolute satisfaction in the end." As in *Pym*, then, that which is lost will be recovered.

Early chapters of *Pym*, identified as Poe's writing, appeared in the January and February 1837 issues of the *Southern Literary Messenger*. However, Poe's editorial work on the periodical came to an end in January 1837, probably because of his drinking, and he finished the novel while he lived in New York City in 1837 and the first half of 1838. Publisher Thomas W. White thought poorly of *Pym*: remarking on the January 1837 issue of the *Messenger*, he wrote, "A great deal of it is good matter—and all far better than [Poe's] Gordon Pym for which I apparently pay him now—$3 per page, but which in reality has and still costs me $20 per page." Meanwhile, to build verisimilitude in his novel, Poe significantly qualified his authorship of the *Messenger* section—he provided the preface by the supposedly real Pym, who explained that Poe had written the *Messenger* portion of the narrative to prove that readers would believe Pym's story; evidence of their belief supposedly persuaded Pym to write the rest of the work. And Poe added the note about Pym's death, perhaps to strengthen readers' belief in Pym's existence. Poe's novel was published on July 30, 1838, by Harper & Brothers; a British edition was published in October of the same year by Wiley and Putnam. However, in the British edition, the remarkable final journal entry (later to be termed by Malcolm Cowley "the finest passage in all [Poe's] works") was omitted—perhaps because of its seeming inexplicability. A pirated edition of *Pym* was published by John Cunningham in 1841.

Pym did sell—better in England than in the United States—but it was not the popular success for which Poe had hoped. It did win critical commendation, but expressions of appreciative amazement were complemented by those of annoyed incredulity. Yet while Poe attempted to ingratiate himself with William Burton, author of that angry review of *Pym*, by terming the novel, in an 1840 letter, "a very silly book," and while, according to the Duyckinck brothers, Poe did not express pride about the book in conversation, he did, shortly after the book's publication, begin to plan the first modern detective story, "The Murders in the Rue Morgue"—almost as if he understood from responses to *Pym* the need to suggest to his readers some of the most effective methods of reading (including a very close attention to the most unusual details). And it is striking to see that Poe, living in Philadelphia in mid-1838 and ever avid for reviews of his work, found adjacent to a highly positive notice of *Pym* in the August 4, 1838, issue of the Philadelphia *Saturday News* ("... it abounds in the wild and wonderful, and it is apparently written with great ability") the story of a murder on Broadway in New York City—a story that came to serve as a vital source for "Rue Morgue." Thus, Poe repeated his experience with the Norfolk *Herald*: seeking a review, he found a source; seeking both a popular readership and a learned one, he turned news into literature. The two audiences of antebellum America are still with us today; the richness of Poe's work for both audiences may help to explain the extraordinary endurance of that work.

The Narrative of Arthur Gordon Pym endures as a classic for students of American literature both in and out of the classroom; it endures, as well, in dissertations and scholarly journals and books, in myriad translations and illustrated reprints (and in Henri Magritte's celebrated 1937 painting, *La Reproduction Interdite*), and in the literature that it helped to shape. Many scholars agree that *Pym* influenced Herman Melville's *Moby-Dick* (1851), especially the chapter "The Whiteness of the Whale," and clearly the novel influenced Henry James's *The Golden Bowl* (1904). And *Pym* is a touchstone for James De Mille's *A Strange Manuscript Found in a Copper Cylinder* (1888), Arthur Conan Doyle's "The Captain of the 'Polestar' " (1894), Jules Verne's *The Sphinx of the Ice-Fields* (1897), Charles Romyn Dake's *A Strange Discovery* (1899), Walter de la Mare's *The Three Mulla-Mulgars* (1910), B. Traven's *Death Ship* (1926), H. P. Lovecraft's *At the Mountains of Madness* (1939), and Vladimir Nabokov's *Pale Fire* (1962). Modern writers have relied on *Pym*, as well—for example, John Gardner in *The King's Indian* (1973), John Barth in *Sabbatical* (1982), and John Calvin Batchelor in *The Birth of the People's Republic of Antarctica* (1983). Versions of the white shrouded figure in *Pym* may be discovered in such works as David Morrell's novel *Testament* (1975) and John Dunning's novel *Bookman's Wake* (1995). And the eminent fiction writer Jorge Luis Borges once said of *Pym*—as related in Paul Theroux's *The Old Patagonian Express* (1979)—"It is Poe's greatest book."

Doubtless, *Pym* will continue to endure and to be recognized as one of the great achievements of Poe's career—and, indeed, by some as his single greatest achievement. The novel is a work whose story will continue to enthrall and whose complexity, economy, and unity will continue to amaze. Still reaching for a popular readership and a literary one, *The Narrative of Arthur Gordon Pym* will continue to create a community of readers—a community that will also endure.

SUGGESTIONS FOR FURTHER READING

Allan, Hervey, and Thomas Ollive Mabbott. *Poe's Brother: The Poems of William Henry Leonard Poe.* New York: George H. Doran, 1926.

Bezanson, Walter E. "The Troubled Sleep of Arthur Gordon Pym." *Essays in Literary History Presented to J. Milton French.* Edited by Rudolf Kirk and C. F. Main. New Brunswick, N.J.: Rutgers University Press, 1960. 149–75.

Bonaparte, Marie. *The Life and Works of Edgar Allan Poe: A Psycho-Analytic Interpretation.* 1933. Translated by John Rodker. London: Imago, 1949.

Brooks, Douglas. *Number and Pattern in the Eighteenth-Century Novel: Defoe, Fielding, Smollett and Sterne.* London: Routledge & Kegan Paul, 1973.

Carlson, Eric W. *A Companion to Poe Studies.* Westport, Conn.: Greenwood Press, 1996.

Cecil, L. Moffitt. "The Two Narratives of Arthur Gordon Pym." *Texas Studies in Language and Literature* 3 (1963): 232–41.

Cox, James M. "Edgar Poe: Style as Prose." *Virginia Quarterly Review* 44 (1968): 67–89.

Dameron, J. Lasley. "Poe's *Pym* and Scoresby on Polar Cataracts." *Resources for American Literary Study* 21 (1995): 258–60.

Davidson, Edward H. *Poe: A Critical Study.* Cambridge: Harvard University Press, 1964.

Eakin, Paul John. "Poe's Sense of an Ending." *American Literature* 45 (1973): 1–22.

Fiedler, Leslie. *Love and Death in the American Novel.* 2nd ed. New York: Stein and Day, 1966.

Forrest, William Mentzel. *Biblical Allusions in Poe.* New York: Macmillan, 1928.

Frank, Frederick, S. "Polarized Gothic: An Annotated Bibliography of Poe's *Narrative of Arthur Gordon Pym.*" *Bulletin of Bibliography* 38 (1981): 117–27.

Frank, Frederick S., and Anthony Magistrale. *The Poe Encyclopedia.* Westport, Conn.: Greenwood Press, 1997.

Fukuchi, Curtis. "Poe's Providential *Narrative of Arthur Gordon Pym.*" *ESQ* 27 (1981): 147–56.

Hoffman, Daniel. *Poe Poe Poe Poe Poe Poe Poe.* Garden City, N.Y.: Doubleday, 1972.

Irwin, John T. *American Hieroglyphics: The Symbol of the Egyptian Hieroglyphics in the American Renaissance.* New Haven: Yale University Press, 1980.

Kaplan, Sidney. "Introduction" to *The Narrative of Arthur Gordon Pym.* New York: Hill and Wang, 1960.

Kennedy, J. Gerald. The Narrative of Arthur Gordon Pym *and the Abyss of Interpretation.* New York: Twayne, 1995.

———. *Poe, Death, and the Life of Writing.* New Haven: Yale University Press, 1987.

Ketterer, David. *The Rationale of Deception in Poe.* Baton Rouge: Louisiana State University Press, 1979.

Kopley, Richard. "Early Illustrations of *Pym*'s 'Shrouded Human Figure.' " In *The Scope of the Fantastic—Culture, Biography, Themes, Children's Literature.* Edited by Robert A. Collins and Howard D. Pearce. Westport, Conn.: Greenwood Press, 1985. 155–70.

———. *Edgar Allan Poe and* The Philadelphia Saturday News. Baltimore: Enoch Pratt Free Library and The Edgar Allan Poe Society, 1991.

———. "The Hidden Journey of *Arthur Gordon Pym.*" *Studies in the American Renaissance 1982.* Edited by Joel Myerson. Charlottesville: University Press of Virginia, 1982. 29–51.

———. "Poe's *Pym*-esque 'A Tale of the Ragged

Mountains.' " In *Poe and His Times: The Artist and His Milieu*. Edited by Benjamin Franklin Fisher IV. Baltimore: The Edgar Allan Poe Society, 1990. 167–77.

———. "The Secret of *Arthur Gordon Pym*: The Text and the Source." *Studies in American Fiction* 8 (1980): 203–18.

———. "The '*Very* Profound Under-current' of *Arthur Gordon Pym*." In *Studies in the American Renaissance 1987*. Edited by Joel Myerson. Charlottesville: University Press of Virginia, 1987. 143–75.

———, ed. *Poe's* Pym: *Critical Explorations*. Durham, N.C.: Duke University Press, 1992.

[Lee], Grace Farrell. "*Pym* and *Moby-Dick*: Essential Connections." *American Transcendental Quarterly* 37 (1978): 73–86.

———. "The Quest of Arthur Gordon Pym." *Southern Literary Journal* 4 (1972): 22–33.

Lee, Helen. "Possibilities of Pym." *English Journal* 55 (1966): 1149–54.

Levin, Harry. *The Power of Blackness: Hawthorne, Poe, Melville*. New York: Alfred A. Knopf, 1958.

Lévy, Maurice. "*Pym*, Conte Fantastique?" *Études Anglaises* 27 (1974): 38–44.

Liebler, Todd M. "The Apocalyptic Imagination of A. Gordon Pym." *Endless Experiments: Essays on the Heroic Experience in American Romanticism*. Columbus: Ohio State University Press, 1973. 165–89.

Limon, John. *The Place of Fiction in the Time of Science: A Disciplinary History of American Writing*. New York: Cambridge University Press, 1990.

Ljungquist, Kent P. *The Grand and the Fair: Poe's Landscape Aesthetics and Pictorial Techniques*. Potomac, Md.: Scripta Humanistica, 1984.

Moldenhauer, Joseph J. "Imagination and Perversity in *The Narrative of Arthur Gordon Pym*." *Texas Studies in Literature and Language* 13 (1971): 267–80.

Nelson, Dana. *The Word in Black and White: Reading "Race" in American Literature, 1638–1867.* New York: Oxford University Press, 1992.

O'Donnell, Charles. "From Earth to Ether: Poe's Flight into Space." *PMLA* 77 (1962): 85–91.

Peden, William. "Prologue to a Dark Journey: The 'Opening' to Poe's *Pym*." In *Papers on Poe: Essays in Honor of John Ward Ostrom.* Edited by Richard P. Veler. Springfield, Ohio: Chantry Music Press, 1972. 84–91.

Poe, Edgar Allan. *Collected Works of Edgar Allan Poe.* Edited by Thomas Ollive Mabbott. 3 vols. Cambridge: Harvard University Press, 1969–78.

———. *Collected Writings of Edgar Allan Poe.* General editor, Burton R. Pollin. 5 vols. Vol. 1. G. K. Hall, 1981. Revised and Corrected. New York: Gordian Press, 1994. Vols. 2–5. New York: Gordian Press, 1985–98. (Vol. 1, *The Imaginary Voyages*, includes *Pym*.)

———. *The Complete Works of Edgar Allan Poe.* Edited by James A. Harrison. 17 vols. Crowell, 1902. New York: AMS Press, 1979.

———. *The Letters of Edgar Allan Poe.* Edited by John Ward Ostrom. 2 vols. Harvard University Press, 1948. With New Foreword and Supplementary Chapter. New York: Gordian Press, 1966.

Pollin, Burton R. "The Narrative of Benjamin Morrell: Out of the Bucket and into Poe's *Pym*." *Studies in American Fiction* 4 (1976): 157–72.

———. "Poe's *Narrative of Arthur Gordon Pym* and the Contemporary Reviewers." *Studies in American Fiction* 2 (1974): 37–56.

Quinn, Arthur Hobson. *Edgar Allan Poe: A Critical Biography.* 1941. New York: Cooper Square, 1969. Reprint, with an introduction by Shawn Rosenheim. Baltimore: Johns Hopkins University Press, 1997.

Reynolds, David S. *Beneath the American Renaissance: The Subversive Imagination in the Age of Emerson and Melville.* New York: Alfred A. Knopf, 1988.

Rhea, Robert Lee. "Some Observations on Poe's Origins." *University of Texas Studies in English* 10 (1930): 135–46.

Ricardou, Jean. " 'The Singular Character of the Water.' " Translated by Frank Towne. *Poe Studies* 9 (1976): 1–6.

Ridgely, Joseph V. "The Continuing Puzzle of *Arthur Gordon Pym*: Some Notes and Queries." *Poe Newsletter* 3 (1970): 5–6.

———. "The End of Pym and the Ending of *Pym*." In *Papers on Poe: Essays in Honor of John Ward Ostrom.* Edited by Richard P. Veler. Springfield, Ohio: Chantry Music Press, 1972. 104–12.

———. "Tragical-Mythical-Satirical-Hoaxical: Problems of Genre in *Pym*." *American Transcendental Quarterly* 24 (1974): 4–9.

Ridgely, Joseph V., and Iola S. Haverstick. " 'Chartless Voyage': The Many Narratives of Arthur Gordon Pym." *Texas Studies in Literature and Language* 8 (1966): 63–80.

Robinson, Douglas. *American Apocalypses: The Image of the End of the World in American Literature.* Baltimore: Johns Hopkins University Press, 1985.

———. "Reading Poe's Novel: A Speculative Review of *Pym* Criticism, 1950–1980." *Poe Studies* 15 (1982): 47–54.

Rowe, John Carlos. *Through the Custom-House: Nineteenth-Century American Fiction and Modern Theory.* Baltimore: Johns Hopkins University Press, 1982.

Silverman, Kenneth. *Edgar A. Poe: Mournful and Never-ending Remembrance.* New York: HarperCollins, 1991.

Smith, Geddeth. *The Brief Career of Eliza Poe.* Rutherford, N.J.: Fairleigh Dickinson University Press, 1988.

Stroupe, John H. "Poe's Imaginary Voyage: Pym as Hero." *Studies in Short Fiction* 4 (1967): 315–21.

Thomas, Dwight, and David K. Jackson. *The Poe Log: A Doc-
umentary Life of Edgar Allan Poe, 1809–1849.* Boston:
G. K. Hall, 1987.

Thompson, G. R. *Poe's Fiction: Romantic Irony in the Gothic
Tales.* Madison: University of Wisconsin Press, 1973.

Tynan, Daniel J. "J. N. Reynolds' *Voyage of the Potomac*:
Another Source for *The Narrative of Arthur Gordon Pym.*"
Poe Studies 4 (1971): 35–37.

Walker, I. M., ed. *Edgar Allan Poe: The Critical Heritage.*
London: Routledge, 1986.

Wells, Daniel A. "Engraved Within the Hills: Further Per-
spectives on the Ending of *Pym.*" *Poe Studies* 10 (1977):
13–15.

Wilbur, Richard. "Introduction" to *The Narrative of Arthur
Gordon Pym.* Boston: Godine, 1973. vii–xxv.

A NOTE ON THE TEXT

The text selected for this edition of *The Narrative of Arthur Gordon Pym* is that of the 1994 Gordian edition of the *The Imaginary Voyages*, a reissue of the 1981 G. K. Hall edition of that volume, with minor revisions and corrections. *The Imaginary Voyages*, the first volume in the *Collected Writings of Edgar Allan Poe*, features *Pym*, "The Unparalleled Adventure of one Hans Pfaall," and "The Journal of Julius Rodman." The editor of *The Imaginary Voyages* is Burton R. Pollin, the general editor of the *Collected Writings*. The text of *Pym* offered in *The Imaginary Voyages* is that of the 1838 American first edition of the novel, the only complete edition that Poe authorized. No manuscript of the work has survived. Pollin has silently emended several minor errors. Since the first American edition includes two different chapters labeled "XXIII"—probably because of the late insertion of the first of these—the two have been distinguished in the Pollin edition as "23" and "23 bis."

THE NARRATIVE
OF
ARTHUR GORDON PYM.
OF NANTUCKET.

COMPRISING THE DETAILS OF A MUTINY AND ATROCIOUS BUTCHERY
ON BOARD THE AMERICAN BRIG GRAMPUS, ON HER WAY TO
THE SOUTH SEAS, IN THE MONTH OF JUNE, 1827.

WITH AN ACCOUNT OF THE RECAPTURE OF THE VESSEL BY THE
SURVIVERS; THEIR SHIPWRECK AND SUBSEQUENT HORRIBLE
SUFFERINGS FROM FAMINE; THEIR DELIVERANCE BY
MEANS OF THE BRITISH SCHOONER JANE GUY; THE
BRIEF CRUISE OF THIS LATTER VESSEL IN THE
ANTARCTIC OCEAN; HER CAPTURE, AND THE
MASSACRE OF HER CREW AMONG THE
GROUP OF ISLANDS IN THE

EIGHTY-FOURTH PARALLEL OF SOUTHERN LATITUDE;

TOGETHER WITH THE INCREDIBLE ADVENTURES AND
DISCOVERIES

STILL FARTHER SOUTH

TO WHICH THAT DISTRESSING CALAMITY GAVE RISE.

Preface

Upon my return to the United States a few months ago, after the extraordinary series of adventure in the South Seas and elsewhere, of which an account is given in the following pages, accident threw me into the society of several gentlemen in Richmond, Va., who felt deep interest in all matters relating to the regions I had visited, and who were constantly urging it upon me, as a duty, to give my narrative to the public. I had several reasons, however, for declining to do so, some of which were of a nature altogether private, and concern no person but myself; others not so much so. One consideration which deterred me was, that, having kept no journal during a greater portion of the time in which I was absent, I feared I should not be able to write, from mere memory, a statement so minute and connected as to have the *appearance* of that truth it would really possess, barring only the natural and unavoidable exaggeration to which all of us are prone when detailing events which have had powerful influence in exciting the imaginative faculties. Another reason was, that the incidents to be narrated were of a nature so positively marvellous, that, unsupported as my assertions must necessarily be (except by the evidence of a single individual, and he a half-breed Indian), I could only hope for belief among my family, and those of my friends who have had reason, through life, to put faith in my veracity—the probability being that the public at large would regard what I should put forth as merely an impudent and ingenious fiction.[1] A distrust in my own abilities as a writer was, nevertheless, one of the principal causes which prevented me from complying with the suggestions of my advisers.

Among those gentlemen in Virginia who expressed the greatest interest in my statement, more particularly in regard to that portion of it which related to the Antarctic Ocean, was Mr. Poe, lately editor of the Southern Literary Messenger, a monthly magazine, published by Mr. Thomas W. White, in the city of Richmond. He strongly advised me, among others, to prepare at once a full account of what I had seen and undergone, and trust to the shrewdness and common sense of the public—insisting, with great plausibility, that however roughly, as regards mere authorship, my book should be got up, its very uncouthness, if there were any, would give it all the better chance of being received as truth.[2]

Notwithstanding this representation, I did not make up my mind to do as he suggested. He afterward proposed (finding that I would not stir in the matter) that I should allow him to draw up, in his own words, a narrative of the earlier portion of my adventures, from facts afforded by myself, publishing it in the Southern Messenger *under the garb of fiction.* To this, perceiving no objection, I consented, stipulating only that my real name should be retained. Two numbers of the pretended fiction appeared, consequently, in the Messenger for January and February (1837), and, in order that it might certainly be regarded as fiction, the name of Mr. Poe was affixed to the articles in the table of contents of the magazine.[3]

The manner in which this *ruse* was received has induced me at length to undertake a regular compilation and publication of the adventures in question; for I found that, in spite of the air of fable which had been so ingeniously thrown around that portion of my statement which appeared in the Messenger (without altering or distorting a single fact), the public were still not at all disposed to receive it as fable, and several letters were sent to Mr. P.'s address distinctly expressing a conviction to the contrary. I thence concluded that the facts of my narrative would prove of such a nature as to carry with them sufficient evidence of their own authenticity, and that I had consequently little to fear on the score of popular incredulity.

This *exposé* being made, it will be seen at once how much of what follows I claim to be my own writing; and it will also be understood that no fact is misrepresented in the first few pages which were written by Mr. Poe. Even to those readers who have not seen the Messenger, it will be unnecessary to point out where his portion ends and my own commences; the difference in point of style will be readily perceived.[4]

A. G. Pym.

New-York, July, 1838.[5]

Narrative of A. Gordon Pym.

My name is Arthur Gordon Pym.[1] My father was a respectable trader in sea-stores at Nantucket, where I was born. My maternal grandfather was an attorney in good practice. He was fortunate in everything, and had speculated very successfully in stocks of the Edgarton New-Bank,[2] as it was formerly called. By these and other means he had managed to lay by a tolerable sum of money. He was more attached to myself, I believe, than to any other person in the world, and I expected to inherit the most of his property at his death. He sent me, at six years of age, to the school of old Mr. Ricketts, a gentleman with only one arm, and of eccentric manners—he is well known to almost every person who has visited New Bedford. I stayed at his school until I was sixteen,[3] when I left him for Mr. E. Ronald's academy[4] on the hill. Here I became intimate with the son of Mr. Barnard, a sea captain, who generally sailed in the employ of Lloyd and Vredenburgh—Mr. Barnard is also very well known in New Bedford, and has many relations, I am certain, in Edgarton. His son was named Augustus,[5] and he was nearly two years older than myself. He had been on a whaling voyage with his father in the John Donaldson, and was always talking to me of his adventures in the South Pacific Ocean. I used frequently to go home with him, and remain all day, and sometimes all night. We occupied the same bed, and he would be sure to keep me awake until almost light, telling me stories of the natives of the Island of Tinian, and other places he had visited in his travels. At last I could not help being interested in what he said, and by degrees I felt the greatest desire to go to sea. I owned a sail-boat called the Ariel,[6] and worth about seventy-five dollars. She had a half-deck or cuddy, and was rigged sloop-fashion—I forget her tonnage, but she would hold ten persons without much crowding. In this boat we were in the habit of going on some of the maddest freaks in the world; and, when I now think of them, it appears to me a thousand wonders that I am alive to-day.

I will relate one of these adventures by way of introduction to a longer and more momentous narrative.[7] One night there was a party at Mr. Barnard's, and both Augustus and myself were not a little intoxicated towards the close of it. As usual, in such cases, I took part of his bed in preference to going home. He went to sleep, as I thought, very quietly (it being near one when the party broke up), and without saying a word on his favourite topic. It might have been half an hour from the time of our getting in bed, and I was just about falling into a doze, when he suddenly started up, and swore with a terrible oath that he would not go to sleep for any Arthur Pym in Christendom, when there was so glorious a breeze from the southwest. I never was so astonished in my life, not knowing what he intended, and thinking that the wines and liquors he had drunk had set him entirely beside himself. He proceeded to talk very coolly, however, saying he knew that I supposed him intoxicated, but that he was never more sober in his life. He was only tired, he added, of lying in bed on such a fine night like a dog, and was determined to get up and dress, and go out on a frolic with the boat. I can hardly tell what possessed me, but the words were no sooner out of his mouth than I felt a thrill of the greatest excitement and pleasure, and thought his mad idea one of the most delightful and most reasonable things in the world. It was blowing almost a gale, and the weather was very cold—it being late in October. I sprang out of bed, nevertheless, in a kind of ecstasy, and told him I was quite as brave as himself, and quite as tired as he was of lying in bed like a dog, and quite as ready for any fun or frolic as any Augustus Barnard in Nantucket.

We lost no time in getting on our clothes and hurrying down to the boat. She was lying at the old decayed wharf by the lumber-yard of Pankey & Co.,[8] and almost thumping her sides out against the rough logs. Augustus got into her and bailed her, for she was nearly half full of water. This being done, we hoisted jib and mainsail, kept full, and started boldly out to sea.

The wind, as I before said, blew freshly from the south-west. The night was very clear and cold. Augustus had taken the helm, and I stationed myself by the mast, on the deck of the cuddy. We flew along at a great rate—neither of us having said a word since casting loose from the wharf. I now asked my companion what course he intended to steer, and what time he thought it probable we should get back. He whistled for a few minutes, and then said crustily, "*I* am going to sea—*you* may go home if you think proper." Turning my eyes upon him, I perceived at once that, in spite of his assumed *nonchalance*, he was greatly agitated. I could see him distinctly by the light of the moon—his face was paler than any marble, and his hand shook so excessively that he could scarcely retain hold of the tiller. I found that something had gone wrong, and became seriously alarmed. At this period I knew little about the management of a boat, and was now depending entirely upon the nautical skill of my friend. The wind, too, had suddenly increased, as we were fast getting out of the lee of the land—still I was ashamed to betray any trepidation, and for almost half an hour maintained a resolute silence. I could stand it no longer, however, and spoke to Augustus about the propriety of turning back. As before, it was nearly a minute before he made answer, or took any notice of my suggestion. "By-and-by," said he at length—"time enough—home by-and-by." I had expected a similar reply, but there was something in the tone of these words which filled me with an indescribable feeling of dread. I again looked at the speaker attentively. His lips were perfectly livid, and his

knees shook so violently together that he seemed scarcely able
to stand. "For God's sake, Augustus," I screamed, now
heartily frightened, "what ails you?—what is the matter?—
what *are* you going to do?" "Matter!" he stammered, in the
greatest apparent surprise, letting go the tiller at the same
moment, and falling forward into the bottom of the boat—
"matter!—why, nothing is the—matter—going home—
d—d—don't you see?" The whole truth now flashed upon
me. I flew to him and raised him up. He was drunk—beastly
drunk—he could no longer either stand, speak, or see. His
eyes were perfectly glazed; and as I let him go in the extremity
of my despair, he rolled like a mere log into the bilge-water
from which I had lifted him. It was evident that, during the
evening, he had drunk far more than I suspected, and that his
conduct in bed had been the result of a highly-concentrated
state of intoxication—a state which, like madness, frequently
enables the victim to imitate the outward demeanour of one in
perfect possession of his senses. The coolness of the night air,
however, had had its usual effect—the mental energy began to
yield before its influence—and the confused perception which
he no doubt then had of his perilous situation had assisted in
hastening the catastrophe. He was now thoroughly insensible,
and there was no probability that he would be otherwise for
many hours.

It is hardly possible to conceive the extremity of my terror.
The fumes of the wine lately taken had evaporated, leaving me
doubly timid and irresolute. I knew that I was altogether incapable of managing the boat, and that a fierce wind and strong
ebb tide were hurrying us to destruction.[9] A storm was evidently gathering behind us; we had neither compass nor provisions; and it was clear that, if we held our present course, we
should be out of sight of land before daybreak. These
thoughts, with a crowd of others equally fearful, flashed
through my mind with a bewildering rapidity, and for some
moments paralyzed me beyond the possibility of making any

exertion. The boat was going through the water at a terrible rate—full before the wind—no reef in either jib or mainsail—running her bows completely under the foam. It was a thousand wonders she did not broach to—Augustus having let go the tiller, as I said before, and I being too much agitated to think of taking it myself. By good luck, however, she kept steady, and gradually I recovered some degree of presence of mind. Still the wind was increasing fearfully; and whenever we rose from a plunge forward, the sea behind fell combing over our counter, and deluged us with water. I was so utterly benumbed, too, in every limb, as to be nearly unconscious of sensation. At length I summoned up the resolution of despair, and rushing to the mainsail, let it go by the run. As might have been expected, it flew over the bows, and, getting drenched with water, carried away the mast short off by the board. This latter accident alone saved me from instant destruction. Under the jib only, I now boomed along before the wind, shipping heavy seas occasionally over the counter, but relieved from the terror of immediate death. I took the helm, and breathed with greater freedom as I found that there yet remained to us a chance of ultimate escape.[10] Augustus still lay senseless in the bottom of the boat; and as there was imminent danger of his drowning (the water being nearly a foot deep just where he fell), I contrived to raise him partially up, and keep him in a sitting position, by passing a rope round his waist, and lashing it to a ringbolt in the deck of the cuddy. Having thus arranged everything as well as I could in my chilled and agitated condition, I recommended myself to God, and made up my mind to bear whatever might happen with all the fortitude in my power.

Hardly had I come to this resolution, when, suddenly, a loud and long scream or yell, as if from the throats of a thousand demons,[11] seemed to pervade the whole atmosphere around and above the boat. Never while I live shall I forget the intense agony of terror I experienced at that moment. My hair stood erect on my head—I felt the blood congealing in my veins—my heart ceased utterly to beat, and without having once raised my eyes to learn the source of my alarm, I tumbled headlong and insensible upon the body of my fallen companion.

I found myself, upon reviving, in the cabin of a large whaling-ship (the Penguin)[12] bound to Nantucket. Several persons were standing over me, and Augustus, paler than death, was busily occupied in chafing my hands. Upon seeing me open my eyes, his exclamations of gratitude and joy excited alternate laughter and tears from the rough-looking personages who were present. The mystery of our being in existence was now soon explained. We had been run down by the whaling-ship, which was close hauled, beating up to Nantucket with every sail she could venture to set, and consequently running almost at right angles to our own course. Several men were on the look-out forward, but did not perceive our boat until it was an impossibility to avoid coming in contact—their shouts of warning upon seeing us were what so terribly alarmed me. The huge ship, I was told, rode immediately over us with as much ease as our own little vessel would have passed over a feather, and without the least perceptible impediment to her progress. Not a scream arose from the deck of the victim—there was a slight grating sound to be heard mingling with the roar of wind and water, as the frail bark which was swallowed up rubbed for a moment along the keel of her destroyer—but this was all. Thinking our boat (which it will be remembered was dismasted) some mere shell cut adrift as useless, the captain (Captain E. T. V. Block of New London) was for proceeding on his course without troubling himself further about the matter. Luckily, there were two of the look-out who swore positively to having seen some person at our helm, and represented the possibility of yet saving him. A discussion ensued, when Block grew angry, and, after a while, said that "it was no business of his to be eternally watching for egg-shells; that the ship should *not* put about for any such nonsense; and if there was a man run down, it was nobody's fault but his own—he might drown and be d—d," or some language to that effect. Henderson, the first mate, now took the matter up, being justly indignant, as well as the whole ship's crew, at a speech evincing so base a degree of heartless atrocity. He spoke plainly, seeing himself upheld by the men, told the captain he considered him a fit subject for the gallows, and that he would disobey his orders if he were hanged for it the moment he set his foot on shore. He strode aft, jostling Block (who turned very pale and made no answer) on one side, and seizing the helm, gave the word, in a firm voice, *Hard-a-lee!* The men flew to their posts, and the ship went cleverly about. All this had occupied nearly five minutes, and it was supposed to be hardly within the bounds of possibility that any individual could be saved—allowing any to have been on board the boat. Yet, as the reader has seen, both Augustus and myself were rescued; and our deliverance seemed to have been brought about by two of those almost inconceivable pieces of good fortune which are attributed by the wise and pious to the special interference of Providence.[13]

While the ship was yet in stays, the mate lowered the jolly-boat and jumped into her with the very two men, I believe, who spoke up as having seen me at the helm. They had just left the lee of the vessel (the moon still shining brightly) when she made a long and heavy roll to windward, and Henderson, at the same moment, starting up in his seat, bawled out to his crew to *back water.* He would say nothing else—repeating his cry impatiently, *back water! back water!* The men put back as speedily as possible; but by this time the ship had gone round, and gotten fully under headway, although all hands on board were making great exertions to take in sail. In despite of the danger of the attempt, the mate clung to the main-chains as soon as they came within his reach. Another huge lurch now brought the starboard side of the vessel out of water nearly as far as her keel, when the cause of his anxiety was rendered obvious enough. The body of a man was seen to be affixed in the most singular manner to the smooth and shining bottom (the Penguin was coppered and copper-fastened), and beating violently against it with every movement of the hull. After several ineffectual efforts, made during the lurches of the ship, and at the imminent risk of swamping the boat, I was finally disengaged from my perilous situation and taken on board—for the body proved to be my own. It appeared that one of the timber-bolts having started and broken a passage through the copper, it had arrested my progress as I passed under the ship, and fastened me in so extraordinary a manner to her bottom. The head of the bolt had made its way through the collar of the green baize jacket I had on, and through the back part of my neck, forcing itself out between two sinews and just below the right ear. I was immediately put to bed—although life seemed to be totally extinct. There was no surgeon on board. The captain, however, treated me with every attention—to make amends, I presume, in the eyes of his crew, for his atrocious behaviour in the previous portion of the adventure.

In the meantime, Henderson had again put off from the ship, although the wind was now blowing almost a hurricane. He had not been gone many minutes when he fell in with some fragments of our boat, and shortly afterward one of the men with him asserted that he could distinguish a cry for help at intervals amid the roaring of the tempest. This induced the hardy seamen to persevere in their search for more than half an hour, although repeated signals to return were made them by Captain Block, and although every moment on the water in so frail a boat was fraught to them with the most imminent and deadly peril. Indeed, it is nearly impossible to conceive how the small jolly they were in could have escaped destruction for a single instant. She was built, however, for the whaling service, and was fitted, as I have since had reason to believe, with air-boxes, in the manner of some life-boats used on the coast of Wales.[14]

After searching in vain for about the period of time just mentioned, it was determined to get back to the ship. They had scarcely made this resolve when a feeble cry arose from a dark object which floated rapidly by. They pursued and soon overtook it. It proved to be the entire deck of the Ariel's cuddy. Augustus was struggling near it, apparently in the last agonies. Upon getting hold of him it was found that he was attached by a rope to the floating timber. This rope, it will be remembered, I had myself tied round his waist, and made fast to a ringbolt, for the purpose of keeping him in an upright position, and my so doing, it appeared, had been ultimately the means of preserving his life. The Ariel was slightly put together, and in going down her frame naturally went to pieces; the deck of the cuddy, as might be expected, was lifted, by the force of the water rushing in, entirely from the main timbers, and floated (with other fragments, no doubt) to the surface— Augustus was buoyed up with it, and thus escaped a terrible death.

It was more than an hour after being taken on board the Penguin before he could give any account of himself, or be made to comprehend the nature of the accident which had befallen our boat. At length he became thoroughly aroused, and spoke much of his sensations while in the water. Upon his first attaining any degree of consciousness, he found himself beneath the surface, whirling round and round with inconceivable rapidity, and with a rope wrapped in three or four folds tightly about his neck.[15] In an instant afterward he felt himself going rapidly upward, when, his head striking violently against a hard substance, he again relapsed into insensibility. Upon once more reviving he was in fuller possession of his reason—this was still, however, in the greatest degree clouded and confused. He now knew that some accident had occurred, and that he was in the water, although his mouth

was above the surface, and he could breathe with some freedom. Possibly, at this period, the deck was drifting rapidly
before the wind, and drawing him after it, as he floated upon
his back. Of course, as long as he could have retained this position, it would have been nearly impossible that he should be
drowned. Presently a surge threw him directly athwart the
deck; and this post he endeavoured to maintain, screaming at
intervals for help. Just before he was discovered by Mr. Henderson, he had been obliged to relax his hold through exhaustion, and, falling into the sea, had given himself up for lost.
During the whole period of his struggles he had not the
faintest recollection of the Ariel, nor of any matters in connexion with the source of his disaster. A vague feeling of terror and despair had taken entire possession of his faculties.
When he was finally picked up, every power of his mind had
failed him; and, as before said, it was nearly an hour after getting on board the Penguin before he became fully aware of his
condition. In regard to myself—I was resuscitated from a state
bordering very nearly upon death (and after every other
means had been tried in vain for three hours and a half) by
vigorous friction with flannels bathed in hot oil—a proceeding suggested by Augustus. The wound in my neck, although
of an ugly appearance, proved of little real consequence, and I
soon recovered from its effects.

The Penguin got into port about nine o'clock in the morning, after encountering one of the severest gales ever experienced off Nantucket. Both Augustus and myself managed to
appear at Mr. Barnard's in time for breakfast—which, luckily,
was somewhat late, owing to the party over night. I suppose
all at the table were too much fatigued themselves to notice
our jaded appearance—of course, it would not have borne a
very rigid scrutiny. Schoolboys, however, can accomplish
wonders in the way of deception, and I verily believe not one
of our friends in Nantucket had the slightest suspicion that
the terrible story told by some sailors in town of their having

run down a vessel at sea and drowned some thirty or forty poor devils,[16] had reference either to the Ariel, my companion, or myself. We two have since very frequently talked the matter over—but never without a shudder. In one of our conversations Augustus frankly confessed to me, that in his whole life he had at no time experienced so excruciating a sense of dismay, as when on board our little boat he first discovered the extent of his intoxication, and felt himself sinking beneath its influence.

CHAPTER 2

In no affairs of mere prejudice, pro or con, do we deduce in-
ferences with entire certainty even from the most simple data.
It might be supposed that a catastrophe such as I have just related would have effectually cooled my incipient passion for
the sea. On the contrary, I never experienced a more ardent
longing for the wild adventures incident to the life of a navigator than within a week after our miraculous deliverance.
This short period proved amply long enough to erase from
my memory the shadows, and bring out in vivid light all
the pleasurably exciting points of colour, all the picturesque-
ness of the late perilous accident. My conversations with Augustus grew daily more frequent and more intensely full of
interest. He had a manner of relating his stories of the ocean
(more than one half of which I now suspect to have been
sheer fabrications) well adapted to have weight with one of
my enthusiastic temperament, and somewhat gloomy, although glowing imagination. It is strange, too, that he most
strongly enlisted my feelings in behalf of the life of a seaman,
when he depicted his more terrible moments of suffering and
despair. For the bright side of the painting I had a limited
sympathy. My visions were of shipwreck and famine; of death
or captivity among barbarian hordes; of a lifetime dragged out
in sorrow and tears,[1] upon some gray and desolate rock, in an
ocean unapproachable and unknown. Such visions or desires—for they amounted to desires—are common, I have
since been assured, to the whole numerous race of the melancholy among men—at the time of which I speak I regarded
them only as prophetic glimpses of a destiny which I felt

myself in a measure bound to fulfil. Augustus thoroughly entered into my state of mind. It is probable, indeed, that our intimate communion had resulted in a partial interchange of character.[2]

About eighteen months after the period of the Ariel's disaster, the firm of Lloyd and Vredenburgh (a house connected in some manner with the Messieurs Enderby, I believe, of Liverpool) were engaged in repairing and fitting out the brig Grampus[3] for a whaling voyage. She was an old hulk, and scarcely seaworthy when all was done to her that could be done. I hardly know why she was chosen in preference to other good vessels belonging to the same owners—but so it was. Mr. Barnard was appointed to command her, and Augustus was going with him. While the brig was getting ready, he frequently urged upon me the excellency of the opportunity now offered for indulging my desire of travel. He found me by no means an unwilling listener—yet the matter could not be so easily arranged. My father made no direct opposition; but my mother went into hysterics at the bare mention of the design; and, more than all, my grandfather, from whom I expected much, vowed to cut me off with a shilling if I should ever broach the subject to him again.[4] These difficulties, however, so far from abating my desire, only added fuel to the flame. I determined to go at all hazards; and, having made known my intention to Augustus, we set about arranging a plan by which it might be accomplished. In the meantime I forbore speaking to any of my relations in regard to the voyage, and, as I busied myself ostensibly with my usual studies, it was supposed that I had abandoned the design. I have since frequently examined my conduct on this occasion with sentiments of displeasure as well as of surprise. The intense hypocrisy I made use of for the furtherance of my project—an hypocrisy pervading every word and action of my life for so long a period of time—could only have been rendered tolera-

ble to myself by the wild and burning expectation with which
I looked forward to the fulfilment of my long-cherished visions of travel.

In pursuance of my scheme of deception, I was necessarily
obliged to leave much to the management of Augustus, who
was employed for the greater part of every day on board the
Grampus, attending to some arrangements for his father in
the cabin and cabin hold. At night, however, we were sure
to have a conference, and talk over our hopes. After nearly
a month passed in this manner, without our hitting upon
any plan we thought likely to succeed, he told me at last
that he had determined upon everything necessary. I had a
relation living in New Bedford, a Mr. Ross, at whose house
I was in the habit of spending occasionally two or three
weeks at a time. The brig was to sail about the middle of June
(June, 1827),[5] and it was agreed that, a day or two before
her putting to sea, my father was to receive a note, as usual,
from Mr. Ross, asking me to come over and spend a fortnight with Robert and Emmet (his sons). Augustus charged
himself with the enditing of this note and getting it delivered. Having set out, as supposed, for New Bedford, I
was then to report myself to my companion, who would contrive a hiding-place for me in the Grampus. This hiding-place,
he assured me, would be rendered sufficiently comfortable for
a residence of many days, during which I was not to make
my appearance. When the brig had proceeded so far on her
course as to make any turning back a matter out of question, I
should then, he said, be formally installed in all the comforts
of the cabin; and as to his father, he would only laugh heartily
at the joke. Vessels enough would be met with by which a
letter might be sent home explaining the adventure to my
parents.[6]

The middle of June at length arrived, and everything had
been matured. The note was written and delivered, and on a
Monday morning I left the house for the New Bedford

packet, as supposed. I went, however, straight to Augustus, who was waiting for me at the corner of a street. It had been our original plan that I should keep out of the way until dark, and then slip on board the brig; but, as there was now a thick fog in our favour, it was agreed to lose no time in secreting me. Augustus led the way to the wharf, and I followed at a little distance, enveloped in a thick seaman's cloak, which he had brought with him, so that my person might not be easily recognised. Just as we turned the second corner, after passing Mr. Edmund's well, who should appear, standing right in front of me, and looking me full in the face, but old Mr. Peterson, my grandfather. "Why, bless my soul, Gordon," said he, after a long pause, "why, why— *whose* dirty cloak is that you have on?" "Sir!" I replied, assuming, as well as I could, in the exigency of the moment, an air of offended surprise, and talking in the gruffest of all imaginable tones—"sir! you are a sum'mat mistaken—my name, in the first place, bee'nt nothing at all like Goddin,[7] and I'd want you for to know better, you blackguard, than to call my new obercoat a darty one!" For my life I could hardly refrain from screaming with laughter at the odd manner in which the old gentleman received this handsome rebuke. He started back two or three steps, turned first pale and then excessively red, threw up his spectacles, then, putting them down, ran full tilt at me, with his umbrella uplifted. He stopped short, however, in his career, as if struck with a sudden recollection; and presently, turning round, hobbled off down the street, shaking all the while with rage, and muttering between his teeth, "Won't do—new glasses—thought it was Gordon—d____d good-for-nothing salt water Long Tom."[8]

After this narrow escape we proceeded with greater caution, and arrived at our point of destination in safety. There were only one or two of the hands on board, and these were busy forward, doing something to the forecastle combings.

Captain Barnard, we knew very well, was engaged at Lloyd and Vredenburg's (*sic*), and would remain there until late in the evening, so we had little to apprehend on his account. Augustus went first up the vessel's side, and in a short while I followed him, without being noticed by the men at work. We proceeded at once into the cabin, and found no person there. It was fitted up in the most comfortable style—a thing somewhat unusual in a whaling-vessel. There were four very excellent staterooms, with wide and convenient berths. There was also a large stove, I took notice, and a remarkably thick and valuable carpet covering the floor of both the cabin and staterooms. The ceiling was full seven feet high, and, in short, everything appeared of a more roomy and agreeable nature than I had anticipated. Augustus, however, would allow me but little time for observation, insisting upon the necessity of my concealing myself as soon as possible. He led the way into his own stateroom, which was on the starboard side of the brig, and next to the bulkheads. Upon entering, he closed the door and bolted it. I thought I had never seen a nicer little room than the one in which I now found myself. It was about ten feet long, and had only one berth, which, as I said before, was wide and convenient. In that portion of the closet nearest the bulkheads there was a space of four feet square, containing a table, a chair, and a set of hanging shelves full of books, chiefly books of voyages and travels. There were many other little comforts in the room, among which I ought not to forget a kind of safe or refrigerator, in which Augustus pointed out to me a host of delicacies, both in the eating and drinking department.

He now pressed with his knuckles upon a certain spot of the carpet in one corner of the space just mentioned, letting me know that a portion of the flooring, about sixteen inches square, had been neatly cut out and again adjusted. As he pressed, this portion rose up at one end sufficiently to allow the passage of his finger beneath. In this manner he raised the mouth of the trap (to which the carpet was still fastened by tacks), and I found that it led into the after hold. He next lit a small taper by means of a phosphorus match, and, placing the light in a dark lantern, descended with it through the opening, bidding me follow. I did so, and he then pulled the cover upon the hole, by means of a nail driven into the under side— the carpet, of course, resuming its original position on the floor of the stateroom, and all traces of the aperture being concealed.

The taper gave out so feeble a ray, that it was with the greatest difficulty I could grope my way through the confused mass of lumber among which I now found myself. By degrees, however, my eyes became accustomed to the gloom, and I proceeded with less trouble, holding on to the skirts of my friend's coat. He brought me, at length, after creeping and winding through innumerable narrow passages, to an iron-bound box, such as is used sometimes for packing fine earthenware. It was nearly four feet high, and full six long, but very narrow. Two large empty oil-casks lay on the top of it, and above these, again, a vast quantity of straw matting, piled up as high as the floor of the cabin. In every other direction around was wedged as closely as possible, even up to the ceiling, a complete chaos of almost every species of ship-furniture, together with a heterogeneous medley of crates, hampers, barrels, and bales, so that it seemed a matter no less than miraculous that we had discovered any passage at all to the box. I afterward found that Augustus had purposely arranged the stowage in this hold with a view to affording me a thorough concealment, having had only one assistant in the labour, a man not going out in the brig.

My companion now showed me that one of the ends of the box could be removed at pleasure. He slipped it aside and displayed the interior, at which I was excessively amused. A mattress from one of the cabin berths covered the whole of its bottom, and it contained almost every article of mere comfort which could be crowded into so small a space, allowing me, at the same time, sufficient room for my accommodation, either in a sitting position or lying at full length. Among other things, there were some books, pen, ink, and paper, three blankets, a large jug full of water, a keg of sea-biscuit, three or four immense Bologna sausages, an enormous ham, a cold leg of roast mutton, and half a dozen bottles of cordials and liqueurs. I proceeded immediately to take possession of my little apartment, and this with feelings of higher satisfaction, I am sure, than any monarch ever experienced upon entering a new palace. Augustus now pointed out to me the method of fastening the open end of the box, and then, holding the taper close to the deck, showed me a piece of dark whipcord lying along it. This, he said, extended from my hiding-place throughout all the necessary windings among the lumber, to a nail which was driven into the deck of the hold, immediately beneath the trapdoor leading into his stateroom. By means of this cord I should be enabled readily to trace my way out without his guidance, provided any unlooked-for accident should render such a step necessary. He now took his departure, leaving with me the lantern, together with a copious supply of tapers and phosphorus, and promising to pay me a visit as often as he could contrive to do so without observation. This was on the seventeenth of June.

I remained three days and nights (as nearly as I could guess) in my hiding-place without getting out of it at all, except twice for the purpose of stretching my limbs by standing erect between two crates just opposite the opening. During the whole period I saw nothing of Augustus; but this occasioned me little uneasiness, as I knew the brig was expected to put to sea every hour, and in the bustle he would not easily find opportunities of coming down to me. At length I heard the trap open and shut, and presently he called in a low voice, asking if all was well, and if there was anything I wanted. "Nothing," I replied; "I am as comfortable as can be; when will the brig sail?" "She will be under weigh in less than half an hour," he answered. "I came to let you know, and for fear you should be uneasy at my absence. I shall not have a chance of coming down again for some time—perhaps for three or four days more. All is going on right aboveboard. After I go up and close the trap, do you creep along by the whipcord to where the nail is driven in. You will find my watch there—it may be useful to you, as you have no daylight to keep time by. I suppose you can't tell how long you have been buried— only three days—this is the twentieth. I would bring the watch to your box, but am afraid of being missed." With this he went up.

In about an hour after he had gone I distinctly felt the brig in motion, and congratulated myself upon having at length fairly commenced a voyage. Satisfied with this idea, I determined to make my mind as easy as possible, and await the course of events until I should be permitted to exchange the box for the more roomy, although hardly more comfortable, accommodations of the cabin. My first care was to get the watch. Leaving the taper burning, I groped along in the dark, following the cord through windings innumerable, in some of which I discovered that, after toiling a long distance, I was brought back within a foot or two of a former position. At length I reached the nail, and, securing the object of my journey, returned with it in safety. I now looked over the books which had been so thoughtfully provided, and selected the expedition of Lewis and Clarke to the mouth of the Columbia.[9] With this I amused myself for some time, when, growing sleepy, I extinguished the light with great care, and soon fell into a sound slumber.

Upon awaking I felt strangely confused in mind, and some

time elapsed before I could bring to recollection all the various circumstances of my situation. By degrees, however, I remembered all. Striking a light, I looked at the watch; but it was run down, and there were, consequently, no means of determining how long I had slept. My limbs were greatly cramped, and I was forced to relieve them by standing between the crates. Presently, feeling an almost ravenous appetite, I bethought myself of the cold mutton, some of which I had eaten just before going to sleep, and found excellent. What was my astonishment at discovering it to be in a state of absolute putrefaction! This circumstance occasioned me great disquietude; for, connecting it with the disorder of mind I experienced upon awaking, I began to suppose that I must have slept for an inordinately long period of time. The close atmosphere of the hold might have had something to do with this, and might, in the end, be productive of the most serious results. My head ached excessively; I fancied that I drew every breath with difficulty; and, in short, I was oppressed with a multitude of gloomy feelings. Still I could not venture to make any disturbance by opening the trap or otherwise, and, having wound up the watch, contented myself as well as possible.

Throughout the whole of the next tedious twenty-four hours no person came to my relief, and I could not help accusing Augustus of the grossest inattention. What alarmed me chiefly was, that the water in my jug was reduced to about half a pint, and I was suffering much from thirst, having eaten freely of the Bologna sausages after the loss of my mutton. I became very uneasy, and could no longer take any interest in my books. I was overpowered, too, with a desire to sleep, yet trembled at the thought of indulging it, lest there might exist some pernicious influence, like that of burning charcoal, in the confined air of the hold. In the mean time the roll of the brig told me that we were far in the main ocean, and a dull humming sound, which reached my ears as if from an im-

mense distance, convinced me no ordinary gale was blowing. I
could not imagine a reason for the absence of Augustus. We
were surely far enough advanced on our voyage to allow of
my going up. Some accident might have happened to him—
but I could think of none which would account for his suffering me to remain so long a prisoner, except, indeed, his having
suddenly died or fallen overboard, and upon this idea I could
not dwell with any degree of patience. It was possible that we
had been baffled by head winds, and were still in the near
vicinity of Nantucket. This notion, however, I was forced to
abandon; for, such being the case, the brig must have frequently gone about; and I was entirely satisfied from her continual inclination to the larboard, that she had been sailing all
along with a steady breeze on her starboard quarter. Besides,
granting that we were still in the neighbourhood of the island,
why should not Augustus have visited me and informed me of
the circumstance? Pondering in this manner upon the difficulties of my solitary and cheerless condition, I resolved to wait
yet another twenty-four hours, when, if no relief were obtained, I would make my way to the trap, and endeavour either to hold a parley with my friend, or get at least a little
fresh air through the opening, and a further supply of water
from his stateroom. While occupied with this thought, however, I fell, in spite of every exertion to the contrary, into a
state of profound sleep, or rather stupor. My dreams were of
the most terrific description. Every species of calamity and
horror befell me. Among other miseries, I was smothered to
death between huge pillows, by demons of the most ghastly
and ferocious aspect. Immense serpents held me in their em-
brace, and looked earnestly in my face with their fearfully
shining eyes. Then deserts, limitless, and of the most forlorn
and awe-inspiring character, spread themselves out before me.
Immensely tall trunks of trees, gray and leafless, rose up in
endless succession as far as the eye could reach. Their roots
were concealed in wide-spreading morasses, whose dreary

water lay intensely black, still, and altogether terrible, beneath. And the strange trees seemed endowed with a human
vitality, and, waving to and fro their skeleton arms, were crying to the silent waters for mercy, in the shrill and piercing ac-
cents of the most acute agony and despair. The scene changed;
and I stood, naked and alone, amid the burning sand-plains of
Zahara. At my feet lay crouched a fierce lion of the tropics.
Suddenly his wild eyes opened and fell upon me. With a
convulsive bound he sprang to his feet, and laid bare his
horrible teeth. In another instant there burst from his red
throat a roar like the thunder of the firmament, and I fell impetuously to the earth. Stifling in a paroxysm of terror, I at
last found myself partially awake. My dream, then, was not all
a dream. Now, at least, I was in possession of my senses. The
paws of some huge and real monster were pressing heavily
upon my bosom—his hot breath was in my ear—and his
white and ghastly fangs were gleaming upon me through the
gloom.

Had a thousand lives hung upon the movement of a limb
or the utterance of a syllable, I could have neither stirred nor
spoken. The beast, whatever it was, retained his position without attempting any immediate violence, while I lay in an utterly helpless, and, I fancied, a dying condition beneath him. I
felt that my powers of body and mind were fast leaving me—
in a word, that I was perishing, and perishing of sheer fright.
My brain swam—I grew deadly sick—my vision failed—even
the glaring eyeballs above me grew dim. Making a last strong
effort, I at length breathed a faint ejaculation to God, and resigned myself to die. The sound of my voice seemed to arouse
all the latent fury of the animal. He precipitated himself at full
length upon my body; but what was my astonishment, when,
with a long and low whine, he commenced licking my face
and hands with the greatest eagerness, and with the most extravagant demonstrations of affection and joy! I was bewil-

dered, utterly lost in amazement—but I could not forget the peculiar whine of my Newfoundland dog Tiger, and the odd manner of his caresses I well knew. It was he. I experienced a sudden rush of blood to my temples—a giddy and overpowering sense of deliverance and reanimation. I rose hurriedly from the mattress upon which I had been lying, and, throwing myself upon the neck of my faithful follower and friend, relieved the long oppression of my bosom in a flood of the most passionate tears.

As upon a former occasion, my conceptions were in a state of the greatest indistinctness and confusion after leaving the mattress. For a long time I found it nearly impossible to connect any ideas—but, by very slow degrees, my thinking faculties returned, and I again called to memory the several incidents of my condition. For the presence of Tiger I tried in vain to account; and after busying myself with a thousand different conjectures respecting him, was forced to content myself with rejoicing that he was with me to share my dreary solitude, and render me comfort by his caresses. Most people love their dogs—but for Tiger I had an affection far more ardent than common; and never, certainly, did any creature more truly deserve it. For seven years he had been my inseparable companion, and in a multitude of instances had given evidence of all the noble qualities for which we value the animal. I had rescued him, when a puppy, from the clutches of a malignant little villain in Nantucket, who was leading him, with a rope around his neck, to the water; and the grown dog repaid the obligation, about three years afterward, by saving me from the bludgeon of a street-robber.

Getting now hold of the watch, I found, upon applying it to my ear, that it had again run down; but at this I was not at all surprised, being convinced, from the peculiar state of my feelings, that I had slept, as before, for a very long period of time; how long, it was of course impossible to say. I was burning up with fever, and my thirst was almost intolerable. I felt about the box for my little remaining supply of water; for I had no light, the taper having burnt to the socket of the lantern, and the phosphorus-box not coming readily to hand. Upon finding the jug, however, I discovered it to be empty— Tiger, no doubt, having been tempted to drink it, as well as to devour the remnant of mutton, the bone of which lay, well picked, by the opening of the box. The spoiled meat I could well spare, but my heart sank as I thought of the water. I was feeble in the extreme—so much so that I shook all over, as with an ague, at the slightest movement or exertion. To add to my troubles, the brig was pitching and rolling with great violence, and the oil-casks which lay upon my box were in momentary danger of falling down, so as to block up the only way of ingress or egress. I felt, also, terrible sufferings from sea-sickness. These considerations determined me to make my way, at all hazards, to the trap, and obtain immediate relief, before I should be incapacitated from doing so altogether. Having come to this resolve, I again felt about for the phosphorus-box and tapers. The former I found after some little trouble; but, not discovering the tapers as soon as I had expected (for I remembered very nearly the spot in which I had placed them), I gave up the search for the present, and bidding Tiger lie quiet, began at once my journey towards the trap.

In this attempt my great feebleness became more than ever apparent. It was with the utmost difficulty I could crawl along at all, and very frequently my limbs sank suddenly from beneath me; when, falling prostrate on my face, I would remain for some minutes in a state bordering on insensibility. Still I struggled forward by slow degrees, dreading every moment that I should swoon amid the narrow and intricate windings of the lumber, in which event I had nothing but death to expect as the result. At length, upon making a push forward with all the energy I could command, I struck my forehead violently against the sharp corner of an iron-bound crate.[10] The accident only stunned me for a few moments; but I found, to my inexpressible grief, that the quick and violent roll of the vessel had thrown the crate entirely across my path, so as effectually to block up the passage. With my utmost exertions I could not move it a single inch from its position, it being closely wedged in among the surrounding boxes and ship-furniture. It became necessary, therefore, enfeebled as I was, either to leave the guidance of the whipcord and seek out a new passage, or to climb over the obstacle, and resume the path on the other side. The former alternative presented too many difficulties and dangers to be thought of without a shudder. In my present weak state of both mind and body, I should infallibly lose my way if I attempted it, and perish miserably amid the dismal and disgusting labyrinths of the hold. I proceeded, therefore, without hesitation, to summon up all my remaining strength and fortitude, and endeavour, as I best might, to clamber over the crate.

Upon standing erect, with this end in view, I found the undertaking even a more serious task than my fears had led me to imagine. On each side of the narrow passage arose a complete wall of various heavy lumber, which the least blunder on my part might be the means of bringing down upon my head; or, if this accident did not occur, the path might be effectually blocked up against my return by the descending mass, as it was in front by the obstacle there. The crate itself was a long and unwieldy box, upon which no foothold could be obtained. In vain I attempted, by every means in my power, to reach the top, with the hope of being thus enabled to draw myself up. Had I succeeded in reaching it, it is certain that my strength would have proved utterly inadequate to the task of getting over, and it was better in every respect that I failed. At length, in a desperate effort to force the crate from its ground,

I felt a strong vibration in the side next me. I thrust my hand eagerly to the edge of the planks, and found that a very large one was loose. With my pocket-knife, which luckily I had with me, I succeeded, after great labour, in prying it entirely off; and, getting through the aperture, discovered, to my exceeding joy, that there were no boards on the opposite side—in other words, that the top was wanting, it being the bottom through which I had forced my way. I now met with no important difficulty in proceeding along the line until I finally reached the nail. With a beating heart I stood erect, and with a gentle touch pressed against the cover of the trap. It did not rise as soon as I had expected, and I pressed it with somewhat more determination, still dreading lest some other person than Augustus might be in his stateroom. The door, however, to my astonishment, remained steady, and I became somewhat uneasy, for I knew that it had formerly required little or no effort to remove it. I pushed it strongly—it was nevertheless firm: with all my strength—it still did not give way: with rage, with fury, with despair—it set at defiance my utmost efforts; and it was evident, from the unyielding nature of the resistance, that the hole had either been discovered and effectually nailed up, or that some immense weight had been placed upon it, which it was useless to think of removing.

My sensations were those of extreme horror and dismay. In vain I attempted to reason on the probable cause of my being thus entombed. I could summon up no connected chain of reflection, and, sinking on the floor, gave way, unresistingly, to the most gloomy imaginings, in which the dreadful deaths of thirst, famine, suffocation, and premature interment, crowded upon me as the prominent disasters to be encountered. At length there returned to me some portion of presence of mind. I arose, and felt with my fingers for the seams or cracks of the aperture. Having found them, I examined them closely to ascertain if they emitted any light from the stateroom; but none was visible. I then forced the penblade of my knife through them, until I met with some hard obstacle. Scraping against it, I discovered it to be a solid mass of iron, which, from its peculiar wavy feel as I passed the blade along it, I concluded to be a chain-cable. The only course now left me was to retrace my way to the box, and there either yield to my sad fate, or try so to tranquillize my mind as to admit of my arranging some plan of escape. I immediately set about the attempt, and succeeded, after innumerable difficulties, in getting back. As I sank, utterly exhausted, upon the mattress, Tiger threw himself at full length by my side, and seemed as if desirous, by his caresses, of consoling me in my troubles, and urging me to bear them with fortitude.

The singularity of his behaviour at length forcibly arrested my attention. After licking my face and hands for some minutes, he would suddenly cease doing so, and utter a low whine. Upon reaching out my hand towards him, I then invariably found him lying on his back, with his paws uplifted. This conduct, so frequently repeated, appeared strange, and I could in no manner account for it. As the dog seemed distressed, I concluded that he had received some injury; and, taking his paws in my hands, I examined them one by one, but found no sign of any hurt. I then supposed him hungry, and gave him a large piece of ham, which he devoured with avidity—afterward, however, resuming his extraordinary manœuvres. I now imagined that he was suffering, like myself, the torments of thirst, and was about adopting this conclusion as the true one, when the idea occurred to me that I had as yet only examined his paws, and that there might possibly be a wound upon some portion of his body or head. The latter I felt carefully over, but found nothing. On passing my hand, however, along his back, I perceived a slight erection of the hair extending completely across it. Probing this with my finger, I discovered a string, and, tracing it up, found that it encircled the whole body. Upon a closer scrutiny, I came across a small slip of what had the feeling of letter paper, through which the string had been fastened in such a manner as to bring it immediately beneath the left shoulder of the animal.

CHAPTER 3

The thought instantly occurred to me that the paper was a note from Augustus, and that some unaccountable accident having happened to prevent his relieving me from my dungeon, he had devised this method of acquainting me with the true state of affairs. Trembling with eagerness, I now commenced another search for my phosphorus matches and tapers. I had a confused recollection of having put them carefully away just before falling asleep; and, indeed, previously to my last journey to the trap, I had been able to remember the exact spot where I had deposited them. But now I endeavoured in vain to call it to mind, and busied myself for a full hour in a fruitless and vexatious search for the missing articles; never, surely, was there a more tantalizing state of anxiety and suspense. At length, while groping about, with my head close to the ballast, near the opening of the box, and outside of it, I perceived a faint glimmering of light in the direction of the steerage. Greatly surprised, I endeavoured to make my way towards it, as it appeared to be but a few feet from my position. Scarcely had I moved with this intention, when I lost sight of the glimmer entirely, and, before I could bring it into view again, was obliged to feel along by the box until I had exactly resumed my original situation. Now, moving my head with caution to and fro, I found that, by proceeding slowly, with great care, in an opposite direction to that in which I had at first started, I was enabled to draw near the light, still keeping it in view. Presently I came directly upon it, (having squeezed my way through innumerable narrow windings), and found that it proceeded from some fragments of my matches lying in an empty barrel turned upon its side. I was wondering how they came in such a place, when my hand fell upon two or three pieces of taper-wax, which had been evidently mumbled by the dog. I concluded at once that he had devoured the whole of my supply of candles, and I felt hopeless of being ever able to read the note of Augustus. The small remnants of the wax were so mashed up among other rubbish in the barrel, that I despaired of deriving any service from them, and left them as they were. The phosphorus, of which there was only a speck or two, I gathered up as well as I could, and returned with it, after much difficulty, to my box, where Tiger had all the while remained.

What to do next I could not tell. The hold was so intensely dark that I could not see my hand, however close I would hold it to my face. The white slip of paper could barely be discerned, and not even that when I looked at it directly; by turning the exterior portions of the retina towards it, that is to say, by surveying it slightly askance, I found that it became in some measure perceptible. Thus the gloom of my prison may be imagined, and the note of my friend, if indeed it were a note from him, seemed only likely to throw me into further trouble, by disquieting to no purpose my already enfeebled and agitated mind. In vain I revolved in my brain a multitude of absurd expedients for procuring light—such expedients precisely as a man in the perturbed sleep occasioned by opium would be apt to fall upon for a similar purpose—each and all of which appear by turns to the dreamer the most reasonable and the most preposterous of conceptions, just as the reasoning or imaginative faculties flicker, alternately, one above the other. At last an idea occurred to me which seemed rational, and which gave me cause to wonder, very justly, that I had not entertained it before. I placed the slip of paper on the back of a book, and, collecting the fragments of the phosphorus matches which I had brought from the barrel, laid them together upon the paper. I then, with the palm of my hand, rubbed the whole over quickly yet steadily. A clear light diffused itself immediately throughout the whole surface; and had there been any writing upon it, I should not have experienced the least difficulty, I am sure, in reading it. Not a syllable was there, however—nothing but a dreary and unsatisfactory blank; the illumination died away in a few seconds, and my heart died away within me as it went.

I have before stated more than once that my intellect, for some period prior to this, had been in a condition nearly bordering on idiocy. There were, to be sure, momentary intervals of perfect sanity, and, now and then, even of energy; but these were few. It must be remembered that I had been, for many days certainly, inhaling the almost pestilential atmosphere of a close hold in a whaling vessel, and a long portion of that time but scantily supplied with water. For the last fourteen or fifteen hours I had none—nor had I slept during that time. Salt provisions of the most exciting kind had been my chief, and, indeed, since the loss of the mutton, my only supply of food, with the exception of the sea-biscuit; and these latter were utterly useless to me, as they were too dry and hard to be swallowed in the swollen and parched condition of my throat. I was now in a high state of fever, and in every respect exceedingly ill. This will account for the fact that many miserable hours of despondency elapsed after my last adventure with the phosphorus, before the thought suggested itself that I had examined only one side of the paper. I shall not attempt to describe my feelings of rage (for I believe I was more angry than anything else) when the egregious oversight I had committed flashed suddenly upon my perception. The blunder itself would have been unimportant, had not my own folly and impetuosity rendered it otherwise—in my disappointment at not finding some words upon the slip, I had childishly torn it in pieces and thrown it away, it was impossible to say where.

From the worst part of this dilemma I was relieved by the

sagacity of Tiger. Having got, after a long search, a small piece
of the note, I put it to the dog's nose, and endeavoured to
make him understand that he must bring me the rest of it. To
my astonishment (for I had taught him none of the usual
tricks for which his breed are famous), he seemed to enter at
once into my meaning, and, rummaging about for a few moments, soon found another considerable portion. Bringing me
this, he paused a while, and, rubbing his nose against my
hand, appeared to be waiting for my approval of what he had
done. I patted him on the head, when he immediately made
off again. It was now some minutes before he came back—but
when he did come, he brought with him a large slip, which
proved to be all the paper missing—it having been torn, it
seems, only into three pieces. Luckily, I had no trouble in
finding what few fragments of the phosphorus were left—being guided by the indistinct glow one or two of the particles
still emitted. My difficulties had taught me the necessity of
caution, and I now took time to reflect upon what I was about
to do. It was very probable, I considered, that some words
were written upon that side of the paper which had not been
examined—but which side was that? Fitting the pieces together gave me no clew in this respect, although it assured me
that the words (if there were any) would be found all on one
side, and connected in a proper manner, as written. There was
the greater necessity of ascertaining the point in question beyond a doubt, as the phosphorus remaining would be altogether insufficient for a third attempt, should I fail in the one
I was now about to make. I placed the paper on a book as before, and sat for some minutes thoughtfully revolving the
matter over in my mind. At last I thought it barely possible
that the written side might have some unevenness on its surface, which a delicate sense of feeling might enable me to de-
tect. I determined to make the experiment, and passed my
finger very carefully over the side which first presented itself—nothing however, was perceptible, and I turned the

paper, adjusting it on the book. I now again carried my fore-finger cautiously along, when I was aware of an exceedingly slight, but still discernible glow, which followed as it pro-ceeded. This, I knew, must arise from some very minute re-maining particles of the phosphorus with which I had covered the paper in my previous attempt. The other, or under side, then, was that on which lay the writing, if writing there should finally prove to be. Again I turned the note, and went to work as I had previously done. Having rubbed in the phos-phorus, a brilliancy ensued as before—but this time several lines of MS. in a large hand, and apparently in red ink, became distinctly visible. The glimmer, although sufficiently bright, was but momentary. Still, had I not been too greatly excited, there would have been ample time enough for me to peruse the whole three sentences before me—for I saw there were three. In my anxiety, however, to read all at once, I succeeded only in reading the seven concluding words, which thus ap-peared: *"blood—your life depends upon lying close."*[1]

Had I been able to ascertain the entire contents of the note—the full meaning of the admonition which my friend had thus attempted to convey, that admonition, even although it should have revealed a story of disaster the most unspeak-able, could not, I am firmly convinced, have imbued my mind with one tithe of the harrowing and yet indefinable horror with which I was inspired by the fragmentary warning thus received. And *"blood"* too, that word of all words—so rife at all times with mystery, and suffering, and terror—how trebly full of import did it now appear—how chillily and heavily (disjointed, as it thus was, from any foregoing words to qual-ify or render it distinct) did its vague syllables fall, amid the deep gloom of my prison, into the innermost recesses of my soul!

Augustus had, undoubtedly, good reasons for wishing me to remain concealed, and I formed a thousand surmises as to what they could be—but I could think of nothing affording a

satisfactory solution of the mystery. Just after returning from
my last journey to the trap, and before my attention had been
otherwise directed by the singular conduct of Tiger, I had
come to the resolution of making myself heard at all events by
those on board, or, if I could not succeed in this directly, of
trying to cut my way through the orlop deck. The half certainty which I felt of being able to accomplish one of these
two purposes in the last emergency, had given me courage
(which I should not otherwise have had) to endure the evils of
my situation. The few words I had been able to read, however, had cut me off from these final resources, and I now, for
the first time, felt all the misery of my fate. In a paroxysm of
despair I threw myself again upon the mattress, where, for
about the period of a day and night, I lay in a kind of stupor,
relieved only by momentary intervals of reason and recollection.

At length I once more arose, and busied myself in reflection upon the horrors which encompassed me. For another
twenty-four hours it was barely possible that I might exist
without water—for a longer time I could not do so. During
the first portion of my imprisonment I had made free use of
the cordials with which Augustus had supplied me, but they
only served to excite fever, without in the least degree assuag-
ing my thirst. I had now only about a gill left, and this was of
a species of strong peach liqueur at which my stomach re-
volted. The sausages were entirely consumed; of the ham
nothing remained but a small piece of the skin; and all the bis-
cuit, except a few fragments of one, had been eaten by Tiger.
To add to my troubles, I found that my headache was increasing momentarily, and with it the species of delirium which
had distressed me more or less since my first falling asleep.
For some hours past it had been with the greatest difficulty I
could breathe at all, and now each attempt at so doing was attended with the most distressing spasmodic action of the

chest. But there was still another and very different source of disquietude, and one, indeed, whose harassing terrors had been the chief means of arousing me to exertion from my stupor on the mattress. It arose from the demeanour of the dog.

I first observed an alteration in his conduct while rubbing in the phosphorus on the paper in my last attempt. As I rubbed, he ran his nose against my hand with a slight snarl; but I was too greatly excited at the time to pay much attention to the circumstance. Soon afterward, it will be remembered, I threw myself on the mattress, and fell into a species of lethargy. Presently I became aware of a singular hissing sound close at my ears, and discovered it to proceed from Tiger, who was panting and wheezing in a state of the greatest apparent excitement, his eyeballs flashing fiercely through the gloom. I spoke to him, when he replied with a low growl, and then remained quiet. Presently I relapsed into my stupor, from which I was again awakened in a similar manner. This was repeated three or four times, until finally his behaviour inspired me with so great a degree of fear that I became fully aroused. He was now lying close by the door of the box, snarling fearfully, although in a kind of under tone, and grinding his teeth as if strongly convulsed. I had no doubt whatever that the want of water or the confined atmosphere of the hold had driven him mad, and I was at a loss what course to pursue. I could not endure the thought of killing him, yet it seemed absolutely necessary for my own safety. I could distinctly perceive his eyes fastened upon me with an expression of the most deadly animosity, and I expected every instant that he would attack me. At last I could endure my terrible situation no longer, and determined to make my way from the box at all hazards, and despatch him, if his opposition should render it necessary for me to do so. To get out, I had to pass directly over his body, and he already seemed to anticipate my design—raising himself upon his fore legs (as I perceived by the altered position of his eyes), and displaying the whole of his white fangs, which were easily discernible. I took the remains of the ham-skin, and the bottle containing the liqueur, and secured them about my person, together with a large carving-knife which Augustus had left me—then, folding my cloak as closely around me as possible, I made a movement towards the mouth of the box. No sooner did I do this than the dog sprang with a loud growl towards my throat. The whole weight of his body struck me on the right shoulder, and I fell violently to the left, while the enraged animal passed entirely over me. I had fallen upon my knees, with my head buried among the blankets, and these protected me from a second furious assault, during which I felt the sharp teeth pressing vigorously upon the woollen which enveloped my neck—yet, luckily, without being able to penetrate all the folds. I was now beneath the dog, and a few moments would place me completely in his power. Despair gave me strength, and I rose bodily up, shaking him from me by main force, and dragging with me the blankets from the mattress. These I now threw over him, and before he could extricate himself I had got through the door and closed it effectually against his pursuit. In this struggle, however, I had been forced to drop the morsel of ham-skin, and I now found my whole stock of provisions reduced to a single gill of liqueur. As this reflection crossed my mind, I felt myself actuated by one of those fits of perverseness[2] which might be supposed to influence a spoiled child in similar circumstances, and, raising the bottle to my lips, I drained it to the last drop, and dashed it furiously upon the floor.

Scarcely had the echo of the crash died away, when I heard my name pronounced in an eager but subdued voice, issuing from the direction of the steerage. So unexpected was anything of the kind, and so intense was the emotion excited within me by the sound, that I endeavoured in vain to reply.

My powers of speech totally failed, and, in an agony of terror lest my friend should conclude me dead, and return without attempting to reach me, I stood up between the crates near the door of the box, trembling convulsively, and gasping and struggling for utterance. Had a thousand worlds depended upon a syllable, I could not have spoken it. There was a slight movement now audible among the lumber somewhere forward of my station. The sound presently grew less distinct, then again less so, and still less. Shall I ever forget my feelings at this moment? He was going—my friend—my companion, from whom I had a right to expect so much—he was going—he would abandon me—he was gone! He would leave me to perish miserably, to expire in the most horrible and loathsome of dungeons—and one word—one little syllable would save me—yet that single syllable I could not utter! I felt, I am sure, more than ten thousand times the agonies of death itself. My brain reeled, and I fell, deadly sick, against the end of the box.

As I fell, the carving-knife was shaken out from the waist-band of my pantaloons, and dropped with a rattling sound to the floor. Never did any strain of the richest melody come so sweetly to my ears! With the intensest anxiety I listened to ascertain the effect of the noise upon Augustus—for I knew that the person who called my name could be no one but himself. All was silent for some moments. At length I again heard the word *Arthur!* repeated in a low tone, and one full of hesitation. Reviving hope loosened at once my powers of speech, and I now screamed, at the top of my voice, "*Augustus! oh Augustus!*" "Hush—for God's sake be silent!" he replied, in a voice trembling with agitation; "I will be with you immediately—as soon as I can make my way through the hold." For a long time I heard him moving among the lumber, and every moment seemed to me an age. At length I felt his hand upon my shoulder, and he placed at the same moment a bottle of water to my lips. Those only who have been suddenly redeemed from the jaws of the tomb, or who have known the insufferable torments of thirst under circumstances as aggravated as those which encompassed me in my dreary prison, can form any idea of the unutterable transports which that one long draught of the richest of all physical luxuries afforded.

When I had in some degree satisfied my thirst, Augustus produced from his pocket three or four cold boiled potatoes, which I devoured with the greatest avidity. He had brought with him a light in a dark lantern, and the grateful rays afforded me scarcely less comfort than the food and drink. But I was impatient to learn the cause of his protracted absence, and he proceeded to recount what had happened on board during my incarceration.

CHAPTER 4

The brig put to sea, as I had supposed, in about an hour after
he had left the watch. This was on the twentieth of June. It
will be remembered that I had then been in the hold for three
days; and, during this period, there was so constant a bustle
on board, and so much running to and fro, especially in the
cabin and staterooms, that he had had no chance of visiting
me without the risk of having the secret of the trap discovered. When at length he did come, I had assured him that I
was doing as well as possible; and, therefore, for the next two
days he felt but little uneasiness on my account—still, however, watching an opportunity of going down. It was not *until
the fourth day* that he found one. Several times during this interval he had made up his mind to let his father know of the
adventure, and have me come up at once; but we were still
within reaching distance of Nantucket, and it was doubtful,
from some expressions which had escaped Captain Barnard,
whether he would not immediately put back if he discovered
me to be on board. Besides, upon thinking the matter over,
Augustus, so he told me, could not imagine that I was in immediate want, or that I would hesitate, in such case, to make
myself heard at the trap. When, therefore, he considered
everything, he concluded to let me stay until he could meet
with an opportunity of visiting me unobserved. This, as I said
before, did not occur until the fourth day after his bringing
me the watch, and the seventh since I had first entered the
hold. He then went down without taking with him any water
or provisions, intending in the first place merely to call my attention, and get me to come from the box to the trap—when

he would go up to the stateroom and thence hand me down a supply. When he descended for this purpose he found that I was asleep, for it seems that I was snoring very loudly. From all the calculations I can make on the subject, this must have been the slumber into which I fell just after my return from the trap with the watch, and which, consequently, must have lasted *for more than three entire days and nights* at the very least. Latterly, I have had reason, both from my own experience and the assurance of others, to be acquainted with the strong soporific effects of the stench arising from old fish-oil when closely confined; and when I think of the condition of the hold in which I was imprisoned, and the long period during which the brig had been used as a whaling vessel, I am more inclined to wonder that I awoke at all, after once falling asleep, than that I should have slept uninterruptedly for the period specified above.[1]

Augustus called to me at first in a low voice and without closing the trap—but I made him no reply. He then shut the trap, and spoke to me in a louder, and finally in a very loud tone—still I continued to snore. He was now at a loss what to do. It would take him some time to make his way through the lumber to my box, and in the mean while his absence would be noticed by Captain Barnard, who had occasion for his services every minute, in arranging and copying papers connected with the business of the voyage. He determined, therefore, upon reflection, to ascend, and await another opportunity of visiting me. He was the more easily induced to this resolve, as my slumber appeared to be of the most tranquil nature, and he could not suppose that I had undergone any inconvenience from my incarceration. He had just made up his mind on these points when his attention was arrested by an unusual bustle, the sound of which proceeded apparently from the cabin. He sprang through the trap as quickly as possible, closed it, and threw open the door of his stateroom.

No sooner had he put his foot over the threshold than a pistol flashed in his face, and he was knocked down, at the same moment, by a blow from a handspike.

A strong hand held him on the cabin floor, with a tight grasp upon his throat—still he was able to see what was going on around him. His father was tied hand and foot, and lying along the steps of the companion-way with his head down, and a deep wound in the forehead, from which the blood was flowing in a continued stream. He spoke not a word, and was apparently dying. Over him stood the first mate, eying him with an expression of fiendish derision, and deliberately searching his pockets, from which he presently drew forth a large wallet and a chronometer. Seven of the crew (among whom was the cook, a negro) were rummaging the staterooms on the larboard for arms, where they soon equipped themselves with muskets and ammunition. Besides Augustus and Captain Barnard, there were nine men altogether in the cabin, and these among the most ruffianly of the brig's company. The villains now went upon deck, taking my friend with them, after having secured his arms behind his back. They proceeded straight to the forecastle, which was fastened down—two of the mutineers standing by it with axes—two also at the main hatch. The mate called out in a loud voice, "Do you hear there below? tumble up with you—one by one, now, mark that— and no grumbling." It was some minutes before any one appeared: at last an Englishman, who had shipped as a raw hand, came up, weeping piteously, and entreating the mate in the most humble manner to spare his life. The only reply was a blow on the forehead from an axe. The poor fellow fell to the deck without a groan, and the black cook lifted him up in his arms as he would a child, and tossed him deliberately into the sea. Hearing the blow and the plunge of the body, the men below could now be induced to venture on deck neither by threats nor promises, until a proposition

was made to smoke them out. A general rush then ensued, and
for a moment it seemed possible that the brig might be re-
taken. The mutineers, however, succeeded at last in closing the forecastle effectually before more than six of their
opponents could get up. These six, finding themselves so
greatly outnumbered and without arms, submitted after a
brief struggle. The mate gave them fair words—no doubt
with a view of inducing those below to yield, for they had no
difficulty in hearing all that was said on deck. The result
proved his sagacity, no less than his diabolical villany. All in
the forecastle presently signified their intention of submitting,
and, ascending one by one, were pinioned and thrown on
their backs together with the first six—there being in all, of
the crew who were not concerned in the mutiny, twenty-
seven.[2]

A scene of the most horrible butchery ensued. The bound
seamen were dragged to the gangway. Here the cook stood
with an axe, striking each victim on the head as he was forced
over the side of the vessel by the other mutineers. In this manner twenty-two perished, and Augustus had given himself up
for lost, expecting every moment his own turn to come next.
But it seemed that the villains were now either weary, or in
some measure disgusted with their bloody labour; for the four
remaining prisoners, together with my friend, who had been
thrown on the deck with the rest, were respited while the
mate sent below for rum, and the whole murderous party held
a drunken carouse, which lasted until sunset. They now fell to
disputing in regard to the fate of the survivers, who lay not
more than four paces off, and could distinguish every word
said. Upon some of the mutineers the liquor appeared to have
a softening effect, for several voices were heard in favour of
releasing the captives altogether, on condition of joining the
mutiny and sharing the profits. The black cook, however
(who in all respects was a perfect demon, and who seemed to
exert as much influence, if not more, than the mate himself),

would listen to no proposition of the kind, and rose repeatedly for the purpose of resuming his work at the gangway.
Fortunately, he was so far overcome by intoxication as to be
easily restrained by the less blood-thirsty of the party, among
whom was a line-manager, who went by the name of Dirk Peters. This man was the son of an Indian squaw of the tribe of
Upsarokas, who live among the fastnesses of the Black Hills
near the source of the Missouri.[3] His father was a fur-trader, I
believe, or at least connected in some manner with the Indian
trading-posts on Lewis river. Peters himself was one of the
most purely ferocious-looking men I ever beheld. He was
short in stature—not more than four feet eight inches high—
but his limbs were of the most Herculean mould. His hands,
especially, were so enormously thick and broad as hardly to
retain a human shape. His arms, as well as legs, were *bowed* in
the most singular manner, and appeared to possess no flexibil-
ity whatever. His head was equally deformed, being of immense size, with an indentation on the crown (like that on the
head of most negroes), and entirely bald. To conceal this latter
deficiency, which did not proceed from old age, he usually
wore a wig formed of any hair-like material which presented
itself—occasionally the skin of a Spanish dog or American
grizzly bear. At the time spoken of he had on a portion of one
of these bearskins; and it added no little to the natural ferocity
of his countenance, which betook of the Upsaroka character.
The mouth extended nearly from ear to ear; the lips were thin,
and seemed, like some other portions of his frame, to be de-
void of natural pliancy, so that the ruling expression never
varied under the influence of any emotion whatever. This ruling expression may be conceived when it is considered that
the teeth were exceedingly long and protruding, and never
even partially covered, in any instance, by the lips. To pass
this man with a casual glance, one might imagine him to be
convulsed with laughter—but a second look would induce a
shuddering acknowledgment, that if such an expression were

indicative of merriment, the merriment must be that of a demon. Of this singular being many anecdotes were prevalent
among the seafaring men of Nantucket. These anecdotes went
to prove his prodigious strength when under excitement, and
some of them had given rise to a doubt of his sanity. But on
board the Grampus, it seems, he was regarded at the time of
the mutiny with feelings more of derision than of anything
else. I have been thus particular in speaking of Dirk Peters,
because, ferocious as he appeared, he proved the main instru-
ment in preserving the life of Augustus, and because I shall
have frequent occasion to mention him hereafter in the course
of my narrative—a narrative, let me here say, which, in its latter portions, will be found to include incidents of a nature so
entirely out of the range of human experience, and for this
reason so far beyond the limits of human credulity, that I proceed in utter hopelessness of obtaining credence for all that I
shall tell, yet confidently trusting in time and progressing science to verify some of the most important and most improbable of my statements.[4]

After much indecision and two or three violent quarrels, it
was determined at last that all the prisoners (with the exception of Augustus, whom Peters insisted in a jocular manner
upon keeping as his clerk) should be set adrift in one of the
smallest whaleboats. The mate went down into the cabin to
see if Captain Barnard was still living—for, it will be remembered, he was left below when the mutineers came up.
Presently the two made their appearance, the captain pale as
death, but somewhat recovered from the effects of his wound.
He spoke to the men in a voice hardly articulate, entreated
them not to set him adrift, but to return to their duty, and
promising to land them wherever they chose, and to take no
steps for bringing them to justice. He might as well have spoken to the winds. Two of the ruffians seized him by the arms
and hurled him over the brig's side into the boat, which had
been lowered while the mate went below. The four men who

were lying on the deck were then untied and ordered to follow, which they did without attempting any resistance—Augustus being still left in his painful position, although he
struggled and prayed only for the poor satisfaction of being
permitted to bid his father farewell. A handful of sea-biscuit
and a jug of water were now handed down; but neither mast,
sail, oar, nor compass. The boat was towed astern for a few
minutes, during which the mutineers held another consultation—it was then finally cut adrift.[5] By this time night had
come on—there were neither moon nor stars visible—and a
short and ugly sea was running, although there was no great
deal of wind. The boat was instantly out of sight, and little
hope could be entertained for the unfortunate sufferers who
were in it. This event happened, however, in latitude 35° 30'
north, longitude 61° 20' west, and consequently at no very
great distance from the Bermuda Islands. Augustus therefore
endeavoured to console himself with the idea that the boat
might either succeed in reaching the land, or come sufficiently
near to be fallen in with by vessels off the coast.

All sail was now put upon the brig, and she continued her
original course to the southwest—the mutineers being bent
upon some piratical expedition, in which, from all that could
be understood, a ship was to be intercepted on her way from
the Cape Verd Islands to Porto Rico. No attention was paid
to Augustus, who was untied and suffered to go about anywhere forward of the cabin companion-way. Dirk Peters
treated him with some degree of kindness, and on one occasion saved him from the brutality of the cook. His situation
was still one of the most precarious, as the men were continually intoxicated, and there was no relying upon their continued good-humour or carelessness in regard to himself. His
anxiety on my account he represented, however, as the most
distressing result of his condition; and, indeed, I had never
reason to doubt the sincerity of his friendship. More than
once he had resolved to acquaint the mutineers with the secret

of my being on board, but was restrained from so doing, partly through recollection of the atrocities he had already beheld, and partly through a hope of being able soon to bring me relief. For the latter purpose he was constantly on the watch; but, in spite of the most constant vigilance, three days elapsed after the boat was cut adrift before any chance occurred. At length, on the night of the third day, there came on a heavy blow from the eastward, and all hands were called up to take in sail. During the confusion which ensued, he made his way below unobserved, and into the stateroom. What was his grief and horror in discovering that the latter had been rendered a place of deposite for a variety of sea-stores and ship-furniture, and that several fathoms of old chain-cable, which had been stowed away beneath the companion-ladder, had been dragged thence to make room for a chest, and were now lying immediately upon the trap! To remove it without discovery was impossible, and he returned on deck as quickly as he could. As he came up the mate seized him by the throat, and demanding what he had been doing in the cabin, was about flinging him over the larboard bulwark, when his life was again preserved through the interference of Dirk Peters. Augustus was now put in handcuffs (of which there were several pairs on board), and his feet lashed tightly together. He was then taken into the steerage, and thrown into a lower berth next to the forecastle bulkheads, with the assurance that he should never put his foot on deck again "until the brig was no longer a brig." This was the expression of the cook, who threw him into the berth—it is hardly possible to say what precise meaning was intended by the phrase. The whole affair, however, proved the ultimate means of my relief, as will presently appear.

CHAPTER 5

For some minutes after the cook had left the forecastle, Augustus abandoned himself to despair, never hoping to leave the berth alive. He now came to the resolution of acquainting the first of the men who should come down with my situation, thinking it better to let me take my chance with the mutineers than perish of thirst in the hold—for it had been ten days since I was first imprisoned, and my jug of water was not a plentiful supply even for four. As he was thinking on this subject, the idea came all at once into his head that it might be possible to communicate with me by the way of the main hold. In any other circumstances, the difficulty and hazard of the undertaking would have prevented him from attempting it; but now he had, at all events, little prospect of life, and consequently little to lose—he bent his whole mind, therefore, upon the task.

His handcuffs were the first consideration. At first he saw no method of removing them, and feared that he should thus be baffled in the very outset; but, upon a closer scrutiny, he discovered that the irons could be slipped off and on at pleasure with very little effort or inconvenience, merely by squeezing his hands through them—this species of manacle being altogether ineffectual in confining young persons, in whom the smaller bones readily yield to pressure. He now untied his feet, and, leaving the cord in such a manner that it could easily be readjusted in the event of any person's coming down, proceeded to examine the bulkhead where it joined the berth. The partition here was of soft pine board, an inch thick, and he saw that he should have little trouble in cutting his way through. A voice was now heard at the forecastle

companion-way, and he had just time to put his right hand
into its handcuff (the left had not been removed), and to draw
the rope in a slipknot around his ankle, when Dirk Peters
came below, followed by Tiger, who immediately leaped into
the berth and lay down. The dog had been brought on board
by Augustus, who knew my attachment to the animal, and
thought it would give me pleasure to have him with me during
the voyage. He went up to our house for him immediately after first taking me into the hold, but did not think of mentioning the circumstance upon his bringing the watch. Since the
mutiny, Augustus had not seen him before his appearance
with Dirk Peters, and had given him up for lost, supposing
him to have been thrown overboard by some of the malignant
villains belonging to the mate's gang. It appeared afterward
that he had crawled into a hole beneath a whaleboat, from
which, not having room to turn round, he could not extricate
himself. Peters at last let him out, and with a species of good
feeling which my friend knew well how to appreciate, had
now brought him to him in the forecastle as a companion,
leaving at the same time some salt junk and potatoes, with a
can of water; he then went on deck, promising to come down
with something more to eat on the next day.

When he had gone, Augustus freed both hands from the
manacles and unfastened his feet. He then turned down the
head of the mattress on which he had been lying, and with his
penknife (for the ruffians had not thought it worth while to
search him) commenced cutting vigorously across one of the
partition planks, as closely as possible to the floor of the
berth. He chose to cut here, because, if suddenly interrupted,
he would be able to conceal what had been done by letting the
head of the mattress fall into its proper position. For the remainder of the day, however, no disturbance occurred, and by
night he had completely divided the plank. It should here be
observed, that none of the crew occupied the forecastle as a
sleeping-place, living altogether in the cabin since the mutiny,

drinking the wines, and feasting on the sea-stores of Captain Barnard, and giving no more heed than was absolutely necessary to the navigation of the brig. These circumstances proved fortunate both for myself and Augustus; for, had matters been otherwise, he would have found it impossible to reach me. As it was, he proceeded with confidence in his design. It was near daybreak, however, before he completed the second division of the board (which was about a foot above the first cut), thus making an aperture quite large enough to admit his passage through with facility to the main orlop deck. Having got here, he made his way with but little trouble to the lower main hatch, although in so doing he had to scramble over tiers of oil-casks piled nearly as high as the upper deck, there being barely room enough left for his body. Upon reaching the hatch, he found that Tiger had followed him below, squeezing between two rows of the casks. It was now too late, however, to attempt getting to me before dawn, as the chief difficulty lay in passing through the close stowage in the lower hold. He therefore resolved to return, and wait till the next night. With this design he proceeded to loosen the hatch, so that he might have as little detention as possible when he should come again. No sooner had he loosened it than Tiger sprang eagerly to the small opening produced, snuffed for a moment, and then uttered a long whine, scratching at the same time, as if anxious to remove the covering with his paws. There could be no doubt, from his behaviour, that he was aware of my being in the hold, and Augustus thought it possible that he would be able to get to me if he put him down. He now hit upon the expedient of sending the note, as it was especially desirable that I should make no attempt at forcing my way out, at least under existing circumstances, and there could be no certainty of his getting to me himself on the morrow as he intended. After events proved how fortunate it was that the idea occurred to him as it did: for, had it not been for the receipt of the note, I should undoubtedly have fallen upon some plan, however desperate, of alarming the crew, and both our lives would most probably have been sacrificed in consequence.

Having concluded to write, the difficulty was now to procure the materials for so doing. An old toothpick was soon made into a pen; and this by means of feeling altogether, for the between-decks were as dark as pitch. Paper enough was obtained from the back of a letter—a duplicate of the forged letter from Mr. Ross. This had been the original draught; but the handwriting not being sufficiently well imitated, Augustus had written another, thrusting the first, by good fortune, into his coat-pocket, where it was now most opportunely discovered.[1] Ink alone was thus wanting, and a substitute was immediately found for this by means of a slight incision with the penknife on the back of a finger just above the nail—a copious flow of blood ensuing, as usual from wounds in that vicinity. The note was now written, as well as it could be in the dark and under the circumstances. It briefly explained that a mutiny had taken place; that Captain Barnard was set adrift; and that I might expect immediate relief as far as provisions were concerned, but must not venture upon making any disturbance. It concluded with these words, *"I have scrawled this with blood—your life depends upon lying close."*

The slip of paper being tied upon the dog, he was now put down the hatchway, and Augustus made the best of his way back to the forecastle, where he found no reason to believe that any of the crew had been in his absence. To conceal the hole in the partition, he drove his knife in just above it, and hung up a pea-jacket which he found in the berth. His handcuffs were then replaced, and also the rope around his ankles.

These arrangements were scarcely completed when Dirk Peters came below, very drunk, but in excellent humour, and bringing with him my friend's allowance of provision for the day. This consisted of a dozen large Irish potatoes roasted, and a pitcher of water. He sat for some time on a chest by the berth, and talked freely about the mate, and the general con-cerns of the brig. His demeanour was exceedingly capricious and even grotesque. At one time Augustus was much alarmed by his odd conduct. At last, however, he went on deck, muttering a promise to bring his prisoner a good dinner on the morrow. During the day two of the crew (harpooners) came down, accompanied by the cook, all three in nearly the last stage of intoxication. Like Peters, they made no scruple of talking unreservedly about their plans. It appeared that they were much divided among themselves as to their ultimate course, agreeing in no point except the attack on the ship from the Cape Verd Islands, with which they were in hourly expectation of meeting. As far as could be ascertained, the mutiny had not been brought about altogether for the sake of booty; a private pique of the chief mate's against Captain Barnard having been the main instigation. There now seemed to be two principal factions among the crew—one headed by the mate, the other by the cook. The former party were for seizing the first suitable vessel which should present itself, and equipping it at some of the West India Islands for a piratical cruise. The latter division, however, which was the stronger, and included Dirk Peters among its partisans, were bent upon pursuing the course originally laid out for the brig into the South Pacific; there either to take whale, or act otherwise, as circumstances should suggest. The representations of Peters, who had frequently visited these regions, had great weight, apparently, with the mutineers, wavering as they were between half-engendered notions of profit and pleasure. He dwelt on the world of novelty and amusement to be found among the innumerable islands of the Pacific, on the perfect security and freedom from all restraint to be enjoyed, but, more particularly, on the deliciousness of the climate, on the abundant means of good living, and on the voluptuous beauty of the women. As yet, nothing had been absolutely determined upon; but the pictures of the hybrid line-manager were taking strong hold upon the ardent imaginations of the seamen, and

there was every probability that his intentions would be finally carried into effect.

The three men went away in about an hour, and no one
else entered the forecastle that day. Augustus lay quiet until
nearly night. He then freed himself from the rope and irons,
and prepared for his attempt. A bottle was found in one of the
berths, and this he filled with water from the pitcher left by
Peters, storing his pockets at the same time with cold potatoes. To his great joy he also came across a lantern, with a
small piece of tallow candle in it. This he could light at any
moment, as he had in his possession a box of phosphorus
matches. When it was quite dark, he got through the hole in
the bulkhead, having taken the precaution to arrange the bedclothes in the berth so as to convey the idea of a person covered up. When through, he hung up the pea-jacket on his
knife, as before, to conceal the aperture—this manœuvre being easily effected, as he did not readjust the piece of plank
taken out until afterward. He was now on the main orlop
deck, and proceeded to make his way, as before, between the
upper deck and the oil-casks to the main hatchway. Having
reached this, he lit the piece of candle, and descended, groping
with extreme difficulty among the compact stowage of the
hold. In a few moments he became alarmed at the insufferable
stench and the closeness of the atmosphere. He could not
think it possible that I had survived my confinement for so
long a period breathing so oppressive an air. He called my
name repeatedly, but I made him no reply, and his apprehensions seemed thus to be confirmed. The brig was rolling violently, and there was so much noise in consequence, that it
was useless to listen for any weak sound, such as those of my
breathing or snoring. He threw open the lantern, and held it
as high as possible, whenever an opportunity occurred, in order that, by observing the light, I might, if alive, be aware that
succour was approaching. Still nothing was heard from me,

and the supposition of my death began to assume the character of certainty. He determined, nevertheless, to force a passage, if possible, to the box, and at least ascertain beyond a
doubt the truth of his surmises. He pushed on for some time
in a most pitiable state of anxiety, until, at length, he found
the pathway utterly blocked up, and that there was no possibility of making any farther way by the course in which he
had set out. Overcome now by his feelings, he threw himself
among the lumber in despair, and wept like a child. It was at
this period that he heard the crash occasioned by the bottle
which I had thrown down. Fortunate, indeed, was it that the
incident occurred—for, upon this incident, trivial as it appears, the thread of my destiny depended. Many years
elapsed, however, before I was aware of this fact. A natural
shame and regret for his weakness and indecision prevented
Augustus from confiding to me at once what a more intimate
and unreserved communion afterward induced him to reveal.[2]
Upon finding his further progress in the hold impeded by ob-
stacles which he could not overcome, he had resolved to abandon his attempt at reaching me, and return at once to the
forecastle. Before condemning him entirely on this head, the
harassing circumstances which embarrassed him should be
taken into consideration. The night was fast wearing away,
and his absence from the forecastle might be discovered; and,
indeed, would necessarily be so, if he should fail to get back to
the berth by daybreak. His candle was expiring in the socket,
and there would be the greatest difficulty in retracing his way
to the hatchway in the dark. It must be allowed, too, that he
had every good reason to believe me dead; in which event no
benefit could result to me from his reaching the box, and a
world of danger would be encountered to no purpose by himself. He had repeatedly called, and I had made him no answer.
I had been now eleven days and nights with no more water
than that contained in the jug which he had left with me, a

supply which it was not at all probable I had hoarded in the beginning of my confinement, as I had had every cause to expect a speedy release. The atmosphere of the hold, too, must have appeared to him, coming from the comparatively open air of the steerage, of a nature absolutely poisonous, and by far more intolerable than it had seemed to me upon my first taking up my quarters in the box—the hatchways at that time having been constantly open for many months previous. Add to these considerations that of the scene of bloodshed and terror so lately witnessed by my friend; his confinement, privations, and narrow escapes from death; together with the frail and equivocal tenure by which he still existed—circumstances all so well calculated to prostrate every energy of mind—and the reader will be easily brought, as I have been, to regard his apparent falling off in friendship and in faith with sentiments rather of sorrow than of anger.

The crash of the bottle was distinctly heard, yet Augustus was not sure that it proceeded from the hold. The doubt, however, was sufficient inducement to persevere. He clambered up nearly to the orlop deck by means of the stowage, and then watching for a lull in the pitchings of the vessel, he called out to me in as loud a tone as he could command—regardless, for the moment, of the danger of being overheard by the crew. It will be remembered that on this occasion the voice reached me, but I was so entirely overcome by violent agitation as to be incapable of reply. Confident, now, that his worst apprehensions were well founded, he descended, with a view of getting back to the forecastle without loss of time. In his haste some small boxes were thrown down, the noise occasioned by which I heard, as will be recollected. He had made considerable progress on his return when the fall of the knife again caused him to hesitate. He retraced his steps immediately, and, clambering up the stowage a second time, called out my name, loudly as before, having watched for a lull. This time I found voice to answer. Overjoyed at discovering me to be still alive, he now resolved to brave every difficulty and danger in reaching me. Having extricated himself as quickly as possible from the labyrinth of lumber by which he was hemmed in, he at length struck into an opening which promised better, and finally, after a series of struggles, arrived at the box in a state of utter exhaustion.

CHAPTER 6

The leading particulars of this narration were all that Augustus communicated to me while we remained near the box. It was not until afterward that he entered fully into all the details. He was apprehensive of being missed, and I was wild with impatience to leave my detested place of confinement. We resolved to make our way at once to the hole in the bulkhead, near which I was to remain for the present, while he went through to reconnoitre. To leave Tiger in the box was what neither of us could endure to think of; yet, how to act otherwise was the question. He now seemed to be perfectly quiet, and we could not even distinguish the sound of his breathing upon applying our ears closely to the box. I was convinced that he was dead, and determined to open the door. We found him lying at full length, apparently in a deep stupor, yet still alive. No time was to be lost, yet I could not bring myself to abandon an animal who had now been twice instrumental in saving my life, without some attempt at preserving him. We therefore dragged him along with us as well as we could, although with the greatest difficulty and fatigue; Augustus, during part of the time, being forced to clamber over the impediments in our way with the huge dog in his arms—a feat to which the feebleness of my frame rendered me totally inadequate. At length we succeeded in reaching the hole, when Augustus got through, and Tiger was pushed in afterward. All was found to be safe, and we did not fail to return sincere thanks to God for our deliverance from the imminent danger we had escaped. For the present it was agreed that I should remain near the opening, through which my companion could readily supply me with a part of his daily provision, and where I could have the advantages of breathing an atmosphere comparatively pure.

In explanation of some portions of this narrative wherein I have spoken of the stowage of the brig,[1] and which may appear ambiguous to some of my readers who may have seen a proper or regular stowage, I must here state that the manner in which this most important duty had been performed on board the Grampus was a most shameful piece of neglect on the part of Captain Barnard, who was by no means as careful or as experienced a seaman as the hazardous nature of the service on which he was employed would seem necessarily to demand. A proper stowage cannot be accomplished in a careless manner, and many most disastrous accidents, even within the limits of my own experience, have arisen from neglect or ignorance in this particular. Coasting vessels, in the frequent hurry and bustle attendant upon taking in or discharging cargo, are the most liable to mishap from the want of a proper attention to stowage. The great point is to allow no possibility of the cargo or ballast's shifting position even in the most violent rollings of the vessel. With this end, great attention must be paid, not only to the bulk taken in, but to the nature of the bulk, and whether there be a full or only a partial cargo. In most kinds of freight the stowage is accomplished by means of a screw. Thus, in a load of tobacco or flour, the whole is screwed so tightly into the hold of the vessel that the barrels or hogsheads upon discharging are found to be completely flattened, and take some time to regain their original shape. This screwing, however, is resorted to principally with a view of obtaining more room in the hold; for in a *full* load of any such commodities as flour or tobacco, there can be no danger of any shifting whatever, at least none from which inconvenience can result. There have been instances, indeed, where this method of screwing has resulted in the most lamentable consequences, arising from a cause altogether distinct from the danger attendant upon a shifting of cargo. A load of cotton, for example, tightly screwed while in certain conditions, has been known, through the expansion of its bulk, to rend a vessel asunder at sea. There can be no doubt, either, that the same result would ensue in the case of tobacco, while undergoing its usual course of fermentation, were it not for the interstices consequent upon the rotundity of the hogsheads.

It is when a partial cargo is received that danger is chiefly to be apprehended from shifting, and that precautions should be always taken to guard against such misfortune. Only those who have encountered a violent gale of wind, or, rather, who have experienced the rolling of a vessel in a sudden calm after the gale, can form an idea of the tremendous force of the plunges, and of the consequent terrible impetus given to all loose articles in the vessel. It is then that the necessity of a cautious stowage, when there is a partial cargo, becomes obvious. When lying to (especially with a small head sail), a vessel which is not properly modelled in the bows is frequently thrown upon her beam-ends; this occurring even every fifteen or twenty minutes upon an average, yet without any serious consequences resulting, *provided there be a proper stowage.* If this, however, has not been strictly attended to, in the first of these heavy lurches the whole of the cargo tumbles over to the side of the vessel which lies upon the water, and, being thus prevented from regaining her equilibrium, as she would otherwise necessarily do, she is certain to fill in a few seconds and go down. It is not too much to say that at least one half of the instances in which vessels have foundered in heavy gales at sea may be attributed to a shifting of cargo or of ballast.

When a partial cargo of any kind is taken on board, the whole, after being first stowed as compactly as may be, should be covered with a layer of stout shifting-boards, extending completely across the vessel. Upon these boards strong temporary stanchions should be erected, reaching to the timbers above, and thus securing everything in its place. In cargoes consisting of grain, or any similar matter, additional precautions are requisite. A hold filled entirely with grain upon leaving port will be found not more than three fourths full upon reaching its destination—this, too, although the freight, when measured bushel by bushel by the consignee, will overrun by a vast deal (on account of the swelling of the grain) the quantity consigned. This result is occasioned by *settling* during the voyage, and is the more perceptible in proportion to the roughness of the weather experienced. If grain loosely thrown in a vessel, then, is ever so well secured by shifting-boards and stanchions, it will be liable to shift in a long passage so greatly as to bring about the most distressing calamities. To prevent these, every method should be employed before leaving port to *settle* the cargo as much as possible; and for this there are many contrivances, among which may be mentioned the driving of wedges into the grain. Even after all this is done, and unusual pains taken to secure the shifting-boards, no seaman who knows what he is about will feel altogether secure in a gale of any violence with a cargo of grain on board, and, least of all, with a partial cargo. Yet there are hundreds of our coasting vessels, and, it is likely, many more from the ports of Europe, which sail daily with partial cargoes, even of the most dangerous species, and without any precautions whatever. The wonder is that no more accidents occur than do actually happen. A lamentable instance of this heedlessness occurred to my knowledge in the case of Captain Joel Rice of the schooner Firefly, which sailed from Richmond, Virginia, to Madeira, with a cargo of corn, in the year 1825. The captain had gone many voyages without serious accident, although he was in the habit of paying no attention whatever to his stowage, more than to secure it in the ordinary manner. He had never before sailed with a cargo of grain, and on this occasion had the corn thrown on board loosely, when it did not much more than half fill the vessel. For the first portion of the voyage he met with nothing more than light breezes; but when within a day's sail of Madeira there came on a strong

gale from the N. N. E. which forced him to lie to. He brought
the schooner to the wind under a double-reefed foresail alone,
when she rode as well as any vessel could be expected to do,
and shipped not a drop of water. Towards night the gale
somewhat abated, and she rolled with more unsteadiness than
before, but still did very well, until a heavy lurch threw her
upon her beam-ends to starboard. The corn was then heard to
shift bodily, the force of the movement bursting open the
main hatchway. The vessel went down like a shot. This happened within hail of a small sloop from Madeira, which
picked up one of the crew (the only person saved), and which
rode out the gale in perfect security, as indeed a jollyboat
might have done under proper management.

The stowage on board the Grampus was most clumsily
done, if stowage that could be called which was little better
than a promiscuous huddling together of oil-casks* and ship
furniture. I have already spoken of the condition of articles in
the hold. On the orlop deck there was space enough for my
body (as I have stated) between the oil-casks and the upper
deck; a space was left open around the main hatchway; and
several other large spaces were left in the stowage. Near the
hole cut through the bulkhead by Augustus there was room
enough for an entire cask, and in this space I found myself
comfortably situated for the present.

By the time my friend had got safely into the berth, and
readjusted his handcuffs and the rope, it was broad daylight.
We had made a narrow escape indeed; for scarcely had he
arranged all matters, when the mate came below, with Dirk
Peters and the cook. They talked for some time about the vessel from the Cape Verds, and seemed to be excessively anxious
for her appearance. At length the cook came to the berth in
which Augustus was lying, and seated himself in it near the

---

* Whaling vessels are usually fitted with iron oil-tanks—why the Grampus
was not I have never been able to ascertain.

head. I could see and hear everything from my hiding-place, for the piece cut out had not been put back, and I was in momentary expectation that the negro would fall against the pea-jacket, which was hung up to conceal the aperture, in which case all would have been discovered, and our lives would, no doubt, have been instantly sacrificed. Our good fortune prevailed, however; and although he frequently touched it as the vessel rolled, he never pressed against it sufficiently to bring about a discovery. The bottom of the jacket had been carefully fastened to the bulkhead, so that the hole might not be seen by its swinging to one side. All this time Tiger was lying in the foot of the berth, and appeared to have recovered in some measure his faculties, for I could see him occasionally open his eyes and draw a long breath.

After a few minutes the mate and cook went above, leaving Dirk Peters behind, who, as soon as they were gone, came and sat himself down in the place just occupied by the mate. He began to talk very sociably with Augustus, and we could now see that the greater part of his apparent intoxication, while the two others were with him, was a feint. He answered all my companion's questions with perfect freedom; told him that he had no doubt of his father's having been picked up, as there were no less than five sail in sight just before sundown on the day he was cut adrift; and used other language of a consolatory nature, which occasioned me no less surprise than pleasure. Indeed, I began to entertain hopes, that through the instrumentality of Peters we might be finally enabled to regain possession of the brig, and this idea I mentioned to Augustus as soon as I found an opportunity. He thought the matter possible, but urged the necessity of the greatest caution in making the attempt, as the conduct of the hybrid appeared to be instigated by the most arbitrary caprice alone; and, indeed, it was difficult to say if he was at any moment of sound mind. Peters went upon deck in about an hour, and did not return again until noon, when he brought Augustus a plentiful supply of junk beef and pudding. Of this, when we were left alone, I partook heartily, without returning through the hole. No one else came down into the forecastle during the day, and at night I got into Augustus's berth,[2] where I slept soundly and sweetly until nearly daybreak, when he awakened me upon hearing a stir upon deck, and I regained my hiding-place as quickly as possible. When the day was fully broke, we found that Tiger had recovered his strength almost entirely, and gave no indications of hydrophobia, drinking a little water that was offered him with great apparent eagerness. During the day he regained all his former vigour and appetite. His strange conduct had been brought on, no doubt, by the deleterious quality of the air of the hold, and had no connexion with canine madness. I could not sufficiently rejoice that I had persisted in bringing him with me from the box. This day was the thirtieth of June, and the thirteenth since the Grampus made sail from Nantucket.

On the second of July the mate came below, drunk as usual, and in an excessively good-humour. He came to Augustus's berth, and, giving him a slap on the back, asked him if he thought he could behave himself if he let him loose, and whether he would promise not to be going into the cabin again. To this, of course, my friend answered in the affirmative, when the ruffian set him at liberty, after making him drink from a flask of rum which he drew from his coat-pocket. Both now went on deck, and I did not see Augustus for about three hours. He then came below with the good news that he had obtained permission to go about the brig as he pleased anywhere forward of the mainmast, and that he had been ordered to sleep, as usual, in the forecastle. He brought me, too, a good dinner, and a plentiful supply of water. The brig was still cruising for the vessel from the Cape Verds, and a sail was now in sight which was thought to be the one in question. As the events of the ensuing eight days were of little importance, and had no direct bearing upon the main incidents of my narrative, I will here throw them into the form of a journal, as I do not wish to omit them altogether.

July 3. Augustus furnished me with three blankets, with which I contrived a comfortable bed in my hiding-place. No one came below, except my companion, during the day. Tiger took his station in the berth just by the aperture, and slept heavily, as if not yet entirely recovered from the effects of his sickness. Towards night a flaw of wind struck the brig before sail could be taken in, and very nearly capsized her. The puff died away immediately, however, and no damage was done beyond the splitting of the foretopsail. Dirk Peters treated Augustus all this day with great kindness, and entered into a long conversation with him respecting the Pacific Ocean, and the islands he had visited in that region. He asked him whether he would not like to go with the mutineers on a kind of exploring and pleasure voyage in those quarters, and said that the men were gradually coming over to the mate's views. To this Augustus thought it best to reply that he would be glad to go on such an adventure, since nothing better could be done, and that anything was preferable to a piratical life.

July 4*th*. The vessel in sight proved to be a small brig from Liverpool, and was allowed to pass unmolested. Augustus spent most of his time on deck, with a view of obtaining all the information in his power respecting the intentions of the mutineers. They had frequent and violent quarrels among themselves, in one of which a harpooner, Jim Bonner, was thrown overboard. The party of the mate was gaining ground. Jim Bonner belonged to the cook's gang, of which Peters was a partisan.

July 5*th*. About daybreak there came on a stiff breeze from the west, which at noon freshened into a gale, so that the brig could carry nothing more than her trysail and foresail. In taking in the foretopsail, Simms, one of the common hands, and belonging also to the cook's gang, fell overboard, being very much in liquor, and was drowned—no attempt being made to save him. The whole number of persons on board was now thirteen, to wit: Dirk Peters; Seymour, the black cook; ——— Jones; ——— Greely; Hartman Rogers; and William Allen, of the cook's party; the mate, whose name I never learned; Absalom Hicks; ——— Wilson; John Hunt; and Richard Parker, of the mate's party—besides Augustus and myself.[3]

July 6th. The gale lasted all this day, blowing in heavy squalls, accompanied with rain. The brig took in a good deal of water through her seams, and one of the pumps was kept continually going, Augustus being forced to take his turn. Just at twilight a large ship passed close by us, without having been discovered until within hail. This ship was supposed to be the one for which the mutineers were on the look-out. The mate hailed her, but the reply was drowned in the roaring of the gale. At eleven, a sea was shipped amid-ships, which tore away a great portion of the larboard bulwarks, and did some other slight damage. Towards morning the weather moderated, and at sunrise there was very little wind.

July 7th. There was a heavy swell running all this day, during which the brig, being light, rolled excessively, and many articles broke loose in the hold, as I could hear distinctly from my hiding-place. I suffered a great deal from sea-sickness. Peters had a long conversation this day with Augustus, and told him that two of his gang, Greely and Allen, had gone over to the mate, and were resolved to turn pirates. He put several questions to Augustus which he did not then exactly understand. During a part of this evening the leak gained upon the vessel; and little could be done to remedy it, as it was occasioned by the brig's straining, and taking in the water through her seams. A sail was thrummed, and got under the bows, which aided us in some measure, so that we began to gain upon the leak.

July 8th. A light breeze sprung up at sunrise from the eastward, when the mate headed the brig to the southwest, with the intention of making some of the West India islands, in pursuance of his piratical designs. No opposition was made by Peters or the cook; at least none in the hearing of Augustus. All idea of taking the vessel from the Cape Verds was abandoned. The leak was now easily kept under by one pump going every three quarters of an hour. The sail was drawn from beneath the bows. Spoke two small schooners during the day.

July 9th. Fine weather. All hands employed in repairing bulwarks. Peters had again a long conversation with Augustus, and spoke more plainly than he had done heretofore. He said nothing should induce him to come into the mate's views, and even hinted his intention of taking the brig out of his hands. He asked my friend if he could depend upon his aid in such case, to which Augustus said, "Yes," without hesitation. Peters then said he would sound the others of his party upon the subject, and went away. During the remainder of the day Augustus had no opportunity of speaking with him privately.

CHAPTER 7

July 10. Spoke a brig from Rio, bound to Norfolk. Weather hazy, with a light baffling wind from the eastward. To-day Hartman Rogers died, having been attacked on the eighth with spasms after drinking a glass of grog. This man was of the cook's party, and one upon whom Peters placed his main reliance. He told Augustus that he believed the mate had poisoned him, and that he expected, if he did not be on the lookout, his own turn would come shortly. There were now only himself, Jones, and the cook belonging to his own gang—on the other side there were five. He had spoken to Jones about taking the command from the mate; but the project having been coolly received, he had been deterred from pressing the matter any further, or from saying anything to the cook. It was well, as it happened, that he was so prudent, for in the afternoon the cook expressed his determination of siding with the mate, and went over formally to that party; while Jones took an opportunity of quarrelling with Peters, and hinted that he would let the mate know of the plan in agitation. There was now, evidently, no time to be lost, and Peters expressed his determination of attempting to take the vessel at all hazards, provided Augustus would lend him his aid. My friend at once assured him of his willingness to enter into any plan for that purpose, and, thinking the opportunity a favourable one, made known the fact of my being on board. At this the hybrid was not more astonished than delighted, as he had no reliance whatever upon Jones, whom he already considered as belonging to the party of the mate. They went below immediately, when Augustus called to me by name, and Peters and myself were soon made acquainted. It was agreed that we should attempt to retake the vessel upon the first good opportunity, leaving Jones altogether out of our councils. In the event of success we were to run the brig into the first port that offered, and deliver her up. The desertion of his party had frustrated Peters's design of going into the Pacific—an adventure which could not be accomplished without a crew, and he depended upon either getting acquitted upon trial on the score of insanity (which he solemnly averred had actuated him in lending his aid to the mutiny), or upon obtaining a pardon, if found guilty, through the representations of Augustus and myself. Our deliberations were interrupted for the present by the cry of "All hands take in sail," and Peters and Augustus ran up on deck.

As usual, the crew were nearly all drunk; and, before sail could be properly taken in, a violent squall laid the brig on her beam-ends. By keeping her away, however, she righted, having shipped a good deal of water. Scarcely was everything secure, when another squall took the vessel, and immediately afterward another—no damage being done. There was every appearance of a gale of wind, which, indeed, shortly came on, with great fury, from the northward and westward. All was made as snug as possible, and we laid to, as usual, under a close-reefed foresail. As night drew on, the wind increased in violence, with a remarkably heavy sea. Peters now came into the forecastle with Augustus, and we resumed our deliberations.

We agreed that no opportunity could be more favourable than the present for carrying our design into effect, as an attempt at such a moment would never be anticipated. As the brig was snugly laid to, there would be no necessity of manœuvring her until good weather, when, if we succeeded in our attempt, we might liberate one, or perhaps two of the men, to aid us in taking her into port. The main difficulty was the great disproportion in our forces. There were only three of us, and in the cabin there were nine. All the arms on board, too, were in their possession, with the exception of a pair of small pistols which Peters had concealed about his person, and the large seaman's knife which he always wore in the waistband of his pantaloons. From certain indications, too, such, for example, as there being no such thing as an axe or a handspike lying in their customary places, we began to fear that the mate had his suspicions, at least in regard to Peters, and that he would let slip no opportunity of getting rid of him. It was clear, indeed, that what we should determine to do could not be done too soon. Still the odds were too much against us to allow of our proceeding without the greatest caution.

Peters proposed that he should go up on deck, and enter into conversation with the watch (Allen), when he would be able to throw him into the sea without trouble, and without making any disturbance, by seizing a good opportunity; that Augustus and myself should then come up, and endeavour to provide ourselves with some kind of weapons from the deck; and that we should then make a rush together, and secure the companion-way before any opposition could be offered. I objected to this, because I could not believe that the mate (who was a cunning fellow in all matters which did not affect his superstitious prejudices) would suffer himself to be so easily entrapped. The very fact of there being a watch on deck at all was sufficient proof that he was upon the alert—it not being usual, except in vessels where discipline is most rigidly enforced, to station a watch on deck when a vessel is lying to in a gale of wind. As I address myself principally, if not altogether, to persons who have never been to sea, it may be as well to state the exact condition of a vessel under such circumstances. Lying to,[1] or, in sea-parlance "laying to," is a measure resorted to for various purposes, and effected in various manners. In moderate weather, it is frequently done with a view of merely bringing the vessel to a stand-still, to wait for another vessel, or any similar object. If the vessel which lies to is under full sail, the manœuvre is usually accomplished by throwing round some portion of her sails so as to let the wind take them aback, when she becomes stationary. But we are now speaking of lying to in a gale of wind. This is done when the wind is ahead, and too violent to admit of carrying sail without danger of capsizing; and sometimes even when the wind is fair, but the sea too heavy for the vessel to be put before it. If a vessel be suffered to scud before the wind in a very heavy sea, much damage is usually done her by the shipping of water over her stern, and sometimes by the violent plunges she makes forward. This manœuvre, then, is seldom resorted to in such case, unless through necessity. When the vessel is in a leaky condition, she is often put before the wind even in the heaviest seas; for, when lying to, her seams are sure to be greatly opened by her violent straining, and it is not so much the case when scudding. Often, too, it becomes necessary to scud a vessel, either when the blast is so exceedingly furious as to tear in pieces the sail which is employed with a view of bringing her head to the wind, or when, through the false modelling of the frame or other causes, this main object cannot be effected.

Vessels in a gale of wind are laid to in different manners, according to their peculiar construction. Some lie to best under a foresail, and this, I believe, is the sail most usually employed. Large square-rigged vessels have sails for the express purpose, called storm-staysails. But the jib is occasionally employed by itself—sometimes the jib and foresail, or a double-reefed foresail, and not unfrequently the after-sails, are made use of. Foretopsails are very often found to answer the purpose better than any other species of sail. The Grampus was generally laid to under a close-reefed foresail.

When a vessel is to be laid to, her head is brought up to the wind just so nearly as to fill the sail under which she lies, when hauled flat aft, that is, when brought diagonally across the vessel. This being done, the bows point within a few degrees of the direction from which the wind issues, and the windward bow of course receives the shock of the waves. In this situation a good vessel will ride out a very heavy gale of wind without shipping a drop of water, and without any further attention being requisite on the part of the crew. The helm is usually lashed down, but this is altogether unnecessary (except on account of the noise it makes when loose), for the rudder has no effect upon the vessel when lying to. Indeed, the helm had far better be left loose than lashed very fast, for the rudder is apt to be torn off by heavy seas if there be no room for the helm to play. As long as the sail holds, a well-modelled vessel will maintain her situation, and ride every sea, as if instinct with life and reason. If the violence of the wind, however, should tear the sail into pieces (a feat which it requires a perfect hurricane to accomplish under ordinary circumstances), there is then imminent danger. The vessel falls off from the wind, and, coming broadside to the sea, is completely at its mercy: the only resource in this case is to put her quickly before the wind, letting her scud until some other sail can be set. Some vessels will lie to under no sail whatever, but such are not to be trusted at sea.

But to return from this digression. It had never been customary with the mate to have any watch on deck when lying to in a gale of wind, and the fact that he had now one, coupled with the circumstance of the missing axes and handspikes, fully convinced us that the crew were too well on the watch to be taken by surprise in the manner Peters had suggested. Something, however, was to be done, and that with as little delay as practicable, for there could be no doubt that a suspicion having been once entertained against Peters, he would be sacrificed upon the earliest occasion, and one would certainly be either found or made upon the breaking of the gale.

Augustus now suggested that if Peters could contrive to remove, under any pretext, the piece of chain-cable which lay over the trap in the stateroom, we might possibly be able to come upon them unawares by means of the hold; but a little reflection convinced us that the vessel rolled and pitched too violently for any attempt of that nature.

By good fortune I at length hit upon the idea of working upon the superstitious terrors and guilty conscience of the mate. It will be remembered that one of the crew, Hartman Rogers, had died during the morning, having been attacked two days before with spasms after drinking some spirits and water. Peters had expressed to us his opinion that this man had been poisoned by the mate, and for this belief he had reasons, so he said, which were incontrovertible, but which he could not be prevailed upon to explain to us—this wayward refusal being only in keeping with other points of his singular character. But whether or not he had any better grounds for suspecting the mate than we had ourselves, we were easily led to fall in with his suspicion, and determined to act accordingly.

Rogers had died about eleven in the forenoon, in violent convulsions; and the corpse presented in a few minutes after death one of the most horrid and loathsome spectacles I ever remember to have seen. The stomach was swollen immensely, like that of a man who has been drowned and lain under water for many weeks. The hands were in the same condition, while the face was shrunken, shrivelled, and of a chalky whiteness, except where relieved by two or three glaring red splotches, like those occasioned by the erysipelas:[2] one of these splotches extended diagonally across the face, completely covering up an eye as if with a band of red velvet. In this disgusting condition the body had been brought up from the cabin at noon to be thrown overboard, when the mate getting a glimpse of it (for he now saw it for the first time), and being either touched with remorse for his crime or struck with terror at so horrible a sight, ordered the men to sew the body up in its hammock, and allow it the usual rites of sea-burial. Having given these directions he went below, as if to avoid any further sight of his victim. While preparations were making to obey his orders, the gale came on with great fury, and the design was abandoned for the present. The corpse, left to itself, was washed into the larboard scuppers, where it still lay at the time of which I speak, floundering about with the furious lurches of the brig.

Having arranged our plan, we set about putting it in execution as speedily as possible. Peters went upon deck, and, as he had anticipated, was immediately accosted by Allen, who appeared to be stationed more as a watch upon the forecastle than for any other purpose. The fate of this villain, however, was speedily and silently decided; for Peters, approaching him in a careless manner, as if about to address him, seized him by the throat, and, before he could utter a single cry, tossed him over the bulwarks. He then called to us, and we came up. Our first precaution was to look about for something with which to arm ourselves, and in doing this we had to proceed with great care, for it was impossible to stand on deck an instant without holding fast, and violent seas broke over the vessel at every plunge forward. It was indispensable, too, that we should be quick in our operations, for every minute we expected the mate to be up to set the pumps going, as it was evident the brig must be taking in water very fast. After searching about for some time, we could find nothing more fit for our purpose than the two pump-handles, one of which Augustus took, and I the other. Having secured these, we stripped off the shirt of the corpse and dropped the body overboard. Peters and myself then went below, leaving Augustus to watch upon deck, where he took his station just where Allen had been placed, and with his back to the cabin companion-way, so that, if any one of the mate's gang should come up, he might suppose it was the watch.

As soon as I got below I commenced disguising myself so as to represent the corpse of Rogers. The shirt which we had taken from the body aided us very much, for it was of a singular form and character, and easily recognisable—a kind of smock, which the deceased wore over his other clothing. It was a blue stockinett, with large white stripes running across. Having put this on, I proceeded to equip myself with a false stomach, in imitation of the horrible deformity of the swollen corpse. This was soon effected by means of stuffing with some bedclothes. I then gave the same appearance to my hands by drawing on a pair of white woollen mittens, and filling them in with any kind of rags that offered themselves. Peters then arranged my face, first rubbing it well over with white chalk, and afterward splotching it with blood, which he took from a cut in his finger. The streak across the eye was not forgotten, and presented a most shocking appearance.

CHAPTER 8

As I viewed myself in a fragment of looking-glass which hung up in the cabin, and by the dim light of a kind of battle-lantern, I was so impressed with a sense of vague awe at my appearance, and at the recollection of the terrific reality which I was thus representing, that I was seized with a violent tremour, and could scarcely summon resolution to go on with my part. It was necessary, however, to act with decision, and Peters and myself went upon deck.

We there found everything safe, and, keeping close to the bulwarks, the three of us crept to the cabin companion-way. It was only partially closed, precautions having been taken to prevent its being suddenly pushed to from without, by means of placing billets of wood on the upper step so as to interfere with the shutting. We found no difficulty in getting a full view of the interior of the cabin through the cracks where the hinges were placed. It now proved to have been very fortunate for us that we had not attempted to take them by surprise, for they were evidently on the alert. Only one was asleep, and he lying just at the foot of the companion-ladder, with a musket by his side. The rest were seated on several mattresses, which had been taken from the berths and thrown on the floor. They were engaged in earnest conversation; and although they had been carousing, as appeared from two empty jugs, with some tin tumblers which lay about, they were not as much intoxicated as usual. All had knives, one or two of them pistols, and a great many muskets were lying in a berth close at hand.

We listened to their conversation for some time before we could make up our minds how to act, having as yet resolved on nothing determinate, except that we would attempt to paralyze their exertions, when we should attack them, by means of the apparition of Rogers. They were discussing their piratical plans, in which all we could hear distinctly was, that they would unite with the crew of a schooner Hornet,[1] and, if possible, get the schooner herself into their possession preparatory to some attempt on a large scale, the particulars of which could not be made out by either of us.

One of the men spoke of Peters, when the mate replied to him in a low voice which could not be distinguished, and afterward added more loudly, that "he could not understand his being so much forward with the captain's brat in the forecastle, and he thought the sooner both of them were overboard the better." To this no answer was made, but we could easily perceive that the hint was well received by the whole party, and more particularly by Jones. At this period I was excessively agitated, the more so as I could see that neither Augustus nor Peters could determine how to act. I made up my mind, however, to sell my life as dearly as possible, and not to suffer myself to be overcome by any feelings of trepidation.

The tremendous noise made by the roaring of the wind in the rigging and the washing of the sea over the deck prevented us from hearing what was said except during momentary lulls. In one of these we all distinctly heard the mate tell one of the men to "go forward, and order the d—d lubbers to come into the cabin, where he could have an eye upon them, for he wanted no such secret doings on board the brig." It was well for us that the pitching of the vessel at this moment was so violent as to prevent this order from being carried into instant execution. The cook got up from his mattress to go for us, when a tremendous lurch, which I thought would carry away the masts, threw him headlong against one of the larboard stateroom doors, bursting it open, and creating a good deal of other confusion. Luckily, neither of our party was thrown

from his position, and we had time to make a precipitate
retreat to the forecastle, and arrange a hurried plan of action
before the messenger made his appearance, or rather before
he put his head out of the companion-hatch, for he did not
come on deck. From this station he could not notice the
absence of Allen, and he accordingly bawled out as if to
him, repeating the orders of the mate. Peters cried out, "Ay,
ay," in a disguised voice, and the cook immediately went
below, without entertaining a suspicion that all was not
right.

My two companions now proceeded boldly aft and down
into the cabin, Peters closing the door after him in the same
manner he had found it. The mate received them with feigned
cordiality, and told Augustus that, since he had behaved himself so well of late, he might take up his quarters in the cabin,
and be one of them for the future. He then poured him out a
tumbler half full of rum, and made him drink it. All this I saw
and heard, for I followed my friends to the cabin as soon as
the door was shut, and took up my old point of observation. I
had brought with me the two pump-handles, one of which I
secured near the companion-way, to be ready for use when
required.

I now steadied myself as well as possible so as to have a
good view of all that was passing within, and endeavoured to
nerve myself to the task of descending among the mutineers
when Peters should make a signal to me as agreed upon.
Presently he contrived to turn the conversation upon the
bloody deeds of the mutiny, and, by degrees, led the men to
talk of the thousand superstitions which are so universally
current among seamen. I could not make out all that was
said, but I could plainly see the effects of the conversation in
the countenances of those present. The mate was evidently
much agitated, and presently, when some one mentioned the
terrific appearance of Rogers's corpse, I thought he was upon

the point of swooning. Peters now asked him if he did not think it would be better to have the body thrown overboard at once, as it was too horrible a sight to see it floundering about in the scuppers. At this the villain absolutely gasped for breath, and turned his head slowly round upon his companions, as if imploring some one to go up and perform the task. No one, however, stirred, and it was quite evident that the whole party were wound up to the highest pitch of nervous excitement. Peters now made me the signal. I immediately threw open the door of the companion-way, and, descending without uttering a syllable, stood erect in the midst of the party.

The intense effect produced by this sudden apparition is not at all to be wondered at when the various circumstances are taken into consideration. Usually, in cases of a similar nature, there is left in the mind of the spectator some glimmering of doubt as to the reality of the vision before his eyes; a degree of hope, however feeble, that he is the victim of chicanery, and that the apparition is not actually a visitant from the world of shadows. It is not too much to say that such remnants of doubt have been at the bottom of almost every such visitation, and that the appalling horror which has sometimes been brought about, is to be attributed, even in the cases most in point, and where most suffering has been experienced, more to a kind of anticipative horror, lest the apparition *might possibly be* real, than to an unwavering belief in its reality. But, in the present instance, it will be seen immediately, that in the minds of the mutineers there was not even the shadow of a basis upon which to rest a doubt that the apparition of Rogers was indeed a revivification of his disgusting corpse, or at least its spiritual image. The isolated situation of the brig, with its entire inaccessibility on account of the gale, confined the apparently possible means of deception within such narrow and definite limits, that they must have thought them-

selves enabled to survey them all at a glance. They had now
been at sea twenty-four days, without holding more than a
speaking communication with any vessel whatever. The
whole of the crew, too, at least all whom they had the most
remote reason for suspecting to be on board, were assembled
in the cabin, with the exception of Allen, the watch; and his
gigantic stature (he was six feet six inches high) was too familiar in their eyes to permit the notion that he was the apparition before them to enter their minds even for an instant. Add
to these considerations the awe-inspiring nature of the tempest, and that of the conversation brought about by Peters;
the deep impression which the loathsomeness of the actual
corpse had made in the morning upon the imaginations of the
men; the excellence of the imitation in my person; and the uncertain and wavering light in which they beheld me, as the
glare of the cabin lantern, swinging violently to and fro, fell
dubiously and fitfully upon my figure, and there will be no
reason to wonder that the deception had even more than the
entire effect which we had anticipated. The mate sprang up
from the mattress on which he was lying, and, without uttering a syllable, fell back, stone dead, upon the cabin floor, and
was hurled to the leeward like a log by a heavy roll of the brig.
Of the remaining seven there were but three who had at first
any degree of presence of mind. The four others sat for some
time rooted apparently to the floor, the most pitiable objects
of horror and utter despair my eyes ever encountered.[2] The
only opposition we experienced at all was from the cook,
John Hunt, and Richard Parker; but they made but a feeble
and irresolute defence. The two former were shot instantly by
Peters, and I felled Parker with a blow on the head from the
pump-handle which I had brought with me. In the mean time
Augustus seized one of the muskets lying on the floor, and
shot another mutineer (———— Wilson) through the breast.
There were now but three remaining; but by this time they

had become aroused from their lethargy, and perhaps began to see that a deception had been practised upon them, for they fought with great resolution and fury, and, but for the immense muscular strength of Peters, might have ultimately got the better of us. These three men were ———— Jones, ———— Greely, and Absalom Hicks. Jones had thrown Augustus on the floor, stabbed him in several places along the right arm, and would no doubt have soon despatched him (as neither Peters nor myself could immediately get rid of our own antagonists), had it not been for the timely aid of a friend upon whose assistance we surely had never depended. This friend was no other than Tiger. With a low growl he bounded into the cabin, at a most critical moment for Augustus, and throwing himself upon Jones, pinned him to the floor in an instant. My friend, however, was now too much injured to render us any aid whatever,[3] and I was so encumbered with my disguise that I could do but little. The dog would not leave his hold upon the throat of Jones—Peters, nevertheless, was far more than a match for the two men who remained, and would, no doubt, have despatched them sooner, had it not been for the narrow space in which he had to act, and the tremendous lurches of the vessel. Presently he was enabled to get hold of a heavy stool, several of which lay about the floor. With this he beat out the brains of Greely as he was in the act of discharging a musket at me, and immediately afterward a roll of the brig throwing him in contact with Hicks, he seized him by the throat, and, by dint of sheer strength, strangled him instantaneously. Thus, in far less time than I have taken to tell it, we found ourselves masters of the brig.

The only person of our opponents who was left alive was Richard Parker. This man, it will be remembered, I had knocked down with a blow from the pump-handle at the commencement of the attack. He now lay motionless by the door of the shattered stateroom; but, upon Peters touching him with his foot, he spoke, and entreated for mercy. His head was only slightly cut, and otherwise he had received no injury, having been merely stunned by the blow. He now got up, and, for the present, we secured his hands behind his back. The dog was still growling over Jones; but, upon examination, we found him completely dead, the blood issuing in a stream from a deep wound in the throat, inflicted, no doubt, by the sharp teeth of the animal.

It was now about one o'clock in the morning, and the wind was still blowing tremendously. The brig evidently laboured much more than usual, and it became absolutely necessary that something should be done with a view of easing her in some measure. At almost every roll to leeward she shipped a sea, several of which came partially down into the cabin during our scuffle, the hatchway having been left open by myself when I descended. The entire range of bulwarks to larboard had been swept away, as well as the caboose, together with the jollyboat from the counter. The creaking and working of the mainmast, too, gave indication that it was nearly sprung. To make room for more stowage in the after hold, the heel of this mast had been stepped between decks (a very reprehensible practice, occasionally resorted to by ignorant ship-builders), so that it was in imminent danger of working from its step. But, to crown all our difficulties, we plummed the well, and found no less than seven feet water.

Leaving the bodies of the crew lying in the cabin, we got to work immediately at the pumps—Parker, of course, being set at liberty to assist us in the labour. Augustus's arm was bound up as well as we could effect it, and he did what he could, but that was not much. However, we found that we could just manage to keep the leak from gaining upon us by having one pump constantly going. As there were only four of us, this was severe labour; but we endeavoured to keep up our spirits, and looked anxiously for daybreak, when we hoped to lighten the brig by cutting away the mainmast.

In this manner we passed a night of terrible anxiety and fatigue, and, when the day at length broke, the gale had neither abated in the least, nor were there any signs of its abating. We now dragged the bodies on deck and threw them overboard. Our next care was to get rid of the mainmast. The necessary preparations having been made,[4] Peters cut away at the mast (having found axes in the cabin), while the rest of us stood by the stays and lanyards. As the brig gave a tremendous lee-lurch, the word was given to cut away the weather-lanyards, which being done, the whole mass of wood and rigging plunged into the sea, clear of the brig, and without doing any material injury. We now found that the vessel did not labour quite as much as before, but our situation was still exceedingly precarious, and, in spite of the utmost exertions, we could not gain upon the leak without the aid of both pumps. The little assistance which Augustus could render us was not really of any importance. To add to our distress, a heavy sea, striking the brig to windward, threw her off several points from the wind, and, before she could regain her position, another broke completely over her, and hurled her full upon her beam-ends. The ballast now shifted in a mass to leeward (the stowage had been knocking about perfectly at random for some time), and for a few moments we thought nothing could save us from capsizing. Presently, however, we partially righted; but the ballast still retaining its place to larboard, we lay so much along that it was useless to think of working the pumps, which indeed we could not have done much longer in any case, as our hands were entirely raw with the excessive labour we had undergone, and were bleeding in the most horrible manner.

Contrary to Parker's advice, we now proceeded to cut away the foremast, and at length accomplished it after much difficulty, owing to the position in which we lay. In going overboard the wreck took with it the bowsprit, and left us a complete hulk.

So far we had had reason to rejoice in the escape of our longboat, which had received no damage from any of the huge seas which had come on board. But we had not long to congratulate ourselves; for the foremast having gone, and, of course, the foresail with it, by which the brig had been steadied, every sea now made a complete breach over us,[5] and in five minutes our deck was swept from stem to stern, the longboat and starboard bulwarks torn off, and even the windlass shattered into fragments. It was, indeed, hardly possible for us to be in a more pitiable condition.

At noon there seemed to be some slight appearance of the gale's abating, but in this we were sadly disappointed, for it only lulled for a few minutes to blow with redoubled fury. About four in the afternoon it was utterly impossible to stand up against the violence of the blast; and, as the night closed in upon us, I had not a shadow of hope that the vessel would hold together until morning.

By midnight we had settled very deep in the water, which was now up to the orlop deck. The rudder went soon afterward, the sea which tore it away lifting the after portion of the brig entirely from the water, against which she thumped in her descent with such a concussion as would be occasioned by going ashore. We had all calculated that the rudder would hold its own to the last, as it was unusually strong, being rigged as I have never seen one rigged either before or since. Down its main timber there ran a succession of stout iron hooks, and others in the same manner down the stern-post. Through these hooks there extended a very thick wrought-iron rod, the rudder being thus held to the stern-post, and swinging freely on the rod. The tremendous force of the sea which tore it off may be estimated by the fact, that the hooks in the stern-post, which ran entirely through it, being clinched on the inside, were drawn every one of them completely out of the solid wood.

We had scarcely time to draw breath after the violence of this shock, when one of the most tremendous waves I had then ever known broke right on board of us,[6] sweeping the companion-way clear off, bursting in the hatchways, and filling every inch of the vessel with water.

CHAPTER 9

Luckily, just before night, all four of us had lashed ourselves firmly to the fragments of the windlass, lying in this manner as flat upon the deck as possible. This precaution alone saved us from destruction. As it was, we were all more or less stunned by the immense weight of water which tumbled upon us, and which did not roll from above us until we were nearly exhausted. As soon as I could recover breath, I called aloud to my companions. Augustus alone replied, saying, "It is all over with us, and may God have mercy upon our souls." By-and-by both the others were enabled to speak, when they exhorted us to take courage, as there was still hope; it being impossible, from the nature of the cargo, that the brig could go down, and there being every chance that the gale would blow over by the morning. These words inspired me with new life; for, strange as it may seem, although it was obvious that a vessel with a cargo of empty oil-casks would not sink,[1] I had been hitherto so confused in mind as to have overlooked this consideration altogether; and the danger which I had for some time regarded as the most imminent was that of foundering. As hope revived within me, I made use of every opportunity to strengthen the lashings which held me to the remains of the windlass, and in this occupation I soon discovered that my companions were also busy. The night was as dark as it could possibly be, and the horrible shrieking din and confusion which surrounded us it is useless to attempt describing. Our deck lay level with the sea, or rather we were encircled with a towering ridge of foam, a portion of which swept over us every instant. It is not too much to say that our heads were not fairly out of water more than one second in three. Although we lay close together, no one of us could see the other, or, indeed, any portion of the brig itself, upon which we were so tempestuously hurled about. At intervals we called one to the other, thus endeavouring to keep alive hope, and render consolation and encouragement to such of us as stood most in need of it. The feeble condition of Augustus made him an object of solicitude with us all; and as, from the lacerated condition of his right arm, it must have been impossible for him to secure his lashings with any degree of firmness, we were in momentary expectation of finding that he had gone overboard—yet to render him aid was a thing altogether out of the question. Fortunately, his station was more secure than that of any of the rest of us; for the upper part of his body lying just beneath a portion of the shattered windlass, the seas, as they tumbled in upon him, were greatly broken in their violence. In any other situation than this (into which he had been accidentally thrown after having lashed himself in a very exposed spot) he must inevitably have perished before morning. Owing to the brig's lying so much along, we were all less liable to be washed off than otherwise would have been the case. The heel, as I have before stated, was to larboard, about one half of the deck being constantly under water. The seas, therefore, which struck us to starboard were much broken by the vessel's side, only reaching us in fragments as we lay flat on our faces; while those which came from larboard, being what are called back-water seas, and obtaining little hold upon us on account of our posture, had not sufficient force to drag us from our fastenings.

In this frightful situation we lay until the day broke so as to show us more fully the horrors which surrounded us. The brig was a mere log, rolling about at the mercy of every wave; the gale was upon the increase, if anything, blowing indeed a complete hurricane, and there appeared to us no earthly prospect of deliverance. For several hours we held on in silence, expecting every moment that our lashings would either give way, that the remains of the windlass would go by the board, or that some of the huge seas, which roared in every direction around us and above us, would drive the hulk so far beneath the water that we should be drowned before it could regain the surface. By the mercy of God, however, we were preserved from these imminent dangers, and about midday were cheered by the light of the blessed sun.[2] Shortly afterward we could perceive a sensible diminution in the force of the wind, when, now for the first time since the latter part of the evening before, Augustus spoke, asking Peters, who lay closest to him, if he thought there was any possibility of our being saved. As no reply was at first made to this question, we all concluded that the hybrid had been drowned where he lay; but presently, to our great joy, he spoke, although very feebly, saying that he was in great pain, being so cut by the tightness of his lashings across the stomach, that he must either find means of loosening them or perish, as it was impossible that he could endure his misery much longer. This occasioned us great distress, as it was altogether useless to think of aiding him in any manner while the sea continued washing over us as it did. We exhorted him to bear his sufferings with fortitude, and promised to seize the first opportunity which should offer itself to relieve him. He replied that it would soon be too late; that it would be all over with him before we could help him; and then, after moaning for some minutes, lay silent, when we concluded that he had perished.

As the evening drew on, the sea had fallen so much that scarcely more than one wave broke over the hulk from windward in the course of five minutes, and the wind had abated a great deal, although still blowing a severe gale. I had not heard any of my companions speak for hours, and now called to Augustus. He replied, although very feebly, so that I could not distinguish what he said. I then spoke to Peters and to Parker, neither of whom returned any answer.

Shortly after this period I fell into a state of partial insensibility, during which the most pleasing images floated in my imagination; such as green trees, waving meadows of ripe grain, processions of dancing girls, troops of cavalry, and other phantasies. I now remember that, in all which passed before my mind's eye, *motion* was a predominant idea. Thus, I never fancied any stationary object, such as a house, a mountain, or anything of that kind; but windmills, ships, large birds, balloons, people on horseback, carriages driving furiously, and similar moving objects, presented themselves in endless succession. When I recovered from this state, the sun was, as near as I could guess, an hour high. I had the greatest difficulty in bringing to recollection the various circumstances connected with my situation, and for some time remained firmly convinced that I was still in the hold of the brig, near the box, and that the body of Parker was that of Tiger.[3]

When I at length completely came to my senses, I found that the wind blew no more than a moderate breeze, and that the sea was comparatively calm; so much so that it only washed over the brig amidships. My left arm had broken loose from its lashings, and was much cut about the elbow; my right was entirely benumbed, and the hand and wrist swollen prodigiously by the pressure of the rope, which had worked from the shoulder downward. I was also in great pain from another rope which went about my waist, and had been drawn to an insufferable degree of tightness. Looking round upon my companions, I saw that Peters still lived, although a thick line was pulled so forcibly around his loins as to give him the appearance of being cut nearly in two; as I stirred, he made a feeble motion to me with his hand, pointing to the rope. Augustus gave no indication of life whatever, and was bent nearly double across a splinter of the windlass. Parker spoke to me when he saw me moving, and asked me if I had not sufficient strength to release him from his situation; saying, that if I would summon up what spirits I could, and contrive to untie him, we might yet save our lives; but that otherwise we must all perish. I told him to take courage, and I would endeavour to free him. Feeling in my pantaloons' pocket, I got hold of my penknife, and, after several ineffectual attempts, at length succeeded in opening it. I then, with my left hand, managed to free my right from its fastenings, and afterward cut the other ropes which held me. Upon attempting, however, to move from my position, I found that my legs failed me altogether, and that I could not get up; neither could I move my right arm in any direction. Upon mentioning this to Parker, he advised me to lie quiet for a few minutes, holding on to the windlass with my left hand, so as to allow time for the blood to circulate. Doing this, the numbness presently began to die away, so that I could move first one of my legs, and then the other; and, shortly afterward, I regained the partial use of my right arm. I now crawled with great caution towards Parker, without getting on my legs, and soon cut loose all the lashings about him, when, after a short delay, he also recovered the partial use of his limbs. We now lost no time in getting loose the rope from Peters. It had cut a deep gash through the waistband of his woollen pantaloons, and through two shirts, and made its way into his groin, from which the blood flowed out copiously as we removed the cordage. No sooner had we removed it, however, than he spoke, and seemed to experience instant relief—being able to move with much greater ease than either Parker or myself—this was no doubt owing to the discharge of blood.

We had little hope that Augustus would recover, as he evinced no signs of life; but, upon getting to him, we discovered that he had merely swooned from loss of blood, the bandages we had placed around his wounded arm having been torn off by the water; none of the ropes which held him to the windlass were drawn sufficiently tight to occasion his death. Having relieved him from the fastenings, and got him clear of the broken wood about the windlass, we secured him in a dry place to windward, with his head somewhat lower than his body, and all three of us busied ourselves in chafing his limbs. In about half an hour he came to himself, although it was not until the next morning that he gave signs of recognising any of us, or had sufficient strength to speak. By the time we had thus got clear of our lashings it was quite dark, and it began to cloud up, so that we were again in the greatest agony lest it should come on to blow hard, in which event nothing could have saved us from perishing, exhausted as we were. By good fortune it continued very moderate during the night, the sea subsiding every minute, which gave us great hopes of ultimate preservation. A gentle breeze still blew from the N. W., but the weather was not at all cold. Augustus was lashed carefully to windward in such a manner as to prevent him from slipping overboard with the rolls of the vessel, as he was still too weak to hold on at all. For ourselves there was no such necessity. We sat close together, supporting each other with the aid of the broken ropes about the windlass, and devising methods of escape from our frightful situation. We derived much comfort from taking off our clothes and wringing the water from them. When we put them on after this, they felt remarkably warm and pleasant, and served to invigorate us in no little de-gree. We helped Augustus off with his, and wrung them for him, when he experienced the same comfort.

Our chief sufferings were now those of hunger and thirst, and, when we looked forward to the means of relief in this re-spect, our hearts sunk within us, and we were induced to re-gret that we had escaped the less dreadful perils of the sea. We endeavoured, however, to console ourselves with the hope of being speedily picked up by some vessel, and encouraged each other to bear with fortitude the evils that might happen.

The morning of the fourteenth at length dawned, and the weather still continued clear and pleasant, with a steady but very light breeze from the N. W. The sea was now quite smooth, and as, from some cause which we could not deter-mine, the brig did not lie so much along as she had done be-

fore, the deck was comparatively dry, and we could move
about with freedom. We had now been better than three entire days and nights without either food or drink, and it became absolutely necessary that we should make an attempt to
get up something from below. As the brig was completely full
of water, we went to this work despondingly, and with but
little expectation of being able to obtain anything. We made a
kind of drag by driving some nails which we broke out from
the remains of the companion-hatch into two pieces of wood.
Tying these across each other, and fastening them to the end
of a rope, we threw them into the cabin, and dragged them to
and fro, in the faint hope of being thus able to entangle some
article which might be of use to us for food, or which might at
least render us assistance in getting it. We spent the greater
part of the morning in this labour without effect, fishing
up nothing more than a few bedclothes, which were readily
caught by the nails. Indeed, our contrivance was so very
clumsy, that any greater success was hardly to be anticipated.

We now tried the forecastle, but equally in vain, and were
upon the brink of despair, when Peters proposed that we
should fasten a rope to his body, and let him make an attempt
to get up something by diving into the cabin. This proposition
we hailed with all the delight which reviving hope could inspire. He proceeded immediately to strip off his clothes with
the exception of his pantaloons; and a strong rope was then
carefully fastened around his middle, being brought up over
his shoulders in such a manner that there was no possibility of
its slipping. The undertaking was one of great difficulty and
danger; for, as we could hardly expect to find much, if any
provision in the cabin itself, it was necessary that the diver, after letting himself down, should make a turn to the right, and
proceed under water a distance of ten or twelve feet, in a narrow passage, to the storeroom, and return, without drawing
breath.

Everything being ready, Peters now descended into the

cabin, going down the companion-ladder until the water reached his chin. He then plunged in, head first, turning to the right as he plunged, and endeavouring to make his way to the storeroom. In this first attempt, however, he was altogether unsuccessful. In less than half a minute after his going down we felt the rope jerked violently (the signal we had agreed upon when he desired to be drawn up). We accordingly drew him up instantly, but so incautiously as to bruise him badly against the ladder. He had brought nothing with him, and had been unable to penetrate more than a very little way into the passage, owing to the constant exertions he found it necessary to make in order to keep himself from floating up against the deck. Upon getting out he was very much exhausted, and had to rest full fifteen minutes before he could again venture to descend.

The second attempt met with even worse success; for he remained so long under water without giving the signal, that, becoming alarmed for his safety, we drew him out without it, and found that he was almost at the last gasp, having, as he said, repeatedly jerked at the rope without our feeling it. This was probably owing to a portion of it having become entangled in the balustrade at the foot of the ladder. This balustrade was, indeed, so much in the way, that we determined to remove it, if possible, before proceeding with our design. As we had no means of getting it away except by main force, we all descended into the water as far as we could on the ladder, and, giving a pull against it with our united strength, succeeded in breaking it down.

The third attempt was equally unsuccessful with the two first, and it now became evident that nothing could be done in this manner without the aid of some weight with which the diver might steady himself, and keep to the floor of the cabin while making his search. For a long time we looked about in vain for something which might answer this purpose; but at length, to our great joy, we discovered one of the weather-forechains so loose that we had not the least difficulty in wrenching it off. Having fastened this securely to one of his ankles, Peters now made his fourth descent into the cabin, and this time succeeded in making his way to the door of the steward's room. To his inexpressible grief, however, he found it locked, and was obliged to return without effecting an entrance, as, with the greatest exertion, he could remain under water not more, at the utmost extent, than a single minute. Our affairs now looked gloomy indeed, and neither Augustus nor myself could refrain from bursting into tears, as we thought of the host of difficulties which encompassed us, and the slight probability which existed of our finally making an escape. But this weakness was not of long duration. Throwing ourselves on our knees to God, we implored his aid in the many dangers which beset us; and arose with renewed hope and vigour to think what could yet be done by mortal means towards accomplishing our deliverance.

CHAPTER 10

Shortly afterward an incident occurred which I am induced to look upon as more intensely productive of emotion, as far more replete with the extremes first of delight and then of horror, than even any of the thousand chances which afterward befell me in nine long years,[1] crowded with events of the most startling, and, in many cases, of the most unconceived and unconceivable character. We were lying on the deck near the companion-way, and debating the possibility of yet making our way into the storeroom, when, looking towards Augustus, who lay fronting myself, I perceived that he had become all at once deadly pale, and that his lips were quivering in the most singular and unaccountable manner. Greatly alarmed, I spoke to him, but he made me no reply, and I was beginning to think that he was suddenly taken ill, when I took notice of his eyes, which were glaring apparently at some object behind me. I turned my head, and shall never forget the ecstatic joy which thrilled through every particle of my frame, when I perceived a large brig bearing down upon us, and not more than a couple of miles off. I sprung to my feet as if a musket bullet had suddenly struck me to the heart; and, stretching out my arms in the direction of the vessel, stood in this manner, motionless, and unable to articulate a syllable. Peters and Parker were equally affected, although in different ways. The former danced about the deck like a madman, uttering the most extravagant rhodomontades, intermingled with howls and imprecations, while the latter burst into tears, and continued for many minutes weeping like a child.[2]

The vessel in sight was a large hermaphrodite brig, of a Dutch build,[3] and painted black, with a tawdry gilt figurehead. She had evidently seen a good deal of rough weather, and, we supposed, had suffered much in the gale which had proved so disastrous to ourselves; for her foretopmast was gone, and some of her starboard bulwarks. When we first saw her, she was, as I have already said, about two miles off and to windward, bearing down upon us. The breeze was very gentle, and what astonished us chiefly was, that she had no other sails set than her foresail and mainsail, with a flying jib— of course she came down but slowly, and our impatience amounted nearly to phrensy. The awkward manner in which she steered, too, was remarked by all of us, even excited as we were. She yawed about so considerably, that once or twice we thought it impossible she could see us, or imagined that, having seen us, and discovered no person on board, she was about to tack and make off in another direction. Upon each of these occasions we screamed and shouted at the top of our voices, when the stranger would appear to change for a moment her intention, and again hold on towards us—this singular conduct being repeated two or three times, so that at last we could think of no other manner of accounting for it than by supposing the helmsman to be in liquor.

No person was seen upon her decks until she arrived within about a quarter of a mile of us.[4] We then saw three seamen, whom by their dress we took to be Hollanders. Two of these were lying on some old sails near the forecastle, and the third, who appeared to be looking at us with great curiosity, was leaning over the starboard bow near the bowsprit. This last was a stout and tall man, with a very dark skin. He seemed by his manner to be encouraging us to have patience, nodding to us in a cheerful although rather odd way, and smiling constantly so as to display a set of the most brilliantly white teeth. As his vessel drew nearer, we saw a red flannel cap which he had on fall from his head into the water; but of this he took little or no notice, continuing his odd smiles and gesticulations. I relate these things and circumstances minutely, and I relate them, it must be understood, precisely as they *appeared* to us.[5]

The brig came on slowly, and now more steadily than before, and—I cannot speak calmly of this event—our hearts leaped up wildly within us, and we poured out our whole souls in shouts and thanksgiving to God for the complete, unexpected, and glorious deliverance that was so palpably at hand. Of a sudden, and all at once, there came wafted over the ocean from the strange vessel (which was now close upon us) a smell, a stench, such as the whole world has no name for— no conception of—hellish—utterly suffocating—insufferable, inconceivable. I gasped for breath, and, turning to my companions, perceived that they were paler than marble. But we had now no time left for question or surmise—the brig was within fifty feet of us, and it seemed to be her intention to run under our counter, that we might board her without her putting out a boat. We rushed aft, when, suddenly, a wide yaw threw her off full five or six points from the course she had been running, and, as she passed under our stern at the distance of about twenty feet, we had a full view of her decks. Shall I ever forget the triple horror of that spectacle? Twenty-five or thirty human bodies, among whom were several females, lay scattered about between the counter and the galley, in the last and most loathsome state of putrefaction! We plainly saw that not a soul lived in that fated vessel! Yet we could not help shouting to the dead for help![6] Yes, long and loudly did we beg, in the agony of the moment, that those silent and disgusting images would stay for us, would not abandon us to become like them, would receive us among their goodly company! We were raving with horror and despair—thoroughly mad through the anguish of our grievous disappointment.

As our first loud yell of terror broke forth, it was replied to by something, from near the bowsprit of the stranger, so closely resembling the scream of a human voice that the nicest ear might have been startled and deceived. At this instant another sudden yaw brought the region of the forecastle for a moment into view, and we beheld at once the origin of the sound. We saw the tall stout figure still leaning on the bulwark, and still nodding his head to and fro, but his face was now turned from us so that we could not behold it. His arms were extended over the rail, and the palms of his hands fell outward. His knees were lodged upon a stout rope, tightly stretched, and reaching from the heel of the bowsprit to a cathead. On his back, from which a portion of the shirt had been torn, leaving it bare, there sat a huge seagull, busily gorging itself with the horrible flesh, its bill and talons deep buried, and its white plumage spattered all over with blood. As the brig moved further round so as to bring us close in view, the bird, with much apparent difficulty, drew out its crimsoned head, and, after eying us for a moment as if stupified, arose lazily from the body upon which it had been feasting, and, flying directly above our deck, hovered there a while with a portion of clotted and liver-like substance in its beak. The horrid morsel dropped at length with a sullen splash immediately at the feet of Parker. May God forgive me, but now, for the first time, there flashed through my mind a thought, a thought which I will not mention,[7] and I felt myself making a step towards the ensanguined spot. I looked upward, and the eyes of Augustus met my own with a degree of intense and eager meaning which immediately brought me to my senses. I sprang forward quickly, and, with a deep shudder, threw the frightful thing into the sea.

The body from which it had been taken, resting as it did upon the rope, had been easily swayed to and fro by the exertions of the carnivorous bird, and it was this motion which had at first impressed us with the belief of its being alive. As the gull relieved it of its weight, it swung round and fell partially over, so that the face was fully discovered. Never, surely, was any object so terribly full of awe! The eyes were gone, and the whole flesh around the mouth, leaving the teeth utterly naked. This, then, was the smile which had cheered us on to hope! this the—but I forbear. The brig, as I have already told, passed under our stern, and made its way slowly but steadily to leeward. With her and with her terrible crew went all our gay visions of deliverance and joy. Deliberately as she went by, we might possibly have found means of boarding her, had not our sudden disappointment, and the appalling nature of the discovery which accompanied it, laid entirely prostrate every active faculty of mind and body. We had seen and felt, but we could neither think nor act, until, alas, too late. How much our intellects had been weakened by this incident may be estimated by the fact, that, when the vessel had proceeded so far that we could perceive no more than the half of her hull, the proposition was seriously entertained of attempting to overtake her by swimming!

I have, since this period, vainly endeavoured to obtain some clew to the hideous uncertainty which enveloped the fate of the stranger. Her build and general appearance, as I have before stated, led us to the belief that she was a Dutch trader, and the dresses of the crew also sustained this opinion. We might have easily seen the name upon her stern, and, indeed, taken other observations which would have guided us in making out her character; but the intense excitement of the moment blinded us to everything of that nature. From the saffron-like hue of such of the corpses as were not entirely decayed, we concluded that the whole of her company had perished by the yellow fever, or some other virulent disease of the same fearful kind.[8] If such were the case (and I know not what else to imagine), death, to judge from the positions of the bodies, must have come upon them in a manner awfully sudden and overwhelming, in a way totally distinct from that which generally characterizes even the most deadly pestilences with which mankind are acquainted. It is possible, indeed, that poison, accidentally introduced into some of their sea-stores, may have brought about the disaster; or that the eating some unknown venomous species of fish, or other marine animal, or oceanic bird, might have induced it—but it is utterly useless to form conjectures where all is involved, and will, no doubt, remain for ever involved, in the most appalling and unfathomable mystery.

CHAPTER 11

We spent the remainder of the day in a condition of stupid lethargy, gazing after the retreating vessel until the darkness, hiding her from our sight, recalled us in some measure to our senses. The pangs of hunger and thirst then returned, absorbing all other cares and considerations. Nothing, however, could be done until the morning, and, securing ourselves as well as possible, we endeavoured to snatch a little repose. In this I succeeded beyond my expectation, sleeping until my companions, who had not been so fortunate, aroused me at daybreak to renew our attempts at getting up provision from the hull.

It was now a dead calm, with the sea as smooth as I have ever known it—the weather warm and pleasant. The brig was out of sight. We commenced our operations by wrenching off, with some trouble, another of the forechains; and having fastened both to Peters's feet, he again made an endeavour to reach the door of the storeroom, thinking it possible that he might be able to force it open, provided he could get at it in sufficient time; and this he hoped to do, as the hulk lay much more steadily than before.

He succeeded very quickly in reaching the door, when, loosening one of the chains from his ankle, he made every exertion to force a passage with it, but in vain, the framework of the room being far stronger than was anticipated. He was quite exhausted with his long stay under water, and it became absolutely necessary that some other one of us should take his place. For this service Parker immediately volunteered; but, after making three ineffectual efforts, found that he could never even succeed in getting near the door. The condition of

Augustus's wounded arm rendered it useless for him to attempt going down, as he would be unable to force the room open should he reach it, and it accordingly now devolved upon me to exert myself for our common deliverance.

Peters had left one of the chains in the passage, and I found, upon plunging in, that I had not sufficient ballast to keep me firmly down. I determined, therefore, to attempt no more, in my first effort, than merely to recover the other chain. In groping along the floor of the passage for this I felt a hard substance, which I immediately grasped, not having time to ascertain what it was, but returning and ascending instantly to the surface. The prize proved to be a bottle, and our joy may be conceived when I say that it was found to be full of Port wine.[1] Giving thanks to God for this timely and cheering assistance, we immediately drew the cork with my penknife, and, each taking a moderate sup, felt the most indescribable comfort from the warmth, strength, and spirits with which it inspired us. We then carefully recorked the bottle, and, by means of a handkerchief, swung it in such a manner that there was no possibility of its getting broken.

Having rested a while after this fortunate discovery, I again descended, and now recovered the chain, with which I instantly came up. I then fastened it on and went down for the third time, when I became fully satisfied that no exertions whatever, in that situation, would enable me to force open the door of the storeroom. I therefore returned in despair.

There seemed now to be no longer any room for hope, and I could perceive in the countenances of my companions that they had made up their minds to perish. The wine had evidently produced in them a species of delirium, which, perhaps, I had been prevented from feeling by the immersion I had undergone since drinking it. They talked incoherently, and about matters unconnected with our condition, Peters repeatedly asking me questions about Nantucket. Augustus, too, I remember, approached me with a serious air, and requested me to lend him a pocket-comb, as his hair was full of fish scales, and he wished to get them out before going on shore. Parker appeared somewhat less affected, and urged me to dive at random into the cabin, and bring up any article which might come to hand. To this I consented, and, in the first attempt, after staying under a full minute, brought up a small leather trunk belonging to Captain Barnard. This was immediately opened in the faint hope that it might contain something to eat or drink. We found nothing, however, except a box of razors and two linen shirts. I now went down again, and returned without any success. As my head came above water I heard a crash on deck, and, upon getting up, saw that my companions had ungratefully taken advantage of my absence to drink the remainder of the wine, having let the bottle fall in the endeavour to replace it before I saw them. I remonstrated with them on the heartlessness of their conduct, when Augustus burst into tears. The other two endeavoured to laugh the matter off as a joke, but I hope never again to behold laughter of such a species: the distortion of countenance was absolutely frightful. Indeed, it was apparent that the stimulus, in the empty state of their stomachs, had taken instant and violent effect, and that they were all exceedingly intoxicated. With great difficulty I prevailed upon them to lie down, when they fell very soon into a heavy slumber, accompanied with loud stertorous breathing.

I now found myself, as it were, alone in the brig, and my reflections, to be sure, were of the most fearful and gloomy nature. No prospect offered itself to my view but a lingering death by famine, or, at the best, by being overwhelmed in the first gale which should spring up, for in our present exhausted condition we could have no hope of living through another.

The gnawing hunger which I now experienced was nearly insupportable, and I felt myself capable of going to any lengths in order to appease it. With my knife I cut off a small portion of the leather trunk, and endeavoured to eat it, but

found it utterly impossible to swallow a single morsel, although I fancied that some little alleviation of my suffering
was obtained by chewing small pieces of it and spitting them
out. Towards night my companions awoke, one by one, each
in an indescribable state of weakness and horror, brought on
by the wine, whose fumes had now evaporated. They shook
as if with a violent ague, and uttered the most lamentable cries
for water. Their condition affected me in the most lively degree, at the same time causing me to rejoice in the fortunate
train of circumstances which had prevented me from indulging in the wine, and consequently from sharing their
melancholy and most distressing sensations. Their conduct,
however, gave me great uneasiness and alarm; for it was evident that, unless some favourable change took place, they
could afford me no assistance in providing for our common
safety. I had not yet abandoned all idea of being able to get up
something from below; but the attempt could not possibly be
resumed until some one of them was sufficiently master of
himself to aid me by holding the end of the rope while I went
down. Parker appeared to be somewhat more in possession of
his senses than the others, and I endeavoured, by every means
in my power, to arouse him. Thinking that a plunge in the
seawater[2] might have a beneficial effect, I contrived to fasten
the end of a rope around his body, and then, leading him to
the companion-way (he remaining quite passive all the while),
pushed him in, and immediately drew him out. I had good
reason to congratulate myself upon having made this experiment; for he appeared much revived and invigorated, and,
upon getting out, asked me, in a rational manner, why I had
so served him. Having explained my object, he expressed himself indebted to me, and said that he felt greatly better from
the immersion, afterward conversing sensibly upon our situation. We then resolved to treat Augustus and Peters in the
same way, which we immediately did, when they both experienced much benefit from the shock. This idea of sudden im-

mersion had been suggested to me by reading in some medical work the good effect of the shower-bath in a case where the patient was suffering from *mania a potu.*[3]

Finding that I could now trust my companions to hold the end of the rope, I again made three or four plunges into the cabin, although it was now quite dark, and a gentle but long swell from the northward rendered the hulk somewhat unsteady. In the course of these attempts I succeeded in bringing up two case-knives, a three-gallon jug, empty, and a blanket, but nothing which could serve us for food. I continued my efforts, after getting these articles, until I was completely exhausted, but brought up nothing else. During the night Parker and Peters occupied themselves by turns in the same manner; but nothing coming to hand, we now gave up this attempt in despair, concluding that we were exhausting ourselves in vain.

We passed the remainder of this night in a state of the most intense mental and bodily anguish that can possibly be imagined. The morning of the sixteenth at length dawned, and we looked eagerly around the horizon for relief, but to no purpose. The sea was still smooth, with only a long swell from the northward, as on yesterday. This was the sixth day since we had tasted either food or drink, with the exception of the bottle of Port wine, and it was clear that we could hold out but a very little while longer unless something could be obtained. I never saw before, nor wish to see again, human beings so utterly emaciated as Peters and Augustus. Had I met them on shore in their present condition I should not have had the slightest suspicion that I had ever beheld them. Their countenances were totally changed in character, so that I could not bring myself to believe them really the same individuals with whom I had been in company but a few days before. Parker, although sadly reduced, and so feeble that he could not raise his head from his bosom, was not so far gone as the other two. He suffered with great patience, making no complaint, and endeavouring to inspire us with hope in every manner he could devise. For myself, although at the commencement of the voyage I had been in bad health, and was at all times of a delicate constitution, I suffered less than any of us, being much less reduced in frame, and retaining my powers of mind in a surprising degree, while the rest were completely prostrated in intellect, and seemed to be brought to a species of second childhood, generally simpering in their expressions, with idiotic smiles, and uttering the most absurd platitudes. At intervals, however, they would appear to revive suddenly, as if inspired all at once with a consciousness of their condition, when they would spring upon their feet in a momentary flash of vigour, and speak, for a short period, of their prospects, in a manner altogether rational, although full of the most intense despair. It is possible, however, that my companions may have entertained the same opinion of their own condition as I did of mine, and that I may have unwittingly been guilty of the same extravagances and imbecilities as themselves—this is a matter which cannot be determined.

About noon Parker declared that he saw land off the larboard quarter, and it was with the utmost difficulty I could restrain him from plunging into the sea with the view of swimming towards it. Peters and Augustus took little notice of what he said, being apparently wrapped up in moody contemplation. Upon looking in the direction pointed out I could not perceive the faintest appearance of the shore—indeed, I was too well aware that we were far from any land to indulge in a hope of that nature. It was a long time, nevertheless, before I could convince Parker of his mistake. He then burst into a flood of tears, weeping like a child, with loud cries and sobs, for two or three hours, when, becoming exhausted, he fell asleep.

Peters and Augustus now made several ineffectual efforts to swallow portions of the leather. I advised them to chew it and spit it out; but they were too excessively debilitated to be able to follow my advice. I continued to chew pieces of it at intervals, and found some relief from so doing; my chief distress was for water, and I was only prevented from taking a draught from the sea by remembering the horrible consequences which thus have resulted to others who were similarly situated with ourselves.

The day wore on in this manner, when I suddenly discovered a sail to the eastward, and on our larboard bow. She appeared to be a large ship, and was coming nearly athwart us, being probably twelve or fifteen miles distant. None of my companions had as yet discovered her, and I forbore to tell them of her for the present, lest we might again be disappointed of relief. At length, upon her getting nearer, I saw distinctly that she was heading immediately for us, with her light sails filled. I could now contain myself no longer, and pointed her out to my fellow-sufferers. They immediately sprang to their feet, again indulging in the most extravagant demonstrations of joy, weeping, laughing in an idiotic manner, jumping, stamping upon the deck, tearing their hair, and praying and cursing by turns. I was so affected by their conduct, as well as by what I now considered a sure prospect of deliverance, that I could not refrain from joining in with their madness, and gave way to the impulses of my gratitude and ecstasy by lying and rolling on the deck, clapping my hands, shouting, and other similar acts, until I was suddenly called to my recollection, and once more to the extreme of human misery and despair, by perceiving the ship all at once with her stern fully presented towards us, and steering in a direction nearly opposite to that in which I had at first perceived her.[4]

It was some time before I could induce my poor companions to believe that this sad reverse in our prospects had actually taken place. They replied to all my assertions with a stare and a gesture implying that they were not to be deceived by such misrepresentations. The conduct of Augustus most sensibly affected me. In spite of all I could say or do to the contrary, he persisted in saying that the ship was rapidly nearing us, and in making preparations to go on board of her. Some seaweed floating by the brig, he maintained that it was the ship's boat, and endeavoured to throw himself upon it, howling and shrieking in the most heartrending manner, when I forcibly restrained him from thus casting himself into the sea.[5]

Having become in some degree pacified, we continued to watch the ship until we finally lost sight of her, the weather becoming hazy, with a light breeze springing up. As soon as she was entirely gone, Parker turned suddenly towards me with an expression of countenance which made me shudder. There was about him an air of self-possession which I had not noticed in him until now, and before he opened his lips my heart told me what he would say. He proposed, in a few words, that one of us should die to preserve the existence of the others.[6]

CHAPTER 12

I had, for some time past, dwelt upon the prospect of our being reduced to this last horrible extremity, and had secretly made up my mind to suffer death in any shape or under any circumstances rather than resort to such a course. Nor was this resolution in any degree weakened by the present intensity of hunger under which I laboured. The proposition had not been heard by either Peters or Augustus. I therefore took Parker aside; and mentally praying to God for power to dissuade him from the horrible purpose he entertained, I expostulated with him for a long time and in the most supplicating manner, begging him in the name of everything which he held sacred, and urging him by every species of argument which the extremity of the case suggested, to abandon the idea, and not to mention it to either of the other two.

He heard all I said without attempting to controvert any of my arguments, and I had begun to hope that he would be prevailed upon to do as I desired. But when I had ceased speaking, he said that he knew very well all I had said was true, and that to resort to such a course was the most horrible alternative which could enter into the mind of man; but that he had now held out as long as human nature could be sustained; that it was unnecessary for all to perish, when, by the death of one, it was possible, and even probable, that the rest might be finally preserved; adding that I might save myself the trouble of trying to turn him from his purpose, his mind having been thoroughly made up on the subject even before the appearance of the ship, and that only her heaving in sight had prevented him from mentioning his intention at an earlier period.

I now begged him, if he would not be prevailed upon to

abandon his design, at least to defer it for another day, when some vessel might come to our relief; again reiterating every argument I could devise, and which I thought likely to have influence with one of his rough nature. He said, in reply, that he had not spoken until the very last possible moment; that he could exist no longer without sustenance of some kind; and that therefore in another day his suggestion would be too late, as regarded himself at least.

Finding that he was not to be moved by anything I could say in a mild tone, I now assumed a different demeanour, and told him that he must be aware I had suffered less than any of us from our calamities; that my health and strength, consequently, were at that moment far better than his own, or than that either of Peters or Augustus; in short, that I was in a condition to have my own way by force if I found it necessary; and that, if he attempted in any manner to acquaint the others with his bloody and cannibal designs, I would not hesitate to throw him into the sea. Upon this he immediately seized me by the throat, and drawing a knife, made several ineffectual efforts to stab me in the stomach; an atrocity which his excessive debility alone prevented him from accomplishing. In the mean time, being roused to a high pitch of anger, I forced him to the vessel's side, with the full intention of throwing him overboard. He was saved from this fate, however, by the interference of Peters, who now approached and separated us, asking the cause of the disturbance. This Parker told before I could find means in any manner to prevent him.

The effect of his words was even more terrible than what I had anticipated. Both Augustus and Peters, who, it seems, had long secretly entertained the same fearful idea which Parker had been merely the first to broach, joined with him in his design, and insisted upon its being immediately carried into effect. I had calculated that one at least of the two former would be found still possessed of sufficient strength of mind to side with myself in resisting any attempt to execute so dreadful a purpose; and, with the aid of either one of them, I had no fear of being able to prevent its accomplishment. Being disappointed in this expectation, it became absolutely necessary that I should attend to my own safety, as a further resistance on my part might possibly be considered by men in their frightful condition a sufficient excuse for refusing me fair play in the tragedy that I knew would speedily be enacted.

I now told them I was willing to submit to the proposal, merely requesting a delay of about one hour, in order that the fog which had gathered around us might have an opportunity of lifting, when it was possible that the ship we had seen might be again in sight. After great difficulty I obtained from them a promise to wait thus long; and, as I had anticipated (a breeze rapidly coming in), the fog lifted before the hour had expired, when, no vessel appearing in sight, we prepared to draw lots.[1]

It is with extreme reluctance that I dwell upon the appalling scene which ensued; a scene which, with its minutest details, no after events have been able to efface in the slightest degree from my memory, and whose stern recollection will imbitter every future moment of my existence. Let me run over this portion of my narrative with as much haste as the nature of the events to be spoken of will permit. The only method we could devise for the terrific lottery, in which we were to take each a chance, was that of drawing straws. Small splinters of wood were made to answer our purpose, and it was agreed that I should be the holder. I retired to one end of the hulk, while my poor companions silently took up their station in the other with their backs turned towards me. The bitterest anxiety which I endured at any period of this fearful drama was while I occupied myself in the arrangement of the lots. There are few conditions into which man can possibly fall where he will not feel a deep interest in the preservation of his existence; an interest momentarily increasing with the frailness of the tenure by which that existence may be held.

But now that the silent, definite, and stern nature of the business in which I was engaged (so different from the tumultuous dangers of the storm or the gradually approaching horrors of famine) allowed me to reflect on the few chances I had of escaping the most appalling of deaths—a death for the most appalling of purposes—every particle of that energy which had so long buoyed me up departed like feathers before the wind, leaving me a helpless prey to the most abject and pitiable terror. I could not, at first, even summon up sufficient strength to tear and fit together the small splinters of wood, my fingers absolutely refusing their office, and my knees knocking violently against each other. My mind ran over rapidly a thousand absurd projects by which to avoid becoming a partner in the awful speculation. I thought of falling on my knees to my companions, and entreating them to let me escape this necessity; of suddenly rushing upon them, and, by putting one of them to death, of rendering the decision by lot useless—in short, of everything but of going through with the matter I had in hand. At last, after wasting a long time in this imbecile conduct, I was recalled to my senses by the voice of Parker, who urged me to relieve them at once from the terrible anxiety they were enduring. Even then I could not bring myself to arrange the splinters upon the spot, but thought over every species of finesse by which I could trick some one of my fellow-sufferers to draw the short straw, as it had been agreed that whoever drew the shortest of four splinters from my hand was to die for the preservation of the rest. Before any one condemn me for this apparent heartlessness, let him be placed in a situation precisely similar to my own.

At length delay was no longer possible, and, with a heart almost bursting from my bosom, I advanced to the region of the forecastle, where my companions were awaiting me. I held out my hand with the splinters, and Peters immediately drew. He was free—*his*, at least, was not the shortest; and there was now another chance against my escape. I summoned up all my strength, and passed the lots to Augustus. He also drew immediately, and he also was free; and now, whether I should live or die, the chances were no more than precisely even. At this moment all the fierceness of the tiger possessed my bosom, and I felt towards my poor fellow-creature, Parker, the most intense, the most diabolical hatred. But the feeling did not last; and, at length, with a convulsive shudder and closed eyes, I held out the two remaining splinters towards him. It was full five minutes before he could summon resolution to draw, during which period of heartrending suspense I never once opened my eyes. Presently one of the two lots was quickly drawn from my hand. The decision was then over, yet I knew not whether it was for me or against me. No one spoke, and still I dared not satisfy myself by looking at the splinter I held. Peters at length took me by the hand, and I forced myself to look up, when I immediately saw by the countenance of Parker that I was safe, and that he it was who had been doomed to suffer. Gasping for breath, I fell senseless to the deck.

I recovered from my swoon in time to behold the consummation of the tragedy in the death of him who had been chiefly instrumental in bringing it about. He made no resistance whatever, and was stabbed in the back by Peters, when he fell instantly dead. I must not dwell upon the fearful repast which immediately ensued. Such things may be imagined, but words have no power to impress the mind with the exquisite horror of their reality. Let it suffice to say that, having in some measure appeased the raging thirst which consumed us by the blood of the victim, and having by common consent taken off the hands, feet, and head, throwing them, together with the entrails, into the sea, we devoured the rest of the body piecemeal, during the four ever memorable days of the seventeenth, eighteenth, nineteenth, and twentieth of the month.

On the nineteenth, there coming on a smart shower which

lasted fifteen or twenty minutes, we contrived to catch some water by means of a sheet which had been fished up from the cabin by our drag just after the gale. The quantity we took in all did not amount to more than half a gallon; but even this scanty allowance supplied us with comparative strength and hope.

On the twenty-first we were again reduced to the last necessity. The weather still remained warm and pleasant, with occasional fogs and light breezes, most usually from N. to W.

On the twenty-second, as we were sitting close huddled together, gloomily revolving over our lamentable condition, there flashed through my mind all at once an idea which inspired me with a bright gleam of hope. I remembered that, when the foremast had been cut away, Peters, being in the windward chains, passed one of the axes into my hand, requesting me to put it, if possible, in a place of security, and that a few minutes before the last heavy sea struck the brig and filled her I had taken this axe into the forecastle, and laid it in one of the larboard berths. I now thought it possible that, by getting at this axe, we might cut through the deck over the storeroom, and thus readily supply ourselves with provisions.

When I communicated this project to my companions, they uttered a feeble shout of joy, and we all proceeded forthwith to the forecastle. The difficulty of descending here was greater than that of going down in the cabin, the opening being much smaller, for it will be remembered that the whole framework about the cabin companion-hatch had been carried away, whereas the forecastle-way, being a simple hatch of only about three feet square, had remained uninjured. I did not hesitate, however, to attempt the descent; and, a rope being fastened round my body as before, I plunged boldly in, feet foremost, made my way quickly to the berth, and, at the very first attempt, brought up the axe. It was hailed with the most ecstatic joy and triumph, and the ease with which it had been obtained was regarded as an omen of our ultimate preservation.

We now commenced cutting at the deck with all the energy of rekindled hope, Peters and myself taking the axe by turns, Augustus's wounded arm not permitting him to aid us in any degree. As we were still so feeble as to be scarcely able to stand unsupported, and could consequently work but a minute or two without resting, it soon became evident that many long hours would be requisite to accomplish our task— that is, to cut an opening sufficiently large to admit of a free access to the storeroom. This consideration, however, did not discourage us; and, working all night by the light of the moon, we succeeded in effecting our purpose by daybreak on the morning of the twenty-third.

Peters now volunteered to go down; and, having made all arrangements as before, he descended, and soon returned, bringing up with him a small jar, which, to our great joy, proved to be full of olives. Having shared these among us, and devoured them with the greatest avidity, we proceeded to let him down again. This time he succeeded beyond our utmost expectations, returning instantly with a large ham and a bottle of Madeira wine. Of the latter we each took a moderate sup, having learned by experience the pernicious consequences of indulging too freely. The ham, except about two pounds near the bone, was not in a condition to be eaten, having been entirely spoiled by the salt water. The sound part was divided among us. Peters and Augustus, not being able to restrain their appetite, swallowed theirs upon the instant; but I was more cautious, and ate but a small portion of mine, dreading the thirst which I knew would ensue. We now rested a while from our labours, which had been intolerably severe.

By noon, feeling somewhat strengthened and refreshed, we again renewed our attempt at getting up provision, Peters and myself going down alternately, and always with more or less success, until sundown. During this interval we had the good fortune to bring up, altogether, four more small jars of olives, another ham, a carboy containing nearly three gallons of excellent Cape Madeira wine, and, what gave us still more delight, a small tortoise of the Gallipago breed, several of which had been taken on board by Captain Barnard, as the Grampus was leaving port, from the schooner Mary Pitts, just returned from a sealing voyage in the Pacific.

In a subsequent portion of this narrative I shall have frequent occasion to mention this species of tortoise.[2] It is found principally, as most of my readers may know, in the group of islands called the Gallipagos, which, indeed, derive their name from the animal—the Spanish word Gallipago meaning a fresh-water terapin. From the peculiarity of their shape and action they have been sometimes called the elephant tortoise. They are frequently found of an enormous size. I have myself seen several which would weigh from twelve to fifteen hundred pounds, although I do not remember that any navigator speaks of having seen them weighing more than eight hundred. Their appearance is singular, and even disgusting. Their steps are very slow, measured, and heavy, their bodies being carried about a foot from the ground. Their neck is long, and exceedingly slender; from eighteen inches to two feet is a very common length, and I killed one, where the distance from the shoulder to the extremity of the head was no less than three feet ten inches. The head has a striking resemblance to that of a serpent. They can exist without food for an almost incredible length of time, instances having been known where they have been thrown into the hold of a vessel and lain two years without nourishment of any kind—being as fat, and, in every respect, in as good order at the expiration of the time as when they were first put in. In one particular these extraordinary animals bear a resemblance to the dromedary, or camel of the desert. In a bag at the root of the neck they carry with them a constant supply of water. In some instances, upon killing them after a full year's deprivation of all nourishment, as much as three gallons of perfectly sweet and fresh water have been found in their bags. Their food is chiefly wild parsley and celery, with purslain, sea-kelp, and prickly pears, upon which latter vegetable they thrive wonderfully, a great quantity of it being usually found on the hillsides near the shore wherever the animal itself is discovered. They are excellent and highly nutritious food, and have, no doubt, been the means of preserving the lives of thousands of seamen employed in the whale-fishery and other pursuits in the Pacific.

The one which we had the good fortune to bring up from the storeroom was not of a large size, weighing probably sixty-five or seventy pounds. It was a female, and in excellent condition, being exceedingly fat, and having more than a quart of limpid and sweet water in its bag. This was indeed a treasure; and, falling on our knees with one accord, we returned fervent thanks to God for so seasonable a relief.

We had great difficulty in getting the animal up through the opening, as its struggles were fierce and its strength prodigious. It was upon the point of making its escape from Peters's grasp, and slipping back into the water, when Augustus, throwing a rope with a slip-knot around its throat, held it up in this manner until I jumped into the hole by the side of Peters, and assisted him in lifting it out.

The water we drew carefully from the bag into the jug, which, it will be remembered, had been brought up before from the cabin. Having done this, we broke off the neck of a bottle so as to form, with the cork, a kind of glass, holding not quite half a gill. We then each drank one of these measures full, and resolved to limit ourselves to this quantity per day as long as it should hold out.

During the last two or three days, the weather having been dry and pleasant, the bedding we had obtained from the cabin, as well as our clothing, had become thoroughly dry, so that we passed this night (that of the twenty-third) in comparative

comfort, enjoying a tranquil repose, after having supped plen-
tifully on olives and ham, with a small allowance of the wine.
Being afraid of losing some of our stores overboard during the
night, in the event of a breeze springing up, we secured them
as well as possible with cordage to the fragments of the windlass. Our tortoise, which we were anxious to preserve alive as
long as we could, we threw on his back, and otherwise carefully fastened.

CHAPTER 13

July 24. This morning saw us wonderfully recruited in spirits and strength. Notwithstanding the perilous situation in which we were still placed, ignorant of our position, although certainly at a great distance from land, without more food than would last us for a fortnight even with great care, almost entirely without water, and floating about at the mercy of every wind and wave, on the merest wreck in the world, still the infinitely more terrible distresses and dangers from which we had so lately and so providentially been delivered caused us to regard what we now endured as but little more than an ordinary evil—so strictly comparative is either good or ill.

At sunrise we were preparing to renew our attempts at getting up something from the storeroom, when, a smart shower coming on, with some lightning, we turned our attention to the catching of water by means of the sheet we had used before for this purpose. We had no other means of collecting the rain than by holding the sheet spread out with one of the forechain-plates in the middle of it. The water, thus conducted to the centre, was drained through into our jug. We had nearly filled it in this manner, when, a heavy squall coming on from the northward, obliged us to desist, as the hulk began once more to roll so violently that we could no longer keep our feet. We now went forward, and, lashing ourselves securely to the remnant of the windlass as before, awaited the event with far more calmness than could have been anticipated, or would have been imagined possible under the circumstances. At noon the wind had freshened into a two-reef breeze, and by night into a stiff gale, accompanied with a tremendously heavy swell. Experience having taught us, however, the best method of arranging our lashings, we weathered this dreary night in tolerable security, although thoroughly drenched at almost every instant by the sea, and in momentary dread of being washed off. Fortunately, the weather was so warm as to render the water rather grateful than otherwise.

July 25. This morning the gale had diminished to a mere ten-knot breeze, and the sea had gone down with it so considerably that we were able to keep ourselves dry upon the deck. To our great grief, however, we found that two jars of our olives, as well as the whole of our ham, had been washed overboard, in spite of the careful manner in which they had been fastened. We determined not to kill the tortoise as yet, and contented ourselves for the present with a breakfast on a few of the olives, and a measure of water each, which latter we mixed, half and half, with wine, finding great relief and strength from the mixture, without the distressing intoxication which had ensued upon drinking the Port. The sea was still far too rough for the renewal of our efforts at getting up provision from the storeroom. Several articles, of no importance to us in our present situation, floated up through the opening during the day, and were immediately washed overboard. We also now observed that the hulk lay more along than ever, so that we could not stand an instant without lashing ourselves. On this account we passed a gloomy and uncomfortable day. At noon the sun appeared to be nearly vertical, and we had no doubt that we had been driven down by the long succession of northward and northwesterly winds into the near vicinity of the equator. Towards evening saw several sharks, and were somewhat alarmed by the audacious manner in which an enormously large one approached us. At one time, a lurch throwing the deck very far beneath the water, the monster actually swam in upon us, floundering for some moments just over the companion-hatch, and striking Peters violently with his tail. A heavy sea at length hurled him overboard, much to our relief. In moderate weather we might have easily captured him.

July 26. This morning, the wind having greatly abated, and the sea not being very rough, we determined to renew our exertions in the storeroom. After a great deal of hard labour during the whole day, we found that nothing further was to be expected from this quarter, the partitions of the room having been stove during the night, and its contents swept into the hold. This discovery, as may be supposed, filled us with despair.

July 27. The sea nearly smooth, with a light wind, and still from the northward and westward. The sun coming out hotly in the afternoon, we occupied ourselves in drying our clothes. Found great relief from thirst, and much comfort otherwise, by bathing in the sea; in this, however, we were forced to use great caution, being afraid of sharks, several of which were seen swimming around the brig during the day.

July 28. Good weather still. The brig now began to lie along so alarmingly that we feared she would eventually roll bottom up. Prepared ourselves as well as we could for this emergency, lashing our tortoise, water-jug, and two remaining jars of olives as far as possible over to the windward, placing them outside the hull, below the main-chains. The sea very smooth all day, with little or no wind.

July 29. A continuance of the same weather. Augustus's wounded arm began to evince symptoms of mortification. He complained of drowsiness and excessive thirst, but no acute pain. Nothing could be done for his relief beyond rubbing his wounds with a little of the vinegar from the olives,[1] and from this no benefit seemed to be experienced. We did everything in our power for his comfort, and trebled his allowance of water.

July 30. An excessively hot day, with no wind. An enormous shark kept close by the hulk during the whole of the forenoon. We made several unsuccessful attempts to capture him by means of a noose. Augustus much worse, and evidently sinking as much from want of proper nourishment as from the effect of his wounds. He constantly prayed to be released from his sufferings, wishing for nothing but death. This evening we ate the last of our olives, and found the water in our jug so putrid that we could not swallow it at all without the addition of wine. Determined to kill our tortoise in the morning.

July 31. After a night of excessive anxiety and fatigue, owing to the position of the hulk, we set about killing and cutting up our tortoise. He proved to be much smaller than we had supposed, although in good condition—the whole meat about him not amounting to more than ten pounds. With a view of preserving a portion of this as long as possible, we cut it into fine pieces, and filled with them our three remaining olive-jars and the wine-bottle (all of which had been kept), pouring in afterward the vinegar from the olives. In this manner we put away about three pounds of the tortoise, intending not to touch it until we had consumed the rest. We concluded to restrict ourselves to about four ounces of the meat per day; the whole would thus last us thirteen days. A brisk shower, with severe thunder and lightning, came on about dusk, but lasted so short a time that we only succeeded in catching about half a pint of water. The whole of this, by common consent, was given to Augustus, who now appeared to be in the last extremity. He drank the water from the sheet as we caught it (we holding it above him as he lay so as to let it run into his mouth), for we had now nothing left capable of holding water, unless we had chosen to empty out our wine from the carboy, or the stale water from the jug. Either of these expedients would have been resorted to had the shower lasted.

The sufferer seemed to derive but little benefit from the draught. His arm was completely black from the wrist to the shoulder, and his feet were like ice. We expected every moment to see him breathe his last. He was frightfully emaciated; so much so that, although he weighed a hundred and twenty-seven pounds upon his leaving Nantucket, he now did not weigh more than *forty or fifty at the farthest.*[2] His eyes were sunk far in his head, being scarcely perceptible, and the skin of his cheeks hung so loosely as to prevent his masticating any food, or even swallowing any liquid, without great difficulty.

August 1. A continuance of the same calm weather, with an oppressively hot sun. Suffered exceedingly from thirst, the water in the jug being absolutely putrid and swarming with vermin. We contrived, nevertheless, to swallow a portion of it by mixing it with wine—our thirst, however, was but little abated. We found more relief by bathing in the sea, but could not avail ourselves of this expedient except at long intervals, on account of the continual presence of sharks. We now saw clearly that Augustus could not be saved; that he was evidently dying. We could do nothing to relieve his sufferings, which appeared to be great. About twelve o'clock he expired in strong convulsions, and without having spoken for several hours.[3] His death filled us with the most gloomy forebodings, and had so great an effect upon our spirits that we sat motionless by the corpse during the whole day, and never addressed each other except in a whisper. It was not until some time after dark that we took courage to get up and throw the body overboard. It was then loathsome beyond expression, and so far decayed that, as Peters attempted to lift it, an entire leg came off in his grasp. As the mass of putrefaction slipped over the vessel's side into the water, the glare of phosphoric light with which it was surrounded plainly discovered to us seven or eight large sharks, the clashing of whose horrible teeth, as their prey was torn to pieces among them, might have been heard at the distance of a mile. We shrunk within ourselves in the extremity of horror at the sound.

August 2. The same fearfully calm and hot weather. The dawn found us in a state of pitiable dejection as well as bodily exhaustion. The water in the jug was now absolutely useless, being a thick gelatinous mass; nothing but frightful-looking worms mingled with slime. We threw it out, and washed the jug well in the sea, afterward pouring a little vinegar in it from our bottles of pickled tortoise. Our thirst could now scarcely be endured, and we tried in vain to relieve it by wine, which seemed only to add fuel to the flame, and excited us to a high degree of intoxication. We afterward endeavoured to relieve our sufferings by mixing the wine with seawater; but this instantly brought about the most violent retchings, so that we never again attempted it. During the whole day we anxiously sought an opportunity of bathing, but to no purpose; for the hulk was now entirely besieged on all sides with sharks—no doubt the identical monsters who had devoured our poor companion on the evening before, and who were in momentary expectation of another similar feast. This circumstance occasioned us the most bitter regret, and filled us with the most depressing and melancholy forebodings. We had experienced indescribable relief in bathing, and to have this resource cut off in so frightful a manner was more than we could bear. Nor, indeed, were we altogether free from the apprehension of immediate danger, for the least slip or false movement would have thrown us at once within reach of these voracious fish, who frequently thrust themselves directly upon us, swimming up to leeward. No shouts or exertions on our part seemed to alarm them. Even when one of the largest was struck with an axe by Peters, and much wounded, he persisted in his attempts to push in where we were. A cloud came up at dusk, but, to our extreme anguish, passed over without discharging itself. It is quite impossible to conceive our sufferings from thirst at this period. We passed a sleepless night, both on this account and through dread of the sharks.[4]

August 3. No prospect of relief, and the brig lying still more and more along, so that now we could not maintain a footing upon deck at all. Busied ourselves in securing our wine and tortoise-meat, so that we might not lose them in the event of our rolling over. Got out two stout spikes from the forechains, and, by means of the axe, drove them into the hull to windward within a couple of feet of the water; this not being very far from the keel, as we were nearly upon our beamends. To these spikes we now lashed our provisions, as being more secure than their former position beneath the chains. Suffered great agony from thirst during the whole day—no chance of bathing on account of the sharks, which never left us for a moment. Found it impossible to sleep.

August 4. A little before daybreak we perceived that the hulk was heeling over, and aroused ourselves to prevent being thrown off by the movement. At first the roll was slow and gradual, and we contrived to clamber over to windward very well, having taken the precaution to leave ropes hanging from the spikes we had driven in for the provision. But we had not calculated sufficiently upon the acceleration of the impetus; for presently the heel became too violent to allow of our keeping pace with it; and, before either of us knew what was to happen, we found ourselves hurled furiously into the sea, and struggling several fathoms beneath the surface, with the huge hull immediately above us.

In going under the water I had been obliged to let go my hold upon the rope; and finding that I was completely beneath the vessel, and my strength utterly exhausted, I scarcely made a struggle for life, and resigned myself, in a few seconds, to die. But here again I was deceived, not having taken into consideration the natural rebound of the hull to windward. The whirl of the water upward, which the vessel occasioned in rolling partially back, brought me to the surface still more violently than I had been plunged beneath. Upon coming up, I found myself about twenty yards from the hulk, as near as I could judge. She was lying keel up, rocking furiously from

side to side, and the sea in all directions around was much agitated, and full of strong whirlpools. I could see nothing of
Peters. An oil-cask was floating within a few feet of me, and
various other articles from the brig were scattered about.

My principal terror was now on account of the sharks,
which I knew to be in my vicinity. In order to deter these, if
possible, from approaching me, I splashed the water vigorously with both hands and feet as I swam towards the hulk,
creating a body of foam. I have no doubt that to this expedient, simple as it was, I was indebted for my preservation; for
the sea all around the brig, just before her rolling over, was so
crowded with these monsters, that I must have been, and really was, in actual contact with some of them during my
progress. By great good fortune, however, I reached the side
of the vessel in safety, although so utterly weakened by the violent exertion I had used that I should never have been able to
get upon it but for the timely assistance of Peters, who now,
to my great joy, made his appearance (having scrambled up to
the keel from the opposite side of the hull), and threw me the
end of a rope—one of those which had been attached to the
spikes.

Having barely escaped this danger, our attention was now
directed to the dreadful imminency of another; that of absolute starvation. Our whole stock of provision had been
swept overboard in spite of all our care in securing it; and seeing no longer the remotest possibility of obtaining more, we
gave way both of us to despair, weeping aloud like children,
and neither of us attempting to offer consolation to the other.
Such weakness can scarcely be conceived, and to those who
have never been similarly situated will, no doubt, appear un-
natural; but it must be remembered that our intellects were so
entirely disordered by the long course of privation and terror
to which we had been subjected, that we could not justly be
considered, at that period, in the light of rational beings. In
subsequent perils, nearly as great, if not greater, I bore up

with fortitude against all the evils of my situation, and Peters, it will be seen, evinced a stoical philosophy nearly as incredible as his present childlike supineness and imbecility—the mental condition made the difference.

The overturning of the brig, even with the consequent loss of the wine and turtle, would not, in fact, have rendered our situation more deplorable than before, except for the disappearance of the bedclothes by which we had been hitherto enabled to catch rainwater, and of the jug in which we had kept it when caught; for we found the whole bottom, from within two or three feet of the bends as far as the keel, together with the keel itself, *thickly covered with large barnacles, which proved to be excellent and highly nutritious food.* Thus, in two important respects, the accident we had so greatly dreaded proved a benefit rather than an injury; it had opened to us a supply of provisions, which we could not have exhausted, using it moderately, in a month; and it had greatly contributed to our comfort as regards position, we being much more at our ease, and in infinitely less danger, than before.

The difficulty, however, of now obtaining water blinded us to all the benefits of the change in our condition. That we might be ready to avail ourselves, as far as possible, of any shower which might fall, we took off our shirts, to make use of them as we had of the sheets—not hoping, of course, to get more in this way, even under the most favourable circumstances, than half a gill at a time. No signs of a cloud appeared during the day, and the agonies of our thirst were nearly intolerable. At night Peters obtained about an hour's disturbed sleep, but my intense sufferings would not permit me to close my eyes for a single moment.

August 5. To-day, a gentle breeze springing up carried us through a vast quantity of seaweed, among which we were so fortunate as to find eleven small crabs, which afforded us several delicious meals.[5] Their shells being quite soft, we ate them entire, and found that they irritated our thirst far less than the barnacles. Seeing no trace of sharks among the seaweed, we also ventured to bathe, and remained in the water for four or five hours, during which we experienced a very sensible diminution of our thirst. Were greatly refreshed, and spent the night somewhat more comfortably than before, both of us snatching a little sleep.

August 6. This day we were blessed by a brisk and continual rain, lasting from about noon until after dark. Bitterly did we now regret the loss of our jug and carboy; for, in spite of the little means we had of catching the water, we might have filled one, if not both of them. As it was, we contrived to satisfy the cravings of thirst by suffering the shirts to become saturated, and then wringing them so as to let the grateful fluid trickle into our mouths. In this occupation we passed the entire day.

August 7. Just at daybreak we both at the same instant descried a sail to the eastward, and *evidently coming towards us!* We hailed the glorious sight with a long, although feeble shout of rapture; and began instantly to make every signal in our power, by flaring the shirts in the air, leaping as high as our weak condition would permit, and even by hallooing with all the strength of our lungs, although the vessel could not have been less than fifteen miles distant. However, she still continued to near our hulk, and we felt that, if she but held her present course, she must eventually come so close as to perceive us. In about an hour after we first discovered her we could clearly see the people on her decks. She was a long, low, and rakish-looking topsail schooner, with a black ball in her foretopsail, and had, apparently, a full crew. We now became alarmed, for we could hardly imagine it possible that she did not observe us, and were apprehensive that she meant to leave us to perish as we were—an act of fiendish barbarity, which, however incredible it may appear, has been repeatedly perpetrated at sea, under circumstances very nearly similar, and by beings who were regarded as belonging to the human species.* In this instance, however, by the mercy of God, we were destined to be most happily deceived; for presently we were aware of a sudden commotion on the deck of the stranger, who immediately afterward run up a British flag, and, hauling her wind, bore up directly upon us. In half an hour more we found ourselves in her cabin. She proved to be the Jane Guy, of Liverpool, Captain Guy, bound on a sealing and trading voyage to the South Seas and Pacific.[7]

---

* The case of the brig Polly, of Boston, is one so much in point,[6] and her fate, in many respects, so remarkably similar to our own, that I cannot forbear alluding to it here. This vessel, of one hundred and thirty tons burden, sailed from Boston, with a cargo of lumber and provisions, for Santa Croix, on the twelfth of December, 1811, under the command of Captain Casneau. There were eight souls on board besides the captain—the mate, four seamen, and the cook, together with a Mr. Hunt, and a negro girl belonging to him. On the fifteenth, having cleared the shoal of Georges, she sprung a leak in a gale of wind from the southeast, and was finally capsized; but, the mast going by the board, she afterward righted. They remained in this situation, without fire, and with very little provision, for the period of *one hundred and ninety-one days* (from December the fifteenth to June the twentieth) when Captain Casneau and Samuel Badger, the only survivors, were taken off the wreck by the Fame, of Hull, Captain Featherstone, bound home from Rio Janeiro. When picked up they were in latitude 28°N., *longitude 13°W., having drifted above two thousand miles.* On the ninth of July the Fame fell in with the brig Dromeo, Captain Perkins, who landed the two sufferers in Kennebeck. The narrative from which we gather these details ends in the following words.

"It is natural to inquire how they could float such a vast distance, upon the most frequented part of the Atlantic, and not be discovered all this time. *They were passed by more than a dozen sail, one of which came so nigh them that they could distinctly see the people on deck and on the rigging looking at them; but, to the inexpressible disappointment of the starving and freezing men, they stifled the dictates of compassion, hoisted sail, and cruelly abandoned them to their fate.*"

CHAPTER 14

The Jane Guy was a fine-looking topsail schooner of a hundred and eighty tons burden.[1] She was unusually sharp in the bows, and on a wind, in moderate weather, the fastest sailer I have ever seen. Her qualities, however, as a rough sea-boat, were not so good, and her draught of water was by far too great for the trade to which she was destined. For this peculiar service a larger vessel, and one of a light proportionate draught, is desirable—say a vessel of from three to three hundred and fifty tons. She should be barque-rigged, and in other respects of a different construction from the usual South Sea ships. It is absolutely necessary that she should be well armed. She should have, say ten or twelve twelve pound carronades, and two or three long twelves, with brass blunderbusses, and water-tight arm-chests for each top. Her anchors and cables should be of far greater strength than is required for any other species of trade, and, above all, her crew should be numerous and efficient—not less, for such a vessel as I have described, than fifty or sixty able-bodied men. The Jane Guy had a crew of thirty-five, all able seamen, besides the captain and mate, but she was not altogether as well armed or otherwise equipped as a navigator acquainted with the difficulties and dangers of the trade could have desired.

Captain Guy was a gentleman of great urbanity of manner, and of considerable experience in the southern traffic, to which he had devoted a great portion of his life. He was deficient, however, in energy, and, consequently, in that spirit of enterprise which is here so absolutely requisite. He was part owner of the vessel in which he sailed, and was invested with discretionary powers to cruise in the South Seas for any cargo which might come most readily to hand. He had on board, as usual in such voyages, beads, looking-glasses, tinder-works, axes, hatchets, saws, adzes, planes, chisels, gouges, gimlets, files, spokeshaves, rasps, hammers, nails, knives, scissors, razors, needles, thread, crockery-ware, calico, trinkets, and other similar articles.

The schooner sailed from Liverpool on the tenth of July, crossed the Tropic of Cancer on the twenty-fifth, in longitude twenty degrees west, and reached Sal, one of the Cape Verd Islands, on the twenty-ninth, where she took in salt and other necessaries for the voyage. On the third of August she left the Cape Verds and steered southwest, stretching over towards the coast of Brazil so as to cross the equator between the meridians of twenty-eight and thirty degrees west longitude. This is the course usually taken by vessels bound from Europe to the Cape of Good Hope, or by that route to the East Indies. By proceeding thus they avoid the calms and strong contrary currents which continually prevail on the coast of Guinea, while, in the end, it is found to be the shortest track, as westerly winds are never wanting afterward by which to reach the Cape. It was Captain Guy's intention to make his first stoppage at Kerguelen's Land—I hardly know for what reason. On the day we were picked up the schooner was off Cape St. Roque,[2] in longitude 31° W.; so that, when found, we had drifted probably, from north to south, *not less than five-and-twenty degrees.*

On board the Jane Guy we were treated with all the kindness our distressed situation demanded. In about a fortnight, during which time we continued steering to the southeast, with gentle breezes and fine weather, both Peters and myself recovered entirely from the effects of our late privation and dreadful suffering, and we began to remember what had passed rather as a frightful dream from which we had been happily awakened, than as events which had taken place in sober and naked reality. I have since found that this species of partial oblivion is usually brought about by sudden transition, whether from joy to sorrow or from sorrow to joy—the degree of forgetfulness being proportioned to the degree of difference in the exchange. Thus, in my own case, I now feel it impossible to realize the full extent of the misery which I endured during the days spent upon the hulk. The incidents are remembered, but not the feelings which the incidents elicited at the time of their occurrence. I only know that, when they did occur, I *then* thought human nature could sustain nothing more of agony.

We continued our voyage for some weeks without any incidents of greater moment than the occasional meeting with whaling-ships, and more frequently with the black or right whale, so called in contradistinction to the spermaceti.[3] These, however, were chiefly found south of the twenty-fifth parallel. On the sixteenth of September, being in the vicinity of the Cape of Good Hope, the schooner encountered her first gale of any violence since leaving Liverpool. In this neighbourhood, but more frequently to the south and east of the promontory (we were to the westward), navigators have often to contend with storms from the northward which rage with great fury. They always bring with them a heavy sea, and one of their most dangerous features is the instantaneous chopping round of the wind, an occurrence almost certain to take place during the greatest force of the gale. A perfect hurricane will be blowing at one moment from the northward or northeast, and in the next not a breath of wind will be felt in that direction, while from the southwest it will come out all at once with a violence almost inconceivable. A bright spot to the southward is the sure forerunner of the change, and vessels are thus enabled to take the proper precautions.

It was about six in the morning when the blow came on with a white squall, and, as usual, from the northward. By eight it had increased very much, and brought down upon us one of the most tremendous seas I had then ever beheld.

Everything had been made as snug as possible, but the schooner laboured excessively, and gave evidence of her bad qualities as a seaboat, pitching her forecastle under at every plunge, and with the greatest difficulty struggling up from one wave before she was buried in another. Just before sunset the bright spot for which we had been on the lookout made its appearance in the southwest, and in an hour afterward we perceived the little headsail we carried flapping listlessly against the mast. In two minutes more, in spite of every preparation, we were hurled on our beam-ends as if by magic, and a perfect wilderness of foam made a clear breach over us as we lay. The blow from the southwest, however, luckily proved to be nothing more than a squall, and we had the good fortune to right the vessel without the loss of a spar. A heavy cross sea[4] gave us great trouble for a few hours after this, but towards morning we found ourselves in nearly as good condition as before the gale. Captain Guy considered that he had made an escape little less than miraculous.

On the thirteenth of October we came in sight of Prince Edward's Island, in latitude 46° 53′ S., longitude 37° 46′ E.[5] Two days afterward we found ourselves near Possession Island, and presently passed the islands of Crozet, in latitude 42° 59′ S., longitude 48° E. On the eighteenth we made Kerguelen's or Desolation Island, in the Southern Indian Ocean, and came to anchor in Christmas Harbour, having four fathoms of water.

This island, or rather group of islands, bears southeast from the Cape of Good Hope, and is distant therefrom nearly eight hundred leagues. It was first discovered in 1772, by the Baron de Kergulen, or Kerguelen, a Frenchman, who, thinking the land to form a portion of an extensive southern continent, carried home information to that effect, which produced much excitement at the time. The government, taking the matter up, sent the baron back in the following year for the purpose of giving his new discovery a critical examination, when the mistake was discovered. In 1777, Captain Cook fell in with the same group, and gave to the principal one the name of Desolation Island, a title which it certainly well deserves. Upon approaching the land, however, the navigator might be induced to suppose otherwise, as the sides of most of the hills, from September to March, are clothed with very brilliant verdure. This deceitful appearance is caused by a small plant resembling saxifrage, which is abundant, growing in large patches on a species of crumbling moss. Besides this plant there is scarcely a sign of vegetation on the island, if we except some coarse rank grass near the harbour, some lichen, and a shrub which bears resemblance to a cabbage shooting into seed, and which has a bitter and acrid taste.

The face of the country is hilly, although none of the hills can be called lofty. Their tops are perpetually covered with snow. There are several harbours, of which Christmas Harbour is the most convenient. It is the first to be met with on the northeast side of the island after passing Cape François, which forms the northern shore, and, by its peculiar shape, serves to distinguish the harbour. Its projecting point terminates in a high rock, through which is a large hole, forming a natural arch. The entrance is in latitude 48° 40′ S., longitude 69° 6′ E. Passing in here, good anchorage may be found under the shelter of several small islands, which form a sufficient protection from all easterly winds. Proceeding on eastwardly from this anchorage you come to Wasp Bay, at the head of the harbour. This is a small basin, completely landlocked, into which you can go with four fathoms, and find anchorage in from ten to three, hard clay bottom. A ship might lie here with her best bower ahead all the year round without risk. To the westward, at the head of Wasp Bay, is a small stream of excellent water, easily procured.

Some seal of the fur and hair species are still to be found on Kerguelen's Island, and sea elephants abound. The feathered tribes are discovered in great numbers. Penguins are very plenty, and of these there are four different kinds. The royal penguin, so called from its size and beautiful plumage, is the largest. The upper part of the body is usually gray, sometimes of a lilach tint; the under portion of the purest white imaginable. The head is of a glossy and most brilliant black, the feet also. The chief beauty of the plumage, however, consists in two broad stripes of a gold colour, which pass along from the head to the breast. The bill is long, and either pink or bright scarlet. These birds walk erect, with a stately carriage. They carry their heads high, with their wings drooping like two arms, and, as their tails project from their body in a line with the legs, the resemblance to a human figure is very striking, and would be apt to deceive the spectator at a casual glance or in the gloom of the evening.[6] The royal penguins which we met with on Kerguelen's Land were rather larger than a goose. The other kinds are the macaroni, the jackass, and the rookery penguin. These are much smaller, less beautiful in plumage, and different in other respects.

Besides the penguin many other birds are here to be found, among which may be mentioned seahens, blue peterels, teal, ducks, Port Egmont hens, shags, Cape pigeons, the nelly, seaswallows, terns, seagulls, Mother Carey's chickens, Mother Carey's geese, or the great peterel, and, lastly, the albatross.

The great peterel is as large as the common albatross, and is carnivorous. It is frequently called the breakbones, or osprey peterel. They are not at all shy, and, when properly cooked, are palatable food. In flying they sometimes sail very close to the surface of the water, with the wings expanded, without appearing to move them in the least degree, or make any exertion with them whatever.

The albatross is one of the largest and fiercest of the South Sea birds. It is of the gull species, and takes its prey on the wing, never coming on land except for the purpose of breeding. Between this bird and the penguin the most singular friendship exists.[7] Their nests are constructed with great uniformity, upon a plan concerted between the two species—that of the albatross being placed in the centre of a little square formed by the nests of four penguins. Navigators have agreed in calling an assemblage of such encampments *a rookery*. These rookeries have been often described, but, as my readers may not all have seen these descriptions, and as I shall have occasion hereafter to speak of the penguin and albatross,[8] it will not be amiss to say something here of their mode of building and living.

When the season for incubation arrives, the birds assemble in vast numbers, and for some days appear to be deliberating upon the proper course to be pursued. At length they proceed to action. A level piece of ground is selected, of suitable extent, usually comprising three or four acres, and situated as near the sea as possible, being still beyond its reach. The spot is chosen with reference to its evenness of surface, and that is preferred which is the least encumbered with stones. This matter being arranged, the birds proceed, with one accord, and actuated apparently by one mind, to trace out, with mathematical accuracy, either a square or other parallelogram, as may best suit the nature of the ground, and of just sufficient size to accommodate easily all the birds assembled, and no more—in this particular seeming determined upon preventing the access of future stragglers who have not participated in the labour of the encampment. One side of the place thus marked out runs parallel with the water's edge, and is left open for ingress or egress.

Having defined the limits of the rookery, the colony now begin to clear it of every species of rubbish, picking up stone by stone, and carrying them outside of the lines, and close by them, so as to form a wall on the three inland sides. Just within this wall a perfectly level and smooth walk is formed, from six to eight feet wide, and extending around the encampment—thus serving the purpose of a general promenade.

The next process is to partition out the whole area into small squares exactly equal in size. This is done by forming narrow paths, very smooth, and crossing each other at right angles throughout the entire extent of the rookery. At each intersection of these paths the nest of an albatross is constructed, and a penguin's nest in the centre of each square—thus every penguin is surrounded by four albatrosses, and each albatross by a like number of penguins. The penguin's nest consists of a hole in the earth, very shallow, being only just of sufficient depth to keep her single egg from rolling. The albatross is somewhat less simple in her arrangements, erecting a hillock about a foot high and two in diameter. This is made of earth, seaweed, and shells. On its summit she builds her nest.

The birds take especial care never to leave their nests unoccupied for an instant during the period of incubation, or, indeed, until the young progeny are sufficiently strong to take care of themselves. While the male is absent at sea in search of food, the female remains on duty, and it is only upon the return of her partner that she ventures abroad. The eggs are never left uncovered at all—while one bird leaves the nest, the other nestling in by its side. This precaution is rendered necessary by the thievish propensities prevalent in the rookery, the inhabitants making no scruple to purloin each other's eggs at every good opportunity.

Although there are some rookeries in which the penguin and albatross are the sole population, yet in most of them a variety of oceanic birds are to be met with, enjoying all the privileges of citizenship, and scattering their nests here and there, wherever they can find room, never interfering, however, with the stations of the larger species. The appearance of such encampments, when seen from a distance, is exceedingly singular. The whole atmosphere just above the settlement is darkened with the immense number of the albatross[9] (mingled with the smaller tribes) which are continually hovering over it, either going to the ocean or returning home. At the same time a crowd of penguins are to be observed, some passing to and fro in the narrow alleys, and some marching, with the military strut so peculiar to them, around the general promenade-ground which encircles the rookery. In short, survey it as we will, nothing can be more astonishing than the spirit of reflection evinced by these feathered beings,[10] and nothing surely can be better calculated to elicit reflection in every well-regulated human intellect.

On the morning after our arrival in Christmas Harbour the chief mate, Mr. Patterson, took the boats, and (although it was somewhat early in the season) went in search of seal, leaving the captain and a young relation of his on a point of barren land to the westward, they having some business, whose nature I could not ascertain, to transact in the interior of the island. Captain Guy took with him a bottle, in which was a sealed letter, and made his way from the point on which he was set on shore towards one of the highest peaks in the place. It is probable that his design was to leave the letter on that height for some vessel which he expected to come after him.[11] As soon as we lost sight of him we proceeded (Peters and myself being in the mate's boat) on our cruise around the coast, looking for seal.[12] In this business we were occupied about three weeks, examining with great care every nook and corner, not only of Kerguelen's Land, but of the several small islands in the vicinity. Our labours, however, were not crowned with any important success. We saw a great many fur seal, but they were exceedingly shy, and, with the greatest exertions, we could only procure three hundred and fifty skins in all. Sea elephants were abundant, especially on the western coast of the main island, but of these we killed only twenty, and this with great difficulty. On the smaller islands we discovered a good many of the hair seal, but did not molest them. We returned to the schooner on the eleventh, where we found Captain Guy and his nephew, who gave a very bad account of the interior, representing it as one of the most dreary and utterly barren countries in the world. They had remained two nights on the island, owing to some misunderstanding, on the part of the second mate, in regard to the sending a jollyboat from the schooner to take them off.

CHAPTER 15

On the twelfth we made sail from Christmas Harbour, re-tracing our way to the westward, and leaving Marion's Island, one of Crozet's group, on the larboard.[1] We after-ward passed Prince Edward's Island, leaving it also on our left; then, steering more to the northward, made, in fifteen days, the islands of Tristan d'Acunha, in latitude 37° 8′ S., longitude 12° 8′ W.

This group, now so well known, and which consists of three circular islands, was first discovered by the Portuguese, and was visited afterward by the Dutch in 1643, and by the French in 1767. The three islands together form a triangle, and are distant from each other about ten miles, there being fine open passages between. The land in all of them is very high, especially in Tristan d'Acunha, properly so called. This is the largest of the group, being fifteen miles in circumference, and so elevated that it can be seen in clear weather at the distance of eighty or ninety miles. A part of the land towards the north rises more than a thousand feet perpendicularly from the sea. A tableland at this height extends back nearly to the centre of the island, and from this tableland arises a lofty cone like that of Teneriffe. The lower half of this cone is clothed with trees of good size, but the upper region is barren rock, usually hid-den among the clouds, and covered with snow during the greater part of the year. There are no shoals or other dangers about the island, the shores being remarkably bold and the water deep. On the northwestern coast is a bay, with a beach of black sand, where a landing with boats can be easily ef-fected, provided there be a southerly wind. Plenty of excellent water may here be readily procured; also cod, and other fish, may be taken with hook and line.

The next island in point of size, and the most westwardly of the group, is that called the Inaccessible. Its precise situation is 37° 17′ S. latitude, longitude 12° 24′ W. It is seven or eight miles in circumference, and on all sides presents a forbidding and precipitous aspect. Its top is perfectly flat, and the whole region is steril, nothing growing upon it except a few stunted shrubs.

Nightingale Island, the smallest and most southerly, is in latitude 37° 26′ S., longitude 12° 12′ W. Off its southern extremity is a high ledge of rocky islets; a few also of a similar appearance are seen to the northeast. The ground is irregular and steril, and a deep valley partially separates it.

The shores of these islands abound, in the proper season, with sea lions, sea elephants, the hair and fur seal, together with a great variety of oceanic birds. Whales are also plenty in their vicinity. Owing to the ease with which these various animals were here formerly taken, the group has been much visited since its discovery. The Dutch and French frequented it at a very early period. In 1790, Captain Patten, of the ship Industry, of Philadelphia, made Tristan d'Acunha, where he remained seven months (from August, 1790, to April, 1791) for the purpose of collecting sealskins. In this time he gathered no less than five thousand six hundred, and says that he would have had no difficulty in loading a large ship with oil in three weeks. Upon his arrival he found no quadrupeds, with the exception of a few wild goats—the island now abounds with all our most valuable domestic animals, which have been introduced by subsequent navigators.

I believe it was not long after Captain Patten's visit that Captain Colquhoun, of the American brig Betsey, touched at the largest of the islands for the purpose of refreshment. He planted onions, potatoes, cabbages, and a great many other vegetables, an abundance of all which are now to be met with.

In 1811, a Captain Heywood, in the Nereus, visited Tristan. He found there three Americans, who were residing upon the islands to prepare sealskins and oil. One of these men was named Jonathan Lambert, and he called himself the sovereign of the country. He had cleared and cultivated about sixty acres of land, and turned his attention to raising the coffee-plant and sugar-cane, with which he had been furnished by the American minister at Rio Janeiro. This settlement, however, was finally abandoned, and in 1817 the islands were taken possession of by the British government, who sent a detachment for that purpose from the Cape of Good Hope. They did not, however, retain them long; but, upon the evacuation of the country as a British possession, two or three English families took up their residence there independently of the government. On the twenty-fifth of March, 1824, the Berwick, Captain Jeffrey, from London to Van Diemen's Land, arrived at the place, where they found an Englishman of the name of Glass, formerly a corporal in the British artillery. He claimed to be supreme governor of the islands, and had under his control twenty-one men and three women. He gave a very favourable account of the salubrity of the climate and of the productiveness of the soil. The population occupied themselves chiefly in collecting sealskins and sea elephant oil, with which they traded to the Cape of Good Hope, Glass owning a small schooner. At the period of our arrival the governor was still a resident, but his little community had multiplied, there being fifty-six persons upon Tristan, besides a smaller settlement of seven on Nightingale Island. We had no difficulty in procuring almost every kind of refreshment which we required—sheep, hogs, bullocks, rabbits, poultry, goats, fish in great variety, and vegetables were abundant. Having come to anchor close in with the large island, in eighteen fathoms, we took all we wanted on board very conveniently. Captain Guy also purchased of Glass five hundred sealskins and some ivory. We remained here a week, during which the prevailing winds were from the northward and westward, and the weather somewhat hazy. On the fifth of November[2] we made sail to the southward and westward, with the intention of having a thorough search for a group of islands called the Auroras, respecting whose existence a great diversity of opinion has existed.

These islands are said to have been discovered as early as 1762, by the commander of the ship Aurora. In 1790, Captain Manuel de Oyarvido, in the ship Princess, belonging to the Royal Philippine Company, sailed, as he asserts, directly among them. In 1794, the Spanish corvette Atrevida went with the determination of ascertaining their precise situation, and, in a paper published by the Royal Hydrographical Society of Madrid in the year 1809, the following language is used respecting this expedition. "The corvette Atrevida practised, in their immediate vicinity, from the twenty-first to the twenty-seventh of January, all the necessary observations, and measured by chronometers the difference of longitude between these islands and the port of Soledad in the Malninas. The islands are three; they are very nearly in the same meridian; the centre one is rather low, and the other two may be seen at nine leagues distance." The observations made on board the Atrevida give the following results as the precise situation of each island. The most northern is in latitude 52° 37′ 24″ S., longitude 47° 43′ 15″ W.; the middle one in latitude 53° 2′ 40″ S., longitude 47° 55′ 15″ W.; and the most southern in latitude 53° 15′ 22″ S., longitude 47° 57′ 15″ W.

On the twenty-seventh of January, 1820, Captain James Weddel, of the British navy, sailed from Staten Land also in search of the Auroras. He reports that, having made the most diligent search, and passed not only immediately over the spots indicated by the commander of the Atrevida, but in every direction throughout the vicinity of these spots, he could discover no indication of land. These conflicting statements have induced other navigators to look out for the islands; and, strange to say, while some have sailed through every inch of sea where they are supposed to lie without finding them, there have been not a few who declare positively that they have seen them, and even been close in with their shores. It was Captain Guy's intention to make every exertion within his power to settle the question so oddly in dispute.*

We kept on our course, between the south and west, with variable weather, until the twentieth of the month, when we found ourselves on the debated ground, being in latitude 53° 15′ S., longitude 47° 58′ W.—that is to say, very nearly upon the spot indicated as the situation of the most southern of the group. Not perceiving any sign of land, we continued to the westward in the parallel of fifty-three degrees south, as far as the meridian of fifty degrees west. We then stood to the north as far as the parallel of fifty-two degrees south, when we turned to the eastward, and kept our parallel by double altitudes, morning and evening, and meridian altitudes of the planets and moon. Having thus gone eastwardly to the meridian of the western coast of Georgia, we kept that meridian until we were in the latitude from which we set out. We then took diagonal courses throughout the entire extent of sea circumscribed, keeping a lookout constantly at the masthead, and repeating our examination with the greatest care for a period of three weeks, during which the weather was remarkably pleasant and fair, with no haze whatsoever. Of course we were thoroughly satisfied that, whatever islands might have

---

* Among the vessels which at various times have professed to meet with the Auroras may be mentioned the ship San Miguel, in 1769; the ship Aurora, in 1774; the brig Pearl, in 1779; and the ship Dolores, in 1790. They all agree in giving the mean latitude fifty-three degrees south.

existed in this vicinity at any former period, no vestige of them remained at the present day. Since my return home I find that the same ground was traced over with equal care in 1822 by Captain Johnson, of the American schooner Henry, and by Captain Morrell,[3] in the American schooner Wasp—in both cases with the same result as in our own.

CHAPTER 16

It had been Captain Guy's original intention, after satisfying himself about the Auroras, to proceed through the Strait of Magellan, and up along the western coast of Patagonia; but information received at Tristan d'Acunha induced him to steer to the southward, in the hope of falling in with some small islands said to lie about the parallel of 60° S., longitude 41° 20′ W. In the event of his not discovering these lands, he designed, should the season prove favourable, to push on towards the pole.[1] Accordingly, on the twelfth of December, we made sail in that direction. On the eighteenth we found ourselves about the station indicated by Glass, and cruised for three days in that neighbourhood without finding any traces of the islands he had mentioned. On the twenty-first, the weather being unusually pleasant, we again made sail to the southward, with the resolution of penetrating in that course as far as possible. Before entering upon this portion of my narrative, it may be as well, for the information of those readers who have paid little attention to the progress of discovery in these regions, to give some brief account of the very few attempts at reaching the southern pole which have hitherto been made.

That of Captain Cook was the first of which we have any distinct account.[2] In 1772 he sailed to the south in the Resolution, accompanied by Lieutenant Furneaux in the Adventure. In December he found himself as far as the fifty-eighth parallel of south latitude, and in longitude 26° 57′ E. Here he met with narrow fields of ice, about eight or ten inches thick, and running northwest and southeast. This ice was in large cakes, and usually it was packed so closely that the vessels had great difficulty in forcing a passage. At this period Captain Cook supposed, from the vast number of birds to be seen, and from other indications, that he was in the near vicinity of land. He kept on to the southward, the weather being exceedingly cold, until he reached the sixty-fourth parallel, in longitude 38° 14′ E. Here he had mild weather, with gentle breezes, for five days, the thermometer being at thirty-six. In January, 1773, the vessels crossed the Antarctic circle, but did not succeed in penetrating much farther; for, upon reaching latitude 67° 15′, they found all farther progress impeded by an immense body of ice, extending all along the southern horizon as far as the eye could reach. This ice was of every variety—and some large floes of it, miles in extent, formed a compact mass, rising eighteen or twenty feet above the water. It being late in the season, and no hope entertained of rounding these obstructions, Captain Cook now reluctantly turned to the northward.

In the November following he renewed his search in the Antarctic. In latitude 59° 40′ he met with a strong current setting to the southward. In December, when the vessels were in latitude 67° 31′, longitude 142° 54′ W., the cold was excessive, with heavy gales and fog. Here also birds were abundant; the albatross, the penguin,[3] and the peterel especially. In latitude 70° 23′ some large islands of ice were encountered, and shortly afterward, the clouds to the southward were observed to be of a snowy whiteness, indicating the vicinity of field ice. In latitude 71° 10′, longitude 106° 54′ W., the navigators were stopped, as before, by an immense frozen expanse, which filled the whole area of the southern horizon. The northern edge of this expanse was ragged and broken, so firmly wedged together as to be utterly impassable, and extending about a mile to the southward. Behind it the frozen surface was comparatively smooth for some distance, until terminated in the extreme back-ground by gigantic ranges of ice mountains, the one towering above the other. Captain Cook concluded that this vast field reached the southern pole or was joined to a continent. Mr. J. N. Reynolds,[4] whose great exertions and perseverance have at length succeeded in getting set on foot a national expedition, partly for the purpose of exploring these regions, thus speaks of the attempt of the Resolution. "We are not surprised that Captain Cook was unable to go beyond 71° 10′, but we are astonished that he did attain that point on the meridian of 106° 54′ west longitude. Palmer's Land lies south of the Shetland, latitude sixty-four degrees, and tends to the southward and westward farther than any navigator has yet penetrated. Cook was standing for this land when his progress was arrested by the ice; which, we apprehend, must always be the case in that point, and so early in the season as the sixth of January—and we should not be surprised if a portion of the icy mountains described was attached to the main body of Palmer's Land, or to some other portions of land lying farther to the southward and westward."

In 1803, Captains Kreutzenstern and Lisiausky were despatched by Alexander of Russia for the purpose of circumnavigating the globe. In endeavouring to get south, they made no farther than 59° 58′, in longitude 70° 15′ W. They here met with strong currents setting eastwardly. Whales were abundant, but they saw no ice. In regard to this voyage, Mr. Reynolds observes that, if Kreutzenstern had arrived where he did earlier in the season, he must have encountered ice—it was March when he reached the latitude specified. The winds prevailing, as they do, from the southward and westward, had carried the floes, aided by currents, into that icy region bounded on the north by Georgia, east by Sandwich Land and the South Orkneys, and west by the South Shetland Islands.

In 1822, Captain James Weddell, of the British navy, with two very small vessels, penetrated farther to the south than any previous navigator, and this too, without encountering extraordinary difficulties. He states that although he was frequently hemmed in by ice *before* reaching the seventy-second parallel, yet, upon attaining it, not a particle was to be discovered, and that, upon arriving at the latitude of 74° 15′, no fields, and only three islands of ice were visible. It is somewhat remarkable that, although vast flocks of birds were seen, and other usual indications of land, and although, south of the Shetlands, unknown coasts were observed from the masthead tending southwardly, Weddell discourages the idea of land existing in the polar regions of the south.

On the eleventh of January, 1823, Captain Benjamin Morrell, of the American schooner Wasp, sailed from Kerguelen's Land with a view of penetrating as far south as possible.[5] On the first of February he found himself in latitude 64° 52′ S., longitude 118° 27′ E. The following passage is extracted from his journal of that date. "The wind soon freshened to an eleven-knot breeze, and we embraced this opportunity of making to the west; being however convinced that the farther we went south beyond latitude sixty-four degrees the less ice was to be apprehended, we steered a little to the southward, until we crossed the Antarctic circle, and were in latitude 69° 15′ E. In this latitude there was *no field ice,* and very few ice islands in sight."

Under the date of March fourteenth I find also this entry. "The sea was now entirely free of field ice, and there were not more than a dozen ice islands in sight. At the same time the temperature of the air and water was at least thirteen degrees higher (more mild) than we had ever found it between the parallels of sixty and sixty-two south. We were now in latitude 70° 14′ S., and the temperature of the air was forty-seven, and that of the water forty-four. In this situation I found the variation to be 14° 27′ easterly, per azimuth. . . . . (*sic*) I have several times passed within the Antarctic circle on different meridians, and have uniformly found the temperature, both of the air and the water, to become more and more mild the farther I advanced beyond the sixty-fifth degree of south latitude, and that the variation decreases in the same proportion.

While north of this latitude, say between sixty and sixty-five south, we frequently had great difficulty in finding a passage for the vessel between the immense and almost innumerable ice islands, some of which were from one to two miles in circumference, and more than five hundred feet above the surface of the water."

Being nearly destitute of fuel and water, and without proper instruments, it being also late in the season, Captain Morrell was now obliged to put back, without attempting any farther progress to the southward, although an entirely open sea lay before him. He expresses the opinion that, had not these overruling considerations obliged him to retreat, he could have penetrated, if not to the pole itself, at least to the eighty-fifth parallel. I have given his ideas respecting these matters somewhat at length, that the reader may have an opportunity of seeing how far they were borne out by my own subsequent experience.

In 1831, Captain Briscoe, in the employ of the Messieurs Enderby, whale-ship owners of London, sailed in the brig Lively for the South Seas, accompanied by the cutter Tula.[6] On the twenty-eighth of February, being in latitude 66° 30′ S., longitude 47° 31′ E., he descried land, and "clearly discovered through the snow the black peaks of a range of mountains running E. S. E." He remained in this neighbourhood during the whole of the following month, but was unable to approach the coast nearer than within ten leagues, owing to the boisterous state of the weather. Finding it impossible to make farther discovery during this season, he returned northward to winter in Van Diemen's Land.

In the beginning of 1832 he again proceeded southwardly, and on the fourth of February land was seen to the southeast in latitude 67° 15′, longitude 69° 29′ W. This was soon found to be an island near the headland of the country he had first discovered. On the twenty-first of the month he succeeded in landing on the latter, and took possession of it in the name of

William IV., calling it Adelaide's Island, in honour of the English queen. These particulars being made known to the Royal Geographical Society of London, the conclusion was drawn by that body "that there is a continuous tract of land extending from 47° 30' E. to 69° 29' W. longitude, running the parallel of from sixty-six to sixty-seven degrees south latitude." In respect to this conclusion Mr. Reynolds observes, "In the correctness of it we by no means concur; nor do the discoveries of Briscoe warrant any such inference. It was within these limits that Weddell proceeded south on a meridian to the east of Georgia, Sandwich Land, and the South Orkney and Shetland Islands." My own experience will be found to testify most directly to the falsity of the conclusion arrived at by the society.

These are the principal attempts which have been made at penetrating to a high southern latitude, and it will now be seen that there remained, previous to the voyage of the Jane, nearly three hundred degrees of longitude in which the Antarctic circle had not been crossed at all. Of course a wide field lay before us for discovery, and it was with feelings of most intense interest that I heard Captain Guy express his resolution of pushing boldly to the southward.[7]

We kept our course southwardly for four days after giving up the search for Glass's Islands, without meeting with any ice at all. On the twenty-sixth, at noon, we were in latitude 63° 23′ S., longitude 41° 25′ W. We now saw several large ice islands, and a floe of field ice, not, however, of any great extent. The winds generally blew from the southeast, or the northeast, but were very light. Whenever we had a westerly wind, which was seldom, it was invariably attended with a rain squall. Every day we had more or less snow. The thermometer, on the twenty-seventh, stood at thirty-five.[1]

January 1, 1828. This day we found ourselves completely hemmed in by the ice, and our prospects looked cheerless indeed. A strong gale blew, during the whole forenoon, from the northeast, and drove large cakes of the drift against the rudder and counter with such violence that we all trembled for the consequences. Towards evening, the gale still blowing with fury, a large field in front separated, and we were enabled, by carrying a press of sail, to force a passage through the smaller flakes into some open water beyond. As we approached this space we took in sail by degrees, and having at length got clear, lay to under a single reefed foresail.

January 2. We had now tolerably pleasant weather. At noon we found ourselves in latitude 69° 10′ S., longitude 42° 20′ W., having crossed the Antarctic circle. Very little ice was to be seen to the southward, although large fields of it lay behind us. This day we rigged some sounding gear, using a large iron pot capable of holding twenty gallons, and a line of two hundred fathoms. We found the current setting to the north, about a quarter of a mile per hour. The temperature of the air was now about thirty-three. Here we found the variation to be 14° 28' easterly, per azimuth.

January 5. We had still held on to the southward without any very great impediments. On this morning, however, being in latitude 73° 15' E., longitude 42° 10' W., we were again brought to a stand by an immense expanse of firm ice. We saw, nevertheless, much open water to the southward, and felt no doubt of being able to reach it eventually. Standing to the eastward along the edge of the floe, we at length came to a passage of about a mile in width, through which we warped our way by sundown. The sea in which we now were was thickly covered with ice islands, but had no field ice, and we pushed on boldly as before. The cold did not seem to increase, although we had snow very frequently, and now and then hail squalls of great violence. Immense flocks of the albatross flew over the schooner this day, going from southeast to northwest.

January 7. The sea still remained pretty well open, so that we had no difficulty in holding on our course. To the westward we saw some icebergs of incredible size, and in the afternoon passed very near one whose summit could not have been less than four hundred fathoms from the surface of the ocean. Its girth was probably, at the base, three quarters of a league, and several streams of water were running from crevices in its sides. We remained in sight of this island two days, and then only lost it in a fog.

January 10. Early this morning we had the misfortune to lose a man overboard. He was an American, named Peter Vredenburgh, a native of New-York, and was one of the most valuable hands on board the schooner. In going over the bows his foot slipped, and he fell between two cakes of ice, never rising again. At noon of this day we were in latitude 78° 30', longitude 40° 15' W. The cold was now excessive, and we had hail squalls continually from the northward and eastward. In this direction also we saw several more immense icebergs, and the whole horizon to the eastward appeared to be blocked up with field ice, rising in tiers, one mass above the other. Some driftwood floated by during the evening, and a great quantity of birds flew over, among which were Nellies, peterels, albatrosses, and a large bird of a brilliant blue plumage. The variation here, per azimuth, was less than it had been previously to our passing the Antarctic circle.

January 12. Our passage to the south again looked doubtful, as nothing was to be seen in the direction of the pole but one apparently limitless floe, backed by absolute mountains of ragged ice,[2] one precipice of which arose frowningly above the other. We stood to the westward until the fourteenth, in the hope of finding an entrance.

January 14. This morning we reached the western extremity of the field which had impeded us, and, weathering it, came to an open sea, without a particle of ice. Upon sounding with two hundred fathoms, we here found a current setting southwardly at the rate of half a mile per hour. The temperature of the air was forty-seven, that of the water thirty-four. We now sailed to the southward, without meeting any interruption of moment until the sixteenth, when, at noon, we were in latitude 81° 21′, longitude 42° W. We here again sounded, and found a current setting still southwardly, and at the rate of three quarters of a mile per hour. The variation per azimuth had diminished, and the temperature of the air was mild and pleasant, the thermometer being as high as fifty-one. At this period not a particle of ice was to be discovered. All hands on board now felt certain of attaining the pole.

January 17. This day was full of incident. Innumerable flights of birds flew over us from the southward, and several were shot from the deck; one of them, a species of pelican, proved to be excellent eating. About midday a small floe of ice was seen from the masthead off the larboard bow, and upon it there appeared to be some large animal. As the weather was good and nearly calm, Captain Guy ordered out two of the boats to see what it was. Dirk Peters and myself accompanied the mate in the larger boat. Upon coming up with the floe, we perceived that it was in the possession of a gigantic creature of the race of the Arctic bear, but far exceeding in size the largest of these animals. Being well armed, we made no scruple of attacking it at once. Several shots were fired in quick succession, the most of which took effect, apparently, in the head and body. Nothing discouraged, however, the monster threw himself from the ice, and swam, with open jaws, to the boat in which were Peters and myself. Owing to the confusion which ensued among us at this unexpected turn of the adventure, no person was ready immediately with a second shot, and the bear had actually succeeded in getting half his vast bulk across our gunwale, and seizing one of the men by the small of his back, before any efficient means were taken to repel him. In this extremity nothing but the promptness and agility of Peters saved us from destruction. Leaping upon the back of the huge beast, he plunged the blade of a knife behind the neck, reaching the spinal marrow at a blow. The brute tumbled into the sea lifeless, and without a struggle, rolling over Peters as he fell. The latter soon recovered himself, and a rope being thrown him, he secured the carcass before entering the boat. We then returned in triumph to the schooner, towing our trophy behind us. This bear, upon admeasurement, proved to be full fifteen feet in his greatest length. His wool was perfectly white, and very coarse, curling tightly.[3] The eyes were of a blood red, and larger than those of the Arctic bear—the snout also more rounded, rather resembling the snout of the bulldog. The meat was tender, but excessively rank and fishy, although the men devoured it with avidity, and declared it excellent eating.

Scarcely had we got our prize alongside, when the man at the masthead gave the joyful shout of *"land on the starboard bow!"* All hands were now upon the alert, and, a breeze springing up very opportunely from the northward and eastward, we were soon close in with the coast. It proved to be a low rocky islet, of about a league in circumference, and altogether destitute of vegetation, if we except a species of prickly pear. In approaching it from the northward, a singular ledge of rock is seen projecting into the sea, and bearing a strong resemblance to corded bales of cotton.[4] Around this ledge to the westward is a small bay, at the bottom of which our boats effected a convenient landing.

It did not take us long to explore every portion of the island, but, with one exception, we found nothing worthy of observation. In the southern extremity, we picked up near the shore, half buried in a pile of loose stones, a piece of wood, which seemed to have formed the prow of a canoe. There had been evidently some attempt at carving upon it, and Captain Guy fancied that he made out the figure of a tortoise, but the resemblance did not strike me very forcibly. Besides this prow, if such it were, we found no other token that any living creature had ever been here before. Around the coast we discovered occasional small floes of ice—but these were very few. The exact situation of this islet (to which Captain Guy gave the name of Bennett's Islet, in honour of his partner in the ownership of the schooner) is 82° 50′ S. latitude, 42° 20′ W. longitude.

We had now advanced to the southward more than eight degrees farther than any previous navigators, and the sea still lay perfectly open before us. We found, too, that the variation uniformly decreased as we proceeded, and, what was still more surprising, that the temperature of the air, and latterly of the water, became milder. The weather might even be called pleasant, and we had a steady but very gentle breeze always from some northern point of the compass. The sky was usually clear, with now and then a slight appearance of thin vapour in the southern horizon—this, however, was invariably of brief duration. Two difficulties alone presented themselves to our view; we were getting short of fuel, and symptoms of scurvy had occurred among several of the crew. These considerations began to impress upon Captain Guy the necessity of returning, and he spoke of it frequently. For my own part, confident as I was of soon arriving at land of some description upon the course we were pursuing, and having every reason to believe, from present appearances, that we should not find it the steril soil met with in the higher Arctic latitudes, I warmly pressed upon him the expediency of persevering, at least for a few days longer, in the direction we were now holding. So tempting an opportunity of solving the great problem in regard to an Antarctic continent had never yet been afforded to man, and I confess that I felt myself bursting with indignation at the timid and ill-timed suggestions of our commander. I believe, indeed, that what I could not refrain from saying to him on this head had the effect of inducing him to push on. While, therefore, I cannot but lament the most unfortunate and bloody events which immediately arose from my advice, I must still be allowed to feel some degree of gratification at having been instrumental, however remotely, in opening to the eye of science one of the most intensely exciting secrets which has ever engrossed its attention.[5]

CHAPTER 18

January 18. This morning* we continued to the southward, with the same pleasant weather as before. The sea was entirely smooth, the air tolerably warm and from the northeast, the temperature of the water fifty-three. We now again got our sounding-gear in order, and, with a hundred and fifty fathoms of line, found the current setting towards the pole at the rate of a mile an hour. This constant tendency to the southward, both in the wind and current, caused some degree of specula-tion, and even of alarm, in different quarters of the schooner, and I saw distinctly that no little impression had been made upon the mind of Captain Guy. He was exceedingly sensitive to ridicule, however, and I finally succeeded in laughing him out of his apprehensions. The variation was now very trivial. In the course of the day we saw several large whales of the right species, and innumerable flights of the albatross passed over the vessel. We also picked up a bush, full of red berries, like those of the hawthorn, and the carcass of a singular-looking land-animal. It was three feet in length, and but six inches in height, with four very short legs, the feet armed with long claws of a brilliant scarlet, and resembling coral in sub-stance. The body was covered with a straight silky hair, per-

---

* The terms *morning* and *evening,* which I have made use of to avoid confu-sion in my narrative, as far as possible, must not, of course, be taken in their ordinary sense. For a long time past we had had no night at all, the daylight being continual. The dates throughout are according to nautical time, and the bearings must be understood as per compass. I would also remark in this place, that I cannot, in the first portion of what is here written, pretend to strict accuracy in respect to dates, or latitudes and longitudes, having kept no regular journal until after the period of which this first portion treats. In many instances I have relied altogether upon memory.

fectly white. The tail was peaked like that of a rat, and about a foot and a half long. The head resembled a cat's, with the exception of the ears—these were flapped like the ears of a dog. The *teeth* were of the same brilliant scarlet as the claws.[1]

January 19.[2] To-day, being in latitude 83° 20', longitude 43° 5' W. (the sea being of an extraordinarily dark colour), we again saw land from the masthead, and, upon a closer scrutiny, found it to be one of a group of very large islands. The shore was precipitous, and the interior seemed to be well wooded, a circumstance which occasioned us great joy. In about four hours from our first discovering the land we came to anchor in ten fathoms, sandy bottom, a league from the coast, as a high surf, with strong ripples here and there, rendered a nearer approach of doubtful expediency. The two largest boats were now ordered out, and a party, well armed (among whom were Peters and myself), proceeded to look for an opening in the reef which appeared to encircle the island. After searching about for some time, we discovered an inlet, which we were entering, when we saw four large canoes put off from the shore, filled with men who seemed to be well armed. We waited for them to come up, and, as they moved with great rapidity, they were soon within hail. Captain Guy now held up a white handkerchief on the blade of an oar,[3] when the strangers made a full stop, and commenced a loud jabbering all at once, intermingled with occasional shouts, in which we could distinguish the words *Anamoo-moo!* and *Lama-Lama!*[4] They continued this for at least half an hour, during which we had a good opportunity of observing their appearance.

In the four canoes, which might have been fifty feet long and five broad, there were a hundred and ten savages in all. They were about the ordinary stature of Europeans, but of a more muscular and brawny frame, their complexion a jet black, with thick and long woolly hair.[5] They were clothed in skins of an unknown black animal, shaggy and silky, and made to fit the body with some degree of skill, the hair being inside, except where turned out about the neck, wrists, and ankles. Their arms consisted principally of clubs, of a dark, and apparently very heavy wood. Some spears, however, were observed among them, headed with flint, and a few slings. The bottoms of the canoes were full of black stones about the size of a large egg.

When they had concluded their harangue (for it was clear they intended their jabbering for such), one of them who seemed to be the chief stood up in the prow of his canoe, and made signs for us to bring our boats alongside of him. This hint we pretended not to understand, thinking it the wiser plan to maintain, if possible, the interval between us, as their number more than quadrupled our own. Finding this to be the case, the chief ordered the three other canoes to hold back, while he advanced towards us with his own. As soon as he came up with us he leaped on board the largest of our boats, and seated himself by the side of Captain Guy, pointing at the same time to the schooner, and repeating the words *Anamoo-moo!* and *Lama-Lama!* We now put back to the vessel, the four canoes following at a little distance.

Upon getting alongside the chief evinced symptoms of extreme surprise and delight, clapping his hands, slapping his thighs and breast, and laughing obstreperously. His followers behind joined in his merriment, and for some minutes the din was so excessive as to be absolutely deafening. Quiet being at length restored, Captain Guy ordered the boats to be hoisted up, as a necessary precaution, and gave the chief (whose name we soon found to be *Too-wit*)[6] to understand that we could admit no more than twenty of his men on deck at one time. With this arrangement he appeared perfectly satisfied, and gave some directions to the canoes, when one of them approached, the rest remaining about fifty yards off. Twenty of the savages now got on board, and proceeded to ramble over every part of the deck, and scramble about among the rigging, making themselves much at home, and examining every article with great inquisitiveness.

It was quite evident that they had never before seen any of the white race—from whose complexion, indeed, they appeared to recoil.[7] They believed the Jane to be a living creature, and seemed to be afraid of hurting it with the points of their spears, carefully turning them up. Our crew were much amused with the conduct of Too-wit in one instance. The cook was splitting some wood near the galley, and, by accident, struck his axe into the deck, making a gash of considerable depth. The chief immediately ran up, and pushing the cook on one side rather roughly, commenced a half whine, half howl, strongly indicative of sympathy in what he considered the sufferings of the schooner, patting and smoothing the gash with his hand, and washing it from a bucket of seawater which stood by. This was a degree of ignorance for which we were not prepared, and for my part I could not help thinking some of it affected.

When the visiters had satisfied, as well as they could, their curiosity in regard to our upper works, they were admitted below, when their amazement exceeded all bounds. Their astonishment now appeared to be far too deep for words, for they roamed about in silence, broken only by low ejaculations. The arms afforded them much food for speculation, and they were suffered to handle and examine them at leisure. I do not believe that they had the least suspicion of their actual use, but rather took them for idols, seeing the care we had of them, and the attention with which we watched their movements while handling them. At the great guns their wonder was redoubled. They approached them with every mark of the profoundest reverence and awe, but forbore to examine them minutely. There were two large mirrors in the cabin, and here was the acme of their amazement. Too-wit was the first to approach them, and he had got in the middle of the cabin, with his face to one and his back to the other, before he fairly per-

ceived them. Upon raising his eyes and seeing his reflected self
in the glass, I thought the savage would go mad; but, upon
turning short round to make a retreat, and beholding himself a
second time in the opposite direction, I was afraid he would
expire upon the spot.[8] No persuasions could prevail upon him
to take another look; but, throwing himself upon the floor,
with his face buried in his hands, he remained thus until we
were obliged to drag him upon deck.

The whole of the savages were admitted on board in this
manner, twenty at a time, Too-wit being suffered to remain
during the entire period. We saw no disposition to thievery
among them, nor did we miss a single article after their departure. Throughout the whole of their visit they evinced the
most friendly manner. There were, however, some points in
their demeanour which we found it impossible to understand:
for example, we could not get them to approach several very
harmless objects—such as the schooner's sails, an egg, an open
book, or a pan of flour. We endeavoured to ascertain if they
had among them any articles which might be turned to account in the way of traffic, but found great difficulty in being
comprehended. We made out, nevertheless, what greatly astonished us, that the islands abounded in the large tortoise of
the Gallipagos, one of which we saw in the canoe of Too-wit.
We saw also some *biche de mer* in the hands of one of the savages, who was greedily devouring it in its natural state. These
anomalies, for they were such when considered in regard to
the latitude, induced Captain Guy to wish for a thorough in-
vestigation of the country, in the hope of making a profitable
speculation in his discovery. For my own part, anxious as I
was to know something more of these islands, I was still more
earnestly bent on prosecuting the voyage to the southward
without delay. We had now fine weather, but there was no
telling how long it would last; and being already in the eighty-
fourth parallel, with an open sea before us, a current setting
strongly to the southward, and the wind fair, I could not lis-

ten with any patience to a proposition of stopping longer than was absolutely necessary for the health of the crew and the taking on board a proper supply of fuel and fresh provisions. I represented to the captain that we might easily make this group on our return, and winter here in the event of being blocked up by the ice. He at length came into my views (for in some way, hardly known to myself, I had acquired much influence over him), and it was finally resolved that, even in the event of our finding *biche de mer,* we should only stay here a week to recruit, and then push on to the southward while we might. Accordingly we made every necessary preparation, and, under the guidance of Too-wit, got the Jane through the reef in safety, coming to anchor about a mile from the shore, in an excellent bay, completely landlocked, on the southeastern coast of the main island, and in ten fathoms of water, black sandy bottom. At the head of this bay there were three fine springs (we were told) of good water, and we saw abundance of wood in the vicinity. The four canoes followed us in, keeping, however, at a respectful distance. Too-wit himself remained on board, and, upon our dropping anchor, invited us to accompany him on shore, and visit his village in the interior.[9] To this Captain Guy consented; and ten savages being left on board as hostages, a party of us, twelve in all, got in readiness to attend the chief. We took care to be well armed, yet without evincing any distrust. The schooner had her guns run out, her boarding-nettings up, and every other proper precaution was taken to guard against surprise. Directions were left with the chief mate to admit no person on board during our absence, and, in the event of our not appearing in twelve hours, to send the cutter, with a swivel, round the island in search of us.

At every step we took inland the conviction forced itself upon us that we were in a country differing essentially from any hitherto visited by civilized men. We saw nothing with which we had been formerly conversant. The trees resembled no growth of either the torrid, the temperate, or the northern frigid zones, and were altogether unlike those of the lower southern latitudes we had already traversed. The very rocks were novel in their mass, their colour, and their stratification; and the streams themselves, utterly incredible as it may appear, had so little in common with those of other climates, that we were scrupulous of tasting them, and, indeed, had difficulty in bringing ourselves to believe that their qualities were purely those of nature. At a small brook which crossed our path (the first we had reached) Too-wit and his attendants halted to drink. On account of the singular character of the water,[10] we refused to taste it, supposing it to be polluted; and it was not until some time afterward we came to understand that such was the appearance of the streams throughout the whole group. I am at a loss to give a distinct idea of the nature of this liquid, and cannot do so without many words. Although it flowed with rapidity in all declivities where common water would do so, yet never, except when falling in a cascade, had it the customary appearance of *limpidity*. It was, nevertheless, in point of fact, as perfectly limpid as any limestone water in existence, the difference being only in appearance. At first sight, and especially in cases where little declivity was found, it bore resemblance, as regards consistency, to a thick infusion of gum Arabic in common water. But this was only the least remarkable of its extraordinary qualities. It was *not* colourless, nor was it of any one uniform colour—presenting to the eye, as it flowed, every possible shade of purple, like the hues of a changeable silk. This variation in shade was produced in a manner which excited as profound astonishment in the minds of our party as the mirror had done in the case of Too-wit. Upon collecting a basinful, and allowing it to settle thoroughly, we perceived that the whole mass of liquid was made up of a number of distinct veins, each of a distinct hue; that these veins did not commingle; and that their cohesion was perfect in regard to their own particles among themselves, and imperfect in regard to neigh-bouring veins. Upon passing the blade of a knife athwart the veins, the water closed over it immediately, as with us, and also, in withdrawing it, all traces of the passage of the knife were instantly obliterated. If, however, the blade was passed down accurately between two veins, a perfect separation was effected, which the power of cohesion did not immediately rectify. The phenomena of this water formed the first definite link in that vast chain of apparent miracles with which I was destined to be at length encircled.

CHAPTER 19

We were nearly three hours in reaching the village, it being more than nine miles in the interior, and the path lying through a rugged country. As we passed along, the party of Too-wit (the whole hundred and ten savages of the canoes) was momentarily strengthened by smaller detachments, of from two to six or seven, which joined us, as if by accident, at different turns in the road. There appeared so much of system in this that I could not help feeling distrust, and I spoke to Captain Guy of my apprehensions. It was now too late, however, to recede, and we concluded that our best security lay in evincing a perfect confidence in the good faith of Too-wit. We accordingly went on, keeping a wary eye upon the manœuvres of the savages, and not permitting them to divide our numbers by pushing in between. In this way, passing through a precipitous ravine, we at length reached what we were told was the only collection of habitations upon the island. As we came in sight of them, the chief set up a shout, and frequently repeated the word *Klock-Klock;*[1] which we supposed to be the name of the village, or perhaps the generic name for villages.

The dwellings were of the most miserable description imaginable, and, unlike those of even the lowest of the savage races with which mankind are acquainted, were of no uniform plan. Some of them (and these we found belonged to the *Wampoos* or *Yampoos,*[2] the great men of the land) consisted of a tree cut down at about four feet from the root, with a large black skin thrown over it, and hanging in loose folds upon the ground. Under this the savage nestled. Others were formed by means of rough limbs of trees, with the withered foliage upon them, made to recline, at an angle of forty-five degrees, against a bank of clay, heaped up, without regular form, to the height of five or six feet. Others, again, were mere holes dug in the earth perpendicularly, and covered over with similar branches, these being removed when the tenant was about to enter, and pulled on again when he had entered. A few were built among the forked limbs of trees as they stood, the upper limbs being partially cut through, so as to bend over upon the lower, thus forming thicker shelter from the weather. The greater number, however, consisted of small shallow caverns, apparently scratched in the face of a precipitous ledge of dark stone, resembling fuller's earth, with which three sides of the village was bounded. At the door of each of these primitive caverns was a small rock, which the tenant carefully placed before the entrance upon leaving his residence, for what purpose I could not ascertain, as the stone itself was never of sufficient size to close up more than a third of the opening.

This village, if it were worthy of the name, lay in a valley of some depth, and could only be approached from the southward, the precipitous ledge of which I have already spoken cutting off all access in other directions. Through the middle of the valley ran a brawling stream of the same magical-looking water which has been described. We saw several strange animals about the dwellings, all appearing to be thoroughly domesticated. The largest of these creatures resembled our common hog in the structure of the body and snout; the tail, however, was bushy, and the legs slender as those of the antelope. Its motion was exceedingly awkward and indecisive, and we never saw it attempt to run. We noticed also several animals very similar in appearance, but of a greater length of body, and covered with a black wool. There were a great variety of tame fowls running about, and these seemed to constitute the chief food of the natives. To our astonishment we saw black albatross among these birds in a state of entire domestication, going to sea periodically for food, but always returning to the village as a home, and using the southern shore in the vicinity as a place of incubation. There they were joined by their friends the pelicans as usual,[3] but these latter never followed them to the dwellings of the savages. Among the other kinds of tame fowls were ducks, differing very little from the canvass-back of our own country, black gannets, and a large bird not unlike the buzzard in appearance, but not carnivorous. Of fish there seemed to be a great abundance. We saw, during our visit, a quantity of dried salmon, rock cod, blue dolphins, mackerel, blackfish, skate, conger eels, elephantfish, mullets, soles, parrotfish, leather-jackets, gurnards, hake, flounders, paracutas, and innumerable other varieties.[4] We noticed, too, that most of them were similar to the fish about the group of the Lord Auckland Islands, in a latitude as low as fifty-one degrees south. The Gallipago tortoise was also very plentiful. We saw but few wild animals, and none of a large size, or of a species with which we were familiar. One or two serpents of a formidable aspect crossed our path, but the natives paid them little attention, and we concluded that they were not venomous.

As we approached the village with Too-wit and his party, a vast crowd of the people rushed out to meet us, with loud shouts, among which we could only distinguish the everlasting *Anamoo-moo!* and *Lama-Lama!* We were much surprised at perceiving that, with one or two exceptions, these new comers were entirely naked, the skins being used only by the men of the canoes. All the weapons of the country seemed also to be in the possession of the latter, for there was no appearance of any among the villagers. There were a great many women and children, the former not altogether wanting in what might be termed personal beauty.[5] They were straight, tall, and well formed, with a grace and freedom of carriage not to be found in civilized society. Their lips, however, like those of the men, were thick and clumsy, so that, even when laughing, the teeth were never disclosed. Their hair was of a finer texture than that of the males. Among these naked villagers there might have been ten or twelve who were clothed, like the party of Too-wit, in dresses of black skin, and armed with lances and heavy clubs. These appeared to have great influence among the rest, and were always addressed by the title *Wampoo*. These, too, were the tenants of the black skin palaces. That of Too-wit was situated in the centre of the village, and was much larger and somewhat better constructed than others of its kind. The tree which formed its support was cut off at a distance of twelve feet or thereabout from the root, and there were several branches left just below the cut, these serving to extend the covering, and in this way prevent its flapping about the trunk. The covering, too, which consisted of four very large skins fastened together with wooden skewers, was secured at the bottom with pegs driven through it and into the ground. The floor was strewed with a quantity of dry leaves by way of carpet.

To this hut we were conducted with great solemnity, and as many of the natives crowded in after us as possible. Too-wit seated himself on the leaves, and made signs that we should follow his example. This we did, and presently found ourselves in a situation peculiarly uncomfortable, if not indeed critical. We were on the ground, twelve in number, with the savages, as many as forty, sitting on their hams so closely around us that, if any disturbance had arisen, we should have found it impossible to make use of our arms, or indeed to have risen on our feet. The pressure was not only inside the tent, but outside, where probably was every individual on the whole island, the crowd being prevented from trampling us to death only by the incessant exertions and vociferations of Too-wit. Our chief security lay, however, in the presence of Too-wit himself among us, and we resolved to stick by him closely, as the best chance of extricating ourselves from the dilemma, sacrificing him immediately upon the first appearance of hostile design.

After some trouble a certain degree of quiet was restored,

when the chief addressed us in a speech of great length, and
very nearly resembling the one delivered in the canoes, with
the exception that the *Anamoo-moos!* were now somewhat
more strenuously insisted upon than the *Lama-Lamas!* We
listened in profound silence until the conclusion of his harangue, when Captain Guy replied by assuring the chief of his
eternal friendship and goodwill, concluding what he had to
say by a present of several strings of blue beads and a knife. At
the former the monarch, much to our surprise, turned up his
nose with some expression of contempt; but the knife gave
him the most unlimited satisfaction, and he immediately ordered dinner. This was handed into the tent over the heads of
the attendants, and consisted of the palpitating entrails of a
species of unknown animal, probably one of the slim-legged
hogs which we had observed in our approach to the village.[6]
Seeing us at a loss how to proceed, he began, by way of setting
us an example, to devour yard after yard of the enticing food,
until we could positively stand it no longer, and evinced such
manifest symptoms of rebellion of stomach as inspired his
majesty with a degree of astonishment only inferior to that
brought about by the looking-glasses. We declined, however,
partaking of the delicacies before us, and endeavoured to
make him understand that we had no appetite whatever, having just finished a hearty *déjeuner*.

When the monarch had made an end of his meal, we commenced a series of cross-questioning[7] in every ingenious manner we could devise, with a view of discovering what were the
chief productions of the country, and whether any of them
might be turned to profit. At length he seemed to have some
idea of our meaning, and offered to accompany us to a part of
the coast where he assured us the *biche de mer* (pointing to a
specimen of that animal) was to be found in great abundance.
We were glad at this early opportunity of escaping from the
oppression of the crowd, and signified our eagerness to proceed. We now left the tent, and, accompanied by the whole

population of the village, followed the chief to the southeastern extremity of the island, not far from the bay where our
vessel lay at anchor. We waited here for about an hour, until
the four canoes were brought round by some of the savages to
our station. The whole of our party then getting into one of
them, we were paddled along the edge of the reef before mentioned, and of another still farther out, where we saw a far
greater quantity of *biche de mer* than the oldest seaman
among us had ever seen in those groups of the lower latitudes
most celebrated for this article of commerce. We stayed near
these reefs only long enough to satisfy ourselves that we could
easily load a dozen vessels with the animal if necessary, when
we were taken alongside the schooner, and parted with Too-
wit after obtaining from him a promise that he would bring
us, in the course of twenty-four hours, as many of the
canvass-back ducks and Gallipago tortoises as his canoes
would hold. In the whole of this adventure we saw nothing in
the demeanour of the natives calculated to create suspicion,
with the single exception of the systematic manner in which
their party was strengthened during our route from the
schooner to the village.

CHAPTER 20

The chief was as good as his word, and we were soon plenti-
fully supplied with fresh provision. We found the tortoises as
fine as we had ever seen, and the ducks surpassed our best
species of wild fowl, being exceedingly tender, juicy, and
well-flavoured. Besides these, the savages brought us, upon
our making them comprehend our wishes, a vast quantity of
brown celery and scurvy grass, with a canoe-load of fresh fish
and some dried. The celery was a treat indeed, and the scurvy
grass proved of incalculable benefit in restoring those of our
men who had shown symptoms of disease. In a very short
time we had not a single person on the sick-list. We had also
plenty of other kinds of fresh provision, among which may be
mentioned a species of shellfish resembling the muscle in
shape, but with the taste of an oyster. Shrimps, too, and
prawns were abundant, and albatross and other birds' eggs
with dark shells. We took in, too, a plentiful stock of the flesh
of the hog which I have mentioned before. Most of the men
found it a palatable food, but I thought it fishy and otherwise
disagreeable. In return for these good things we presented the
natives with blue beads, brass trinkets, nails, knives, and
pieces of red cloth, they being fully delighted in the exchange.
We established a regular market on shore, just under the guns
of the schooner, where our barterings were carried on with
every appearance of good faith, and a degree of order which
their conduct at the village of *Klock-klock* had not led us to
expect from the savages.

Matters went on thus very amicably for several days, during which parties of the natives were frequently on board the
schooner, and parties of our men frequently on shore, making

long excursions into the interior, and receiving no molestation whatever. Finding the ease with which the vessel might be loaded with *biche de mer,* owing to the friendly disposition of the islanders, and the readiness with which they would render us assistance in collecting it, Captain Guy resolved to enter into negotiation with Too-wit for the erection of suitable houses in which to cure the article, and for the services of himself and tribe in gathering as much as possible, while he himself took advantage of the fine weather to prosecute his voyage to the southward. Upon mentioning this project to the chief he seemed very willing to enter into an agreement. A bargain was accordingly struck, perfectly satisfactory to both parties, by which it was arranged that, after making the necessary preparations, such as laying off the proper grounds, erecting a portion of the buildings, and doing some other work in which the whole of our crew would be required, the schooner should proceed on her route, leaving three of her men on the island to superintend the fulfilment of the project, and instruct the natives in drying the *biche de mer.* In regard to terms, these were made to depend upon the exertions of the savages in our absence. They were to receive a stipulated quantity of blue beads, knives, red cloth, and so forth, for every certain number of piculs of the *biche de mer* which should be ready on our return.[1]

A description of the nature of this important article of commerce, and the method of preparing it, may prove of some interest to my readers, and I can find no more suitable place than this for introducing an account of it. The following comprehensive notice of the substance is taken from a modern history of a voyage to the South Seas.

"It is that *mollusca* from the Indian Seas which is known in commerce by the French name *bouche de mer* (a nice morsel from the sea). If I am not much mistaken, the celebrated Cuvier calls it *gasteropeda pulmonifera.* It is abundantly gathered in the coasts of the Pacific Islands, and gathered especially for the Chinese market, where it commands a great price, perhaps as much as their much-talked-of edible bird's nests, which are probably made up of the gelatinous matter picked up by a species of swallow from the body of these molluscæ. They have no shell, no legs, nor any prominent part, except an *absorbing* and an *excretory,* opposite organs; but, by their elastic wings,[2] like caterpillars or worms, they creep in shallow waters, in which, when low, they can be seen by a kind of swallow, the sharp bill of which, inserted in the soft animal, draws a gummy and filamentous substance, which, by drying, can be wrought into the solid walls of their nest. Hence the name of *gasteropeda pulmonifera.*

"This mollusca is oblong, and of different sizes, from three to eighteen inches in length; and I have seen a few that were not less than two feet long. They are nearly round, a little flattish on one side, which lies next the bottom of the sea; and they are from one to eight inches thick. They crawl up into shallow water at particular seasons of the year, probably for the purpose of gendering, as we often find them in pairs. It is when the sun has the most power on the water, rendering it tepid, that they approach the shore; and they often go up into places so shallow, that, on the tide's receding, they are left dry, exposed to the heat of the sun. But they do not bring forth their young in shallow water, as we never see any of their progeny, and the full-grown ones are always observed coming in from deep water. They feed principally on that class of zoophytes which produce the coral.

"The *biche de mer* is generally taken in three or four feet water; after which they are brought on shore, and split at one end with a knife, the incision being one inch or more, according to the size of the mollusca. Through this opening the entrails are forced out by pressure, and they are much like those of any other small tenant of the deep. The article is then washed, and afterward boiled to a certain degree, which must not be too much or too little. They are then buried in the ground for four hours, then boiled again for a short time, after which they are dried, either by the fire or the sun. Those cured by the sun are worth the most; but where one picul (133⅓ lbs.) can be cured that way, I can cure thirty piculs by the fire. When once properly cured, they can be kept in a dry place for two or three years without any risk; but they should be examined once in every few months, say four times a year, to see if any dampness is likely to affect them.

"The Chinese, as before stated, consider *biche de mer* a very great luxury, believing that it wonderfully strengthens and nourishes the system, and renews the exhausted system of the immoderate voluptuary. The first quality commands a high price in Canton, being worth ninety dollars a picul; the second quality seventy-five dollars; the third fifty dollars; the fourth thirty dollars; the fifth twenty dollars; the sixth twelve dollars; the seventh eight dollars; and the eighth four dollars; small cargoes, however, will often bring more in Manilla, Singapore, and Batavia."

An agreement having been thus entered into, we proceeded immediately to land everything necessary for preparing the buildings and clearing the ground. A large flat space near the eastern shore of the bay was selected, where there was plenty both of wood and water, and within a convenient distance of the principal reefs on which the *biche de mer* was to be procured. We now all set to work in good earnest, and soon, to the great astonishment of the savages, had felled a sufficient number of trees for our purpose, getting them quickly in order for the framework of the houses, which in two or three days were so far under way that we could safely trust the rest of the work to the three men whom we intended to leave behind. These were John Carson, Alfred Harris, and ——— Peterson (all natives of London, I believe), who volunteered their services in this respect.

By the last of the month we had everything in readiness for departure. We had agreed, however, to pay a formal visit of leavestaking to the village, and Too-wit insisted so pertinaciously upon our keeping the promise, that we did not think it advisable to run the risk of offending him by a final refusal. I believe that not one of us had at this time the slightest suspicion of the good faith of the savages. They had uniformly behaved with the greatest decorum, aiding us with alacrity in our work, offering us their commodities frequently without price, and never, in any instance, pilfering a single article, although the high value they set upon the goods we had with us was evident by the extravagant demonstrations of joy always manifested upon our making them a present. The women especially were most obliging in every respect, and, upon the whole, we should have been the most suspicious of human beings had we entertained a single thought of perfidy on the part of a people who treated us so well. A very short while sufficed to prove that this apparent kindness of disposition was only the result of a deeply-laid plan for our destruction, and that the islanders for whom we entertained such inordinate feelings of esteem were among the most barbarous, subtle, and bloodthirsty wretches that ever contaminated the face of the globe.

It was on the first of February that we went on shore for the purpose of visiting the village. Although, as said before, we entertained not the slightest suspicion, still no proper precaution was neglected. Six men were left in the schooner with instructions to permit none of the savages to approach the vessel during our absence, under any pretence whatever, and to remain constantly on deck. The boarding-nettings were up, the guns double-shotted with grape and canister, and the swivels loaded with canisters of musket-balls. She lay, with her anchor apeak, about a mile from the shore, and no canoe could approach her in any direction without being distinctly seen and exposed to the full fire of our swivels immediately.

The six men being left on board, our shore-party consisted of thirty-two persons in all. We were armed to the teeth,[3] having with us muskets, pistols, and cutlasses, besides each a long kind of seaman's knife, somewhat resembling the Bowie knife now so much used throughout our western and southern country. A hundred of the black skin warriors met us at the landing for the purpose of accompanying us on our way. We noticed, however, with some surprise, that they were now entirely without arms; and, upon questioning Too-wit in relation to this circumstance, he merely answered that *Mattee non we pa pa si*—meaning that there was no need of arms where all were brothers.[4] We took this in good part, and proceeded.

We had passed the spring and rivulet of which I before spoke, and were now entering upon a narrow gorge leading through the chain of soapstone hills among which the village was situated.[5] This gorge was very rocky and uneven, so much so that it was with no little difficulty we scrambled through it on our first visit to Klock-klock. The whole length of the ravine might have been a mile and a half, or probably two miles. It wound in every possible direction through the hills (having apparently formed, at some remote period, the bed of a torrent), in no instance proceeding more than twenty yards without an abrupt turn. The sides of this dell would have averaged, I am sure, seventy or eighty feet in perpendicular altitude throughout the whole of their extent, and in some portions they arose to an astonishing height, overshadowing the pass so completely that but little of the light of day could penetrate. The general width was about forty feet, and occasionally it diminished so as not to allow the passage of more than five or six persons abreast. In short, there could be no place in the world better adapted for the consummation of an ambuscade, and it was no more than natural that we should look carefully to our arms as we entered upon it. When I now think of our egregious folly, the chief subject of astonishment seems to be, that we should have ever ventured, under any circumstances, so completely into the power of unknown savages as to permit them to march both before and behind us in our progress through this ravine. Yet such was the order we blindly took up, trusting foolishly to the force of our party, the unarmed condition of Too-wit and his men, the certain efficacy of our firearms (whose effect was yet a secret to the natives), and, more than all, to the long-sustained pretension of friendship kept up by these infamous wretches. Five or six of them went on before, as if to lead the way, ostentatiously busying themselves in removing the larger stones and rubbish from the path. Next came our own party. We walked closely together, taking care only to prevent separation. Behind followed the main body of the savages, observing unusual order and decorum.

Dirk Peters, a man named Wilson Allen, and myself were on the right of our companions, examining, as we went along, the singular stratification of the precipice which overhung us. A fissure in the soft rock attracted our attention. It was about wide enough for one person to enter without squeezing, and extended back into the hill some eighteen or twenty feet in a straight course, sloping afterward to the left. The height of the opening, as far as we could see into it from the main gorge, was perhaps sixty or seventy feet. There were one or two stunted shrubs growing from the crevices, bearing a species of filbert, which I felt some curiosity to examine, and pushed in briskly for that purpose, gathering five or six of the nuts at a grasp, and then hastily retreating. As I turned, I found that Peters and Allen had followed me. I desired them to go back, as there was not room for two persons to pass, saying they should have some of my nuts. They accordingly turned, and were scrambling back, Allen being close to the mouth of the fissure, when I was suddenly aware of a concussion resembling nothing I had ever before experienced, and which impressed me with a vague conception, if indeed I then thought of anything, that the whole foundations of the solid globe were suddenly rent asunder, and that the day of universal dissolution was at hand.[6]

CHAPTER 21

As soon as I could collect my scattered senses, I found myself nearly suffocated, and grovelling in utter darkness among a quantity of loose earth, which was also falling upon me heavily in every direction, threatening to bury me entirely. Horribly alarmed at this idea, I struggled to gain my feet, and at length succeeded. I then remained motionless for some moments, endeavouring to conceive what had happened to me, and where I was. Presently I heard a deep groan just at my ear, and afterward the smothered voice of Peters calling to me for aid in the name of God. I scrambled one or two paces forward, when I fell directly over the head and shoulders of my companion, who, I soon discovered, was buried in a loose mass of earth as far as his middle, and struggling desperately to free himself from the pressure. I tore the dirt from around him with all the energy I could command, and at length succeeded in getting him out.

As soon as we sufficiently recovered from our fright and surprise to be capable of conversing rationally, we both came to the conclusion that the walls of the fissure in which we had ventured had, by some convulsion of nature, or probably from their own weight, caved in overhead, and that we were consequently lost for ever, being thus entombed alive. For a long time we gave up supinely to the most intense agony and despair, such as cannot be adequately imagined by those who have never been in a similar situation. I firmly believe that no incident ever occurring in the course of human events is more adapted to inspire the supremeness of mental and bodily distress than a case like our own, of living inhumation. The blackness of darkness which envelops the victim, the terrific oppression of lungs, the stifling fumes from the damp earth, unite with the ghastly considerations that we are beyond the remotest confines of hope, and that such is the allotted portion of *the dead,* to carry into the human heart a degree of appalling awe and horror not to be tolerated—never to be conceived.[1]

At length Peters proposed that we should endeavour to ascertain precisely the extent of our calamity, and grope about our prison; it being barely possible, he observed, that some opening might be yet left us for escape. I caught eagerly at this hope, and, arousing myself to exertion, attempted to force my way through the loose earth. Hardly had I advanced a single step before a glimmer of light became perceptible, enough to convince me that, at all events, we should not immediately perish for want of air. We now took some degree of heart, and encouraged each other to hope for the best. Having scrambled over a bank of rubbish which impeded our farther progress in the direction of the light, we found less difficulty in advancing, and also experienced some relief from the excessive oppression of lungs which had tormented us. Presently we were enabled to obtain a glimpse of the objects around, and discovered that we were near the extremity of the straight portion of the fissure, where it made a turn to the left. A few struggles more, and we reached the bend, when, to our inexpressible joy, there appeared a long seam or crack extending upward a vast distance, generally at an angle of about forty-five degrees, although sometimes much more precipitous. We could not see through the whole extent of this opening; but, as a good deal of light came down it, we had little doubt of finding at the top of it (if we could by any means reach the top) a clear passage into the open air.

I now called to mind that three of us had entered the fissure from the main gorge, and that our companion, Allen, was still missing; we determined at once to retrace our steps and look for him. After a long search, and much danger from the far-

ther caving in of the earth above us, Peters at length cried out
to me that he had hold of our companion's foot, and that his
whole body was deeply buried beneath the rubbish, beyond a
possibility of extricating him. I soon found that what he said
was too true, and that, of course, life had been long extinct.
With sorrowful hearts, therefore, we left the corpse to its fate,
and again made our way to the bend.

The breadth of the seam was barely sufficient to admit us,
and, after one or two ineffectual efforts at getting up, we began once more to despair. I have before said that the chain of
hills through which ran the main gorge was composed of a
species of soft rock resembling soapstone. The sides of the
cleft we were now attempting to ascend were of the same material, and so excessively slippery, being wet, that we could get
but little foothold upon them even in their least precipitous
parts; in some places, where the ascent was nearly perpendicular, the difficulty was, of course, much aggravated; and, indeed, for some time we thought it insurmountable.[2] We took
courage, however, from despair; and what, by dint of cutting
steps in the soft stone with our Bowie knives, and swinging, at
the risk of our lives, to small projecting points of a harder
species of slaty rock which now and then protruded from the
general mass, we at length reached a natural platform, from
which was perceptible a patch of blue sky, at the extremity of
a thickly-wooded ravine. Looking back now, with somewhat
more leisure, at the passage through which we had thus far
proceeded, we clearly saw, from the appearance of its sides,
that it was of late formation, and we concluded that the concussion, whatever it was, which had so unexpectedly overwhelmed us, had also, at the same moment, laid open this path
for escape. Being quite exhausted with exertion, and, indeed,
so weak that we were scarcely able to stand or articulate, Peters now proposed that we should endeavour to bring our
companions to the rescue by firing the pistols which still remained in our girdles—the muskets as well as cutlasses had

been lost among the loose earth at the bottom of the chasm. Subsequent events proved that, had we fired, we should have sorely repented it; but, luckily, a half suspicion of foul play had by this time arisen in my mind, and we forbore to let the savages know of our whereabouts.

After having reposed for about an hour, we pushed on slowly up the ravine, and had gone no great way before we heard a succession of tremendous yells. At length we reached what might be called the surface of the ground; for our path hitherto, since leaving the platform, had lain beneath an arch-way of high rock and foliage, at a vast distance overhead. With great caution we stole to a narrow opening, through which we had a clear sight of the surrounding country, when the whole dreadful secret of the concussion broke upon us in one moment and at one view.

The spot from which we looked was not far from the summit of the highest peak in the range of the soapstone hills. The gorge in which our party of thirty-two had entered ran within fifty feet to the left of us. But, for at least one hundred yards, the channel or bed of this gorge was entirely filled up with the chaotic ruins of more than a million tons of earth and stone that had been artificially tumbled within it. The means by which the vast mass had been precipitated were not more simple than evident, for sure traces of the murderous work were yet remaining. In several spots along the top of the eastern ridge of the gorge (we were now on the western) might be seen stakes of wood driven into the earth.[3] In these spots the earth had not given way; but throughout the whole extent of the face of the precipice from which the mass *had* fallen, it was clear, from marks left in the soil resembling those made by the drill of the rock-blaster, that stakes similar to those we saw standing had been inserted, at not more than a yard apart, for the length of perhaps three hundred feet, and ranging at about ten feet back from the edge of the gulf. Strong cords of grape vine were attached to the stakes still remaining on the hill, and it was evident that such cords had also been attached to each of the other stakes. I have already spoken of the singular stratification of these soapstone hills; and the description just given of the narrow and deep fissure through which we effected our escape from inhumation will afford a further conception of its nature. This was such that almost every natural convulsion would be sure to split the soil into perpendicular layers or ridges running parallel with one another; and a very moderate exertion of art would be sufficient for effecting the same purpose. Of this stratification the savages had availed themselves to accomplish their treacherous ends. There can be no doubt that, by the continuous line of stakes, a partial rupture of the soil had been brought about, probably to the depth of one or two feet, when, by means of a savage pulling at the end of each of the cords (these cords being attached to the tops of the stakes, and extending back from the edge of the cliff), a vast leverage power was obtained, capable of hurling the whole face of the hill, upon a given signal, into the bosom of the abyss below. The fate of our poor companions was no longer a matter of uncertainty. We alone had escaped from the tempest of that overwhelming destruction. We were the only living white men upon the island.[4]

CHAPTER 22

Our situation, as it now appeared, was scarcely less dreadful than when we had conceived ourselves entombed for ever. We saw before us no prospect but that of being put to death by the savages, or of dragging out a miserable existence in captivity among them.[1] We might, to be sure, conceal ourselves for a time from their observation among the fastnesses of the hills, and, as a final resort, in the chasm from which we had just issued; but we must either perish in the long Polar winter through cold and famine, or be ultimately discovered in our efforts to obtain relief.

The whole country around us seemed to be swarming with savages, crowds of whom, we now perceived, had come over from the islands to the southward on flat rafts, doubtless with a view of lending their aid in the capture and plunder of the Jane. The vessel still lay calmly at anchor in the bay, those on board being apparently quite unconscious of any danger awaiting them. How we longed at that moment to be with them! either to aid in effecting their escape, or to perish with them in attempting a defence. We saw no chance even of warning them of their danger without bringing immediate destruction upon our own heads, with but a remote hope of benefit to them. A pistol fired might suffice to apprize them that something wrong had occurred; but the report could not possibly inform them that their only prospect of safety lay in getting out of the harbour forthwith—it could not tell them that no principles of honour now bound them to remain, that their companions were no longer among the living. Upon hearing the discharge they could not be more thoroughly prepared to meet the foe, who were now getting ready to attack,

than they already were, and always had been. No good, therefore, and infinite harm, would result from our firing, and, after mature deliberation, we forbore.

Our next thought was to attempt a rush towards the vessel,
to seize one of the four canoes which lay at the head of the
bay, and endeavour to force a passage on board. But the utter
impossibility of succeeding in this desperate task soon became
evident. The country, as I said before, was literally swarming
with the natives, skulking among the bushes and recesses of
the hills, so as not to be observed from the schooner. In our
immediate vicinity especially, and blockading the sole path[2]
by which we could hope to attain the shore in the proper
point, were stationed the whole party of the black skin warriors, with Too-wit at their head, and apparently only waiting
for some re-enforcement to commence his onset upon the
Jane. The canoes, too, which lay at the head of the bay were
manned with savages, unarmed, it is true, but who undoubtedly had arms within reach. We were forced, therefore, however unwillingly, to remain in our place of concealment, mere
spectators of the conflict which presently ensued.

In about half an hour we saw some sixty or seventy rafts,
or flatboats, with outriggers, filled with savages, and coming
round the southern bight of the harbour. They appeared to
have no arms except short clubs, and stones which lay in the
bottom of the rafts. Immediately afterward another detachment, still larger, approached in an opposite direction, and
with similar weapons. The four canoes, too, were now quickly
filled with natives, starting up from the bushes at the head of
the bay, and put off swiftly to join the other parties. Thus, in
less time than I have taken to tell it,[3] and as if by magic, the
Jane saw herself surrounded by an immense multitude of des-
peradoes evidently bent upon capturing her at all hazards.

That they would succeed in so doing could not be doubted
for an instant.[4] The six men left in the vessel, however res-
olutely they might engage in her defence, were altogether un-

equal to the proper management of the guns, or in any manner to sustain a contest at such odds. I could hardly imagine
that they would make resistance at all, but in this was deceived; for presently I saw them get springs upon the cable,
and bring the vessel's starboard broadside to bear upon the
canoes, which by this time were within pistol range, the rafts
being nearly a quarter of a mile to windward. Owing to some
cause unknown, but most probably to the agitation of our
poor friends at seeing themselves in so hopeless a situation,
the discharge was an entire failure. Not a canoe was hit or a
single savage injured, the shots striking short and *ricochêting*
over their heads. The only effect produced upon them was astonishment at the unexpected report and smoke, which was so
excessive that for some moments I almost thought they would
abandon their design entirely, and return to the shore. And
this they would most likely have done had our men followed
up their broadside by a discharge of small arms, in which, as
the canoes were now so near at hand, they could not have
failed in doing some execution, sufficient, at least, to deter this
party from a farther advance, until they could have given the
rafts also a broadside. But, in place of this, they left the canoe
party to recover from their panic, and, by looking about them,
to see that no injury had been sustained, while they flew to
the larboard to get ready for the rafts.

The discharge to larboard produced the most terrible effect. The star and double-headed shot of the large guns cut
seven or eight of the rafts completely asunder, and killed, perhaps, thirty or forty of the savages outright,[5] while a hundred
of them, at least, were thrown into the water, the most of
them dreadfully wounded. The remainder, frightened out of
their senses, commenced at once a precipitate retreat, not even
waiting to pick up their maimed companions, who were
swimming about in every direction, screaming and yelling for
aid. This great success, however, came too late for the salva-
tion of our devoted people. The canoe party were already on

board the schooner to the number of more than a hundred and fifty, the most of them having succeeded in scrambling up the chains and over the boarding nettings even before the matches had been applied to the larboard guns. Nothing could now withstand their brute rage. Our men were borne down at once, overwhelmed, trodden under foot, and absolutely torn to pieces in an instant.

Seeing this, the savages on the rafts got the better of their fears, and came up in shoals to the plunder. In five minutes the Jane was a pitiable scene indeed of havoc and tumultuous outrage. The decks were split open and ripped up; the cordage, sails, and everything moveable on deck demolished as if by magic; while, by dint of pushing at the stern, towing with the canoes, and hauling at the sides, as they swam in thousands around the vessel, the wretches finally forced her on shore (the cable having been slipped), and delivered her over to the good offices of Too-wit, who, during the whole of the engagement, had maintained, like a skilful general, his post of security and reconnoissance among the hills, but, now that the victory was completed to his satisfaction, condescended to scamper down with his warriors of the black skin, and become a partaker in the spoils.

Too-wit's descent left us at liberty to quit our hiding-place and reconnoitre the hill in the vicinity of the chasm. At about fifty yards from the mouth of it we saw a small spring of water, at which we slaked the burning thirst that now consumed us. Not far from the spring we discovered several of the filbert-bushes which I mentioned before. Upon tasting the nuts we found them palatable, and very nearly resembling in flavour the common English filbert. We collected our hats full immediately, deposited them within the ravine, and returned for more. While we were busily employed in gathering these, a rustling in the bushes alarmed us, and we were upon the point of stealing back to our covert, when a large black bird of the bittern species strugglingly and slowly arose above the shrubs.[6] I was so much startled that I could do nothing, but Peters had sufficient presence of mind to run up to it before it could make its escape, and seize it by the neck. Its struggles and screams were tremendous, and we had thoughts of letting it go, lest the noise should alarm some of the savages who might be still lurking in the neighbourhood. A stab with a Bowie knife, however, at length brought it to the ground, and we dragged it into the ravine, congratulating ourselves that, at all events, we had thus obtained a supply of food enough to last us for a week.

We now went out again to look about us, and ventured a considerable distance down the southern declivity of the hill, but met with nothing else which could serve us for food. We therefore collected a quantity of dry wood and returned, seeing one or two large parties of the natives on their way to the village, laden with the plunder of the vessel, and who, we were apprehensive, might discover us in passing beneath the hill.

Our next care was to render our place of concealment as secure as possible, and, with this object, we arranged some brushwood over the aperture which I have before spoken of as the one through which we saw the patch of blue sky, on reaching the platform from the interior of the chasm. We left only a very small opening, just wide enough to admit of our seeing the bay, without the risk of being discovered from below. Having done this, we congratulated ourselves upon the security of the position; for we were now completely excluded from observation, as long as we chose to remain within the ravine itself, and not venture out upon the hill. We could perceive no traces of the savages having ever been within this hollow; but, indeed, when we came to reflect upon the probability that the fissure through which we attained it had been only just now created by the fall of the cliff opposite, and that no other way of attaining it could be perceived, we were not

so much rejoiced at the thought of being secure from molestation as fearful lest there should be absolutely no means left us
for descent. We resolved to explore the summit of the hill
thoroughly, when a good opportunity should offer. In the
mean time we watched the motions of the savages through
our loophole.

They had already made a complete wreck of the vessel, and
were now preparing to set her on fire.[7] In a little while we
saw the smoke ascending in huge volumes from her main-
hatchway, and, shortly afterward, a dense mass of flame burst
up from the forecastle. The rigging, masts, and what remained
of the sails caught immediately, and the fire spread rapidly
along the decks. Still a great many of the savages retained their
stations about her, hammering with large stones, axes, and
cannon balls at the bolts and other copper and iron work. On
the beach, and in canoes and rafts, there were not less, altogether, in the immediate vicinity of the schooner, than ten
thousand natives, besides the shoals of them who, laden with
booty, were making their way inland and over to the neigh-
bouring islands. We now anticipated a catastrophe, and were
not disappointed. First of all there came a smart shock (which
we felt distinctly where we were as if we had been slightly gal-
vanized), but unattended with any visible signs of an explosion. The savages were evidently startled, and paused for an
instant from their labours and yellings. They were upon the
point of recommencing, when suddenly a mass of smoke
puffed up from the decks, resembling a black and heavy
thunder-cloud—then, as if from its bowels, arose a tall stream
of vivid fire to the height, apparently, of a quarter of a mile—
then there came a sudden circular expansion of the flame—
then the whole atmosphere was magically crowded, in a single
instant, with a wild chaos of wood, and metal, and human
limbs—and, lastly, came the concussion in its fullest fury,
which hurled us impetuously from our feet, while the hills
echoed and re-echoed the tumult, and a dense shower of the

minutest fragments of the ruins tumbled headlong in every direction around us.

The havoc among the savages far exceeded our utmost expectation, and they had now, indeed, reaped the full and perfect fruits of their treachery. Perhaps a thousand perished by the explosion, while at least an equal number were desperately mangled. The whole surface of the bay was literally strewn with the struggling and drowning wretches, and on shore matters were even worse. They seemed utterly appalled by the suddenness and completeness of their discomfiture, and made no efforts at assisting one another. At length we observed a total change in their demeanour. From absolute stupor they appeared to be, all at once, aroused to the highest pitch of excitement, and rushed wildly about, going to and from a certain point on the beach, with the strangest expressions of mingled horror, rage, and intense curiosity depicted on their countenances, and shouting, at the top of their voices, *Tekeli-li! Tekeli-li!*[8]

Presently we saw a large body go off into the hills, whence they returned in a short time, carrying stakes of wood. These they brought to the station where the crowd was the thickest, which now separated so as to afford us a view of the object of all this excitement. We perceived something white lying on the ground, but could not immediately make out what it was. At length we saw that it was the carcass of the strange animal with the scarlet teeth and claws which the schooner had picked up at sea on the eighteenth of January. Captain Guy had had the body preserved for the purpose of stuffing the skin and taking it to England. I remember he had given some directions about it just before our making the island, and it had been brought into the cabin and stowed away in one of the lockers. It had now been thrown on shore by the explosion; but why it had occasioned so much concern among the savages was more than we could comprehend. Although they crowded around the carcass at a little distance, none of them

seemed willing to approach it closely. By-and-by the men
with the stakes drove them in a circle around it, and, no
sooner was this arrangement completed, than the whole of the
vast assembly rushed into the interior of the island, with loud
screams of *Tekeli-li! Tekeli-li!*

During the six or seven days immediately following we remained in our hiding-place upon the hill, going out only occasionally, and then with the greatest precaution, for water and filberts. We had made a kind of penthouse on the platform, furnishing it with a bed of dry leaves, and placing in it three large flat stones, which served us for both fireplace and table. We kindled a fire without difficulty by rubbing two pieces of dry wood together, the one soft, the other hard. The bird we had taken in such good season proved excellent eating, although somewhat tough. It was not an oceanic fowl, but a species of bittern, with jet black and grizzly plumage, and diminutive wings in proportion to its bulk. We afterward saw three of the same kind in the vicinity of the ravine, apparently seeking for the one we had captured; but, as they never alighted, we had no opportunity of catching them.

As long as this fowl lasted we suffered nothing from our situation; but it was now entirely consumed, and it became absolutely necessary that we should look out for provision. The filberts would not satisfy the cravings of hunger, afflicting us, too, with severe gripings of the bowels, and, if freely indulged in, with violent headache. We had seen several large tortoises near the seashore to the eastward of the hill, and perceived they might be easily taken, if we could get at them without the observation of the natives. It was resolved, therefore, to make an attempt at descending.

We commenced by going down the southern declivity, which seemed to offer the fewest difficulties, but had not proceeded a hundred yards before (as we had anticipated from appearances on the hill-top) our progress was entirely arrested

by a branch of the gorge in which our companions had perished. We now passed along the edge of this for about a quarter of a mile, when we were again stopped by a precipice of
immense depth, and, not being able to make our way along
the brink of it, we were forced to retrace our steps by the
main ravine.

We now pushed over to the eastward, but with precisely
similar fortune. After an hour's scramble, at the risk of breaking our necks, we discovered that we had merely descended
into a vast pit of black granite, with fine dust at the bottom,
and whence the only egress was by the rugged path in which
we had come down. Toiling again up this path, we now tried
the northern edge of the hill. Here we were obliged to use the
greatest possible caution in our manœuvres, as the least indis-
cretion would expose us to the full view of the savages in the
village. We crawled along, therefore, on our hands and knees,
and, occasionally, were even forced to throw ourselves at full
length, dragging our bodies along by means of the shrubbery.
In this careful manner we had proceeded but a little way,
when we arrived at a chasm far deeper than any we had yet
seen, and leading directly into the main gorge. Thus our fears
were fully confirmed, and we found ourselves cut off entirely
from access to the world below. Thoroughly exhausted by
our exertions, we made the best of our way back to the platform, and, throwing ourselves upon the bed of leaves, slept
sweetly and soundly for some hours.

For several days after this fruitless search we were occupied
in exploring every part of the summit of the hill, in order to
inform ourselves of its actual resources. We found that it
would afford us no food, with the exception of the unwhole-
some filberts, and a rank species of scurvy grass which grew in
a little patch of not more than four rods square, and would be
soon exhausted. On the fifteenth of February, as near as I can
remember, there was not a blade of this left, and the nuts were
growing scarce; our situation, therefore, could hardly be more

lamentable.* On the sixteenth we again went round the walls of our prison, in hope of finding some avenue of escape, but to no purpose. We also descended the chasm in which we had been overwhelmed, with the faint expectation of discovering, through this channel, some opening to the main ravine. Here, too, we were disappointed, although we found and brought up with us a musket.

On the seventeenth we set out with the determination of examining more thoroughly the chasm of black granite into which we had made our way in the first search. We remembered that one of the fissures in the sides of this pit had been but partially looked into, and we were anxious to explore it, although with no expectation of discovering here any opening.

We found no great difficulty in reaching the bottom of the hollow as before, and were now sufficiently calm to survey it with some attention. It was, indeed, one of the most singular-looking places imaginable, and we could scarcely bring ourselves to believe it altogether the work of nature. The pit, from its eastern to its western extremity, was about five hundred yards in length, when all its windings were threaded; the distance from east to west in a straight line not being more (I should suppose, having no means of accurate examination) than forty or fifty yards. Upon first descending into the chasm, that is to say, for a hundred feet downward from the summit of the hill, the sides of the abyss bore little resemblance to each other, and, apparently, had at no time been connected, the one surface being of the soapstone and the other of marl, granulated with some metallic matter. The average breadth, or interval between the two cliffs, was probably here sixty feet, but there seemed to be no regularity of formation. Passing down, however, beyond the limit spoken of, the

* This day was rendered remarkable by our observing in the south several huge wreaths of the grayish vapour I have before spoken of.

interval rapidly contracted, and the sides began to run parallel, although, for some distance farther, they were still dissimilar in their material and form of surface. Upon arriving within fifty feet of the bottom, a perfect regularity commenced. The sides were now entirely uniform in substance, in colour, and in lateral direction, the material being a very black and shining granite, and the distance between the two sides, at all points facing each other, exactly twenty yards. The precise formation of the chasm will be best understood by means of a delineation taken upon the spot; for I had luckily with me a pocketbook and pencil, which I preserved with great care through a long series of subsequent adventure, and to which I am indebted for memoranda of many subjects which would otherwise have been crowded from my remembrance.

FIGURE 1

This figure (see figure 1) gives the general outlines of the chasm, without the minor cavities in the sides, of which there were several, each cavity having a corresponding protuberance opposite.[2] The bottom of the gulf was covered to the depth of three or four inches with a powder almost impalpable, beneath which we found a continuation of the black granite. To the right, at the lower extremity, will be noticed the appearance of a small opening; this is the fissure alluded to above, and to examine which more minutely than before was the object of our second visit. We now pushed into it with vigour, cutting away a quantity of brambles which impeded us, and removing a vast heap of sharp flints somewhat resembling arrowheads in shape. We were encouraged to persevere, however, by perceiving some little light proceeding from the farther end. We at length squeezed our way for about thirty feet, and found that the aperture was a low and regularly-formed arch, having a bottom of the same impalpable powder as that in the main chasm. A strong light now broke upon us, and, turning a short bend, we found ourselves in another lofty chamber, similar to the one we had left in every respect but longitudinal form. Its general figure is here given. (See figure 2.)

FIGURE 2

The total length of this chasm, commencing at the opening *a* and proceeding round the curve *b* to the extremity *d*, is five hundred and fifty yards. At *c* we discovered a small aperture similar to the one through which we had issued from the other chasm, and this was choked up in the same manner with brambles and a quantity of the white arrowhead flints. We forced our way through it, finding it about forty feet long, and emerged into a third chasm. This, too, was precisely like the first, except in its longitudinal shape, which was thus. (See figure 3.)

FIGURE 3

FIGURE 5

We found the entire length of the third chasm three hundred and twenty yards. At the point *a* was an opening about six feet wide, and extending fifteen feet into the rock, where it terminated in a bed of marl, there being no other chasm beyond, as we had expected. We were about leaving this fissure, into which very little light was admitted, when Peters called my attention to a range of singular-looking indentures in the surface of the marl forming the termination of the *cul-de-sac*. With a very slight exertion of the imagination, the left, or most northerly of these indentures might have been taken for the intentional, although rude, representation of a human figure standing erect, with outstretched arm.[3] The rest of them bore also some little resemblance to alphabetical characters, and Peters was willing, at all events, to adopt the idle opinion that they were really such. I convinced him of his error, finally, by directing his attention to the floor of the fissure, where, among the powder, we picked up, piece by piece, several large flakes of the marl, which had evidently been broken off by some convulsion from the surface where the indentures were found, and which had projecting points exactly fitting the indentures; thus proving them to have been the work of nature. Figure 4 presents an accurate copy of the whole.

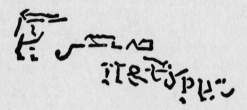

FIGURE 4

After satisfying ourselves that these singular caverns afforded us no means of escape from our prison, we made our way back, dejected and dispirited, to the summit of the hill. Nothing worth mentioning occurred during the next twenty-four hours, except that, in examining the ground to the eastward of the third chasm, we found two triangular holes of great depth, and also with black granite sides. Into these holes we did not think it worth while to attempt descending, as they had the appearance of mere natural wells, without outlet. They were each about twenty yards in circumference, and their shape, as well as relative position in regard to the third chasm, is shown in figure 5, preceding page.

CHAPTER 23 bis

On the twentieth of the month, finding it altogether impossible to subsist any longer upon the filberts, the use of which occasioned us the most excruciating torment, we resolved to make a desperate attempt at descending the southern declivity of the hill. The face of the precipice was here of the softest species of soapstone, although nearly perpendicular throughout its whole extent (a depth of a hundred and fifty feet at the least), and in many places even overarching. After long search we discovered a narrow ledge about twenty feet below the brink of the gulf; upon this Peters contrived to leap, with what assistance I could render him by means of our pocket-handkerchiefs tied together. With somewhat more difficulty I also got down; and we then saw the possibility of descending the whole way by the process in which we had clambered up from the chasm when we had been buried by the fall of the hill—that is, by cutting steps in the face of the soapstone with our knives. The extreme hazard of the attempt can scarcely be conceived; but, as there was no other resource, we determined to undertake it.

Upon the ledge where we stood there grew some filbert-bushes; and to one of these we made fast an end of our rope of handkerchiefs. The other end being tied round Peters's waist, I lowered him down over the edge of the precipice until the handkerchiefs were stretched tight. He now proceeded to dig a deep hole in the soapstone (as far in as eight or ten inches), sloping away the rock above to the height of a foot, or thereabout, so as to allow of his driving, with the butt of a pistol, a tolerably strong peg into the levelled surface. I then drew him up for about four feet, when he made a hole similar to the one below, driving in a peg as before, and having thus a resting-place for both feet and hands. I now unfastened the handkerchiefs from the bush, throwing him the end, which he tied to the peg in the uppermost hole, letting himself down gently to a station about three feet lower than he had yet been, that is, to the full extent of the handkerchiefs. Here he dug another hole, and drove another peg. He then drew himself up, so as to rest his feet in the hole just cut, taking hold with his hands upon the peg in the one above. It was now necessary to untie the handkerchiefs from the topmost peg, with the view of fastening them to the second; and here he found that an error had been committed in cutting the holes at so great a distance apart. However, after one or two unsuccessful and dangerous attempts at reaching the knot (having to hold on with his left hand while he laboured to undo the fastening with his right), he at length cut the string, leaving six inches of it affixed to the peg. Tying the handkerchiefs now to the second peg, he descended to a station below the third, taking care not to go too far down. By these means (means which I should never have conceived of myself, and for which we were indebted altogether to Peters's ingenuity and resolution) my companion finally succeeded, with the occasional aid of projections in the cliff, in reaching the bottom without accident.[1]

It was some time before I could summon sufficient resolution to follow him; but I did at length attempt it. Peters had taken off his shirt before descending, and this, with my own, formed the rope necessary for the adventure. After throwing down the musket found in the chasm, I fastened this rope to the bushes, and let myself down rapidly, striving, by the vigour of my movements, to banish the trepidation which I could overcome in no other manner. This answered sufficiently well for the first four or five steps; but presently I found my imagination growing terribly excited by thoughts of the vast depth yet to be descended, and the precarious nature of the pegs and soapstone holes which were my only support. It was in vain I endeavoured to banish these reflections, and to keep my eyes steadily bent upon the flat surface of the cliff before me. The more earnestly I struggled *not to think,* the more intensely vivid became my conceptions, and the more horribly distinct. At length arrived that crisis of fancy, so fearful in all similar cases, the crisis in which we begin to anticipate the feelings with which we *shall* fall—to picture to ourselves the sickness, and dizziness, and the last struggle, and the half swoon, and the final bitterness of the rushing and headlong descent. And now I found these fancies creating their own realities, and all imagined horrors crowding upon me in fact. I felt my knees strike violently together, while my fingers were gradually yet certainly relaxing their grasp. There was a ringing in my ears, and I said, "This is my knell of death!" And now I was consumed with the irrepressible desire of looking below. I could not, I would not, confine my glances to the cliff; and, with a wild, indefinable emotion half of horror, half of a relieved oppression, I threw my vision far down into the abyss. For one moment my fingers clutched convulsively upon their hold, while, with the movement, the faintest possible idea of ultimate escape[2] wandered, like a shadow, through my mind—in the next my whole soul was pervaded with *a longing to fall;* a desire, a yearning, a passion utterly uncontrollable.[3] I let go at once my grasp upon the peg, and, turning half round from the precipice, remained tottering for an instant against its naked face. But now there came a spinning of the brain; a shrill-sounding and phantom voice screamed within my ears; a dusky, fiendish, and filmy figure stood immediately beneath me; and, sighing, I sunk down with a bursting heart, and plunged within its arms.

I had swooned, and Peters had caught me as I fell. He had observed my proceedings from his station at the bottom of the cliff; and, perceiving my imminent danger, had endeavoured to inspire me with courage by every suggestion he could devise; although my confusion of mind had been so great as to prevent my hearing what he said, or being conscious that he had even spoken to me at all. At length, seeing me totter, he hastened to ascend to my rescue, and arrived just in time for my preservation. Had I fallen with my full weight, the rope of linen would inevitably have snapped, and I should have been precipitated into the abyss; as it was, he contrived to let me down gently, so as to remain suspended without danger until animation returned. This was in about fifteen minutes. On recovery, my trepidation had entirely vanished; I felt a new being, and, with some little further aid from my companion, reached the bottom also in safety.

We now found ourselves not far from the ravine which had proved the tomb of our friends, and to the southward of the spot where the hill had fallen. The place was one of singular wildness, and its aspect brought to my mind the descriptions given by travellers of those dreary regions marking the site of degraded Babylon.[4] Not to speak of the ruins of the disruptured cliff, which formed a chaotic barrier in the vista to the northward, the surface of the ground in every other direction was strewn with huge tumuli, apparently the wreck of some gigantic structures of art; although, in detail, no semblance of art could be detected. Scoria were abundant, and large shapeless blocks of the black granite, intermingled with others of marl,* and both granulated with metal. Of vegetation there were no traces whatsoever throughout the whole of the desolate area within sight. Several immense scorpions were seen, and various reptiles not elsewhere to be found in the high latitudes.

As food was our most immediate object, we resolved to make our way to the seacoast, distant not more than half a mile, with a view of catching turtle, several of which we had observed from our place of concealment on the hill. We had

---

* The marl was also black; indeed, we noticed no light-coloured substances of any kind upon the island.

proceeded some hundred yards, threading our route cautiously between the huge rocks and tumuli, when, upon turning a corner, five savages sprung upon us from a small cavern, felling Peters to the ground with a blow from a club. As he fell the whole party rushed upon him to secure their victim, leaving me time to recover from my astonishment. I still had the musket, but the barrel had received so much injury in being thrown from the precipice that I cast it aside as useless, preferring to trust my pistols, which had been carefully preserved in order. With these I advanced upon the assailants, firing one after the other in quick succession. Two savages fell, and one, who was in the act of thrusting a spear into Peters, sprung to his feet without accomplishing his purpose. My companion being thus released, we had no further difficulty. He had his pistols also, but prudently declined using them, confiding in his great personal strength, which far exceeded that of any person I have ever known. Seizing a club from one of the savages who had fallen, he dashed out the brains of the three who remained, killing each instantaneously with a single blow of the weapon, and leaving us completely masters of the field.

So rapidly had these events passed, that we could scar[c]ely[5] believe in their reality, and were standing over the bodies of the dead in a species of stupid contemplation, when we were brought to recollection by the sound of shouts in the distance. It was clear that the savages had been alarmed by the firing, and that we had little chance of avoiding discovery. To regain the cliff, it would be necessary to proceed in the direction of the shouts; and even should we succeed in arriving at its base, we should never be able to ascend it without being seen. Our situation was one of the greatest peril, and we were hesitating in which path to commence a flight, when one of the savages whom I had shot, and supposed dead, sprang briskly to his feet, and attempted to make his escape. We overtook him, however, before he had advanced many paces, and were about to put him to death, when Peters suggested that we might derive some benefit from forcing him to accompany us in our attempt at escape. We therefore dragged him with us, making him understand that we would shoot him if he offered resistance. In a few minutes he was perfectly submissive, and ran by our sides as we pushed in among the rocks, making for the seashore.

So far, the irregularities of the ground we had been traversing hid the sea, except at intervals, from our sight, and, when we first had it fairly in view, it was, perhaps, two hundred yards distant. As we emerged into the open beach we saw, to our great dismay, an immense crowd of the natives pouring from the village, and from all visible quarters of the island, making towards us with gesticulations of extreme fury, and howling like wild beasts. We were upon the point of turning upon our steps, and trying to secure a retreat among the fastnesses of the rougher ground, when I discovered the bows of two canoes projecting from behind a large rock which ran out into the water. Towards these we now ran with all speed, and, reaching them, found them unguarded, and without any other freight than three of the large Gallipago turtles and the usual supply of paddles for sixty rowers. We instantly took possession of one of them, and, forcing our captive on board, pushed out to sea with all the strength we could command.

We had not made, however, more than fifty yards from the shore before we became sufficiently calm to perceive the great oversight of which we had been guilty in leaving the other canoe in the power of the savages, who, by this time, were not more than twice as far from the beach as ourselves, and were rapidly advancing to the pursuit. No time was now to be lost. Our hope was, at best, a forlorn one, but we had none other. It was very doubtful whether, with the utmost exertion, we could get back in time to anticipate them in taking possession of the canoe; but yet there was a chance that we could. We might save ourselves if we succeeded, while not to make the attempt was to resign ourselves to inevitable butchery.

The canoe was modelled with the bow and stern alike,[6] and, in place of turning it round, we merely changed our position in paddling. As soon as the savages perceived this they redoubled their yells, as well as their speed, and approached with inconceivable rapidity. We pulled, however, with all the energy of desperation, and arrived at the contested point before more than one of the natives had attained it. This man paid dearly for his superior agility, Peters shooting him through the head with a pistol as he approached the shore. The foremost among the rest of his party were probably some twenty or thirty paces distant as we seized upon the canoe. We at first endeavoured to pull her into the deep water, beyond the reach of the savages, but, finding her too firmly aground, and there being no time to spare, Peters, with one or two heavy strokes from the butt of the musket, succeeded in dashing out a large portion of the bow and of one side. We then pushed off. Two of the natives by this time had got hold of our boat, obstinately refusing to let go, until we were forced to despatch them with our knives. We were now clear off, and making great way out to sea. The main body of the savages, upon reaching the broken canoe, set up the most tremendous yell of rage and disappointment conceivable. In truth, from everything I could see of these wretches, they appeared to be the most wicked, hypocritical, vindictive, bloodthirsty, and altogether fiendish race of men upon the face of the globe. It is clear we should have had no mercy had we fallen into their hands. They made a mad attempt at following us in the fractured canoe, but, finding it useless, again vented their rage in a series of hideous vociferations, and rushed up into the hills.

We were thus relieved from immediate danger, but our situation was still sufficiently gloomy. We knew that four canoes of the kind we had were at one time in the possession of the savages, and were not aware of the fact (afterward ascertained from our captive) that two of these had been blown to

pieces in the explosion of the Jane Guy. We calculated, therefore, upon being yet pursued, as soon as our enemies could
get round to the bay (distant about three miles) where the
boats were usually laid up. Fearing this, we made every exertion to leave the island behind us, and went rapidly through
the water, forcing the prisoner to take a paddle. In about half
an hour, when we had gained, probably, five or six miles to
the southward, a large fleet of the flat-bottomed canoes or
rafts was seen to emerge from the bay, evidently with the design of pursuit. Presently they put back, despairing to overtake us.

CHAPTER 24

We now found ourselves in the wide and desolate Antarctic Ocean, in a latitude exceeding eighty-four degrees, in a frail canoe, and with no provision but the three turtles. The long Polar winter, too, could not be considered as far distant, and it became necessary that we should deliberate well upon the course to be pursued. There were six or seven islands in sight belonging to the same group, and distant from each other about five or six leagues; but upon neither of these had we any intention to venture. In coming from the northward in the Jane Guy we had been gradually leaving behind us the severest regions of ice—this, however little it may be in accordance with the generally-received notions respecting the Antarctic, was a fact experience would not permit us to deny. To attempt, therefore, getting back, would be folly—especially at so late a period of the season. Only one course seemed to be left open for hope. We resolved to steer boldly to the southward, where there was at least a probability of discovering other lands, and more than a probability of finding a still milder climate.

So far we had found the Antarctic, like the Arctic Ocean, peculiarly free from violent storms or immoderately rough water; but our canoe was, at best, of frail structure, although large, and we set busily to work with a view of rendering her as safe as the limited means in our possession would admit. The body of the boat was of no better material than bark—the bark of a tree unknown. The ribs were of a tough osier, well adapted to the purpose for which it was used. We had fifty feet room from stem to stern, from four to six in breadth, and in depth throughout four feet and a half—the boats thus differing vastly in shape from those of any other inhabitants of the Southern Ocean with whom civilized nations are acquainted. We never did believe them the workmanship of the ignorant islanders who owned them; and some days after this period discovered, by questioning our captive, that they were in fact made by the natives of a group to the southwest of the country where we found them, having fallen accidentally into the hands of our barbarians. What we could do for the security of our boat was very little indeed. Several wide rents were discovered near both ends, and these we contrived to patch up with pieces of woollen jacket. With the help of the superfluous paddles, of which there were a great many, we erected a kind of framework about the bow, so as to break the force of any seas which might threaten to fill us in that quarter. We also set up two paddle-blades for masts, placing them opposite each other, one by each gunwale, thus saving the necessity of a yard. To these masts we attached a sail made of our shirts—doing this with some difficulty, as here we could get no assistance from our prisoner whatever, although he had been willing enough to labour in all the other operations. The sight of the linen seemed to affect him in a very singular manner. He could not be prevailed upon to touch it or go near it, shuddering when we attempted to force him, and shrieking out *Tekeli-li!*

Having completed our arrangements in regard to the security of the canoe, we now set sail to the south southeast for the present, with the view of weathering the most southerly of the group in sight. This being done, we turned the bow full to the southward. The weather could by no means be considered disagreeable. We had a prevailing and very gentle wind from the northward, a smooth sea, and continual daylight. No ice whatever was to be seen; *nor did I ever see one particle of this after leaving the parallel of Bennett's Islet.* Indeed, the temperature of the water was here far too warm for its existence in any quantity. Having killed the largest of our tortoises, and obtained from him not only food, but a copious supply of water, we continued on our course, without any incident of moment, for perhaps seven or eight days, during which period we must have proceeded a vast distance to the southward, as the wind blew constantly with us, and a very strong current set continually in the direction we were pursuing.

March 1.* Many unusual phenomena now indicated that we were entering upon a region of novelty and wonder. A high range of light gray vapour appeared constantly in the southern horizon, flaring up occasionally in lofty streaks, now darting from east to west, now from west to east, and again presenting a level and uniform summit—in short, having all the wild variations of the Aurora Borealis. The average height of this vapour, as apparent from our station, was about twenty-five degrees. The temperature of the sea seemed to be increasing momentarily, and there was a very perceptible alteration in its colour.

March 2. To-day, by repeated questioning of our captive, we came to the knowledge of many particulars in regard to the island of the massacre, its inhabitants, and customs—but with these how can I *now* detain the reader? I may say, however, that we learned there were eight islands in the group—that they were governed by a common king, named *Tsalemon* or *Psalemoun*,[1] who resided in one of the smallest of the islands—that the black skins forming the dress of the warriors came from an animal of huge size to be found only in a valley near the court of the king—that the inhabitants of the group fabricated no other boats than the flat-bottomed rafts; the four canoes being all of the kind in their possession, and these having been obtained, by mere accident, from some large is-

* For obvious reasons I cannot pretend to strict accuracy in these dates. They are given principally with a view to perspicuity of narration, and as set down in my pencil memoranda.

land to the southwest—that his own name was Nu-Nu[2]—that he had no knowledge of Bennett's Islet—and that the appellation of the island we had left was *Tsalal.* The commencement of the words *Tsalemon* and *Tsalal* was given with a prolonged hissing sound,[3] which we found it impossible to imitate, even after repeated endeavours, and which was precisely the same with the note of the black bittern we had eaten upon the summit of the hill.

March 3. The heat of the water was now truly remarkable, and its colour was undergoing a rapid change, being no longer transparent, but of a milky consistency and hue. In our immediate vicinity it was usually smooth, never so rough as to endanger the canoe—but we were frequently surprised at perceiving, to our right and left, at different distances, sudden and extensive agitations of the surface—these, we at length noticed, were always preceded by wild flickerings in the region of vapour to the southward.

March 4. To-day, with the view of widening our sail, the breeze from the northward dying away perceptibly, I took from my coat-pocket a white handkerchief. Nu-Nu was seated at my elbow, and the linen accidentally flaring in his face, he became violently affected with convulsions. These were succeeded by drowsiness and stupor, and low murmurings of Tekeli-li! Tekeli-li!

March 5. The wind had entirely ceased, but it was evident that we were still hurrying on to the southward,[4] under the influence of a powerful current. And now, indeed, it would seem reasonable that we should experience some alarm at the turn events were taking—but we felt none. The countenance of Peters indicated nothing of this nature, although it wore at times an expression I could not fathom. The Polar winter appeared to be coming on—but coming without its terrors. I felt a *numbness* of body and mind—a dreaminess of sensation—but this was all.

March 6. The gray vapour had now arisen many more degrees above the horizon, and was gradually losing its grayness of tint. The heat of the water was extreme, even unpleasant to the touch, and its milky hue was more evident than ever. To-day a violent agitation of the water occurred very close to the canoe. It was attended, as usual, with a wild flaring up of the vapour at its summit, and a momentary division at its base. A fine white powder, resembling ashes—but certainly not such—fell over the canoe and over a large surface of the water, as the flickering died away among the vapour and the commotion subsided in the sea. Nu-Nu now threw himself on his face in the bottom of the boat, and no persuasions could induce him to arise.

March 7. This day we questioned Nu-Nu concerning the motives of his countrymen in destroying our companions; but he appeared to be too utterly overcome by terror to afford us any rational reply. He still obstinately lay in the bottom of the boat; and, upon our reiterating the questions as to the motive, made use only of idiotic gesticulations, such as raising with his forefinger the upper lip, and displaying the teeth which lay beneath it. These were black. We had never before seen the teeth of an inhabitant of Tsalal.[5]

March 8. To-day there floated by us one of the white animals whose appearance upon the beach at Tsalal had occasioned so wild a commotion among the savages. I would have picked it up, but there came over me a sudden listlessness, and I forbore. The heat of the water still increased, and the hand could no longer be endured within it. Peters spoke little, and I knew not what to think of his apathy. Nu-Nu breathed, and no more.

March 9. The white ashy material fell now continually around us, and in vast quantities. The range of vapour to the southward had arisen prodigiously in the horizon, and began to assume more distinctness of form. I can liken it to nothing but a limitless cataract,[6] rolling silently into the sea from some immense and far-distant rampart in the heaven. The gigantic curtain ranged along the whole extent of the southern horizon. It emitted no sound.

March 21. A sullen darkness now hovered above us—but from out the milky depths of the ocean a luminous glare arose, and stole up along the bulwarks of the boat.[7] We were nearly overwhelmed by the white ashy shower which settled upon us and upon the canoe, but melted into the water as it fell. The summit of the cataract was utterly lost in the dimness and the distance. Yet we were evidently approaching it with a hideous velocity. At intervals there were visible in it wide, yawning, but momentary rents, and from out these rents, within which was a chaos of flitting and indistinct images, there came rushing and mighty, but soundless winds,[8] tearing up the enkindled ocean in their course.

March 22. The darkness had materially increased, relieved only by the glare of the water thrown back from the white curtain before us. Many gigantic and pallidly white birds flew continuously now from beyond the veil, and their scream was the eternal *Tekeli-li!* as they retreated from our vision. Hereupon Nu-Nu stirred in the bottom of the boat; but, upon touching him, we found his spirit departed. And now we rushed into the embraces of the cataract, where a chasm threw itself open to receive us. But there arose in our pathway a shrouded human figure, very far larger in its proportions than any dweller among men. And the hue of the skin of the figure was of the perfect whiteness of the snow.[9]

Note

The circumstances connected with the late sudden and distressing death of Mr. Pym are already well known to the public through the medium of the daily press. It is feared that the few remaining chapters which were to have completed his narrative, and which were retained by him, while the above were in type, for the purpose of revision, have been irrecoverably lost through the accident by which he perished himself. This, however, may prove not to be the case, and the papers, if ultimately found, will be given to the public.[1]

No means have been left untried to remedy the deficiency. The gentleman whose name is mentioned in the preface, and who, from the statement there made, might be supposed able to fill the vacuum, has declined the task—this for satisfactory reasons connected with the general inaccuracy of the details afforded him, and his disbelief in the entire truth of the latter portions of the narration. Peters, from whom some information might be expected, is still alive, and a resident of Illinois, but cannot be met with at present. He may hereafter be found, and will, no doubt, afford material for a conclusion of Mr. Pym's account.[2]

The loss of the two or three final chapters (for there were but two or three) is the more deeply to be regretted, as, it cannot be doubted, they contained matter relative to the Pole itself, or at least to regions in its very near proximity; and as, too, the statements of the author in relation to these regions may shortly be verified or contradicted by means of the governmental expedition now preparing for the Southern Ocean.[3]

On one point in the Narrative some remarks may be well offered; and it would afford the writer of this appendix much pleasure if what he may here observe should have a tendency to throw credit, in any degree, upon the very singular pages now published. We allude to the chasms found in the island of Tsalal, and to the whole of the figures upon pages 200, 201, 202.

Mr. Pym has given the figures of the chasms without comment, and speaks decidedly of the *indentures* found at the extremity of the most easterly of these chasms as having but a fanciful resemblance to alphabetical characters, and, in short, as being positively *not such.* This assertion is made in a manner so simple, and sustained by a species of demonstration so conclusive (viz., the fitting of the projections of the fragments found among the dust into the indentures upon the wall), that we are forced to believe the writer in earnest; and no reasonable reader should suppose otherwise. But as the facts in relation to *all* the figures are most singular (especially when taken in connexion with statements made in the body of the narrative), it may be as well to say a word or two concerning them all—this, too, the more especially as the facts in question have, beyond doubt, escaped the attention of Mr. Poe.

Figure 1, then, figure 2, figure 3, and figure 5, when conjoined with one another in the precise order which the chasms themselves presented, and when deprived of the small lateral branches or arches (which, it will be remembered, served only as means of communication between the main chambers, and were of totally distinct character), constitute an Ethiopian verbal root—the root ʌᐱᕐ: "To be shady"— whence all the inflections of shadow or darkness.[4]

In regard to the "left or most northwardly" of the indentures in figure 4, it is more than probable that the opinion of Peters was correct, and that the hieroglyphical appearance was really the work of art, and intended as the representation of a human form. The delineation is before the reader, and he may, or may not, perceive the resemblance suggested; but the rest of the indentures afford strong confirmation of Peters's idea. The upper range is evidently the Arabic verbal root ﺳﻼﻣ "To be white," whence all the inflections of brilliancy and whiteness. The lower range is not so immediately perspicuous. The characters are somewhat broken and disjointed; nevertheless, it cannot be doubted that, in their perfect state, they formed the full Egyptian word ΠⲀⲨⲢⲎⳞ, "The region of the south." It should be observed that these interpretations confirm the opinion of Peters in regard to the "most northwardly" of the figures. The arm is outstretched towards the south.

Conclusions such as these open a wide field for speculation and exciting conjecture. They should be regarded, perhaps, in connexion with some of the most faintly-detailed incidents of the narrative; although in no visible manner is this chain of connexion complete. Tekeli-li! was the cry of the affrighted natives of Tsalal upon discovering the carcass of the *white* animal picked up at sea. This also was the shuddering exclamation of the captive Tsalalian upon encountering the *white* materials in possession of Mr. Pym. This also was the shriek of the swift-flying, *white,* and gigantic birds which issued from the vapoury *white* curtain of the South. Nothing *white* was to be found at Tsalal, and nothing otherwise in the subsequent voyage to the region beyond. It is not impossible that "Tsalal," the appellation of the island of the chasms, may be found, upon minute philological scrutiny, to

betray either some alliance with the chasms themselves, or some reference to the Ethiopian characters so mysteriously written in their
windings.[5]

"*I have graven it within the hills, and my vengeance upon the dust
within the rock.*"[6]

EXPLANATORY NOTES

Burton R. Pollin's annotations of *Pym* in *The Imaginary Voyages*, volume 1 of *Collected Writings of Edgar Allan Poe*, have provided some of the factual matter in the following notes.

Preface

1. impudent and ingenious fiction: The epithet "impudent" to describe Poe's narrative was borrowed by William Burton for his review in *Graham's Magazine* and by a British critic for his review in the *Metropolitan Magazine*.
2. received as truth: To build belief in the character Pym and the validity of the narrative, Poe tries to persuade us through Pym that Poe tried to persuade Pym to write his narrative.
3. of the magazine: For the installment of *Pym* in the January 1837 issue of the *Messenger*, see pp. 13–16; for the installment of the novel in the February 1837 issue of the magazine, see pp. 109–16. On January 3, 1837, Poe left the *Messenger*—probably because publisher Thomas W. White had dismissed him (in large part, for drinking). At the close of the January 1837 issue of the *Messenger*, White graciously announced Poe's departure: ". . . Mr. Poe, who has filled the editorial department for the last twelve months, with so much ability, retired from that station on the 3d. inst.; and the entire management of the work again devolves on myself alone. Mr. P, however, will continue to furnish its columns, from time to time, with the effusions of his vigorous and popular pen . . ." (96).
4. readily perceived: Style does not reveal the end of the *Messenger* text of *Pym*. That text closes with the third paragraph of chapter 4.
5. New-York, July, 1838: By July 19, 1838, Poe was living in Philadelphia; his letter to James K. Paulding of that date requests "the most unimportant Clerkship in your gift—*any thing, by sea or land*" (*Letters* 2:681).

Chapter 1

1. Arthur Gordon Pym: The rhythm of this name suggests the rhythm of the name of the author; Arthur Gordon Pym implies Edgar Allan Poe.
2. Edgarton New-Bank: Edgartown is on Martha's Vineyard, an island near Nantucket. The name clearly serves to indicate the novel's author.

3. until I was sixteen: Pym was fourteen, not sixteen, in the *Messenger* text. For all variants in the *Messenger* text, see Pollin's *Imaginary Voyages* (211–14).

4. Mr. E. Ronald's academy: "E. Ronald" suggests E. Arnold—Eliza Arnold—Poe's mother's maiden name, as Richard Wilbur has observed. (Kenneth Silverman notes also that "E. Ronald" is an anagram for "Leonard," one of the middle names of Poe's brother.)

5. His son was named Augustus: Augustus Barnard represents Poe's brother William Henry Leonard Poe, as has been acknowledged since Marie Bonaparte's early Freudian study, *The Life and Works of Edgar Allan Poe*.

6. called the Ariel: As indicated in the introduction, the *Ariel* is probably drawn from the account of the wreck of the Norfolk vessel the *Ariel*, a story appearing in the Norfolk *Beacon* and *Herald* in February 1836. The vessel's name would have yielded a second level of meaning, by way of Isaiah 29:1—Jerusalem. For Poe's brief mention of Jerusalem in his February 1836 short essay "Palæstine" (based on entries in the fifth American edition of J. Lempriere's *Classical Dictionary*, "corrected and improved" by Charles Anthon), see *Collected Writings* 5:106–7.

7. more momentous narrative: This sentence did not appear in the *Messenger* text of *Pym*; it was added for the novel.

8. Pankey & Co.: In 1836, Dr. James Pankey was a correspondent and agent for a Richmond newspaper, the *Southern Religious Telegraph*. Poe may well have borrowed Pankey's name for its intimation of "the key [to] all" (as the introduction proposes that the *Ariel* and the *Penguin* are for the religious allegory of the novel). It is relevant to add that Herman Melville writes, at the beginning of *Moby-Dick*, that the image of Narcissus in that work is "the key to it all."

9. hurrying us to destruction: The close of this sentence, ". . . fierce wind and strong ebb tide were hurrying us to destruction," is later partially echoed by language in the March 5 entry of the final chapter—". . . we were still hurrying on to the southward. . . ." A series of symmetrical phrases in *Pym* frame the center of the novel.

10. a chance of ultimate escape: This phrase corresponds with a phrase in chapter 23 bis, "the faintest possible idea of ultimate escape."

11. of a thousand demons: The scream of what sounds like "a thousand demons" anticipates the many screaming "gigantic and pallidly white birds" of the final journal entry.

    The phrase "a loud and long scream or yell" corresponds with a phrase in chapter 22, "screaming and yelling for aid."

12. (the Penguin): The appearance here of the ship *Penguin* corresponds with the appearance in the final journal entry of the

"shrouded human figure"—the ship *Penguin,* according to the argument of the introduction.

Pym's Penguin may have been borrowed from newspaper accounts and literary treatments of the battle of the British vessel *Penguin* with the American *Hornet* in 1815 and/or from newspaper accounts that mentioned the American vessel *Penguin,* which accompanied the *Seraph* and the *Annawan* in an 1829–30 voyage to the South Seas. J. N. Reynolds, the advocate of South Sea exploration who is mentioned several times in *Pym,* was on that 1829–30 voyage; he wrote about the voyage not only in the May 1839 "Mocha Dick," a source for *Moby-Dick,* but also in the April 21, 1838, "Leaves from an Unpublished Journal," a source for *Pym.* A description of a difficult ascent in "Leaves" resonates with a similar description of a difficult ascent in chapter 21 of *Pym.* Notably, "Leaves" closes with the rescue of marooned men by the *Annawan* and the *Penguin.* In light of his probable acquaintance with Reynolds, Poe may have seen this work prior to publication.

13. the special interference of Providence: The theme of Providence in *Pym,* evident in this passage and later ones, is well elaborated by Curtis Fukuchi. Poe would have been well aware of the theme's importance in Daniel Defoe's *Robinson Crusoe* (1719; rpt. 1835).

14. on the coast of Wales: Mention of "the coast of Wales" in conjunction with the boat of the *Penguin* may well suggest the Welsh etymology of that key word "penguin."

15. about his neck: Poe may be describing his brother's birth, with the umbilical cord caught around Henry's neck.

16. thirty or forty poor devils: Poe's language—"drowned some thirty or forty poor devils"—corresponds with "killed, perhaps, thirty or forty of the savages" in chapter 22—further evidence of the symmetrical phrasing in *Pym.*

Chapter 2

1. in sorrow and tears: Pym's vision "of death or captivity among barbarian hordes; of a lifetime dragged out in sorrow and tears" is reflected at the beginning of chapter 22 in his fear "of being put to death by the savages, or of dragging out a miserable existence in captivity among them."

2. partial interchange of character: When Pym states of his relationship with Augustus, ". . . our intimate communion had resulted in a partial interchange of character," Poe may well be adverting to his own close relationship with his brother, Henry (William Henry Leonard Poe). It is telling to note that while Henry published under his own initials some of Edgar's poetry, Edgar borrowed for his own biography some elements of Henry's life. Henry even

wrote a tale with loose connections to his brother's failed romance with Elmira Royster, and he called the lead character "Edgar-Leonard"; Edgar called himself at one point "Henri Le Rennet."

3. the brig Grampus: Joseph C. Hart's *Miriam Coffin, or The Whale-Fisherman* (1834) featured a ship named *Grampus*.

4. the subject to him again: Pym's grandfather here recalls John Allan, who had inadequately supported his young foster son at college and later left him nothing in his will.

5. (June, 1827): The fictional voyage of "June, 1827" was only shortly after Poe's actual March 1827 voyage north, from Norfolk to Boston, in a coal vessel. And in the *Messenger* text, the date given for Pym's voyage was "(April, 1827)."

6. to my parents: The first installment of *Pym* in the *Messenger* ended at this point.

7. nothing at all like Goddin: The name "Goddin" would have called to mind to Richmonders of Poe's day Goddin's Tavern. In light of the religious dimension of *Pym*, it should be noted that the words "tavern" and "tabernacle" are etymologically linked.

8. "salt water Long Tom": "Long Tom" was a character in James Fenimore Cooper's novel *The Pilot*; it was also the term for a naval gun.

9. to the mouth of the Columbia: Pym's reading "the expedition of Lewis and Clarke to the mouth of the Columbia"—perhaps the *History of the Expedition under the Command of Captains Lewis and Clark* (1814)—calls to mind Poe's later writing a western narrative, "The Journal of Julius Rodman." Six chapters of twelve appeared in the first six months of 1840 in *Burton's Gentleman's Magazine*, but the remaining six chapters were never written, probably because of Poe's falling-out with editor William Burton.

10. of an iron-bound crate: Pym's struggling through the hold and striking his head recall Augustus's whirling through the water and striking his head in chapter 1; perhaps these events are allegories of the births of Edgar and Henry Poe.

Chapter 3

1. *"lying close":* In this context, "lying close" suggests keeping still. In other contexts in the novel, it could imply prevaricating. And in contexts rich with autobiographical subtext, "lying close" might imply Edgar and Henry's sharing the same bed in Maria Clemm's house in Baltimore. In chapter 6, Arthur and Augustus may share a berth.

2. fits of perverseness: Pym's experiencing "one of those fits of perverseness" anticipates Poe's further development of the theme of human perverseness, as in the 1846 tale "The Imp of the Perverse."

Chapter 4

1. for the period specified above: Commenting on the "soporific effects" of fish oil and, indirectly, whale oil, Pym implies that in recent years he has been aboard a fishing vessel—perhaps a whaler.

2. in the mutiny, twenty-seven: The second and final *Messenger* installment of *Pym* ends here. Susan F. Beegel proposes (in Kopley, *Poe's Pym*) a source for the *Grampus* mutiny in the *Globe* mutiny.

3. the source of the Missouri: Poe drew some of his detail here from Washington Irving's *Astoria* (1835), which he reviewed in the January 1837 issue of the *Southern Literary Messenger* (*Collected Writings* 5:345–54). Dirk Peters has been linked to Irving's Pierre Dorian. Kenneth Silverman has noted, alternatively, that the name "Dirk Peters" resembles the name of a woman to whom Poe inscribed a copy of *Pym*: "Mrs. Mary Kirk Petrie." Carol Peirce and Alexander G. Rose III have suggested an Arthurian reading of the name (in Kopley, *Poe's Pym*).

4. most improbable of my statements: Perhaps the final sentence of this paragraph was a late insertion, included to link Pym's adventure story to the later polar approach, as L. Moffitt Cecil first conjectured.

5. finally cut adrift: Poe may owe a debt here to the story of Captain Bligh of the *Bounty*.

Chapter 5

1. most opportunely discovered: Poe may have made an error here—in the hold, Pym had perceived the paper to be blank on one side and carrying Augustus's warning on the other; he had not seen there the "forged letter from Mr. Ross."

2. induced him to reveal: Another possible error, often noticed, is the statement that "Many years elapsed" before Pym learned of Augustus's nearly giving up the search—after all, Augustus would, in fact, soon die. It is possible, as some have suggested, that, years later, Pym learned of Augustus's nearly giving up from Dirk Peters, with whom Augustus had spoken soon after the event, during an "intimate and unreserved communion." But perhaps it is more likely simply that Homer nodded.

Chapter 6

1. stowage of the brig: Joan Tyler Mead, having examined numerous nautical documents that Poe might have seen, has concluded (in Kopley, *Poe's Pym*) that this digression on stowage was probably not drawn from any source, but composed wholly by Poe. Remarkably, she finds Poe's treatment of stowage quoted by John

McLeod Murphy in the 1849 volume by Murphy and W. N. Jeffers Jr., *Nautical Routine and Stowage, with Short Rules in Navigation*. She considers it probable that Murphy understood that he was relying on a work of fiction, but allows the possibility that he took Pym's narrative to be a truthful travel narrative.

2. I got into Augustus's berth: Here Pym and Augustus seem to be literally "lying close."

3. besides Augustus and myself: Some of the names here suggest actual people; for example, "Simms" calls to mind William Gilmore Simms, a South Carolina writer who admired Poe, and "Greely" recalls Horace Greeley, whose *New-Yorker* had praised Poe's criticism in the *Messenger*. (The review of *Pym* in Greeley's *New-Yorker* referred to the book's "extraordinary, freezing interest"—although, amusingly, later in *Pym*, Peters "beat out the brains of Greely.") "Richard Parker" suggests the leader of the 1797 Nore mutiny, who was hanged for his part in that famous event—a man later treated by Walt Whitman in "Richard Parker's Widow" (1845) and drawn on by Herman Melville for *Billy Budd* (a work nearly completed by Melville's death in 1891 and published in 1924).

Chapter 7

1. Lying to: Mead persuasively identifies the source for Poe's "lying to" digression as William Falconer's *A New Universal Dictionary of the Marine* (1769; revised 1804 and 1815). The critical entries were "To lie to," "Lying to," and "Trying." Presumably this digression was designed to increase the verisimilitude of the novel, and perhaps, as Mead contends, to convey a sense of danger.

2. by the erysipelas: "Erysipelas" is an inflammation of the skin.

Chapter 8

1. a schooner Hornet: This reference recalls that possible sources for the *Penguin* were treatments of its battle with the *Hornet*.

2. my eyes ever encountered: This incident may relate to an actual incident involving young Poe, who, disguised as a ghost, surprised his foster father and Allan's friends as they played whist.

3. any aid whatever: Pym's stating that Augustus was "too much injured to render us any aid whatever" recalls Poe's writing to John Allan on August 10, 1829, "Henry [is] entirely given up to drink & unable to help himself, much less me," and then, on February 21, 1831, when Henry was probably drinking excessively and becoming sicker, "I have written to my brother—but he cannot help me. . . ." Readers may call to mind also that, in chapter 1 of the novel, Augustus's excessive drinking led to his being unable to help Pym on the *Ariel*.

4. preparations having been made: Poe was relying here and later, in part, on "The Loss of the Peggy" in R. Thomas's *Remarkable Shipwrecks and Remarkable Events* (1836).

5. a complete breach over us: Poe may well have been relying here and later, also, on "Loss of the Ship Albion" in Thomas.

6. right on board of us: Poe was indebted here and later to "The Loss of the Phoenix" in Thomas.

Chapter 9

1. would not sink: In Poe's 1841 tale "A Descent into the Maelström," the protagonist survives by tying himself to a water cask.

2. blessed sun: The phrase "blessed sun" invites consideration of a possible pun, "blessed Son." Subsequent details will offer further Christian allusions.

3. that of Tiger: This is the last mention of the dog Tiger—presumably he had been washed overboard.

Chapter 10

1. nine long years: This period of time must have covered July 14, 1827, through 1836, before the first installment of *Pym* was published in the January 1837 issue of the *Southern Literary Messenger*. However, the remaining adventures in *Pym* take place in roughly the next eight months.

2. weeping like a child: Details in this passage may well have been drawn from a variety of mariner's chronicles available to Poe.

3. of a Dutch build: A "hermaphrodite brig," also termed a "brigantine," features both a square-rigged foremast and a schooner-rigged mainmast. The fact that the vessel is "of a Dutch build" implies its nature: it is the legendary Flying Dutchman, so powerfully described in Poe's 1833 tale, "MS. Found in a Bottle." Later reference to "Hollanders" and the vessel's identity as a "Dutch trader" reinforce the implication.

4. a quarter of a mile of us: Details of this paragraph and the following three paragraphs were drawn from Michael Scott's novel, *Tom Cringle's Log* (1833). This paragraph, the next two paragraphs, and more than half of the subsequent paragraph were reprinted in the *Southern Literary Messenger* in John M. Daniel's March 1850 review of the first two volumes in the Griswold edition of Poe's works, *The Works of the Late Edgar Allan Poe*. (The third volume appeared later in 1850; the fourth volume, which included *Pym*, was published in 1856.)

5. as they *appeared* to us: Poe's emphasis on the deceptiveness of appearances here and elsewhere in *Pym* may refer, in part, to *Pym*'s seeming to be a mere adventure story when it is actually much more than that.

6. to the dead for help: Pym's stating that "... we could not help shouting to the dead for help!" may be Poe's allusion to his novel's serving as a literary reaching toward his lost mother and brother.

7. which I will not mention: The seagull's horribly feeding on the corpse of the mariner suggests to Pym the possibility of cannibalism among the four survivors of the *Grampus*.

8. same fearful kind: This sentence and the following two sentences offer language that is repeated in the first paragraph of the "Note." Such words and phrases here as "that the," "perished," "If," "the case," "death," "sudden and," "which," "are," "It is," "may," and "will" are found in that first paragraph. Furthermore, this passage's "fearful," "know," "accidentally," and "remain" become the later paragraph's "feared," "known," "accident," and "remaining." The correspondences in language intimate a relationship between the deaths of those to whom Pym could not help shouting for help and the death discussed in that first paragraph in the "Note."

Chapter 11

1. full of Port wine: Chapter 58 of Washington Irving's *Astoria* may be a source for this section on descending into a wrecked ship and bringing up wine.

2. a plunge in the seawater: The immersion of Parker, Augustus, and Peters suggests baptism, as Grace Farrell [Lee] has noted.

3. *mania a potu:* The term "*mania a potu*" signified melancholy brought on by excessive drinking.

4. at first perceived her: Perhaps this portion of the text was drawn, in part, from "Extraordinary Famine in the American Ship Peggy," appearing in various collections of mariner's chronicles, including Thomas.

5. casting himself into the sea: Poe may be alluding to a passage in the Bible—John 21:7—in which Simon Peter "did cast himself into the sea" when he heard that the stranger he saw on the shore of the Sea of Tiberias was the risen Jesus.

6. the existence of the others: In Poe's time, cannibalism did sometimes occur in accounts of dire circumstances on land and sea. In light of the Christian detail in *Pym*, cannibalism may also suggest communion, as Walter E. Bezanson and numerous subsequent scholars have contended.

Chapter 12

1. to draw lots: The drawing of lots, present in several nautical narratives of Poe's time, may suggest in *Pym* the drawing of lots for the clothes of the crucified Jesus (Matthew 27:35, Mark 15:24, Luke 23:34, John 19:23–24), as Grace Farrell [Lee] has suggested.

2. this species of tortoise: Poe's treatment of the Galápagos tortoise is indebted to Benjamin Morrell's 1832 *A Narrative of Four Voyages*, published by the Harpers, the firm that would publish *Pym*. (See pp. 125–26.) Morrell's book, actually ghostwritten by Samuel Woodworth, as Pollin notes in "The Narrative of Benjamin Morrell," is an important source for a number of subsequent passages in *Pym*.

Poe mentions the Galápagos tortoise again in chapters 13, 18, 19, 20, 23, and 24; "the figure of a tortoise" appears in chapter 17. Poe also mentions the turtle, apparently referring still to the Galápagos tortoise, in chapters 13, 23 bis, and 24.

Chapter 13

1. vinegar from the olives: The application of the vinegar from the olives to the wounds of Augustus recalls the offering of vinegar to the crucified Jesus (Matthew 27:48, Mark 15:36, Luke 23:36, John 19:29–30), as Grace Farrell [Lee] has also remarked.

2. *forty or fifty at the farthest:* The excessive emaciation may have been drawn from James Riley's *An Authentic Narrative of the Loss of the American Brig Commerce* (1817; rpt. 1818, 1820, 1828).

3. for several hours: The death of Augustus is literally the central event of Poe's *Pym*. It occurs in the thirteenth of twenty-five chapters, in the eleventh paragraph of the twenty-two paragraphs in the central chapter (not counting the note). The death of Augustus on August 1 represents the death of Poe's brother Henry on August 1. According to the argument of the introduction, Augustus is midway between the facing mirrors at either end of the novel—the ship *Penguin* and the seeming "thousand demons" (chapter 1) and that ship and the "gigantic and pallidly white birds" (chapter 24)—linked, through the penguins and albatrosses in chapter 14, with "the spirit of reflection." Arguably, Augustus is analogous to the native chief Too-wit, who in chapter 18 is also caught between two facing mirrors. The implied infinite reflection of the death of Augustus suggests Poe's ceaseless memory of the death of Henry.

According to the Providence Tradition, symmetrical language and events frame a significant midpoint involving Jesus coming in judgment, appearing at noon as the "Sun of righteousness" (Malachi 4:2). Daniel Defoe's *Robinson Crusoe*, a vital influence on Poe's *Pym*, is written in the Providence Tradition, as Douglas Brooks shows in *Number and Pattern in the Eighteenth-Century Novel* (1973)—the significant midpoint is the discovery of Friday's footprint, an event that does occur at noon. In *Pym*, symmetrical language and events frame the significant midpoint, the death of Augustus, which occurs at noon under "an oppressively hot sun," representing Jesus come in intense judgment. Accordingly, the providential theme in *Pym* is matched by a providential form.

4. of the sharks: Poe's treatment of sharks in this chapter may well be informed by his reading of "Loss of the Magpie," appearing in Thomas's *Remarkable Shipwrecks* and the *Mariner's Chronicle* (one or two vols., 1834).

5. delicious meals: Poe may well have found details about barnacles and crabs in "Loss of the Brig Polly," included in Thomas and other nautical collections of Poe's time.

6. so much in point: This footnote is drawn from "Loss of the Brig Polly."

7. to the South Seas and Pacific: No actual vessel named *Jane Guy* has been identified. If the fictional *Jane Guy* is named after Captain Guy's wife, we should note that Benjamin Morrell's wife was named Abby Jane, and that her name was put to an 1833 Harpers book titled *Narrative of a Voyage to the Ethiopic and South Atlantic Ocean . . .*, actually ghostwritten by Samuel Knapp. Also, Morrell mentioned in *A Narrative of Four Voyages* the vessel *Jane Maria*.

Chapter 14

1. eighty tons burden: For detail and language in this paragraph and numerous subsequent paragraphs, Poe drew on Morrell's *A Narrative of Four Voyages*.

2. Cape St. Roque: For the name "Cape St. Roque," Poe may have consulted *Symzonia: A Voyage of Discovery by Captain Adam Seaborn* (1820), attributed to either John Cleves Symmes Jr. (of whom J. N. Reynolds was a disciple), or Nathaniel Ames.

3. to the spermaceti: Elements of this paragraph and the next were drawn from J. N. Reynolds's *Voyage of the United States Frigate Potomac* (1835), also published by the Harpers. (See pp. 61–62.)

4. A heavy cross sea: The phrase "heavy cross sea," not found in the Reynolds source passage, may well constitute an allusion to Jesus bearing the cross.

5. longitude 37° 46′ E.: Poe here returns to his reliance on Morrell and continues to draw considerably from Morrell in the rest of the chapter.

6. in the gloom of the evening: Much of this paragraph is drawn from Morrell's passages on penguins (50, 63–64), but while Morrell (Woodworth) writes that ". . . they appear at a distance like a company of juvenile soldiers," like "a company of children with white aprons tied round their waists with black strings" (50), like "officers and subalterns on a parade day" (53), Poe writes that ". . . the resemblance [of a penguin] to a human figure is very striking, and would be apt to deceive the spectator at a casual glance or in the

gloom of the evening." Indeed, in the final chapter of *Pym*, it is when "[t]he darkness had materially increased" that Pym sees the "shrouded human figure"—arguably, the *Penguin*.

7. singular friendship exists: Much of this paragraph and the following five paragraphs concerning the friendship of the penguin and the albatross in the rookery is drawn from Morrell (xxiv, 50–53). With regard to the albatross, Poe would surely have thought of Samuel Taylor Coleridge's "Rime of the Ancient Mariner," which appeared in the renowned *Lyrical Ballads* (1798), by Coleridge and William Wordsworth.

8. of the penguin and albatross: Pym maintains that he will speak again of the penguin and the albatross, but he makes only passing reference explicitly, in chapter 16, not warranting the anticipation. If we conjecture that the pelicans appearing with the albatross in chapter 19 should have been penguins, we still have only another passing reference. However, the anticipation of the penguin and the albatross is fully justified by the conclusion of the final chapter of *Pym*, which does offer implicitly, according to the reading presented in the introduction, the ship *Penguin* (rendered as the "shrouded human figure"), and flying above that ship, "gigantic and pallidly white birds"—albatrosses.

9. of the albatross: Perhaps the fact that "The whole atmosphere . . . is darkened with the immense number of the albatross . . ." indicates that the darkness at the conclusion of *Pym* is caused by many flying albatrosses—which may appear, in the words of Morrell, "like a dense cloud" (53).

10. by these feathered beings: Morrell writes that the "order and regularity" of birds in the rookery would prompt an observer to recognize " 'the Divinity which stirs within' them" (53). But Poe offers a different comment on the orderly penguins and albatrosses in the rookery—a comment not found in any source passages: "In short, survey it as we will, nothing can be more astonishing than the spirit of reflection evinced by these feathered beings. . . ." "The spirit of reflection" suggests a mirror, and, as the introduction asserts, the ship *Penguin*, accompanied by a scream of what seem to be "a thousand demons" in chapter 1, and the ship *Penguin*, accompanied by many screaming "gigantic and pallidly white birds" in chapter 24, serve as facing mirrors.

11. to come after him: Captain Guy's leaving a message in a bottle on an island peak recalls Captain Cook's leaving a message in a bottle on an island "eminence"; Poe's source could be a book by James Cook and James King, *A Voyage to the Pacific* (1784), or a piece in *Rees's Cyclopaedia* on Kerguelen's Land.

12. looking for seal: This passage is drawn, in part, from Morrell (61–62).

Chapter 15

1. on the larboard: This chapter, so weighted with details of geography and history, constitutes substantial verisimilar ballast for Poe's novel. Poe is indebted for many elements of this chapter to Morrell's *Narrative*.

2. On the fifth of November: Poe made a mistake here, probably because of excessive reliance on Morrell: "November" should be "December." He continues with his error when he refers to "the twentieth of the month" three paragraphs later.

3. and by Captain Morrell: Poe thus indirectly indicates the purported author of his source text.

Chapter 16

1. towards the pole: Poe's shift toward emphasizing polar exploration is evident here.

2. any distinct account: With this paragraph and subsequent paragraphs, Poe shifts from his Morrell source to a J. N. Reynolds source, *Address, on the Subject of a Surveying and Exploring Expedition . . .* , published by the Harpers in 1836. Robert L. Rhea discusses Poe's debt to Reynolds's *Address*.

3. the albatross, the penguin: Poe offers only a brief reference here to the birds so vital to his novel; the language is drawn from Reynolds's *Address* (92).

4. Mr. J. N. Reynolds: Poe mentions Reynolds explicitly for the first time in *Pym* and soon quotes from his *Address* (92–93). Poe had written of Reynolds in his review of the *Address* in the January 1837 *Messenger*, "He is the originator, the persevering and indomitable advocate, the life, the soul of the design [of the South Sea expedition]. Whatever, of glory at least, accrue therefore from the expedition, this gentleman, whatever post he may occupy in it, or whether none, will be fairly entitled to the lion's share, and will as certainly receive it. . . . He is known, by all who know him at all, as a man of the loftiest principles and of unblemished character. . . . For ourselves, we have frequently borne testimony to his various merits as a gentleman, a writer and a scholar." Presuming that Reynolds would write the narrative of the South Sea expedition, Poe commented, "How admirably well he is qualified for this task, no person can know better than ourselves. His energy, his love of polite literature, his many and various attainments, and above all, his ardent and honorable enthusiasm, point him out as the man of all men for the execution of the task" (*Collected Writings* 5:354, 356). However, because of a dispute with Secretary of the Navy Mahlon Dickerson, Reynolds was not appointed to the expedition. (Another who was turned down was Nathaniel Hawthorne.) The South Sea expedition was led by Lieutenant Charles Wilkes, who

also wrote the *Narrative of the United States Exploring Expedition, during the Years 1838, 1839, 1840, 1841, and 1842* (1845).

5. as far south as possible: Poe here and in the next three paragraphs returns to his Morrell source (64–67).

6. by the cutter Tula: This paragraph and the following two paragraphs are drawn from Reynolds's *Address* (94–96).

7. to the southward: Poe attributes to Captain Guy the keen interest in southern exploration earlier expressed by J. N. Reynolds in his *Address*: "With such a wide field before us [to the south], and such a noble theatre whereon to contend for mastery with the nations of the earth . . . , we confidently indulge the hope that this measure [for southern exploration] will be sanctioned without further delay" (96).

Chapter 17

1. at thirty-five: Poe now returns to his Morrell source, relying on it repeatedly in this chapter.

2. absolute mountains of ragged ice: Poe's phrasing calls to mind the hills southwest of Charlottesville, the Ragged Mountains, about which Poe would have known as a former student at the University of Virginia. Poe used these mountains as the setting for his 1844 work, "A Tale of the Ragged Mountains," with which *Pym* has a thematic and structural affinity.

3. curling tightly: The "perfectly white" "wool" here anticipates "the perfect whiteness" of the "shrouded human figure" at the novel's close.

4. corded bales of cotton: This is the critical detail in Poe's novel suggestive of an association of *Pym* with the American South. Pertinently, the "ledge of rock" that looks like "bales of cotton" is approached "from the northward."

5. has ever engrossed its attention: Poe focuses on the coming revelation of a polar secret, intimated by his novel's subtitle, which includes "INCREDIBLE ADVENTURES AND DISCOVERIES STILL FARTHER SOUTH." Poe's mention of "the eye of science" seems an effort to lend greater validity to the approaching discovery.

Chapter 18

1. as the claws: This "singular-looking land-animal" is clearly a composite of familiar animals—the rat, the cat, the dog. While this creature signals Pym's presence in a strange region, it also reminds us that elements of the familiar shape that region. Indeed, as Poe was to write in his review of Thomas Moore's *Alciphron: A Poem* in *Burton's Gentleman's Magazine* in January 1840, any "creation of intellect" is a griffin, a seemingly new creature that is "resoluble into the old"—into lion and eagle (*Complete Works* 10:62). *Pym* it-

self is composed, in part, of elements of other works. The nature and purpose of the adaptation and arrangement of these disparate elements are uniquely Poe's.

2. *January* 19: Poe uses his own birthday for the date of the discovery of the island of Tsalal, thus calling attention to the covertly personal nature of his novel.

3. on the blade of an oar: Similarly, when Morrell arrived at the Massacre Islands, he held up a white flag at the approach of natives (395). Poe is indebted to Morrell throughout this chapter.

4. *Anamoo-moo!* and *Lama-Lama!:* Both these words seem to be Poe inventions. "Anamoo-moo" was probably derived from the native name for the southern island of New Zealand, *"Tavi Poënam-moo,"* given in Morrell (365). Accordingly, the word would be another reference to the author himself. "Lama-Lama," as Richard Wilbur has suggested, was probably drawn from the final words of Jesus on the cross: "Eli, Eli, lama sabachthani?"—"My God, my God, why has thou forsaken me?" (Matthew 27:46; Mark 15:34). The word would thus intimate the crucifixion motif in *Pym*. According to this view, the two words hint at the autobiographical and Christian allegories of Poe's novel. They seem to function for the Tsalalian natives as expressions of their fear of whiteness.

5. long woolly hair: In the first American edition, the phrase "their complexion" began a new sentence; Pollin has converted a period to a comma and made the uppercase "T" lowercase to eliminate a sentence fragment, caused probably by a printer's error.

6. found to be *Too-wit:* The name of Poe's native chief may have been drawn from Coleridge's "Christabel": at midnight the owls cry "Tu-whit!—Tu-whoo!" Too-wit himself is based, in part, on Morrell's native chief, "Nero" (395–96).

7. appeared to recoil: Poe may have borrowed here from "The Wreck of the British Ship Sidney," in Thomas.

8. upon the spot: Captain Morrell shows Nero and the other natives only one mirror (396). As the introduction argues, Poe employed two mirrors here to render in miniature the shape of his book. Each of the two mirrors is analogous to the *Penguin*, accompanied either by what seem to be a thousand screaming "demons" (chapter 1) or by the many screaming "gigantic and pallidly white birds" (chapter 24), since, according to chapter 14, the penguin and the albatross have "the spirit of reflection." Too-wit, "in the middle of the cabin" and caught between the facing mirrors, is analogous to Augustus, who dies in the middle of the book. (Notably, Pym thinks that Too-wit would "expire upon the spot.") This incident in the cabin of the *Jane Guy*, duplicating the novel itself, may be termed a *"mise en abîme."*

9. village in the interior: The visit to the chief's village was probably

drawn from Morrell's visit to Nero's village and the captain's later
journey with Nero inland (397–99).

10. the singular character of the water: The phrase "the singular char-
    acter of the water" is an adaptation of the phrase "the singular
    character of the city," found in J. L. Stephens's *Incidents of Travel
    in Egypt, Arabia Petræa, and the Holy Land*, a two-volume work
    published by the Harpers in 1837 (2:82). Poe reviewed this work in
    the *New-York Review* in October 1837, commenting on the "*liter-
    alness*" of prophecy. The city that Stephens mentions is forsaken
    Petra, of which he writes that "veins of white, blue, red, purple,
    and sometimes scarlet and light orange" may be found in the rock
    of apartments and in "the whole stony rampart that encircled the
    city" (2:78). Petra may be taken as a type of Jerusalem, whose de-
    struction is allegorized in *Pym*. A passage in Morrell (432) may
    also be linked with Poe's description of the Tsalalian water.

Chapter 19

1. the word *Klock-Klock:* Chapter 19 offers Poe's allegory of his 1831
   work, "A Tale of Jerusalem," published in the Philadelphia *Saturday Courier* on June 9, 1832. That work, one of the pieces in his
   never-published "Tales of the Folio Club," was based on an incident in Horace Smith's novel *Zillah: a Tale of the Holy City*
   (1828). The name "Klock-Klock" may allude to Poe's fictional author of "A Tale of Jerusalem," mentioned in the introduction to
   "Tales of the Folio Club," a man "who admired Horace Smith":
   "Chronologos Chronology."

2. *Wampoos* or *Yampoos:* Perhaps these names were suggested to Poe
   by the name of a port city he would have come upon in *Symzonia*,
   Whampoa. The possible allusion may suggest the author himself.

3. the pelicans as usual: As we know from chapter 14, the friends of
   the albatross are the penguins—presumably Poe made an error
   here. In his 1858 French translation, Charles Baudelaire corrected
   the error.

4. innumerable other varieties: Here Poe relies on Morrell's description of fish (362).

5. termed personal beauty: Poe borrows from Morrell's visit to
   Nero's village and house (397).

6. to the village: Here is Poe's allegory of "A Tale of Jerusalem": the
   twelve men from the *Jane Guy* (the twelve tribes of Israel), confined inside a "hut," a "tent" (etymologically close to the "tabernacle," in the city of Jerusalem) that is besieged by natives (Romans),
   are offered the entrails of "one of the slim-legged hogs" (the for-
   bidden hog). To compare this allegory with the original tale, see
   Poe, *Collected Works* 2:43–48. (We may recall here Poe's allusion
   in chapter 1 to Goddin's Tavern, a name that suggests God in the

tabernacle.) Poe's allegory of an incident occurring during the siege of Jerusalem is consonant with his concern in *Pym* with the destruction of Jerusalem, already suggested by the destruction of the *Ariel*, and soon to be suggested twice more.

7. a series of cross-questioning: With this phrase, Poe continues his pattern of allusions to the crucifixion. The crucifixion was considered resonant with the destruction of Jerusalem. Furthermore, allusions to the crucifixion in *Pym* appropriately anticipate the coded presentation of Jesus come to prophesy the New Jerusalem.

Chapter 20

1. on our return: Poe is relying on Morrell's discussion of bêche-de-mer, the sea cucumber (399–402). Again, Poe presents verisimilar detail to encourage belief—or perhaps an indulgent willingness to accept disbelief—and to heighten the effect of his coming "incredibilities" (as he termed passages of extraordinary incident in his September 1836 review of Robert Montgomery Bird's novel *Sheppard Lee*—see *Collected Writings* 5:286).

2. elastic wings: In the original Morrell passage, this phrase read "elastic rings" (401).

3. armed to the teeth: John Limon points out that the thirty-two men "armed to the teeth" themselves suggest teeth, recalling Poe's 1835 story "Berenice."

4. all were brothers: Pollin suggests the translation "Kill not; we see peace" (330).

5. the village was situated: Elements of this paragraph were drawn from a passage about the approach to Mount Sinai in J. L. Stephens's *Incidents of Travel* (1:250), a passage also appearing in the April 29, 1837, *New-York Mirror*.

6. dissolution was at hand: Language here and in the first three paragraphs of the next chapter echoes language employed in an 1831 story attributed to Poe, "A Dream," concerning the effects of the crucifixion of Jesus: *I heard a muttered groan* ... the fearful thought stole over me, *that the day of retribution had come....* The veil, which had hid its secrets from unhallowed gaze, was now *rent....* The fire, which was to kindle the mangled limbs of the victim, gleamed for a moment, on the distant walls, and then 'twas lost *in utter darkness....* A column of *light* shot athwart the gloom.... There was an *opening* in the *vast* arch of heaven's broad expanse" (*Collected Works* 2:8; emphasis added).

Chapter 21

1. never to be conceived: "The blackness of darkness" is derived from the Epistle of Jude 13, where the term refers to a punishment for evildoers. (The phrase appears also in J. N. Reynolds's 1838 piece

"Leaves from an Unpublished Journal" and Poe's 1842 tale "The Pit and the Pendulum.") Poe is developing here further his recurring theme of burial alive, most famously elaborated in the 1844 tale, "The Premature Burial." See Poe, *Collected Works* 3:954–69 (esp. 961).

2. we thought it insurmountable: Poe here begins to include distinct verbal echoes of a passage in Reynolds's "Leaves from an Unpublished Journal," a narrative appearing in the *New-York Mirror* of April 21, 1838. Poe would have seen the published work at the time of its publication and perhaps, in light of his probable acquaintance with Reynolds, a copy of the piece before publication.

3. driven into the earth: Here Poe begins a new allegory for the destruction of Jerusalem. Isaiah 33:20 states, "Look upon Zion, the city of our solemnities: thine eyes shall see Jerusalem a quiet habitation, a tabernacle that shall not be taken down; not one of the stakes thereof shall ever be removed, neither shall any of the cords thereof be broken." Poe reverses the prophecy through his account of the precipitation of the Tsalalian landslide, which involves the natives' pulling on "cords" (a word employed four times) to dislodge "stakes" (a word employed six times) embedded in the earth, thereby causing the disruption.

   Perhaps suggestive to Poe for this passage would have been excerpts from J. L. Stephens's *Incidents of Travel* appearing in the *New-Yorker* and the *New-York Mirror*.

4. upon the island: Here Poe neglects the fact that Dirk Peters is a "half-breed" Indian. The death of thirty of the thirty-two men who were "armed to the teeth" suggests to John Limon the loss of "individual *ident*ities." Liliane Weissberg has discussed this pun with regard to "Berenice."

Chapter 22

1. captivity among them: Poe completes a symmetrical pair; see note 1 for chapter 2.

2. sole path: Poe offers here a near-spoonerism for Pym's ultimate objective, the "South Pole."

3. than I have taken to tell it: In consultation with the editor of the 1994 Gordian edition of *Pym*, the editor of the present edition of the novel has corrected the erratum "that" to the word "than."

4. for an instant: This paragraph and the following one are indebted to Morrell's description of the natives' attack on the schooner *Antarctic* (412). For the following paragraph, see also pp. 436–37.

5. the savages outright: In this sentence and the following one, Poe completes symmetrical pairs; see notes 11 and 16 for chapter 1.

6. above the shrubs: The bittern is a bird associated in the Bible with

such destroyed cities as Babylon (Isaiah 14:23), Idumea (Isaiah 34:11), and Nineveh (Zephaniah 2:14), calling to mind the destruction of Jerusalem. The bird is mentioned in Alexander Keith's *Evidence of the Truth of the Christian Religion*, a book reprinted by the Harpers in 1832, and in Stephens's *Incidents of Travel*.

7. set her on fire: Details of this paragraph and the following one are drawn from the destruction of the *Tonquin* in Washington Irving's *Astoria*.

8. *Tekeli-li! Tekeli-li!*: The natives respond to the preserved carcass of the "singular-looking land-animal" that appeared in chapter 18. Apparently they are disturbed by the creature's whiteness. This word that the natives repeatedly shout comes from the title of the play in which Poe's mother performed as the bride Christine, *Tekeli, or, The Siege of Montgatz*, by Theodore Hook.

Chapter 23

1. Chapter 23: There are two chapters with this number in the first edition. Probably this chapter, the first of the two and closely related to the final "Note," was inserted late in the composition of the novel. In the Pollin text used here, the second chapter 23 is distinguished from the first one with the name "Chapter 23 bis."

2. protuberance opposite: Perhaps this figure and the next two figures reveal the initials "eAp," as Pollin has suggested (*Collected Writings* 1:343).

3. with outstretched arm: Here again Poe uses the phrase "human figure," presumably linked to the "human figure" in chapter 14 to which a penguin is compared and the "shrouded human figure" of chapter 24, the ship *Penguin*. This sentence bears a resemblance to a sentence in "The Journal of Julius Rodman," chapter 6, concerning lines on cliffs. See *Collected Writings* 1:573.

Chapter 23 bis

1. without accident: Poe may owe a debt here to a wall-climbing passage in Frederick Marryat's novel *Peter Simple* (1834).

2. the faintest possible idea of ultimate escape: Poe completes another pair of symmetrical phrases. See note 10 for chapter 1.

3. a passion utterly uncontrollable: Pym's uncontrollable "*longing to fall*" anticipates Poe's tale "The Imp of the Perverse," especially with regard to the following comment in that work: "There is no passion in nature so demoniacally impatient, as that of him, who shuddering upon the edge of a precipice, thus meditates a plunge" (*Collected Works* 3:1223). Poe's view of man's perverseness is sometimes taken to foreshadow Sigmund Freud's "death instinct."

4. the site of degraded Babylon: Reference to this destroyed city rein-

forces Poe's covert concern in *Pym* with the destruction of Jerusalem. Poe may have relied for this sentence partly on Keith's *Evidence of the Truth of the Christian Religion* (182). He may also have drawn details in this paragraph from Stephens's *Incidents of Travel*. For an earlier instance of Poe's treating a destroyed city, see the 1831 poem "The Doomed City," later revised and titled "The City in the Sea" (*Collected Works* 1:199–202).

5. scar[c]ely: The "c" was mistakenly omitted in the first edition.

6. bow and stern alike: The canoe, with identical bow and stern, is a symbol of the novel itself, which begins with the *Ariel*, the *Penguin*, and the scream of what seem "a thousand demons" and ends with the canoe, the coded *Penguin*, and the screaming "gigantic and pallidly white birds."

Chapter 24

1. *Tsalemon* or *Psalemoun:* The name of the natives' king suggests Solomon, the wise King of Israel who built the Temple in Jerusalem. Both "Tsalemon" and "Psalemoun" feature within them the name "Salem," a familiar shortened form of the name "Jerusalem."

2. his own name was Nu-Nu: Kenneth Silverman points out that "Nunu" was the name of the Indian heroine in the N. P. Willis short story, "The Cherokee's Threat" (474), a tale that appeared in the 1836 *Inklings of Adventure*. In light of the coming allusion to the Book of Revelation by Saint John the Divine, it is relevant to add that in Willis's tale, Nunu is the beloved of "St. John."

3. a prolonged hissing sound: The "hissing sound" is associated with Jerusalem, as in Jeremiah 19:8: "And I will make this city desolate, and an hissing; every one that passeth thereby shall be astonished and hiss because of all the plagues thereof."

4. hurrying on to the southward: Again, Poe completes a pair of symmetrical phrases. See note 9 for chapter 1.

5. an inhabitant of Tsalal: In the October 5, 1833, issue of the Baltimore *Saturday Visiter*, appearing two weeks before that in which Poe was identified as the winner of the short story contest for "MS. Found in a Bottle," a paragraph appeared titled "*Black Teeth.*" Poe would surely have read this.

6. a limitless cataract: Perhaps Poe is suggesting the aurora australis. J. Lasley Dameron suggests a passage in William Scoresby Jr.'s *An Account of the Arctic Regions with a History and Description of the Northern Whale-Fishery* (1820) as a source for the cataract.

7. bulwarks of the boat: The term "bulwarks" appears in the Bible regarding the fortifications of Jerusalem (2 Chronicles 26:15, Psalms 48:13, Isaiah 26:1).

8. **but soundless winds:** That prophecy is imminent is clear from this allusion to "a sound from heaven as of a rushing mighty wind" (Acts 2:2), referring to the Holy Spirit.

9. **the perfect whiteness of the snow:** This celebrated passage has been considered indebted to such works as J. N. Reynolds's "Leaves from an Unpublished Journal" (Kopley, "The Secret of *Arthur Gordon Pym*") and William Scoresby Jr.'s 1823 *Journal of a Voyage to the Northern Whale-Fishery: Including Researches and Discoveries on the Eastern Coast of West Greenland* (Dameron in Kopley, *Poe's Pym*.) *Pym*'s climactic passage has enjoyed diverse interpretations—the "shrouded human figure" has been seen as death (Moldenhauer, Peden) and as a Lazarus figure conquering death (Eakin); as goodness (Stroupe) and as perversity (Cox); as knowledge (O'Donnell, Helen Lee) and as the limits of knowledge (Lévy); as imagination (Liebler, Wells), the narrative itself (Kennedy, *Poe, Death, and the Life of Writing*), and the white at the bottom of the page (Ricardou); as a Titan (Ljungquist), as a divinity (Bonaparte, Fiedler, Bezanson), and as Pym's unrecognized white shadow (Irwin; Robinson, *American Apocalypses*). The analyses of this figure are rich, varied, and provocative. And certainly there will be new analyses yet to come. However, the evidence presented in the introduction and throughout the notes tends to suggest a particular reading involving three levels: the literal, the autobiographical, and the biblical.

On the literal level, the "shrouded human figure" is the ship *Penguin*, surrounded by screaming albatrosses. The critical link is the phrase "human figure," to which Poe compares a penguin in chapter 14. This penguin at the close of *Pym*, "very far larger in its proportions than any dweller among men," is a ship. With the ship *Penguin* and the many screaming "gigantic and pallidly white birds," Poe completes a critical instance of symmetry, repeating thus in chapter 24 the appearance of the *Penguin* and the scream of what seem "a thousand demons" in chapter 1. Furthermore, in both the beginning and end of the novel, the *Penguin* and a small vessel collide, and the *Penguin* rescues Pym and a friend from that vessel. The "bow and stern" of this novel are "alike."

On the autobiographical level, the "shrouded human figure" is male and female—brother and mother. Since the penguins and the albatrosses are distinguished by their "spirit of reflection," the *Penguin* with the apparent screaming demons in the first chapter and the *Penguin* with the screaming white birds in the last chapter constitute mirrors—facing mirrors, as in chapter 18. Even as the facing mirrors in the cabin of the *Jane Guy* are analogous to the reflecting penguin/albatross pair, the native chief Too-wit "in the middle of the cabin" is analogous to Augustus Barnard, who dies at the center of the book. The reflections between facing mirrors are infinite; the infinite reflection of Augustus, who represents Poe's brother, Henry, suggests Poe's infinite memory of his brother's death. The "shrouded human figure" yields reflections of Henry's death—but insofar as the figure is white, appears on March 22, and is surrounded by cries of *"Tekeli-li!,"* it also represents Poe's mother, who was scheduled to perform as a bride on March 22 in the play *Tekeli*. Poe's statement that his love for his brother was owing to the brothers' shared love for the same parent—their mother—tends to support this reading.

Finally, on the biblical level, the "shrouded human figure" represents the response to the biblical loss in *Pym*—the destruction of Jerusalem, allegorically signified by the destruction of the *Ariel* in chapter 1 and that of the canoe in chapter 24, and by the Tsalalian landslide. For such scholars as William Mentzel Forrest, Sidney Kaplan, and Richard Wilbur, the white figure in this biblically cadenced passage may be linked with the Vision of the Seven Candlesticks in the Revelation of Saint John the Divine: Christ come to prophesy. The cataract may well suggest "the sound of many waters" (Revelation 1:15). If, as in the introduction, we return to the identity of the figure as the ship *Penguin*, and if we remember the linking in chapter 1 of the *Penguin* with Wales and bear in mind Poe's love of etymology, we may be led to consider the Welsh origins of the word "penguin": according to the dictionaries of Samuel Johnson and Noah Webster (which Poe mentioned regularly), the word means, in Welsh, "white head." And if we examine the description of that Vision of the Seven Candlesticks, we read, "His head and his hairs were white like wool, as white as snow . . ." (Revelation 1:14). Accordingly, we understand why Poe chose the name *Penguin* for that rescuing vessel. Biblically, the "shrouded human figure" culminates *Pym*'s allegories of the destruction of Jerusalem and the crucifixion of Christ—it is the white head of Christ come to prophesy the "new Jerusalem" (Revelation 3:12). Furthermore, the cries of *"Tekeli-li!"* allude to Eliza Poe's performing as a bride named Christine—that is, she is both bride and bridegroom, Church and Christ, at the end of time. Thus, the providential theme of *The Narrative of Arthur Gordon Pym* is fulfilled.

Clearly, Poe must have had this very complex final image in mind from the beginning of his composition of the novel to render it—and to anticipate it—as effectively as he did. Poe probably planned his novel backward (as he did other literary works), thereby shaping its great aesthetic unity. Compellingly uniting the three levels of *Pym* is the sense of loss—whether of a boat, of a family, or of a holy city. Through *Pym*, Poe grieved—and through *Pym*, Poe brilliantly imagined recovery.

Note

1. given to the public: The first paragraph of the "Note" offers a false lead, relying on the seeming incompleteness of the narrative. However, through the supposed "writer of this appendix," Poe offers in this first paragraph suggestive verbal links with the concluding paragraph of the "Death Ship" chapter. (See note 8 for chapter 10.) The parallel phrasing evident in that final paragraph and this first paragraph intimates a connection between those dead to whom Pym "could not help shouting . . . for help" and the recently deceased Pym himself. Perhaps Poe has imagined that he has died in the same manner as his mother and his brother—or that he is reunited in the hereafter with these two he so deeply loved. That the supposed lost chapters, if found, "will be given to the public," suggest a source for the idea for this "Note": the "Note" at the end of Stephens's *Incidents of Travel*, which closes with the assurance that "details connected with the present exploring of the pyramids will probably soon be given to the public . . ." (2:286).

2. of Mr. Pym's account: Poe encourages attention to the issue of the truthfulness of the narrative, thereby diminishing attention to the work's allegorical character. Impressively, Charles Romyn Dake based his 1899 novel, *A Strange Discovery*, in part, on the premise that Dirk Peters was indeed "still alive" in Illinois; the first nine chapters are titled "How We Found Dirk Peters," and the remaining eleven chapters are called "The Story of Dirk Peters." Dake tells of Pym and Peters's further adventures on an island near the South Pole called "Hili-li."

3. for the Southern Ocean: The "governmental expedition" was the United States Exploring Expedition, also known as the Wilkes Expedition, which lasted from 1838 to 1842.

4. of shadow or darkness: Perhaps Poe closed this "Note" with a linguistic puzzle because of J. L. Stephens's "Note," which offers an Egyptian cartouche. Also possibly contributing were letters by philologists in Reynolds's *Address* and the much analyzed Dighton Rock. (See Moldenhauer in Kopley, *Poe's Pym*.) For the words Poe deciphers, he was indebted to Edward Robinson's *A Hebrew and English Lexicon of the Old Testament from the Latin of William Gesenius* (1836). For Poe's interest in Hebrew for use in his review of Stephens's *Incidents of Travel*, see Charles Anthon's letter to Poe in *Complete Works* 17:42–43.

5. in their windings: Poe's emphasis on whiteness and blackness strengthens the view that *Pym* is a novel concerning, in part, race.

But that final native word cited here, "Tekeli-li," points significantly to some of the other themes developed throughout the novel.

6. *"within the rock":* This final line was probably drawn from Job 19:24, a passage concerning Job's wish regarding his words—"That they were graven with an iron pen and lead in the rock for ever!" It is altogether likely that Poe, who had endured so many troubles, identified with Job and felt that Job's view expressed his own. Also relevant is the verse that immediately precedes Job 19:24: "Oh that my words were now written! oh that they were printed in a book!" (Job 19:23). And, in light of the allegory of Christ prophesying the New Jerusalem at the close of *Pym*, it is interesting to consider the verse that immediately follows Job 19:24, a Christian reading of which is evident: "For I know that my redeemer liveth, and that he shall stand at the latter day upon the earth" (Job 19:25).

CLICK ON A CLASSIC
www.penguinclassics.com

The world's greatest literature at your fingertips

Constantly updated information on more than a thousand titles,
from Icelandic sagas to ancient Indian epics, Russian drama to
Italian romance, American greats to African masterpieces

•

The latest news on recent additions to the list, updated
editions, and specially commissioned translations

•

Original essays by leading writers

•

A wealth of background material, including biographies
of every classic author from Aristotle to Zamyatin, plot
synopses, readers' and teachers' guides, useful web links

•

Online desk and examination copy assistance for academics

•

Trivia quizzes, competitions, giveaways, news on
forthcoming screen adaptations

FOR THE BEST IN PAPERBACKS, LOOK FOR THE

In every corner of the world, on every subject under the sun, Penguin represents quality and variety—the very best in publishing today.

For complete information about books available from Penguin—including Penguin Classics, Penguin Compass, and Puffins—and how to order them, write to us at the appropriate address below. Please note that for copyright reasons the selection of books varies from country to country.

In the United States: Please write to *Penguin Group (USA), P.O. Box 12289 Dept. B, Newark, New Jersey 07101-5289* or call 1-800-788-6262.

In the United Kingdom: Please write to *Dept. EP, Penguin Books Ltd, Bath Road, Harmondsworth, West Drayton, Middlesex UB7 0DA.*

In Canada: Please write to *Penguin Books Canada Ltd, 90 Eglinton Avenue East, Suite 700, Toronto, Ontario M4P 2Y3.*

In Australia: Please write to *Penguin Books Australia Ltd, P.O. Box 257, Ringwood, Victoria 3134.*

In New Zealand: Please write to *Penguin Books (NZ) Ltd, Private Bag 102902, North Shore Mail Centre, Auckland 10.*

In India: Please write to *Penguin Books India Pvt Ltd, 11 Panchsheel Shopping Centre, Panchsheel Park, New Delhi 110 017.*

In the Netherlands: Please write to *Penguin Books Netherlands bv, Postbus 3507, NL-1001 AH Amsterdam.*

In Germany: Please write to *Penguin Books Deutschland GmbH, Metzlerstrasse 26, 60594 Frankfurt am Main.*

In Spain: Please write to *Penguin Books S. A., Bravo Murillo 19, 1° B, 28015 Madrid.*

In Italy: Please write to *Penguin Italia s.r.l., Via Benedetto Croce 2, 20094 Corsico, Milano.*

In France: Please write to *Penguin France, Le Carré Wilson, 62 rue Benjamin Baillaud, 31500 Toulouse.*

In Japan: Please write to *Penguin Books Japan Ltd, Kaneko Building, 2-3-25 Koraku, Bunkyo-Ku, Tokyo 112.*

In South Africa: Please write to *Penguin Books South Africa (Pty) Ltd, Private Bag X14, Parkview, 2122 Johannesburg.*